I0664277

CRYSTALLIZED

The Spectrum Series

SAMANTHA MINA

CRYSTALLIZED

BOOK 3 OF A SERIES

For Bethany Kurtz Sykes

who introduced me to the world of science fiction in the winter of 2003. If it weren't for you, I never would have read a word of military sci-fi, let alone write it.

PRONUNCIATION GUIDE

Acci: *"AX-ee"*
Arrhyth: *"AR-hith"*
Buird: *"Bird"*
Ichthyosis: *"Ik-thee-OH-sis"*
Leavesleft: *"LEEV-ssleft"*
Lechatelierite: *"Luh-shaht-LEER-ahyt"*
(rhymes with "light")
Nuria: *"NER-ee-ah"*
Qui Tsop: *"Key Sop"*

NORTHWESTERN HEMISPHERE OF SECOND EARTH

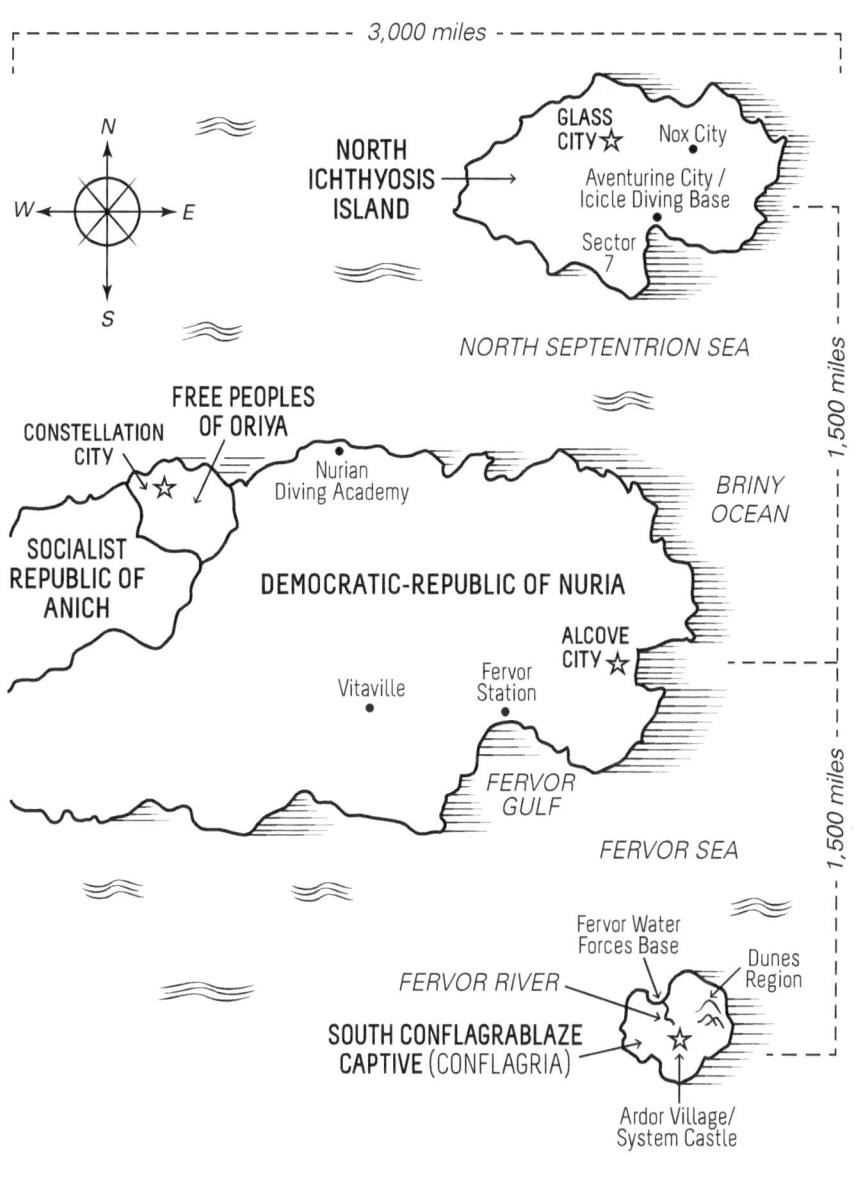

PART I
THE SECOND EPOCH OF THE CRYSTAL-LAND'S END

Seeing the snowman standing all alone
In dusk and cold is more than he can bear.
The small boy weeps to hear the wind prepare
A night of gnashings and enormous moan.
His tearful sight can hardly reach to where
His pale-faced figure with bitumen eyes
Returns him such a god-forsaken stare
As outcast Adam gave to Paradise.

The man of snow is, no nonetheless, content,
Having no wish to go inside and die
Still, he is moved to see the youngster cry.
Though frozen water is his element,
He melts enough to drop from one soft eye
A trickle of the purest rain, a tear
For the child at the bright pane surrounded by
Such warmth, such light, such love, and so much fear.

—*Richard Wilbur*

FAIR GABARDINE

THUD!
THUD!

Right on schedule.

Blackness surrounded me in the narrow tunnel. I cautiously made my way, probing for the unconscious, undressed forms of Rusty Pypes and Cu Twentnine.

That was my inglorious job in this infiltration mission: to collect and oversee the flaccid forms of the System soldiers Scarlet July and Ambrek Coppertus knocked out and stripped down. I'd dress them in spare garments, drag them to the forest, tie them to my scabrous, ride off to Seventh Cabin and keep them drugged-up on some concoction Ambrek brewed until it was time to return them to base after the battle. Yes, we were returning them: taking prisoners wasn't the purpose of our mish and there was no need to give the System additional reasons to be suspicious. Our only objectives today were to retrieve the fragment of the Core Crystal from the Septentrion Sea and firebomb the System Mage Castle.

Handling Rusty and Cu was a long, difficult and noisy ordeal. Even after five-plus months sans magic, I hadn't become accustomed to the physical limitations. Every minute of every day, I felt like something was missing—my most useful limb. It was incredibly annoying to have this limp mop of strings hanging from my head. Without spectrum, hair was good for nothing.

Moreover, my powersource wasn't the only thing contending with the diffusion. My entire body ached, all the time. Living without an aura was like being sick. It was like decaying alive. No wonder the System had so many supporters, these days. I doubted anyone outside the Tincture administration really agreed with the idea of mind-suppression, but a whole lot of people were understandably upset over losing their magic, for physical *and* financial reasons. Society longed to regain the comforts of ordered life—an illusion the System maintained. Our culture was so spectrally-dependent, Conflagria's socioeconomic structure fell apart the moment the Crystal ended. When you were unemployed, poor, hungry, cold and weak, it only got easier to resent Scarlet for what she did. Even I grew frustrated sometimes.

And, if I was having this much trouble coping without magic, I could only imagine how rough things were for Scarlet, who faced the challenge of physical littleness on top of it all. *She* certainly couldn't lift Rusty or Cu without spectrum. Without her dual sources, could sub-five-foot, eighty-pound, sixteen-age-old Scarlet carry the weight of the world?

That begged the question: was Scarlet really responsible for 'taking from the fallen children of Second Earth what was no longer rightfully theirs'? She took the spectrum from Conflagria—did that mean the prophecy was fulfilled? But, if the spectrum didn't 'rightfully' belong to us, why did diffusion feel like death? Why did the nation dissolve into chaos the instant the Crystal detonated? Why should a young, small girl shoulder all the burdens of her people?

Scarlet took her job as Red Leader very seriously and never cut herself any slack. She wasn't the best at delegating, either. She threw herself into every challenge the revolution faced, following each task from drawing board to completion. In front of her men, she was a fearless warrior and a never-ceasing wellspring of ideas. Everyone believed she was unstoppable and unbreakable.

Except Ambrek and I.

We knew the truth: her exhaustion and fear manifested itself in hidden tears, almost nightly. When we were kids, she hardly ever cried. But, I supposed, her family's execution followed by six rocky ages in the Nordic world changed her. Harsh circumstances forged her into a furiously-creative fighter with a tough outer shell but an insecure heart. So, she turned to none other than the Commander of the Ichthyothian Diving Fleet to fill the vacuum of love in her lonely, tormented life. But, Cease Lechatelierite obviously couldn't give her the security and stability she desperately needed. The blunt truth was, a Nordic technophile and a tribal mage could never build a future together. Which was why I hardened my heart toward Inexor, when he was around. Now that he was gone, I didn't miss him. I didn't miss anyone. I didn't have to: everyone I loved was right here in Conflagria, with me, to stay.

But, then, there was Scarlet. Scarlet, who let herself attach to a Nordic. And, not just any Nordic, but the *Leader of the Ichthyothian Resistance*—a man who'd never leave his icy nation. A man who was simply too busy and needed by his people to have time or energy for love. A man who probably didn't have the emotional capacity to love, in the first place. Scarlet acted like distance was the only thing separating her and Cease. But, in truth, those three-thousand miles were but mere candles in a conflagration.

Sometimes, I wondered what'd happen if a mage and an Ichthyothian actually tried to reproduce, pre-diffusion. In all of Second Earth history, there'd never been a single, documented case of 'covalence.' I wondered, what would this hypothetical child's body-temperature be? Conflagrians generally ran at one-oh-six degrees Fahrenheit, which would induce heatstroke on Ichthyothians. Ichthyothians usually ran at about ninety-three degrees, which would make mages hypothermic. And, would the half-blood's magical powers be weakened? Would it have an aura, at all? Suffer from spectral poisoning? Survive until birth, in the first place?

Well, those questions were moot, even if the spectral web ever did recrystallize. Because, it'd be a miracle if Ichthyothians and Conflagrians ever stopped slaughtering each other, let alone start interbreeding.

Scarlet needed to forget about Cease. She'd be much better off with someone like Ambrek, anyway. Ambrek was perfect for her, on every level. Not to mention, they were obviously crazy about each other. Yet, Scarlet rejected him because she wanted to be true to Cease. But, why on Second Earth should she stay faithful to a man she'd never see again? A man who probably forgot all about her as soon as she left, heart re-calloused and re-consumed by the war? Unlike Cease, Ambrek could offer Scarlet stability, security and a future. A future right *here*, in Conflagria—the only place Scarlet could possibly belong.

BOOM!

Rusty and Cu tumbled to the cabin floor, in a heap. Prunus Persica and his green grandfather, Ivan 'Ivy' Leaf, goggled at them.

"So, July and Coppertus made it inside the hangar?" Ivy exclaimed in his strong southeastern-Conflagrian accent.

"They got their hands on a Nordic fighter?" Prunus chimed, flashing his handsome smile.

I only nodded, not really sharing their enthusiasm. I was still worried sick. To use a funny Nordic expression, Scarlet and Ambrek weren't 'out of the woods' yet—snagging a ship was only the beginning. Who knew if they'd actually find the crystal-fragment or make it back from battle alive. But, of course, Prunus and Ivy didn't have a clue about the shard. No one besides Scarlet, Ambrek and I were aware of its existence; that part of the op was classified.

"Coppertus came here at two o'clock for the incendiary," Ivy commented, folding his spindly arms across his chest.

What? Why so early? Ambrek was already gone when Scarlet and I got up at dawn this morning, but we'd assumed we just missed him by minutes. So, by now, he'd been out and about for nearly two-dozen hours? Doing what? Installing the firebomb in Rusty and Cu's fighter wouldn't take very long, especially considering he now had a random, mysterious, ever-convenient underground tunnel at his disposition.

Really, what was the deal with that tunnel?

"Don't like being in the dark, do you, Gabardine?" Ivy asked.

"What're you talking about?" I snapped.

"You don't feel left out, sometimes?"

"From what?"

"July and Coppertus don't make you feel… peripheral?" He observed me closely with his astute, hazel-green eyes.

Peripheral? Tincture, Ivy had some nerve. Irritated, I trudged to the pantry to retrieve Ambrek's sleep-inducing chemicals.

Ivy tailed me. "I see you, trying to busy yourself, ignoring me…"

"I'm not 'trying to busy myself'!" I retorted, imitating his stupid accent. "I'm doing my job!" Returning to the lobby, I dropped to my knees beside Rusty and Cu. "I'm supposed to keep these two under until—"

"Until the dream team returns. Your job is to supervise unconscious bodies while the red girl and the iridescent boy do the real work."

Real work? I whirled around. "Are you always this spiteful, grandpa, or are you *trying* to piss me off?"

"Why do you need to keep them alive?" he suddenly demanded.

I rolled my eyes. "Because the System might think something's up, if their fighter miraculously materializes in the hangar without them, after the battle."

"Will the System have time to get suspicious, though? Aren't July and Coppertus bombing the Castle as soon as they get back? Will there be a base for these men to return to?"

I sat up straighter. Oh, Tincture.

"There's flaw in the plan," he pressed. "Fix it, Gabardine: kill them."

I hesitated. "Hold the torch, Ivy. There's got to be a reason Ambrek would tell me to do this. He's not dumb. Let me think about it, for a moment."

"Coppertus told you?" Ivy cocked a thin brow.

"Yes, he's the one who came up with this whole bombing scheme."

"Not July?"

"No."

"Of course." He nodded. "July doesn't make mistakes. Had to be Coppertus."

"Oh, believe me, Scarlet makes plenty of mistakes," I muttered darkly.

"Coppertus is a stone wall. Doesn't explain much," Ivy said, somberly. "Not to you, not to July, not to my grandson, not to me, not to anyone. Stays quiet. Keeps to himself. Gives orders. Acts like a commander."

"Well, he *is* one of our leaders."

"July is our commander. Not Coppertus. But, July only makes one mistake."

"I thought you said Scarlet doesn't make mistakes?"

Ivy ignored me. "She listens to everything Coppertus says."

I blinked. "Is that a bad thing? Scarlet listens to everyone, no matter how green. She blends all our ideas into hers. That's why people love to follow her."

"No, July listens to *everything* Coppertus says. She does whatever he wants. Always."

My stomach twisted. "That's not true. When Ambrek first suggested infiltrating the Water Forces, Scarlet refused. She had us contact the Nurian manufacturers, first."

"But, her plan didn't exactly work out, did it?"

"What difference does that make?" I tossed my hair over my shoulder. "The point is, Scarlet overrules Ambrek sometimes. She's not some *puppet* of his!"

My words rang in the dusty air.

"Isn't she, though?"

"Shut up, Ivy!" I hissed. "Of course, she isn't. She's too strong-willed. She wouldn't let anyone manipulate her, ever." But, the more I thought about it now, the more I remembered incident after incident in which Scarlet bent to Ambrek's will, without question. She only stood up to him maybe once or twice since the revolution began. How was that possible? Scarlet was an *Ichthyothian-trained military leader.* How could the former Second of the Nordic Diving Fleet be malleable? Unless—

Ivy nodded as the truth hit me like a torch to the face.

Cease Lechatelierite. My mind conjured terrible images of him from last summer, towering over me, torturing me, inflicting physical and emotional pain as I'd never experienced before. Cease Lechatelierite, with his brutal dominance, broke Scarlet down while she was under his thumb, propelling her into a state of perpetual insecurity. She obeyed everything *he* said, heeded every word from *his* mouth. And, now, in Scarlet's mind, that authority had subconsciously transferred to Ambrek.

Ivy didn't know Cease. He knew *of* him—everyone in this war did—but, the two never met. He didn't spend a whole lot of time around Scarlet or Ambrek, either. Yet, with a fraction of the puzzle pieces, Ivy managed to put the picture together before me.

He crouched beside me. "I don't trust Coppertus," he whispered. "Perhaps, the two-toned man has two faces."

"Why'd you say that?" I whimpered. "Just because he influences Scarlet and gave me orders we don't understand?"

"Not just because of that. Since August, there's just… something. Something my mind chokes on, every time I see him."

"You have no evidence," I objected. Ambrek had to be trustworthy. He had to be. He was the co-leader of the Reds. He was like a brother to me. He cared deeply for Scarlet. And, he knew everything, absolutely everything, about the revolution. "Scarlet's brilliant; you said so yourself. If she trusts him, we all should!"

"July," Ivy spoke in a low tone, "is blind."

Blind. By her naïveté. By her past. By her insecurities. By her love for Cease. Her love for Ambrek.

Ivy was wise. At seventy-seven ages old, he was still an active participant in the revolution. He'd seen the Conflagrian throne pass from Pekoe to Tincture, and recently watched his entire family—except for his grandson, Prunus—turn against him in favor of the System. His age and experience gave him insight even geniuses like Scarlet couldn't possibly have, yet.

Even so, the fact there was an aura of mystery surrounding Ambrek didn't justify going rogue all of a sudden and taking a knife to my POWs' throats. After being a prisoner myself, I wasn't exactly hankering to blow the Geneva Convention to hell on a hunch. I needed to investigate the Ambrek situation further before taking such drastic action. So, tonight, I decided I'd quietly keep Rusy and Cu alive, as I was told to.

Hours passed. Whenever the men stirred, I administered more medicine. Then, just as I was about to fetch myself a glass of scabrous milk, powerful heat inexplicably shot through my scalp. Gasping, I kneeled over, hair emitting white light. Ivy and Prunus followed suit, respectfully exuding green and peach mist. Red-orange waves undulated from Rusty's head as Cu's throat glowed copper-brown.

Suddenly, the pain vanished, replaced by strength, unparalleled strength. And, everything seemed so simple now, so black and white. Because I was myself, again. A hair mage. A loyalist to Tincture's throne. A true patriot.

INEXOR BUIRD

"Commander Lechatelierite!" I called into my helmet's intercom for the umpteenth time, to no avail. If only we had the PAVLAK navigation system already, as we should've by now. Damn development got delayed, *again*.

"Commander Leavesleft?"

Silence.

Suspicions piqued, the two of them went off about an hour ago to tail a low-flying enemy scout with downcast searchlights. What took them so long and why were my cries falling on deaf ears?

I found the answer near the shore of sector seven. Shreds of charred metal danced like stormclouds on the frosted, uneven surface of the reef. And, shining like a beacon through the dust, was a single globe of white and silver. A helmet.

I anchored my crystalline, dove from the shaft, stream-lined to the seabed and seized the helmet with trembling hands. It was small. Only one man in this fleet wore one so small. I returned to my shuttle, throwing it violently against the wall.

"Buird!" Illia's voice sounded.

"Yes, Frappe?"

"I've been calling the Commanders for fifteen minutes! Where are they?"

"Leavesleft was shot down," I answered, numbly, "by the shore of sector seven."

There was a pause.

"Where's Lechatelierite, then?"

"He was surface-riding on Leavesleft's crystalline." I swallowed. "I found his helmet among the debris."

Another tense silence ensued.

"Well, our strategy is falling apart, if you haven't noticed!" Illia growled. "Are you going to take charge of this battle, or should I?"

My eyes blurred. "Be my guest."

"Lechatelierite was right; you have lost your touch," he spat.

"Take command and leave me the hell alone!"

"I need you to cooperate. The breakthrough in sector eighty-seven needs reinforcement. Move!"

"Yes, sir."

* * *

A long line snaked the hall. Five-hundred-three Nurians cradled the contents of their lockers, awaiting their turns to toss them in the bins by the exit. Tears streaked the faces of Dither Maine and Arrhyth Link, the very last in the procession. Base-raised divers would never weep openly, like that. But, these two had no shame. They were crying for Nurtic Leavesleft, no doubt.

I was never close to Maine, Link or any Nurians, for that matter. But, something compelled me to approach them, now. They straightened up when I drew near, wiping their faces in the uniforms that were no longer theirs.

"Leavesleft would've insisted on flying you all home, if he were here," I told them. "At least, he died doing what he was born for. He loved piloting more than anything else in the world."

Link blew his nose into the chest of his diving suit; mucus slipped down the waxy, arrhythmic fabric. "That's not true, sir," he said.

"Yeah, there's something Nurtic loved more than flying," Maine chimed.

"What's that?"

"God." Link fingered his collar, probably thinking of the cross Leavesleft always wore. "He wanted to join an aviation ministry, when we got home. It was his next dream. Now, he'll never get to do it."

"No, he won't," I said. "But, he's doing something better now, isn't he? He's with the Father in heaven as we speak, right?"

They stared.

"You don't believe that," Link breathed. "None of you Ichthyothians do. You're mocking us now, aren't you?"

"No, that wasn't my intention." True, I wasn't religious myself—it's not like the Childhood Program supplied its students with bibles or anything—but, I knew a lot of the Nurians believed in a higher power. I only meant to 'speak their language' to them now, to encourage and comfort.

"You think Nurtic's nothing but a frozen corpse bobbing in the sea, don't you?" Maine asked.

I didn't know what to say. This was going all wrong. Why did I bother coming over here? In about thirty seconds, the Nurians weren't going to be my problem, anymore. I shouldn't have wasted my breath.

"Aw, why are we giving you a hard time when we know you're suffering as much as us?" Link frowned. "Lechatelierite was your friend, wasn't he?"

I was startled. How did they know? It's not like the Nurians got to witness the heyday of our friendship. Since my return from captivity, Cease and I were constantly at each other's throats, upset over everything that went down with Fair and Scarlet.

"We figured it out from little hints, here and there," Link smiled, sadly, "like the look on your face when he got arrested. Sure, everybody was shaken up by that, but none as much as you."

"And, you always called him by his first name when you didn't think anyone else could hear," Maine added, "even when he specifically asked you not to."

"And, Frappe took charge of the battle after Lechatelierite went MIA, though you're next in the chain-of-command."

I stayed quiet. I wasn't about to admit to a breach of the Laws of Emotional Protection, though I doubted Link and Maine were a real threat.

At last, they made it to the bins, where they dumped their things. Link watched as the sleeve of his diving suit got swallowed by the mechanical flap, melancholy in his gaze.

"Sir, thanks for coming over," he murmured. He glanced back at the tables where the rest of the Ichthyothians sat in silence, eating breakfast, completely ignoring them.

I saluted, firmly. They returned the gesture, then disappeared into the snow.

Ichthyosis depended on Nuria. With the Conflagrian sea-blockade in full swing and our fleet too small to break through, my people were about to face the biggest struggle in nearly five eras. As the Nurians boarded their plane, I couldn't help but despair a little. Was Ichthyosis's last hope literally walking out the door?

No. The twenty-seven divers left here wouldn't give up. The majority of the Ichthyothian population got wiped out during the Epoch of the Crystal-Land's End—the seven-month period between Ichthyosis's declaration of independence from Nuria and acceptance into the Second

Earth Order. Yet, our ancestors survived. And, so would we. We'd find a way.

I heard movement, behind me. I turned and saw, with much surprise, every last one of my Ichthyothian comrades gathering to see the Nurians' jet take off.

SCARLET JULY

I'd never felt like this before. Like… absolutely nothing. It was hard to describe. Emptiness surrounded me and penetrated every aspect of my existence. It was like, I was both conscious and unconscious. I was hovering in a vortex, a vacuum, a space of whiteness.

Was this death? Well, how should I know? I couldn't hear, see or feel. But, I was aware. I could think. That had to mean something. Right?

The flesh over my collarbone seared—

Pain! I felt pain! I was elated; there was now something more than emptiness in my world. My ribs throbbed, my chest stung and my extremities felt as though pressed into a bed of thorns. And, I was cold. Unbearably cold. I'd never been so happy to be so uncomfortable.

Nothing made sense. I should've been dead, by now. I let go. Willingly. I knew I didn't stand a chance. Yet, here I was, stuck in-between a dead life and a living death. Why? What kept me here? I could feel the answer in my aura. Something—or, someone—else refused to let me go. I sensed a black wavelength relentlessly twisting around my red one, stubbornly holding it here, keeping me going.

Wait, aura? Wavelength? What!?

The paralyzing cold relented and sensation returned to my extremities. I grew… warm. Then, suddenly, I was hot. Too hot. I didn't expect to have *that* problem. It was scalding.

Especially my scalp and eyes—how they burned! Then, almost as quickly as the unbearable heat came, it went.

I opened my eyes.

Something wiry and dark filled my sight, tickling my nose. Fur? Hair? Hair!

My heart soared as I struggled to find my voice. "Cease?"

His head lifted from my collarbone with a jolt. His frost-bitten face, forehead smeared with my own blood, gaped at me.

"Scarlet!" he cried, silver-grey eyes alight. "You're alive!"

"Cease, what on earth is—"

But, his lips cut me off, coarse and cold and aggressive. I kissed back, desperately, hungrily, ignoring the pain striking my ribs. When he pulled back, his gaze dropped to my torso. He gasped. The wound was gone.

Curious, tiny, tear-drop-shaped bits of ice fell from my chest as I sat up.

"So, the spectral web crystallized," I said, quietly. Which meant Ambrek did it. He reinstated the Core Crystal. My people were enslaved. Everything the Diving Fleet accomplished in the past age was undone. Ichthyosis was back to square one. My throat tightened. "But, the new Crystal is young and we're three-thousand miles away, so my aura feels weak and—"

At that moment, my gaze landed on Cease's body. His right arm and leg stuck out at disturbing angles. Oh, Tincture! I'd forgotten about that. And, of course, my spectrum could only mend flesh. My cracked rib and his broken bones would have to heal the good old-fashioned way.

"I'm not in pain," Cease lied, expression deadpan. "But, this'll complicate our journey to civilization. We're in sector seven." Sector seven. Ichthyosis's seismically-unstable, uninhabited southwestern peninsula. "I'd say we're about... eighty miles from Icicle."

"Seventy-seven miles," I corrected. I guessed my eidetic memory was back.

I surveyed the blinding-white expanse that stretched endlessly in all directions except that of the seashore. Without Cease's intercom, we had no way to communicate with his men. Cease could hardly hold his head up, let alone walk. How would we hike seventy-seven miles in the snow?

I eyed his utility belt. "Cease, I'm going to use your deadline to make splints, okay?"

"You know how to do that?" he asked, sharply.

My pulse hammered. "When I studied in Nuria, I read some medical and wilderness-survival stuff."

"When you studied six ages ago, you mean?"

I tapped the side of my head and tried to smile reassuringly. "Spectral memory, remember?" I said, all too aware of the difference between knowing something in theory and actually executing it. "I can do this. Y-you're going to be alright."

"Who're you trying to convince, me or you?" he barked, voice like a blade. It was hard to believe he was kissing me, mere minutes ago.

I removed the flippers from my boots since I doubted I'd go swimming anytime soon. Then, crouching over Cease, I reached for his wire dispenser and unraveled several feet. It was weirdly nerve-wracking to be so close to his body. Was it just me, or did Cease seem even thinner than when we'd parted, last summer? Well, my memory didn't lie. In the last five months, Cease apparently dropped weight he couldn't afford. A lot. His joints protruded and his cheeks seemed to sink up into his face. He was downright gaunt. Tincture. I could only imagine what his life had been like, since I saw him last. The war he thought he won... amped back up. The nation he gave his life to... condemned him. The woman he loved... left him without intention to return...

Severing the cable, I imagined a diagram from page seven-hundred-twenty-five of *The Essentials of Orthopedic Surgery*.

"Here goes," I murmured, trying not to think about the immobility or limp I could inflict on Cease if I messed up.

I snaked a lock of hair down my arm, to my palm. Then, I touched Cease's knobby knee, sending a swell of pain-relieving spectrum into his leg.

Cease actually slapped my hand away, hard.

"Cease?"

"Don't waste your spectrum!" he growled. "You said your aura's weak!"

Waste? "You expect me to operate on you without using *any* anesthetic magic?" Was he kidding? Or, a masochist?

"It's not an *operation*. And, we've got bigger problems here than my pain!" Masochist it was.

"I-I'm just trying to help! I don't want to hurt you." Tears of stress involuntarily stung my lashes. "I can't do this knowing how much it'll hurt you!"

"I said no, Scarlet!"

My hands shook. I inhaled and waited until I was calm—or, as calm as possible, considering—before touching Cease again. Holding my breath, I guided the bone back into position and bound his leg with deadline. Then, I got to work on his arm.

Of course, Cease said nothing the entire time. He just pursed his thin lips.

"Done," I finally breathed.

Cease nodded. "Thank you," he said, curtly.

"I need to roll you onto your back. I can't help you up if you're on your stomach like this."

I slid my hands beneath his chest and right thigh and pushed him over his left side. His right arm and leg swung spectacularly, smacking into the ground. Oh, Tincture.

Cease grunted, loudly.

"I'm so sorry, sir!" I whimpered.

"It's fine!" His voice came out a couple octaves too high. "Don't use any magic!" He struggled to sit up, without my help.

"Wait, no," I squeaked. "Be careful!"

"There's work to do! We're not just going to sit here, are we?"

"Well, don't we have to, um, make a survival plan or something, first?"

"Talk *while* working."

Cease pulled some deadline from his belt and shoved a loop in his mouth.

"What're you doing?"

He snatched the coil with his left hand. "Weaving a fishing-net," he shot. "Either help me or find something else productive to do."

"O-okay." I scooted beside him. He sure was being short with me. Yes, we were in a tight fix and all, but what did he hope to gain from being nasty to the one person he was stranded with? It was almost as if he were the same man as when we first met. Not the man who said he loved me.

No. I pushed the unpleasant thought from my mind. His snappiness was just the injuries talking.

Making a net wasn't as tough as I expected. Cease knew what to do and I had the dexterity to do it. We made a good team. Though I could've easily done all the weaving myself, he insisted on using his mouth and left hand to help. All things considered, he was surprisingly quick and precise. But, I could tell how frustrated he was with himself. This whole fiasco probably brought back memories of his paralysis. I could see the agitation in his dangerous, diamond stare.

Fist full of wire now, he struggled to use his pinky to pull his visual band from his belt. When that didn't work, he actually tried to use the fingers of his broken arm.

I quickly grabbed it, melted its frost with my hair and snapped it across his face.

"Whenever you need help with things like that, just ask, okay?"

His mouth hardened. We continued to labor in silence, light flashing across his silver strip. I hated not being able to see his eyes, the most emotive part of his default-deadpan face. The band made it even harder to tell what he was thinking and feeling.

When we were done, he started to tie the net around his narrow waist.

"No, when it dangles, it'll bump into your leg," I said. "I'll carry it." I tried to take it from him, but he seized my arm, roughly.

I blinked. "Did you hear me? I said, I'll carry it."

"It's fine where it is."

I sighed, wrenching myself from his grasp. "I have a better idea." I got to my feet, pulled him up, wound the net around both of our waists and pulled his left arm over my shoulders.

"Lean on me," I instructed.

He didn't shift.

"Come on, all your weight," I insisted.

I knew how ridiculous that must've sounded, but how else was he expecting to walk?

He reluctantly leaned. I staggered a little and had to sacrifice a bit of spectrum to wind a reinforcing lock around his body. We could walk after that, but only about as well as a three-legged, era-old scabrous. We inched across the slippery ice, following Cease's compass north-east. After only a couple hours, I was exhausted beyond belief. With a fractured rib, a weak aura, an empty stomach and an eighteen-age-old man to support, I was on the verge of tears.

My hands and feet grew heavy and numb. My eyes rolled to the back of my head as my hair began to droop. Gait dragging, my foot caught on a small crack. I pitched backward, dragging Cease down with me. He was heavier, so he fell faster and struck ice first... with me landing smack-dab on his broken leg.

He swore at the top of his lungs in Ichthyothian, shoving me.

"Watch where you're going!"

"I'm so sorry, sir!"

He laboriously stood, yanking me up like a rag.

"Careful!" I cried. "Don't put any weight on that foot!"

"It can't *take* any weight," he snarled, "and, you've already proven you can't support me."

"I *tripped*. It was an *accident!*"

"So was Apha Edenta's little slip."

Cease's loaded words hung in the frigid air. I couldn't believe he'd say that. He knew what a sore spot Apha's death was for me. What a low blow. I closed my watering eyes and bit my lip. I couldn't take this. Not from him. Not now.

"Scarlet," he said, voice deadened by the wind, "Scarlet, I'm sorry. That was below the belt."

Lids still scrunched, I only nodded.

"This isn't supposed to be easy," he went on, tone monotonous. "I know that. It's just... hard for me to accept help, sometimes."

Only sometimes? I nodded again, still not looking at him.

"I see a rift in the landmass, over there." He gestured with his chin, voice suddenly businesslike. "Time to fish."

The white land was interrupted by a streak of sparkling blue—a river five feet wide and countless miles in twisting length.

Per Cease's request, I unraveled the net from our waists and lay him down on the ice so he was perpendicular to the rift, head about an inch from the edge. Cease stuck one end of the cable in his mouth, held the other in his left hand and swung the net into the water. In seconds, he pulled it out. It bore two fish.

I gaped. "That was… quick."

Quick? Try ridiculously amazing.

"Well, don't just *stand* there," he said crossly, killing the fish with a single stab of his deadline-sheering razor. He slid the blade toward me, across the ice. "I'll fish, you flay," he ordered.

I shook my head. "You shouldn't be straining yourself like that; I'll fish."

He tossed the net back over his head.

"Cease?" My face burned despite the bitter wind. "Did you hear me?" Was he always this stubborn and aggravating?

Visual band slipping, he regarded me with icicle-eyes. He spat the wire. "Fine, if you want to fish, be my guest. But, I'm not handing over the net."

I understood what he didn't say. So, pain-management when setting broken bones wasn't a worthy use of spectrum, but fishing was? Very well, then. I'd show him.

I put several yards between us and squatted by the river, surprised to find myself actually breathing a sigh of relief. I couldn't believe it; after five months of missing Cease desperately and longing to be reunited, I was actually glad to get away from him for a little while. Part of me even wished I was marooned with someone else— someone who cooperated with me, spoke kindly to me and wasn't too prideful to accept help. Someone like… Ambrek.

My empty stomach churned. No, not Ambrek. The real Ambrek, I didn't know. I worked with an imposter, all along. I still couldn't digest it. Just thinking about him made me want to cry.

And, now, I was stuck here with this cold man who was nothing like the Cease I left behind last summer. *That* Cease was certainly rough around the edges, yet still the type of person to draw undying devotion and awe. He was the kind of leader soldiers would follow to the bottom of the Fire Pit. His authority was born of trust and respect. He made you believe you were needed. That you were capable. That you couldn't dare to give him anything less than your absolute best because that's simply what it took to succeed together. He made you want to be excellent. He made you hunger for his approval. When I was his subordinate, I didn't dare dream of letting him down. And, it was this very allegiance and amazement he stirred in me as my military commander that wound up planting the seeds for the romantic feelings I eventually developed.

But, *this* Cease—the Cease with me today—seemed to have lost the compelling side of his otherwise hash personality. The side that made him tolerable. Now, he wasn't just stern, but downright disrespectful and mean. I was the girl he supposedly loved yet, here he was, walking all over me like I were some straggler in bootcamp. He manipulated me by instilling fear, not respect… like the System.

He was lost.

The thought filled me with dread. He came so far, over the summer. But, now, he was worse off than ever before. How? Why? I swallowed. Was I to blame? Perhaps. Maybe, our relationship screwed with his head until he became too vulnerable to handle the brutality of war. So, to cope, he tried to re-callous his conscience… and wound up overdoing it. Human nature always favored overcompensation and extremism. Political isolationism was a glaring example of that; Second Earth certainly went too far, trying to avoid First Earth's mistakes.

Was the Cease who loved me still in there, behind those glassy eyes? Could I salvage his humanity, again? *Should* I? My heart pounded in my throat. He wasn't mine to change. He belonged to the Ichthyothian military. He was officially their property. They decided, eighteen ages ago, he was born for this war. He spent his entire life cultivating a stoic spirit, to serve his country. What right did I have to mess with his militancy and undo everything he worked for, just because I wanted him for myself? Was I really that selfish?

My hair plunged into the water, weaving itself into a grid. Face only inches from the surface, I scanned the cobalt-blue depths. It was a long while before I caught something. Exhausted from the magical exertion, I carried my dinky fish to where Cease lay. Carefully avoiding his banded stare, I looked down at his net. It was full.

Apparently, the Multi-Source Enchant was no match for a half-incapacitated Cease.

He smirked, shaking off his band. "How exactly did you manage to survive alone on the city streets for five ages?"

I was silent.

He blinked. "It was a joke."

I shifted my weight from one foot to the other.

He sat up. "Well, I'm not sure I did the best thing, either. We can't eat all that now, so..." More to carry. Great. "Not to mention, our leftovers could attract wildlife."

I froze. "Wildlife?"

He gave me a strange look. "We're out here in the open; why wouldn't there be wildlife?"

"I don't know." A red lock spontaneously twisted around my finger. "Ichthyosis just seems so... barren. I guess I never considered the possibility of there being animals around, or anything."

Cease blinked, again. "Of course, there'd be animals in an ecosystem. Especially out here, where industry doesn't reach." It must've been strange for him to hear something so dumb from the mouth of the person who once read every nonfiction book in southeastern Nuria. "I suppose, compared to Conflagria, Ichthyosis just seems like a wasteland to you." His voice was actually… sad. It was as if he wanted me to like being here. With him.

My gaze dropped.

"You hate it here. You don't want to stay on this island a minute longer than you have to, do you?" he asked, cutting right to the heart of it.

Cheeks burning, I nodded.

"Well, if the System mind-control is back, the Red Revolution is gone and you don't have a home to go back to. Not yet, anyway. You can't leave until we take care of the new Core Crystal. I'm sorry."

There was a long, uncomfortable pause. I wanted to tell him how much I missed him when I was away, how his presence made even Ichthyosis beautiful, how I wished with all my heart that I could go home without having to say goodbye. I wanted to tell him, if it were up to me, I'd never leave his side again. But, the words got caught in my throat. Instead, I just reached for the pile of fish and murmured, "Let's start cleaning these up."

Using Cease's razor and lance, we flayed a few. Then, we staked them on the end of the lance and I roasted them with my eye-fire. It didn't work too well. Spectral fire wasn't exactly slow-cooking material. The outer layer of the meat blackened in seconds while the insides stayed cold and pink.

But, it was food, the only food we had, so we sat down and ate. In silence.

This was so surreal. I never thought I'd set foot on this icy shore again, yet here I was, and with—

"Cease," I suddenly spurted, mouth full, "why are you here? What were you doing in battle, yesterday? Aren't you supposed to be on trial in Nuria?"

Cease bit his fish's head off. "So, you heard about that."

I nodded.

"Know what my charges are?"

"Yes."

"How did you find out?"

How exactly did he turn this into an interrogation? "*The Alcove City Post.*"

His eyes narrowed to diamond slits. "I'm guessing they don't deliver to Conflagria. What were you doing in Alcove City?"

"I went to the Centerscraper to ask to borrow a ship."

He froze in mid-chew. Did he know who his father was?

"Your dad is the CEO of the Underwater Vessel Manu-facturing Company," I blurted.

"I know," his voice was hard, "we've met."

They did? "I met him, too."

"How'd it go?"

"Not well. He denied my request, almost immediately."

"No surprise there," he snorted. "He hated you from the moment he learned your name."

I felt slapped. "Cease, how does he even know a-about… us… in the first place?"

"Well, *I* didn't tell him," he grumbled, spitting a nee-dle-like fish bone. "No one's supposed to know."

His command was on the line. The Laws of Emotional Protection forbade soldiers from making friends, let alone acting on romantic interests. But, wait, *what* command…?

"Cease, what happened at your court-martial?"

He looked away. "I was discharged."

The wind leaked from my lungs. I stared at his angular profile in shock.

"I could only command yesterday's battle because Leavesleft—whom I promoted in my place—leveraged the national state-of-emergency to request my temporary release—"

"State-of-emergency?" I sat up straighter.

"To put it short, the System found out about the alliance, firebombed the Centerscraper and initiated a sea blockade. The Order threatened blacklisting if Nuria doesn't sever its relations with Ichthyosis, right away. Nuria is complying. We're alone in the war, now."

The stench of half-burnt-half-raw fish suddenly nauseated me as a lump the size of a hobnail egg formed in my throat. How else did the System find out about the alliance but through Ambrek, who learned it from me? How else did they get their hands on a firebomb? Cease's dad was dead. Thousands of Nurian civilians burned alive. Ichthyosis lost its lifeline. And, it was all my fault!

I could hardly bear it. I started to cry.

"Stop it!" Cease shouted. "We can't afford weakness when we must fight to survive, out here!"

But, his words only pushed me further over the edge. I sobbed harder.

"I said, cut that out, right now!"

How were tears an unreasonable response to news like this? Wasn't he upset, too? Fear, sorrow, anger and stress welled in my chest, all at once. "Unlike you," I found myself yelling, "I'm not a robot who never shed a tear in his life for anyone!"

Cease's blinked. "That's not true; I've cried at least twice in my li—"

"I can't watch the world end and feel *nothing!*" I screamed in his face.

His eyes were molten-iron. "Do you know what it's like to 'feel nothing'? To hurt someone, to destroy them, to know what you did was bad, to *will* yourself to regret it, but still draw a blank?"

I was taken aback. "N-no."

"At my court-martial yesterday, I had to look at countless photos of Fair Gabardine's wounds and listen to Nurse Raef go on and on about how I scarred her for life." Terror prickled through me. "And, you know what I felt?" He raised his voice. "Nothing. You know how hard it is to see something like that, know you're responsible and not feel a shred of remorse no matter how much you tell yourself to?" His words rang in the crisp air.

"Sir," I whispered. "I-I'm sorry... I didn't mean to—"

"Yes, you did!" he cut across me. Then, looking at his boots, he added in a quieter tone, "And, you're right to."

Silence.

"Cease, I—"

He held up his hand. "Scarlet, it's not easy being the way I am, being *aware* of what I am. I was blissfully ignorant, before you came along. And, sometimes, I wish I could go back. Back to how things were before I knew what was missing. But, I can't. Try as I might, I can't erase your influence from my life—not completely. And, believe me, I've tried. I've tried every damn day, since the war rekindled."

I didn't dare blink or breathe. He was having a rare, vulnerable moment and I was afraid any movement or sound on my part would snap him out of it.

"Being around you again after all these months also isn't easy for me, you know," he went on, voice barely above a whisper, as though afraid the fish would overhear, "because you make it harder to ignore what I'm lacking. You remind me every minute what it looks like to be... different. Real. Alive."

I didn't know what to say. I just sat there, staring stupidly, heart swelling with promise. Cease wasn't lost, after all. There was hope for him, yet. His old self never would've fathomed of there being another way to see the world. But, now, he recognized there was something wrong. He felt incomplete.

Even after five months of silent separation, he couldn't snuff out the fire I lit in his heart.

* * *

The miles stretched before us, endless as the blinding-white horizon. Cease and I struggled side-by-side through the snow, clinging to one another, watching over each other. What an odd sight we'd be, to an onlooker—a white-and-blue-suited Ichthyothian diver with an orange-and-green-clad Conflagrian mage. Not even seven eras of worldwide isolationism could stand between us.

MARY-ESTHER LEAVESLEFT

If you'd told me just a couple ages ago that my sweet, gentle son would grow up to be a soldier, I would've had a good laugh.

Since childhood, Nurtic was a jack of many trades. He was athletic, smart and almost annoyingly charismatic. His personality drew an eclectic assortment of friends, from jocks to nerds. His teachers couldn't get enough of him. His stellar academic record was accompanied by an impressive list of extracurricular activities like lacrosse, basketball, church and viola. He still made time for relaxing and hanging out with the boys, though. He and his two longtime best friends, Ecivon Wen and Tnerruc Ruetama, were regulars at the train-station arcade.

Even-keel and placid, Nurtic was never the type to shake things up without provocation. He tended to roll with the status-quo. Which was why my husband, John-Paul, and I thought it odd when everything suddenly changed during Nurtic's senior age of high school.

It all started with Nurtic's political-science class. His teacher, Oke Addle, had a stroke about two weeks into the school-age and got replaced by an illegal Ichthyothian named Enahc Ecreoc whose son, Diving Commander Ecrof Ecreoc, had recently died in combat. Enahc hated the international Isolationist Laws, flagrantly disregarding them by teaching his students about the Ichthyo-Conflagrian Wars. It wasn't long before he got discovered, fired from Bay River Secondary and deported back to Ichthyosis. But, the damage was done.

Almost overnight, Nurtic quit the lacrosse and basketball teams in favor of the swim team, alongside his new friends, Arrhyth Link and Dither Maine. He started spending a whole lot of time at the Link mansion. Whenever he went there, he'd come home very late, backpack bulging. Then, he'd hole up in his room for hours, door shut.

His father and I grew concerned. It was very unlike Nurtic to drop his favorite sports, stay out so late and barely speak a word to his parents, day-in and day-out.

One evening at dinner, John-Paul, grinning over a bowl of spaghetti, asked Nurtic, out-of-the-blue, "Alright, what's her name?"

Nurtic looked up from his food, face blank.

"What's her name, the girl you like?" John-Paul insisted.

Nurtic blinked.

"Is it Linkeree?" Linkeree was Arrhyth's little sister, a couple ages his junior. That'd explain why Nurtic was constantly over at their place.

"There's no girl, dad," Nurtic said. "I don't like Ree. Not like that, anyway."

John-Paul chuckled. "Nothing wrong if you did. Your mother and I were already sweethearts, at your age."

Nurtic stared.

Time for some damage-control. "We've just noticed a lot of changes with you, lately," I jumped in. "Quitting lacrosse and basketball, coming home after dark each day, refusing to commit to the college that's been your dream since you were in diapers. It's not like you." Since early childhood, Nurtic had always expressed an interest in the University of Vita, the top public school in the country.

"I'm just exploring my options, mom," he said, head in his plate. "I'm not sure what I want to do with my life." He twirled his fork in his left hand. "I don't want to do 'early admission' to UVA, anymore."

"How come?"

He was silent, fingers fluttering to the stainless-steel cross around his neck.

The next day, after Nurtic left for school and John-Paul went to work, I did some housekeeping. Working my way around Nurtic's bed, the front of my vacuum-cleaner bumped into something. Frowning, I got down on my knees and peeked under the wooden frame.

There lay half a dozen books, the nearest of which was titled, *The Legacy of the Lechatelierites.* Lechatelierite. That didn't ring any bells. I opened it and peered at a black-and-white photograph of a boy probably about two or three ages younger than Nurtic. He wore a peculiar suit, covered in bands, cords and medals. He had a pointed face, messy hair and eerie, colorless eyes. His high cheekbones and angular jaw would've made him conventionally handsome, if it weren't for the intense anger in his stare. And, his body was much too lean. Almost emaciated. I suppressed a shudder. Why would Nurtic want to learn about this man? I read the caption: *'Cease Terminus Lechatelierite, when first promoted to Commander of the Ichthyothian Diving Fleet at the age of fifteen (December of the 90th age).'*

I looked up. Ichthyothian Diving Fleet? My pulse quickened. Ichthyothian? It was as though I found drugs under Nurtic's bed. This book was contraband. My son violated the Isolationist Laws. I couldn't believe it. Where did he even get this? I snapped it shut, spotting a sticker on the back cover: 'PROPERTY OF THE SECOND EARTH ORDER. ON LOAN TO: Arnold Link.' I breathed a sigh of relief; Nurtic didn't break the law. He just borrowed material from his friend's father. But, why?

I flipped through, catching terms, names and phrases like, 'crystalline shuttle,' 'vitreous silica,' 'Arrete Lechatelierite,' 'Ichthyo-Conflagrian War,' 'Terminus Lechatelierite,' 'Finis Lechatelierite' and a whole lot about 'Cease Lechatelierite,' the scary man in the first picture I saw. My confusion only grew. Why would Nurtic read about the military figures of some random country? Why learn about any nation but your own? Unless considering a future in the Second Earth Order—something Nurtic never expressed an interest in, before—studying foreign affairs was a waste of time.

I pulled out another volume. *The Ichthyo-Conflagrian War: An In-Depth Study of the Current Conflict Between the North Ichthyosis Island and the South Conflagrablaze Captive.* Another book about war! I rolled my eyes. Boys will be boys, I supposed.

The next one was curiously titled, *Fire vs. Ice: Predicted Outcomes of the Ongoing Ichthyo-Conflagrian War.* I exhaled through my nostrils. Current conflict. Predicted outcomes. Ongoing war. And, the picture of the young Ichthyothian Diving Commander was recent, taken in the ninetieth age. My lips parted. The two countries directly to our north and south were at war. Right now.

Gnawing my lip, I prowled under Nurtic's bed, retrieving the last two books in his stash. They had nothing to do with history or current events.

The Nurian-Ichthyothian Dictionary.

Learn to Speak and Write Basic Ichthyothian in One Age.

I froze. It was one thing for a boy to be interested in war and quite another for a busy student to want to learn a foreign language in his free time.

I shoved everything back under Nurtic's bed and stood up, bumping into his desk. His computer screen flicked on, displaying an instant-message window from last night:

1&OnlyNurroOrion: i got something 2 tell u

LeftyLeaf: ur new screen name makes no sense. u arent the only nurro orion. what about ree

1&OnlyNurroOrion: nevermind her, ive got big news

LeftyLeaf: whats up?

1&OnlyNurroOrion: u may want 2 sit down 4 this

LeftyLeaf: um already am...

1&OnlyNurroOrion: drumroll pls

LeftyLeaf: ur killing me. spill

LeftyLeaf: come on! >_<

1&OnlyNurroOrion: diving commander cease something is coming here in sept right b4 we graduate 2 convince nuria 2 b an ally :-)

LeftyLeaf: r u kidding!!?? hes coming HERE? :-O

1&OnlyNurroOrion: well not *here* but northern nuria somewhere

LeftyLeaf: omg so crazy. how u know?

1&OnlyNurroOrion: dad duh :-)

LeftyLeaf: im in shock

1&OnlyNurroOrion: me 2

LeftyLeaf: wouldnt that blacklist nuria?

1&OnlyNurroOrion: like hell. but u think dad'll let that happen? he supports the war mvmnt & will hush it all up :-P

LeftyLeaf: he can keep a secret that big from rest of world?

1&OnlyNurroOrion: sure y not? he has lots of power

LeftyLeaf: O_o thats not just a big lie, its international conspiracy

1&OnlyNurroOrion: so what? this is what we wanted. we want 2 join up remember

LeftyLeaf: i know but it still makes me nervous. do u think cease will win over nuria?

1&OnlyNurroOrion: well hes never lost a fight b4

I sank back to the floor. Nuria was going to war. My son—who'd never even step on a worm—was going to war. He wanted to participate in an international conspiracy, throwing himself in the middle of a violent clash between two blacklisted nations.

Everything made sense, now. Why Nurtic was no longer dead-set on UVA. Why he joined the swim-team. Why he spent hours with the Links, every other day.

Nurtic was full of energy at dinner, that night. About halfway through the meal, he unearthed a pamphlet from nowhere, blurting, "The airport isn't too far from home; I can bike there, after school. And, I have enough saved up to pay for everything myself. I promise it won't cut into practice or homework, either. Not to mention, it'll look great on my resume—"

"Hold on, Nurtic, we don't even know what you're talking about, yet," John-Paul breathed, taking the brochure from him.

It was for the Alcove City Flight School. My stomach disappeared.

John-Paul's brows raised. "What's this all about?"

Nurtic hesitated.

"It sounds very expensive and time-consuming," my husband went on. "Not to mention, I don't think you have to worry about your resume. UVA—or any college you may be considering, these days—would be lucky to have a student like you."

Nurtic took a deep breath. "Mom, dad, I have something to tell you." He swallowed, pushing aside his bowl of soup. "After graduating, I want to go to an Ichthyothian military academy. I want to grow up to be a Diving Fleet pilot."

John-Paul looked at Nurtic as though he spontaneously sprouted a second head. "And, I want to be a Conflagrian mage. Doesn't mean I can just hop out the window, swinging from the trees by my hair." He tossed the brochure on the table. "Sorry, son, but you're forgetting a little something called isolationism. No Ichthyothian school would accept a Nurian citizen. You saw what happened to your civics teacher."

"They could accept me," Nurtic said, "if Nuria and Ichthyosis become allies."

John-Paul took a draught of milk. "The Briggesh administration will agree to that the day I start growing magical hair."

"The Leader of the Ichthyothian Resistance himself is coming to the northern coast in September to meet with the Briggesh administration. Arrhyth's dad said so. And, he thinks the officer stands a good chance of convincing the president."

John-Paul froze in mid-gulp.

Nurtic shrugged, slurping his soup. "I dunno, the Diving Fleet may not even take me. I'm trying not to get my hopes up too high, and I'll still apply to normal schools like UVA, of course, just not 'early admission.' Because this is what I really want. I'm sure. I want to fight. I want to defend the northwestern hemisphere from imperialism."

By the fall, Nurtic left for the Nurian Diving Academy on the northern shore. We didn't hear a word from or about him until the spring of the ninety-third age, when the Commander with the impossible last name sent us a brief form letter relaying Nurtic's acceptance into the Nurro-Ichthyothian Diving Fleet, prompting his relocation to Icicle Base in Aventurine City, Ichthyosis, across the Septentrion Sea. Our little boy was all grown up.

Only six or so weeks later, we received another note, conveying Nurtic's promotion to unit two officer. We were floored. By the end of the age, the scary-eyed Commander was court-martialed, leaving none other than our son in charge. We couldn't believe it.

And, then, about a week after that, the Nurian Trade Centerscraper was firebombed and the alliance crumbled. The five-hundred-some surviving Nurian divers came home.

Nurtic wasn't among them.

FAIR GABARDINE

Captain Anapes Patrici assigned me to Seventh Cabin, to oversee a POW Ambrek brought back from the sea. An Ichthyothian diver. So, Ambrek managed to find the crystal shard, kill Lechatelierite and Scarlet, restore the spectral web *and* seize a prisoner, all in one night. He was a war hero. The most important mage in Conflagrian history.

The door creaked open.

"Prunus?" I called into the dusty darkness. "Ivy?"

Silence.

"They aren't here," a voice answered in Ichthyothian, to my left.

I turned on my heel, hair poised defensively, and laid eyes on a white-suited, hazel-eyed, long-limbed, sandy-haired man bound to a bench. I recognized him, immediately. It was Nurtic Leavesleft, the pilot who took Scarlet and I back to Conflagria after the Crystal's end, last summer.

He actually grinned. So weird. "I'd shake your hand if I could, but, well…" He glanced down at his ropes and shrugged.

I wasn't sure what to say. I didn't expect my prisoner to chat and joke like we were old friends meeting for a drink of coconut milk. That threw me for a loop.

He squinted. "Hey, I know you," he said, slowly. "Lechatelierite brought you back to Icicle with Buird, last July."

How very kind of him to remind me of my imprisonment. I swore loudly, in Conflagrian.

"Sorry, I don't speak mage."

Of course, he didn't. Those elitist Nordics didn't bother to learn *our* language. Not that I spoke his too well—my speech was slow and my accent was thick.

Leavesleft's eyes were sad. "You were Scarlet July's best friend. Her co-leader. Weren't you?"

"I was a fool!" I spat in Ichthyothian. "The Red Revolution is dead."

"Fair Gabardine," he said. "I remember, now. It means 'white threads,' right?"

"An Ichthyothian who actually understands the art of language; I'm impressed," I sneered.

"I'm Nurian."

I snorted. "I almost feel sorry for you, then. You're one of those naïve high-schoolers who got brainwashed at a career fair—"

"Brainwashed? Interesting word-choice for a System soldier whose every move is controlled by the Core Crystal."

I didn't answer.

"Scarlet July was my friend and comrade, too," he went on. "I care a lot about her, just like you."

"Scarlet means nothing to me."

"You spent the last five months working with her, to rebuild your nation. She was your leader, your confidant. You grew up with her, you looked after her, you missed her when she was taken away. Tell me this, Fair Gabardine: what would Scarlet say if she could see you, now?"

I kicked the insufferable Nurian in the chest. He took the blow without so much as a flinch. "Scarlet's a traitor!" I screamed.

"Once again, interesting word choice," he plowed on. "Because, I know all about the real Fair Gabardine. I know she's still there, standing right in front of me. She's a brave warrior who'd rather die than betray her people.

She pledged her life to defending her country. I know what that's like. I made a promise like that, too. It's not something I take lightly. I'm committed—mind, body and soul. So are you. To the Reds, to Scarlet. Not to the System. The System only wants to enslave you. But, you're stronger than that. The right hand of the Multi-Source Enchant is no one's slave. She's listening to me now, agreeing with me, pleading with you to set her free—"

"Shut up!" I cried, hair-whipping his face.

"Why do my words bother you?" he grunted. "Because you know I'm right. Fair, you can break out of it—at least for a little while—I know you can! You want to. Fight it off and go help Scarlet! Help her destroy the Crystal! Come on!"

Terror shot through me as I thought of Scarlet. I panted with an open mouth, eyes tracking.

"Where is she?" Nurtic boomed. "Find her and help her. Find her and help her."

Shaking from head to toe, I fell to my knees. "I-I can't!"

"Why not?"

"Because she's dead!" I heaved. "Ambrek killed her and Lechatelierite!"

"No." Nurtic's hazel eyes went wide. "No, I don't believe that."

"Ambrek came back from the sea alone, suit dripping in their blood!"

He shook his head, blonde hair flying. "No, Scarlet's not dead. She can't be. Scarlet is linked to the prophecy. So, until it's fulfilled, she can't go."

Did he really believe that? "H-how can you be sure?"

"I can't. I don't even know anymore if Scarlet is the one, Fair. But, I do believe she's a chapter in the story, at least. She *and* Lechatelierite. So, they can't die. Not yet. Mark my words," he insisted, as I felt my brief mental freedom come to a close. "Second Earth hasn't seen the last of Scarlet July and Cease Lechatelierite."

CEASE LECHATELIERITE

It'd been three days since Scarlet and I began our journey across sector seven. Progress was slow. We were going at a rate of about seven miles per thirty-six hours.

Eight days to go.

I hated being so helpless. Since recovering from my paralysis, I'd forgotten what it was like to depend on others for my every need, great or small.

Scarlet was clearly bending beneath the pressure of being my fulltime caretaker. It was hard to see her so anxious in my presence. She apologized for every whim, wrung her hands, spoke to her boots and often called me 'sir' though I had no formal authority over her, anymore. Knowing what was at stake if we didn't make it back to base sooner than later, I found myself easily irritated by her bumbling insecurity, prone to snapping and giving her more reasons to fret. It was a vicious cycle.

I'd dreamt of reuniting with Scarlet almost every day since she left. But, I never thought it'd be like this.

INEXOR BUIRD

"Commander Buird, Dr. Calibre says Tose Acci's in a coma," reported Illia, my Second-in-Command.

"Thank you, Frappe," I sighed. "Please alert Tacit."

"Yes, sir."

Tose was in Quiesce Tacit's unit. The fleet now had three units of seven and one unit of six. Without Tose, unit four was down to five divers. It needed a transfer in.

We'd just come home from battle. Shuttle hit, Tose got knocked upside the head while ejecting. With Cease and Leavesleft both MIA, Tose was the best pilot we had. When the Nurians arrived at Icicle and Tose saw Leavesleft in action, he asked to be reassigned to unit two just to observe him more closely. Leavesleft was happy to take Tose under his wing. The two of them were liable to stay out in the sea all night, practicing pilotry. Cease never offered Tose a unit, but was quick to call on him to perform his Leavesleft-like feints in battle, engaging enemy ships in a dizzying game of tag. Leavesleft was the master of what the Nurians liked to call the 'horsefly maneuver.' It was practically impossible to get a target-lock on him.

Wait a minute...

"Frappe!"

Illia turned on his heel and jogged back down the corridor. "Commander?"

"Frappe, how did they hit Leavesleft?" I blurted.

He blinked. "Excuse me, sir?"

"How did the System shoot down Leavesleft?" My mind raced. "He was pretty far off the grid. Not at all in the thick of things. He wasn't surrounded, cornered or outnumbered. He was up against a single enemy fighter. How could one fighter take him out?"

Was that an eye-roll? "One is all it takes, sir."

"For anybody else, sure. But, not Leavesleft."

Illia's nostrils flared. "He really wasn't that brilliant, you know. The kid had trouble with pre-calculus, for crying out loud. Could hardly sit in class for two minutes without whispering to Scarlet for help."

"And, Leavesleft wasn't alone, either," I went on. "He had Lechatelierite with him. The best tactician this fleet has ever seen. So, we had our top pilot and best strategist, together on one craft, dogfighting a single enemy. The odds were really in their favor. Their crystalline wasn't bombarded; it took a single hit, in the engine. A clean shot."

Illia shrugged. "So, the System has a good sharpshooter."

"A great sharpshooter. One who's a match for both Leavesleft and Lechatelierite, combined. Who on Second Earth fits that description?"

He folded his arms. "Sir, we don't *know* any Conflagrians. We can't begin to guess who in the Water Forces is responsible. What does it matter, anyway?"

"We do know a Conflagrian. You actually know her a lot better than me because you got to see her fight, firsthand."

There was a long pause.

"That's impossible, sir," Illia said, flatly. "She couldn't. She wouldn't."

"Who else could it be? Leavesleft can't be hit, but Scarlet July can't miss. I've watched her practice videos. I've read Lechatelierite's logs, analyzing her. I've seen her files and test scores. It all adds up."

Illia shook his head. "Sir, Scarlet July would never fight for the System."

"Frappe, can we really trust any Conflagrian completely?"

Now, Illia looked enraged. The loyalty Scarlet cultivated from everyone in such a short space of time was incredible. She spent, what, seven months at the academy and a measly two-and-a-half months at Icicle? Yet, every diver who knew her, Nurian and Ichthyothian alike, was fully committed to her. Despite the brevity of her service, Scarlet was a legend among my comrades.

"You don't even know her, sir," Illia shot. "You never went into battle with your life in her hands. She isn't like other Conflagrians. Everything the Childhood Program taught us about *them* doesn't apply to her. She's one of us. Period."

"I hope you're right."

If he wasn't, Ichthyosis was up against one hell of an enemy.

NURTIC LEAVESLEFT

Sand stung my throat. Sweat burned my eyes. Magically-fortified ropes chaffed my wrists. The air was stale and hazy and probably about one-hundred-twenty degrees. My tongue was a thick wad of sandpaper in my mouth.

But, this was what I wanted, wasn't it? Despite my dust allergy, I wanted to move—at least for a few ages—to Conflagria one day to reach out to magekind. Well, here I was. No time like the present. Right?

If only the System weren't mentally enslaving everyone I interacted with.

The prophecy said that the Multi-Source Enchant would, 'take from all the fallen children of Second Earth what was no longer rightfully theirs.' I used to think that meant Scarlet would strip Conflagria of spectrum. I thought the prophecy got fulfilled when Scarlet and Lechatelierite destroyed the Core Crystal in July. But, after watching all their work come undone, I was no longer sure what to believe. Because when prophecies got fulfilled, they *stayed* fulfilled. So, maybe, God didn't want to do away with the spectral web. Magic was a central part of Conflagrian life and culture, after all. Perhaps it was just the dominion of the System that the Multi-Source Enchant was meant to revoke? I wondered, must the spectrum and the mind-control be a packaged deal?

Fair Gabardine was the engineer of the Underwater Fire. She was a brilliant spectroscoper. I couldn't think of a better brain to pick.

"Excuse me, Miss Gabardine?" I called.

The wooden door creaked and Fair's head poked in.

"What?" she snapped.

"I just wanted to ask you something, if now's a good time."

"Quit feigning decency, will you?" She hugged a scroll to her chest. "No, now isn't a good time. So, shut the hell up!"

"You know, you really *could* shut me up. You could bind my mouth. Beat me blue. Interrogate me. Hand me over to higher authorities so the System can really have its way with me. But, you don't. You just put me to work a few hours a day, then leave me be. Why?"

Fair blinked. "I've been… busy."

"Busy," I echoed. "Is that it, or are you religiously following the Geneva Convention because you remember all too well what it's like to be held by a captor who doesn't?"

She glared at me the way she always did, whenever the topic of Cease Lechatelierite came up. "You son of a—"

"If you're not going to use me for anything, why do you keep me around? Why don't you just kill me?"

Her oil-black eyes went wide.

"My labor hasn't been too valuable; I can hardly function in this heat," I went on. "Keeping me alive probably costs more than I'm worth. I'm an enemy of the System, a Nordic. And, I'm completely at your mercy."

I could practically see the gears turn in Fair's mind as she blinked again and again, a white lock autonomously twisting around her finger. I recognized what was going on—she was slowly starting to break back through the Crystal's fog.

"Why are you keeping me alive, Fair?" I boomed. "Why haven't you killed me, yet?"

Shaking, she sank to her knees. "I just… c-can't," she choked.

"You can't because you know, deep down, you don't want to serve the System. You know you're only doing it because you feel forced. But, you remember who Fair Gabardine really is and what she stands for. Not for an evil dictatorship."

"They t-tell me they're th-the ones p-protecting Conflagria." Was it just me, or did Fair's aura suddenly adopt a peculiar, reddish tint? "P-protecting it from the Nordic t-technophiles who w-want to steal our spectrum and c-condemn Conflagria to i-international obscurity–"

The door banged open and Fair leapt to her feet. Ambrek Coppertus stomped inside, carrying a thick, ancient-looking book with gilded pages. He spurted a string of rapid Conflagrian. Fair shrugged and blurted something back. Ambrek squared his jaw, fury in his gold gaze. He threw his massive hands up, muttered under his breath and stalked out the door. Fair smiled as she watched him retreat. Then, she whirled around, ran to the fireplace and threw her scroll into it. Scarlet flames consumed the amber parchment in a matter of seconds. Soon, it was nothing but a lump of blackened ash.

Something flickered in Fair's stare. "I just… lied to Ambrek and destroyed my work," she whispered. "I told him I hit a bump in my assignment. But, I was actually almost done. It was a big project, too. Something that'd turn this whole war on its head. And, now, it's just… gone." She turned toward me, eyes raking my face. "Because of *you*."

"Stay with me, Fair," I pleaded. "Fight off those thoughts; they aren't yours. Listen to me."

"Why should I?" she growled. "Why am I either a tool of the System or a tool of the Nordics?"

"This is war, Fair. You have to pick a side if you want to fight. That's how it works."

"So, I'm either doing what you say, or what Ambrek and Tincture say?" She balled her fists. "When I was in the Water Forces, I did whatever Crimson Cerise said. During the Red Revolution, I did whatever Scarlet said. All my life, I've never been anything more than a puppet."

"That's not true. You're a soldier, not a puppet. Soldiers follow orders; that's in the job description. I do it, too."

"I gave the System the Underwater Fire. The most powerful spectral weapon to date. And, now, I was *about* to give them a solid plan to outfit their blockade ships with the ability to strengthen the spectral web across Ichthyosis, melting all its ice and preparing it for Conflagrian occupation. But, then, in came holy-man Nurtic Leavesleft, prophet from Nuria, telling me I'm nothing but a slave, that my hard work is a crime against humanity!"

Oh my goodness, she was about to give them *what?*

"Fair, you don't have to be anyone's slave, puppet or tool. My people want to free yours. That's what we've been fighting for."

Fair let out a hollow laugh. "Maybe, that's why *Scarlet* got involved in this war, but that sure as hell isn't the reason Ichthyosis destroyed the Crystal. Ichthyosis didn't diffuse the spectrum to free us. They did it to weaken us. To take away our sustenance and way-of-life. Think about it, Nordic: what would your world be like, without technology? What would happen to your quality of life? Without spectrum, Conflagrian society falls apart. Without auras, so do our bodies. When Scarlet and I came home last August to start the Red Revolution, there was barely a nation left to salvage. Forget the 'Reign of Terror' in First-Earth France; things here were way worse. Starvation, violence, rape, theft, murder. No magic, no tech, no stable government, no tools nor resources nor faint idea of how to cope with the diffusion. We didn't even know any medical-science—we always relied on magic for that. Imagine an entire society with no doctors, no medicine, no diagnostic tools, no fancy x-ray machines, no surgeons. Everywhere you looked, people were dying of infections, malaria, scarlet fever, measles, you name it. Scarlet was the only one among us who knew any health-science, but she's still no doctor and she certainly couldn't take care of an entire country on her own. In the midst of all the chaos, it got pretty damn hard not to hate Ichthyosis for doing this to us. You see, *Scarlet's* intention in destroying the Core Crystal was to free her people. But, *Ichthyosis's* intention was to rob us blind and leave us to die."

I didn't know what to say. I hadn't a clue just how bad things were in diffused Conflagria. Magic was everything, here. And, after taking it away, my people didn't lift a finger to help the Island of Fire stand on its own two feet. The alliance did nothing for the country whose world they single-handedly turned upside-down.

Lechatelierite tried. He pleaded with the alliance to assist the revolution and was about to go against his superiors' word and take matters into his own hands regardless of the consequences. But, he never got the chance. The Alliance Committee threw him in jail before he could do a thing. And, I busted him out for nothing—who knew where he was now or if he was even alive.

"Fair, is there a way to extract the mind-control from the spectral web?" I got down to business. "Is it possible to extinguish it without destroying the entire magical network?"

"The System bound up the web, eras ago. I wouldn't have the faintest idea where to begin with something like that."

Wait a minute. "How long has it been, now?"

"Since the System took over? Like, forever."

"No, since we started this conversation?"

She looked down at her magical sundial. "Almost fifteen minutes."

No way. "You did it, Fair; you broke through the seven-minute limit!"

"Tincture, you're right," she breathed.

"But, how?"

"I have a theory, but there's no time to get into it now," she hastily replied. "Let's run!"

Fair severed my bindings with her hair and pulled me to my feet. Quickly stowing her bow, quiver and sword under her cloak, we scurried out the door and into the forest.

"Let's grab a ship and head for Ichthyosis," Fair panted.

I breathed with an open mouth. It was really hard to run in a hundred-twenty degrees, especially while hungry and dehydrated. "How will we get to the hangar without being intercepted?"

"I know of an underground tunnel from the forest to the Castle basement."

Huh. "Sounds real shady and dangerous."

"No, it should be okay; the System has no clue about it."

A secret passage into the heart of the enemy turf? Seriously? How convenient. Something smelled fishy.

"What? Did the Reds build it?" How did they manage that?

"No."

So, neither the Reds nor the System was responsible for it? "Then, who did?"

"Crimson Cerise."

That only raised more questions. "Why would the Captain of the Water Forces need a secret path to her own base?"

"I don't know."

"How did you find out about it?"

"Ambrek."

Pieces fell into place. Crimson built the passage to help facilitate Ambrek's double-agent role. I grabbed Fair's arm, stopping us dead in our tracks.

"We can't use the tunnel; it isn't safe."

Fair wasn't listening. "Oh, Tincture," she stared over my shoulder, "someone's headed our way!"

FAIR GABARDINE

"Quick!" My hair seized Nurtic's wrists, pulling them behind his back. "Act like a prisoner!"

"Shouldn't be too hard," he muttered.

I shoved him. "Keep moving, Nordic!" I barked, loudly. Nurtic cast me a surprisingly-convincing glower.

The mage approaching us had a rust-colored moustache and wore an orange robe and a stupid green hat. Great. Of all people to take a stroll in the woods today, it had to be Principal Tiki Tincture himself!

"Gabardine." He yielded me a curt nod.

I bowed, deeply. "Your Majesty."

"State your business with this Ichthyothian." Nurtic visibly recoiled as Tincture surveyed him closely. I fought the urge to laugh—the kid was one hell of an actor. Then again, maybe, he didn't need to feign disgust when staring pure evil in the face.

"I'm taking him to Ambrek Coppertus for interrogation, Your Grace."

"Coppertus tells me you're having difficulty with the project." His eyes scoured mine. "Perhaps, you should spend less time parading around with your little capture and more time researching."

"Yes, of course, Orange One." I bowed again.

With that, Tincture grunted and stormed off.

"That was close," I breathed to Nurtic, once the Principal was out of ear and eyeshot. I released him from my hair.

"What did you tell him?"

"I said I was taking you for interrogation."

"I heard you guys mention Ambrek?"

"I said he's the one questioning you."

Nurtic moaned. "Bad move. What if he sees Ambrek later on and asks him how it went?"

"I had to think fast, Nurtic; sorry if my lie was imperfect!" I looked down at our feet and saw a little knob poking from the shrubbery. "We're here." I stooped.

But, before I could yank the thing, Nurtic grabbed my wrist.

"Where's Ambrek?"

"Right now? I don't know."

"Well, we shouldn't go in there until we do."

"What? Why?"

That's when the door flew open and a large, muscular hand caught my ankle.

AMBREK COPPERTUS

Fair screamed as she fell and hit the ground. I jammed the door shut before Leavesleft could jump in, after us.

"Tell me how you did it, traitor!" I yelled, seizing her neck with one hand and her hair with the other. "How did you break through the seven-minute limit?"

She wheezed and gagged, face changing from brown to yellow.

"Answer me, now, before I twitch my fingers and snap your neck!"

"Ssscarlet," she gagged.

I shook her. "Scarlet's dead! I killed her!" How could she borrow photons from a dead mage? How could she stay twined to a diffused frequency?

Without warning, my vision clouded. When the fog lifted, it was no longer Fair who lay at my feet, but a red-faced, red-haired, green-eyed girl in a ragged red robe, belly protruding like she had tapeworm. My hand was pressed hard against a wound on her chest, as though trying to stop the bleeding.

Terror and confusion shot through me like lightning. "Scarlet?"

"Hurry!" she screamed. "Get your sword! You can save him!"

Save who? From what? Why was there blood everywhere? Who did this to her?

"Scarlet?" I cried, again.

"Hurry, Ambrek!" she screamed, iridescent flashes of red and black light surrounding us.

Then, something whacked me upside the head. And, like magic, I was back in the underground tunnel. World spinning, I blinked repeatedly.

Nurtic Leavesleft landed, catlike, beside me.

NURTIC LEAVESLEFT

I tugged on the knob, to no avail. The door was jammed shut by a hand mage, after all. A hand mage who'd probably snap Fair's neck in about fifteen seconds, if I didn't manage to get inside and stop him. But, I had no weapon, no deadline, no lance, no razor. How'd I open the hatch?

My eyes frantically scoured the forest floor for an item thin but strong enough to use as a lever. I tried a tree branch but, unsurprisingly, it broke. Nothing wooden would work. I needed something stronger. Like, something metal. I bent over and my stainless-steel cross slipped out from beneath my collar, dangling before my eyes. I stared. Of course!

I quickly untied the leather strap and wedged the longer end of the cross into the frame. Sure enough, the hatch cracked open. I leapt inside, kicking Ambrek upside the head as I fell. He crumpled easily. Too easily. Sure, I was big and tall, but Ambrek probably still had a couple dozen pounds on me. He lay on his back, blinking and panting.

"Scarlet!" he yelled.

"He's going mad," Fair cried, eyes wide and fearful and relieved, all at once. "Let's go!"

We scrambled out, picked a direction and ran as fast as we could, putting as much distance as possible between ourselves and the tunnel.

"It's like he was having a fit or something," Fair panted, as we ran.

"He said Scarlet's name," I breathed, heart hammering against my Adam's apple. "Maybe, he's not going crazy. Maybe, he's having a vision."

SCARLET JULY

We hadn't come across a rift in days. Which meant no fishing. I knew my body could live off of spectrum, for a while. When I was a street-urchin, I depended on it. It wasn't a perfect substitute for food, but it was a whole lot better than nothing. But, Cease had no such alternative. Sure, he had somewhat of a black haze for an aura, but it didn't compare to mine. Not to mention, he was already nothing but skin and bones, and some of those bones were broken, to boot. So, clearly, it only made sense that he be the one to eat most of our scant leftovers. I insisted on it. But, of course, he gave me grief. He refused to eat unless I did, first.

Now really wasn't the time to be a gentleman.

"Some survival instinct *we* have," he joked, sourly.

Freezing and famished and exhausted, my patience was wearing thin. "Cut the nice-guy act before I knock your crippled ass to the ice and force-feed you," I snapped.

Was that an eye-roll? Somehow, that infuriated me more than if he yelled. He offered no other answer. We trudged on.

Yawning, I suddenly realized I was on my knees.

"Huh?" I breathed, stupidly.

"You're fainting!" Cease's voice sounded faraway, though his lips were right by my ear.

We awkwardly plopped down on the ice, my head on his lap. I inhaled sharply, cold burning my throat. I could feel another frequency strangling mine, absorbing my photons, leeching energy from my aura.

It was white.

It could only be someone twined to me. Someone who, at this very moment, desperately needed something only the Multi-Source Enchant's aura could offer.

Fair Gabardine was in trouble.

CEASE LECHATELIERITE

I cradled Scarlet's ethereal figure, overcome by the desire to protect her, to save her, somehow. Her frame was so slight, I felt like she'd blow away if I didn't hold on tightly enough. She certainly didn't look like the most powerful mage in Conflagrian history, right now. More like a sleeping, little girl. I touched her flushed face. It was stone-cold. My hand slid to her neck, searching for a pulse. It was weak.

"Scarlet?" I shook her. Her red lashes fluttered.

Swearing under my breath, I activated my glacier-thawing lance and pressed it against her cheek, hoping the heat would revitalize her aura.

"Wake up, Scarlet! That's an order!"

SCARLET JULY

Cease stroked my face and hair with his lance until I slowly came around. I wasn't sure how long I'd stayed under. When I opened my eyes, he threw the rod aside and brushed my jaw with his fingertips.

"How're you feeling, Scarlet?" His voice actually shook. Only once before had I heard him sound like that—when I almost fell into the Fire Pit, last July.

"Better," I croaked.

"You scared me half to death!" he hissed.

"I'm sorry."

I was suddenly very aware of the fact I was lying on his lap. His lap was warm and firm. Abruptly nervous, I quickly sat up. He watched me with cautious eyes.

"Another mage was… is… using my magic," I explained.

"What?" Cease growled, holding the small of my back, as though afraid I'd kneel over again. "How? Why?"

"Well, it doesn't happen often. Or, easily. It's only supposed to be possible for twins or twined mages of the same color. But, as we know all too well by now, my aura doesn't always follow the rules." I exhaled. "It's Fair. She must be in some sort of crisis. It's hard to tell for sure." My stomach knotted up. "She's still using a good portion of my spectrum, now. I can feel it. But, things have stabilized a bit. I've adjusted, for the most part." My gaze dropped to the ice. "I hope she's okay."

Cease snorted. "I'd prefer if *you're* okay, thanks. You need your aura, right now. Every last photon, dammit."

"It's fine, really," I said. "I'm able to cope. I can handle it. And, I'm happy to help her."

His temples pulsed.

"You've borrowed my aura before, too, you know," I said, playfully poking his ribs.

He blinked. "I never stole so much as a photon. Any magic I've used, you volunteered."

"Not true. I only deliberately shared my spectrum with you during the infiltration, when I gave you your black glow and reduced your fever."

"When else have I ever used your spectrum?"

"Cease, we communicated through the web during the battle you lost, remember?"

"Of course. I'll always remember that. You saved my life."

"Well, that implies twining."

"What?"

"Our frequencies are spectrally twined."

"No," he grunted, shaking his head. His objection was like a punch in the gut. "I don't have a place in the spectral web. I don't have a color."

"You do, though. I can feel it, sometimes. Originally, your frequency was infrared, but now it's turning black. I'm no spectroscoper, but I'd guess it probably just started off as you sharing my aura—your infrared lifeline latched onto my red one, enabling you to borrow some of my powers—but, by now, your wavelength seems to be growing more distinct and independent. We're still tightly twined, of course, but you have your own color."

And, there it was, in his eyes: fear. Fear of the magical. And, worse yet, revulsion. He was disgusted. Disturbed. At the prospect of sharing spectrum with *me*, the woman he claimed to love.

I looked away, cut deeply. "Come on," I murmured. "We're losing time. Let's get moving."

But, before I could get up and pull Cease to his feet, he suddenly withdrew a hunk of fish from his pocket and stuffed it into my mouth.

"Just shut up and eat, already."

I shut up and ate.

NURTIC LEAVESLEFT

Buying time—that was all Fair and I could do, these days. Cover blown, we had no choice but to live on the run.

News of Fair's miraculous resistance to the Core Crystal spread like wildfire across the island. Every man, woman and child memorized her face and was on the lookout for her and the tall, blonde Nordic she escaped with. There were bounty-hunters everywhere we turned.

Two kids—a sixteen-age-old mage and a nineteen-age-old Nurian—were all that was left of the Red Revolution. It was us against an entire nation. I didn't have my utility belt but Fair, thankfully, had her hair, bow, quiver and sword. The problem was, I didn't know the first thing about archery or dueling. Accustomed to high-tech side-arms, I was really clumsy with Fair's weapons. We hardly stood a chance of stealing a means to get off the island. And, we really needed to; as long as the Crystal was intact, there wasn't much two rogue teens could accomplish, here. We were nothing but a couple maggots biting the ankles of giants.

* * *

We found ourselves in the northern Dunes. The mages who lived out here were essentially nomads, detached from Conflagrian society. The Crystal kept them loyal to the System, but physical distance from the capital made the Dunes the least politically-charged region of the island.

Physical distance meant nothing on technological nations, where info could spread with the push of a button, but here, word from Ardor Village could take days to arrive. None of the gypsies were ever System soldiers or Reds. They knew and cared less about the wars. This was the safest place to hide.

Life as a wanted man was interesting, to say the least. Fair and I spoke only to each other, kept our faces covered and never stayed in the same hideout twice. We migrated among deserted caves, abandoned shacks, forsaken tents, and sometimes, to the displeasure of my sinuses, in sand valleys. We stole food and clothing from gypsy habitats. It was ludicrous to maraud around in my diving suit; I now wore an itchy burlap robe that we nicked from a random family's clothesline. I hated the sick, twisted cycle my life had become.

Every night, I lay awake, mind racing faster than a semi-vowel. Tonight, at the foothill of a sand dune, I stared up at the mud-brown sky, wondering what would become of Ichthyosis without Nuria. I wondered about the twenty-seven divers left at Icicle. I wondered about the Ichthyothian civilians living under siege. It was the Epoch of the Crystal-Land's End, all over again... only worse, because the Order wasn't going to rescue anybody, this time. I wondered how Nuria was doing, in the wake of terrorism. Without a military infrastructure of its own, how would Nuria defend itself from future Conflagrian attack? I wondered if my parents were okay, since they lived and worked in Alcove City, though thankfully nowhere near the Centerscraper. I wondered what happened to Lechatelierite. And, Scarlet. I was worried sick over Scarlet. Did she, in fact, survive the seventh? Or, did I only hold to that conclusion because I couldn't bear to consider the alternative?

Fair worried a lot, too. About everything. But, unlike me, she didn't privately ruminate, she vocalized her frets. All of them. All the time. Which didn't help my own anxiety, one bit. Of all people to be marooned with, a headstrong warrior honestly wasn't a bad choice—Fair was tough, resourceful and knew a thing or two about wilderness survival. But, our personalities couldn't be more different. We drove each other nuts. She spent tons of energy agonizing and being bitter toward everyone and everything. She constantly vented about her past mistakes and hounded me with pointless questions like—

"How the hell are we supposed to get out of here?" she wrenched me now from my thoughts.

I rolled over, pulling off my damp facial rag—my makeshift dust-filter.

"I don't know," I answered, as always. My voice came out hoarse from all the sand in my throat. "But, you're smart. I'm sure we'll figure something out."

"Well, if I'm so smart, how come that bastard, Ambrek, managed to trick me, all these months?" Fair spat, acidly. "He had all the Reds fooled, even Scarlet. Especially Scarlet. She was totally wrapped around his little finger. He was always flirting with her, putting his hands all over her, telling her exactly how high to jump. I even spotted them kissing once, down by the beach. They never made things official, but I know Ambrek was really gunning for it the entire time he was around, trying to convince Scarlet to love him the way she did Cease. I was positive she'd eventually give in."

Was that so? Uncharacteristic rage suddenly swelled in my chest. How dare someone play with Scarlet's heart like that. How dare someone use her in such a way, feigning romantic interest for an agenda. I couldn't imagine squandering Scarlet's affections like that. It was one thing to pretend to be a comrade and quite another to fake being in love. That took deception to a whole new level. What an evil, disgusting, manipulative son-of-a—

"The Centerscraper thing was also his doing, you know," Fair railed on. "Worse yet, he asked Scarlet to design the incendiary he used, under the pretense of bombing the System Castle."

Wait, what? "When she finds *that* out, she'll take full responsibility, and it'll kill her," I moaned. "She doesn't know what to do with guilt. It breaks her apart. I mean, you should've seen her after Apha Edenta—"

"Yeah, she told me all about that. She blames herself for his death. Never really let it go."

"Exactly. And, this is so much worse!"

Fair pursed her lips. "I've been through the same thing, you know. I engineered the Underwater Fire. Who knows how many my invention killed. If I can get over *that*, Scarlet can forgive herself for this."

"No, Fair, you're not like Scarlet." Oh boy, did that come out all wrong.

"What's *that* supposed to mean?" Fair rounded on me.

"Nothing. I'm sorry, I didn't mean to—"

"Yes, you did!"

"Fair, I'm so sorry—"

"And, quit pretending to care about Scarlet, will you? The only reason you Nordics give a damn about her is because you think the prophecy depends on her!"

"That's not true. I'd care about her, regardless. I cared for her long before I had a clue who she was."

Fair wasn't listening. "Everyone always *wants* something from her. Everyone's always *using* her for one purpose or another!"

Pieces fell into place. "Are we still talking about me?"

There was a pregnant pause. Fair closed her eyes.

"How else am I resisting the Crystal," she whispered, "if not through the aura of the only one who can?"

"So, you also believe she's alive."

"It's the only explanation for what's going on with me. I don't even know where she is or how she's doing, yet, I'm… leeching from her. And, the worst part is, I'm not doing anything productive with it. If I'm going to deplete her aura, at least it should be for a good cause. All we do is run and hide."

"You *did* do something good. You destroyed the System's plans to melt Ichthyosis."

"Okay, that's one thing."

"That's one really, really big thing."

"The System can figure it out without me, you know. I'm not the only decent spectroscoper in their ranks. As long as there's magic on Second Earth, the risk for all sorts of horrors exist. The Crystal needs to be destroyed." Did it? Was that the only way to make things right? Was the prophecy even about the spectral web, at all? "But, the only one who can do that is MIA, plus I'm busy robbing her of her strength."

I chewed my lip. "Well, the new Crystal is still young, isn't it? Maybe, that makes its emissions more malleable, or something. I mean, the original Crystal was enormous. Eras of growth. But, this one's probably only about the size of a basketball by now, right?"

Fair's eyes boggled. "I have no idea what basketball is, but I get your point. Maybe, we don't need a multi-sourced mage to destroy it. Maybe, someone who's twined to her could." She wrung her hands. "But, that means me. I'm all she's got left. Could *I* really end the Crystal? Am I strong enough for that? I mean, just guarding my mind from the System right now is ridiculously exhausting; every night, I'm terrified to go to sleep, for fear I'll wake up re-enslaved."

"You're not all Scarlet's got left," I said, solemnly. "I know someone who's probably more twined to her than you."

"Who? Ambrek?" she snorted.

"Cease Lechatelierite."

Silence.

"He's Nordic," Fair finally spat. "Nordics have infrared electromagnetic fields. Cease Lechatelierite can't twine to anyone, let alone make a dent in the Crystal—" Aura flickering, her voice abruptly died. Scrunching her lids, she covered her face with shaking hands.

"Fair?"

She grabbed my arm. "Disarm me. Now!"

"What?"

"I have to let go, Nurtic. Scarlet needs her aura. All of it. Right now. She's in trouble."

My pulse skyrocketed. "What?" I blurted, again.

"Nurtic, bind me up. Hold me at sword-point. Tie my swathe over my mouth. Quickly. Before I make things really difficult for you."

Stomach summersaulting, I immediately got to work.

"Bye, Nurtic," she whispered. And, then, her eyes changed.

For an hour, we sat there in the sand, my sweaty hands holding her blade to her throat as she squirmed in her ropes and struggled to scream through her gag.

And, with her every gasp and cry, I felt another part of me die.

SCARLET JULY

The milky-white sky gave way to the inky blackness of night. The endless, unblemished expanse of snow glittered like opals beneath the cold fury of the glowing moon. I never thought I'd think this, but Ichthyosis was beautiful. Regal mountains, shimmering glaciers, smoking volcanos, jagged fjords—it was a wintry wonderland.

Goosebumps rose on my skin as I curled beneath an ice cleft. Sleeping under a ridge when the land was seismically-unstable had its risks, but it was either that or wake up inevitably buried under a foot or more of fresh accumulations. Inhaling the polar air, I concentrated on spectrally raising my body temperature so I wouldn't die of hypothermia in my sleep. The heater in Cease's diving suit was still working, but his face was exposed. So, whenever he slept, he set his lance on low and hugged it to his forehead or cheek.

In the near-distance, I saw Cease hobbling on his extended lance. His belt was haphazardly fastened, which meant he'd likely just come from emptying his catheter somewhere. He lowered himself beneath the only other cleft around, a few yards away, and snapped on his visual band. He was on watch first, tonight.

In seconds, fatigue pulled me into a deep slumber. When I awoke and saw it was almost dawn, I felt guilty. We were supposed to switch off after four hours. It'd been at least six. I sat up and nodded to Cease, who pulled off his band and lay down.

Despite my long rest-shift, I was exhausted. I closed my eyes, watching Cease through my lids. Four hours to go before we'd get moving. I exhaled, breath curling into the clouds…

How my collarbone seared! And, my stomach! Oh, my stomach! It was pain as I'd never experienced before. All the while, terrified gold eyes bored through mine.

"Hurry!" I cried to him in Conflagrian, feeling the cold air bite my open wounds—

"Scarlet! SCARLET!" Cease's voice penetrated my consciousness. I snapped out of my dream, only to discover the part about my belly was true.

A gelid—a furry white beast resembling a First Earth polar bear—gnawed my gut, dragging me from beneath the ridge. I screamed.

From behind, a length of deadline lassoed its neck, yanking its head back and forcing its jaws to release me. My blood soaked into the snow like a grotesque paint spill. Everything was red.

Then, it swiveled around and grabbed Cease by his broken leg.

"No!" I shouted.

I squinted my eyes, to no avail. I couldn't create a single flame. Never before had my magic failed me so completely.

Cease let out a roar as he thrust his activated lance into the animal's side, showering his white suit with crimson. Howling, the beast staggered back. With a swipe of its powerful paw, it smashed his visual band into his face with a loud crunch. Then, it teetered and collapsed with a dull thud, a mere foot from Cease's body. Cease retrieved his bloodied lance and used it to pull himself to where I lay, battered and bleeding.

I sobbed as the frigid wind stung my gaping gash. Cease stared at it with wide, scared eyes.

"I f-fell asleep on w-watch," I blubbered. "I'm s-so sorry, s-sir!"

"Scarlet," he croaked, hoarsely, "you've got to heal yourself, now!"

"I-I c-can't," I choked, teeth chattering.

"Hurry! Before you bleed to death!"

But, my aura was too weak!

"Close your eyes!" he barked, grabbing his lance.

I obeyed. He pressed the hot, smelly, bloody metal against my lids. Warmth seeped into my source.

"Concentrate on the heat!" he ordered. "Do you feel it?"

"Mmm."

"Good. Think about where you want it to go. Send it there. *Will* it there. Can you do that?"

I whimpered.

"Picture it in your mind, like waves. Waves feeding your aura. Now, direct your aura to your stomach. Now! Come on, Scarlet, do it!"

Waves. Red heat waves. I could see them, now. I could feel them. This was my spectrum. My aura. It was right here. It was swelling in my eyes, coursing through my veins, collecting in my abdomen…

At last, the pain ebbed. Cease tossed the rod aside. I looked down at my torn suit. My belly was intact.

Cease threw himself against me, hard. "Don't you ever scare me like that again, Scarlet," he cried into my hair.

He held me tight. Too tight. I could feel my fractured rib poke my lung. I gnawed my lip until my mouth was bitter. But, I didn't budge or make a sound. I let Cease hug me as long as he wanted.

When he finally pulled away, I got a better look at his newest battle wounds. His face was slashed where the visual band snapped and his leg-splint was completely undone. Thanks to the arrhythmic suit, his flesh wasn't broken where the beast bit, though there were visible dents in the fabric. And, he was covered in animal blood from head to toe.

"You're a mess," I said, stupidly. "Let's fix you up."

I squatted beside him and got to work, healing his cuts with my hair, slicing away shreds of deadline, resetting the bone and winding new cord around his leg.

And, then, it was time to scrub the blood off his suit. Nerves rigged with anxiety, I grabbed a fistful of snow. I hesitated, feeling Cease's silver stare on my burning face. Then, I slowly placed a trembling hand on his belly. It was warm and firm. I worked my way up to his chest, feeling the texture of his pecs. He closed his eyes, as though soothed by my touch. The blood smeared and coagulated and caked before coming off. This wasn't romantic, this was totally disgusting.

Finally finished, I exhaled.

"All clean, sir," I piped, wiping my gloved hands on my pants.

His eyes popped open. "Thank you." He blinked a couple times. "I can't see too well."

I moaned, internally. Just what he needed. Another handicap.

"Well, at least we have plenty to eat for breakfast." I smiled weakly as I looked at the gelid corpse, still steaming on the ice.

"We should carve out some flesh, then get as far from it as possible," Cease said, whipping out his razor, "just in case it attracts some… friends."

"At least we don't have to worry about the stuff rotting; we're *in* a freezer, right now," I murmured.

Pockets soon heavy with pounds of slimy, raw meat, we got to our tired feet. Spectrally drained and dreary from blood loss, I stumbled beneath Cease's weight.

"Watch it!" he shot.

For Tincture's sake, did Cease always oscillate like this? It was impossible to tell where I stood with him. One minute, he was embracing me until I couldn't breathe, and the next minute, he was biting my head off. He needed to make up his mind before I went crazy.

Hunting for a new place for him to sleep, the day wore on. Cease, face pale as a cadaver's, scrunched his lids shut. Was he passing out?

"Cease?"

He opened his bloodshot eyes a crack. "Yes?"

"Are you dozing off, or what?"

"No."

"Let's take a break—"

"No. Not until we come across another cleft."

"You look like you're about to kneel over. We should stop for a little while—"

"I said, no!"

"Are you okay?" All things considered, anyway.

"*Yes!*"

I halted, forcing Cease to, as well.

"Something's up. I can tell."

"Really? You mean something besides the fact I'm stuck out here with a little girl who almost got eaten by a wild animal before my eyes, who's now literally starving on her feet as she carries a man for miles?" His chin dropped to his bony chest.

"I'm not carrying you," I said, "and quit deflecting my question."

"It's my eyes," he finally admitted. "Without my visual band, they hurt like crazy and I can eventually go blind. I've already started to lose my peripheral vision."

Oh, Tincture. "Is it reversible?"

"Only if I don't wait too long before getting another band."

My heart pounded in my throat. Cease didn't want me spending more spectrum than absolutely necessary on him, but if his sight wasn't worth a few photons, what was? Without asking, I wound a lock around his face and channeled a good portion of my aura—what was left of it, anyway—into his eyes. A black mist hovered around him. My hair withdrew.

"Better?" I asked.

"Like magic."

I hid a smile.

Two miles later, when we finally came across a decent cleft, it was time to let Cease finish his sleep-shift. It took everything in me not to drop him on the ground, but to set him down gently.

"Have a goodnight, sir," I panted, though it was probably around noon. Hugging my knees to my chest, I added, meekly, "I promise I'll stay awake this time."

Without a word, Cease reached up and touched my face. That's when I realized I was crying—tears of exhaustion and stress paved their way through the frost on my cheeks. Cease wiped them away with his fingertips, expression almost deadpan—but, only almost. He stroked my cheek, chin, neck, collarbone. Then, he pulled me down onto the ice, beside him. Winding an arm around my body, he drew my head to his chest. We lay, frozen in time, for just a few minutes.

"I told you not to use any pain-relief on me," Cease said, softly.

I looked up at his closed lids. "I'm not."

"Huh, I guess it's just your presence, then." Eyes still shut, he kissed my forehead and whispered in my ear, "My rescuer."

And, with that, his breathing deepened and he was out cold. He didn't wake once until his shift was over.

QUI TSOP LECHATELIERITE

It all began at seven o'clock on January seventh, when I stepped out of the office to grab breakfast at the Adip Café, a few blocks away. I'd just emerged from an hour-long department meeting about the ever-controversial 'Cobalt-60 Project' and I was famished. As I hurried down the bustling, polluted streets, missing home more with every step, I called Finis to see if he'd like to join me.

"I can't; I'm giving a presentation to the board at nine and I need to finish prepping."

"You can't spare a few minutes for breakfast?"

"I'm sorry."

"We hardly ever spend time together, anymore," I whined. "All you do is work." Well, to be fair, that was pretty much all *I* did, too.

"Please, Qui, I can't have this conversation, right now; I have enough to deal with, as it is."

"I know. I just miss you, that's all. Do you want me to bring something back from the café?"

"I have a stash of crackers and salmon paste, right here in my office."

"But, Adip has pancakes and waffles."

"Don't tell me you actually like Nurian food?"

I shrugged, though he obviously couldn't see. "I'm getting used to it."

"Qui, I've got to go. My slideshow isn't going to revise itself."

"Fine. I'll see you later. I love y—"But, he already hung up.

At the restaurant, I was greeted by a pimply teenager wearing a backward baseball-cap. Probably a recent high-school grad trying to earn some cash for college or a fliv-ver. He looked no older than my son, who spent his entire life bearing the weight of the northwestern hemisphere on his shoulders.

"May I recommend today's special: a one-pound, bacon-and-fried-egg breakfast burrito with a side of hash-browns, served alongside a frothy, twenty-ounce cappuccino with whipped cream and chocolate drizzle?" he asked, grinning.

Ugh, he was kidding, right? "Um, no thank you. I'd like a water bottle and a plain waffle, to go."

"If you're watching those calories, we have low-fat soy lattes and bran muffins—"

"No, thank you. I'll just have the waffle and the water."

"How many packets of butter and syrup?"

"None, please."

"You eat like an Ichthyothian," the kid laughed, looking rather pleased with himself for his worldly reference.

He had no idea.

Five minutes later, he handed me a cup and a grease-stained bag. I checked my cell. It was seven-twenty-five. Great. I told my supervisor I'd be back by seven-thirty.

As I began to jog, I heard a rumble, overhead. I looked up and saw a grey company plane dart across the sky, to-ward the Centerscraper. As it circled the roof, a silver spec dropped from its belly. In seconds, the top of the building erupted into tall, red-orange flames. Large, charred chunks of debris came hurtling in my direction, sweeping me off my feet and out of consciousness.

So, here I was now, a couple days later, at the Alcove City Hospital, widowed and suffering from 'cobalt-60'-induced radiation poisoning.

The door creaked open and in came two teenagers. One had short white-blonde hair and the other, bushy brown curls. The taller boy introduced himself in mildly-accented Ichthyothian as 'Dither Maine,' and his friend, 'Arrhyth Link.' They were Nurian veterans, home from the war.

"Mrs. Lechatelierite, there's something we need to tell you," Maine said, voice grave.

"More bad news?" I murmured. "I don't know how that's even possible."

He cast an uneasy eye at his companion. "Arrhyth, can you help me out?"

I looked at the other boy. I'd never seen curly hair in person, before. Maybe, he had some Orion blood in him. Wait a minute—

"Arrhyth? Arrhyth Link?" I echoed. "Any relation to Order Chairman Arnold Link?"

"Yes, he's my father." What was the son of the SEO leader doing in the Diving Fleet? "Mrs. Lechatelierite," he took a deep breath, "on January seventh, your son went missing-in-action."

I blinked. "Action? He's been arrested. He's in jail, somewhere in this city." It was torture that I couldn't visit him when he was so close.

"Your son was surface-riding on Commander Nurtic Leavesleft's crystalline when they got shot down. I'm sorry."

"Shot down? I thought you said Cease was missing."

Link shifted from one foot to the other. "Well, 'missing-in-action' is the term we use when a body isn't found."

Body? "You must be mistaken, Mr. Link. Cease couldn't have been in battle on the seventh. His court-martial was that day."

Link inhaled. "Nurtic Leavesleft pulled your son out of trial so he could command the last battle before the alliance collapsed."

All air disappeared from my lungs.

Link nodded at Maine, who reached for the duffle bag at his feet.

"This was all we've found of him."

I opened the sack. It contained nothing but a small, silver-and-white helmet with cobalt-blue, triangle insignia.

* * *

After the Nurians left, a doctor came around to tell me that my test results were in and my prognosis was bleak. I had maybe an age left before radiation poisoning would take me. An age felt too long; I wished I could get it over with sooner. Why should I get to spend half an era on this earth when my poor Cease would never see his second decade?

"I'm sorry," the doctor glanced at the clipboard, "Mrs. Quit Stop." He didn't even bother to attempt my last name.

"It's pronounced, 'Key Sop,'" I said automatically, burying my face in my hands.

MARY-ESTHER LEAVESLEFT

I stood in the doorframe of Qui Lechatelierite's room, nervously clutching a handful of chrysanthemums wrapped in cellophane.

"Hello, Mrs. Luhshahtleerahyt," I fumbled over her crazy, foreign last name, resisting the urge to shove my foot in my mouth. And, I'd practiced it all morning, too. "These are for you."

Her windowsill and nightstand were otherwise empty. No cards, no balloons, no flowers. I sat at the foot of her bed. She didn't even look at me.

"My name is Mary-Esther Leavesleft. My son also went missing-in-action on January seventh."

Now, I had her attention. She turned her balding head toward me, thin face covered in red pinpricks. Her bloodshot, blue eyes studied my features.

"Nurian?" she asked.

I nodded.

"Then, your son was a fool," she spat, dabbing her cheeks with a tissue, "an idealistic fool, for choosing to throw his life away for this war. My son never had a choice. He grew up without even knowing his family. He had no identity, no childhood, no roots. They branded him like an animal and tossed him into combat when he was just a kid. They broke him down, killed his humanity, made him into a machine incapable of handling a brief meetup with his parents without getting violent."

"Ma'am—"

"Wait, you said your name's Leavesleft?" she cut across me.

"Yes."

"I met your son, once. Nurtic. He's the pilot who brought my husband and me to Icicle to see Cease for the first time, last August. He's a nice boy, very interesting to talk to."

Qui sure had dramatic mood-swings. One minute, she was biting my head off, and the next minute, she was complementing my son.

"Thank you. Nurtic was always a people-person to the power of ten. Definitely not a shy one."

"No kidding. He didn't have a clue when to shut up."

I froze.

She flicked a frayed lock of dark hair over her shoulder. "He knew private things about Cease that he had no right to, and he just wouldn't stop blabbing and blabbing and blabbing, all about it—"

"Come, now," I interrupted, gently, "there's no need to tread on a man's grave."

She glared at me. "He was the Commander of the Diving Fleet, right? Cease left him in charge, before his arrest?"

I nodded.

"So, he's the reason my son's dead." My pulse quickened. What? "If Nurtic didn't pull Cease from his trial, he wouldn't have gone to battle, that day!"

This was going from bad to worse. "Ma'am, I understand you're upset. Believe me, I get it: Nurtic was my only child, too—"

"If your kid was a halfway-decent leader, he wouldn't have needed to run, crying, to mine! Cease had enough to deal with that day, as it was!"

The door opened and an orderly popped in. "Mrs. Leavesleft, I'm going to have to ask you to leave."

But, I'd only just arrived! "Could I please just have a few more—"

"Now. Before I call security."

As I stood, I cast one last look at Qui's angry face, seeing so much of her son in her pale cheeks, dark hair and glassy eyes. Please, God, if not me, could You send someone else to her bedside before she passed?

INEXOR BUIRD

"Commander Buird," came Frappe's voice from the other side of my room door. Sometimes, I wondered why I had an intercom; no one ever bothered with it. "Dinner ends in ten, sir."

Immersed in an online article, I grunted, "I'm not hungry."

"Fine. More for the rest of us."

No kidding. Without Nurian trade, all anyone had left to eat around here was salmon, salmon and more salmon. The minute the blockade began, supermarkets everywhere got raided. It wasn't long before parliament passed a bunch of ridiculous rationing and conservation laws, making it a crime to throw away 'edibles' without 'valid cause'—not that anyone really had a clue what constituted 'legal spoiling' or how exactly the government would even enforce regulations like that. Starvation was now a real concern for middle-class Ichthyothians. And, our nation's problems extended far beyond just food. The entire economy was in shambles. There were shortages of metals, textiles, woods... just about every natural resource but petroleum. As a result, every product soon had a cheap, dinky, plastic counterpart. It was the Epoch of the Crystal-Land's End, all over again.

The military world wasn't faring any better. The mess halls served almost nothing but salmon paste, leftover stale wheat crackers and the occasional bowl of oatmeal.

Materiel-production screeched to a halt. In our hangar, we had half a dozen crystallines and only one vitreous silica.

As the Leader of the Ichthyothian Resistance, I was under a lot of pressure to miraculously pierce the blockade, overnight. On a daily basis, the media mercilessly compared me to the 'great Commander Lechatelierite who probably would've figured something out, already.' Right, sure, *now*, the public praised Cease. Never mind the mud they continually flung at him for weeks before he went MIA. Where was the adulation when the man was still alive, consecrating himself to the war? Now, an hour couldn't go by without my 'inaction' being mentioned in the news. I wanted to scream. It wasn't inaction, it was careful planning in a high-stakes situation. With so few soldiers and ships, the Diving Fleet couldn't just haphazardly jump into the sea.

Every plan my men and I drew up always required more reinforcements than we had available. What could be done with twenty-seven divers, six crystallines and one vitreous silica? Those were ridiculous odds.

If only we still had the Nurians.

Exhaling, I scrolled Channel Seven's website. Skipping the usual scathing headlines about myself and the military, a rather amusing title caught my eye: 'Eskimos Respond to Sacred Slay.' I decided to read it, if anything, for a distraction. I couldn't remember the last time I laughed or even cracked a smile.

Apparently, about a week ago, a nomadic Eskimo tribe found a fresh gelid corpse in sector seven, only about a couple dozen miles outside Aventurine City—not too far from Icicle. With a punctured stomach and chunks neatly cut from its side, the beast appeared to be slain by men rather than killed by natural causes or predators. As worshippers of the gelid as an earthly incarnation of the Snow God, the tribe was scandalized.

I stopped dead when I read that shreds of orange and green cloth were found in the animal's mouth. Those were the colors of the System Water Forces. This couldn't be a coincidence. Was an enemy taskforce making a covert advance on us, at this very moment?

Icicle, a mostly-underground facility, was both well-concealed and enshrouded in diffusion technology, undetectable by radar or spectrometer. Our coordinates were a fiercely-guarded military secret. The System had never been able to locate us before. How would they have done so now? Was there a security leak?

Who on Second Earth could shoot down Cease and Leavesleft?

It was the same question, I knew.

I grabbed my laptop and hurried to the mess hall.

* * *

"There's Conflagrian presence, on the island," Illia Frappe breathed, the moment I finished reading the news-story aloud, "heading here, as we speak."

"But, how?" asked Autoero Austere Jr. "How would they know where to find us?"

"We've always taken the utmost precaution when transporting POWs to and from base," Quiesce Tacit spoke up. "The only Conflagrian who's been here *without* heavy guard is Scarlet July."

I swallowed. "Exactly."

There was a tense pause.

"That's outrageous, sir," Quiesce snapped. Of course, everyone would leap to Scarlet's defense. "She couldn't. She wouldn't."

An angry murmur of agreement spread across the hall.

"Think about it, soldiers," I interjected into the disgruntled hubbub. "The System Water Forces just took down

Lechatelierite and Leavesleft—our top pilot and our best tactician—with one shot. Who on Second Earth can do that? Perhaps an eye-mage who's familiar with both Leavesleft's flying style and Lechatelierite's strategies? Do you really think it's just a coincidence that, less than a fortnight after the Commanders went MIA, the enemy is at Icicle's doorstep for the first time in history? Which Conflagrian knows where Icicle is? Which Conflagrian can shoot down Leavesleft and Lechatelierite? What if it's the same person? How could it not be?"

Faces all around me went white.

"We need to intercept them," I went on, pacing. "We need to deploy into sector seven, immediately."

At that very moment, the door of the mess hall flew open.

Framed in the entrance was the most baffling sight I'd ever laid eyes upon. Like rictuses of death, there stood a man and a woman—emaciated, dirty, bloodied and bound up with deadline. He was impossibly pale, unshaven and had a paralyzing, silver-grey stare. She had a flushed and freckled face, wild red hair and eyes like enormous green orbs. He wore white and blue and she wore orange and green.

Cease Lechatelierite and Scarlet July.

Immediately, twenty-seven weapons were drawn and leveled at Scarlet's head.

"Freeze, mage!" I boomed. "Yield your prisoner!"

Scarlet's hollow face twisted with surprise. "Prisoner?" she echoed in Ichthyothian, looking at Cease, red brows jumping to her hairline. "Commander Buird," she breathed, "he's not my prisoner."

"Liar!" I spat. "Just look what you've done to him!"

"Me? A System pilot attacked us, sir. A hand mage named Ambrek Coppertus. We barely escaped with our lives."

I advanced on Scarlet, eyes raking her System suit. She glanced down at it with mild surprise, as though just discovering she was wearing it.

"I infiltrated the Water Forces, on the seventh," she squeaked, "as part of an undercover op for the Reds. We had to get to sea. We needed a ship. The System has ships."

"What was your mission objective?" I demanded.

"To find the fragment of the Core Crystal on the seafloor."

Of course.

"Where are the others?" I barked.

"O-others?"

"Your reinforcements!"

"No one else knows we're here, Commander Buird."

I snorted.

"Come on, sir, if I was a System soldier, would I choose to infiltrate Icicle like *this?* Would I really barge in here, in the middle of the evening, injured, unarmed and alone?"

I hesitated, finger still on the trigger. My men didn't stand down, either. I knew, if I gave the order, they'd fire. No matter how much they claimed to love Scarlet, they'd do it. Her life was in my hands.

Cease's bloodshot eyes struggled to fix on my face. He shook out his tangled, matted hair, swallowed and almost gagged before quietly saying, "She's telling the truth, Inexor."

Inexor. So, that's how he was playing this. By calling me—the Commander—by my first name, in front of everybody, he was essentially reassuming his authority. The man was a walking corpse, barely audible, yet he had all of us back under his thumb with one breathy sentence.

"She's not with the System and I'm *no one's* prisoner," he hissed. "Stand down, all of you. Now." How ludicrous those words would seem, coming from anyone else in his condition. But, this wasn't anyone else. This was Cease.

Twenty-seven guns were holstered.

Cease and Scarlet limped to the nearest seats. She carefully let him down, unwinding hair and deadline from his frighteningly-thin waist. How was he alive? I saw his shuttle debris swirling on the seafloor. I found his helmet tumbling in the tide. That battle was nearly two weeks ago.

My pulse hammered like a semi. Something smelled fishy. I needed to speak to Cease. Alone. Now.

But, at that moment, medical personnel burst into the mess hall. They strapped Cease and Scarlet onto stretchers and whisked them off to the hospital wing. I followed suit, ignoring Illia's calls of, "Commander Buird?" And, I barged into Cease's operating room, without knocking. Half a dozen gloved and masked doctors were already huddled around my best friend's broken frame, instruments and IVs in hand.

Everyone stared at me.

Nurse Insouci Raef blocked my path, arms folded, fury in her dark-blue eyes. She yanked off her surgical mask.

"Excuse me, Commander Buird, this is a sterile zone; medical staff only!"

A Nurian? "Mrs. Raef? What are you doing here?"

"I could ask you the same thing," she said, coolly. "This is an OR, and you're a contaminant. Out. Now."

An anesthesiologist strapped a gasmask over Cease's mouth and nose. He'd be out cold, in seconds. My questions really would have to wait. As I turned to leave, I gave his pinched face one last look. Distrust lingered in his silvery eyes before they fluttered shut.

If I couldn't talk to Cease, Scarlet would have to do. Perhaps, she was still awake.

But, Scarlet wasn't allowed to have visitors, yet. I had to wait two hours before I was permitted a fifteen-minute visitation. Fine. That'd be more than enough.

I strode into the room to the sight of Scarlet on her back, feet elevated, IVs in her arms and prongs protruding from beneath her much-too-baggy hospital gown. On her nightstand sat a glass of water and a jar brimming with red flames. I stared at the jar. There was no gas or wick. At first, a blatantly-magical sight like that, here at Icicle, shocked me. But, I supposed, Scarlet had no reason to hide her magehood from the Diving Fleet, anymore. We all already knew what she was.

She laboriously sat up. "Hi, Inexor," she wheezed, saluting. So, we were on a first-name basis, were we?

"Scarlet." I didn't salute back. "How are you doing?"

She blinked, lips tight. Of course, she was on her guard; I'd just accused her of being a traitor, at gunpoint.

She smiled weakly and took a sip. "Malnutrition, hypotension, acid damage to my stomach-lining… the list goes on, but I won't bore you." She placed the glass back on the nightstand. "Sugared water is the only thing I can keep down, at the moment. The next step is diluted milk. The road to solid food will likely be long and perilous." Chuckling dryly, she picked up the jar of fire and held the opening much too close to her face. Flames licked her nose. "We lived off of fish and gelid-meat." Aha, so the gelid was theirs, just as I'd thought. "But, we ran out about a week ago and didn't come across any other places to fish or hunt for the rest of the trip." She raised her head and set her large, glassy eyes on mine. "But, I'm healthy compared to Cease." Her voice grew sad when she mentioned him. By his first name. To my face. "He's getting those crazy, digital casts put on his arm and leg, right now. You know, the kind that gets hardwired to your bone-barrow, injecting calcium and enzymes to speed the healing." She was filled with such childlike awe when she spoke of Ichthyothian technology. "The doctors were hesitant to use much anesthesia on him for the operation because they're afraid he won't ever wake up. Oh, Inexor, I'm so worried, I'm going out of my mind—"

"Scarlet, what the hell's going on here?" I interjected, unable to hold back any longer. "Lechatelierite and Leavesleft were shot down, on the seventh. I found Lechatelierite's helmet on the seafloor."

She swallowed.

"Who took them out?" I demanded.

She didn't answer. Which gave me her answer.

I swore, reaching for my sidearm. "I don't believe this, you mother-f—"

"Inexor, wait," she spoke fast, holding up her hands. "It's just as I told you: I was on an undercover mission. I was in a System ship. And, their crystalline was bombarding us. They were going to blow us out of the water if we didn't fight back. It was self-defense. Believe me, we didn't want to do it."

"We," I echoed. Of course, the Reds wouldn't send her in alone. "Who was with you and where are they, now?"

The jar slipped from Scarlet's hands and rolled across the bed. In a flash, I snatched it up before the flames could sneak onto the sheets.

"Watch it!" I snapped.

She rolled her eyes, took the jar back from me, turned it upside-down and pressed the rim against the mattress.

"What are you doing?" I cried.

"I can generate 'safe flames,'" she explained. "Can't catch onto anything but the inside of this container."

Well, that was all fine and dandy. I refused to let the conversation derail: "I believe I asked you a question. Who was with you?" My heartrate jumped a little when I added, "Was it Fair?'"

Scarlet studied her knees. "No, Fair's back home. It was a man named Ambrek Coppertus. He was my co-leader. At least, I thought he was."

"Until the Crystal subdued his mind, you mean."

She scrunched her lids and shook her head. "No, he was never a Red. He only pretended to be, since we met up in August." I froze. What? "All along, he was a double-agent. He used me to get the shard for the System." No way. Someone duped Scarlet. For five months. How? "Cease actually survived the crash, just fine. Made it to shore, fragment in hand. But, Ambrek took it from him, stabbed me in the chest, broke Cease's arm and leg, and left us both on the ice to die."

"How?" I breathed. "How could one man win a fight against both of you?" This was Cease and Scarlet we were talking about. A military dream-team.

"Well, Cease didn't have his weapon and my aura wasn't responding to the shard's emissions. But, Ambrek had both hand-spectrum and blackmail, on his side."

"Blackmail? With what?" I was nonplused. What could possibly be worth it? Why on Second Earth would Cease fail to guard the stone with his life? The obvious answer hit me like a vitreous silica on full throttle. "That traitorous bastard!" I leapt to my feet. But, before I could take a step, my sleeve... was on fire!

Calling out, I dove for Scarlet's half-empty cup of sugar-water and dumped it on my arm.

The door banged open.

"What's going on, in here?" Raef barged in.

With a sizzle, Scarlet's hair extinguished.

Raef rounded on me. "Are you harassing my patients?" Wait, *Scarlet* lit me on fire, and *I* was the offender? "She can go into shock at any moment! Get out, now!"

With pleasure. I stormed out, heading for the anesthesia-recovery hall.

I was going to kill Cease.

He flushed Ichthyosis down the toilet. He betrayed us. I thought no one on Second Earth cared for the war as much as him. Everyone believed, of all people in this fleet, he was most willing to give up everything for it. How wrong we were.

I threw Cease's door open. Hooked to four IVs and who knew how many monitors, there were bandages all over his sickly body. His right leg was suspended from the ceiling and his right arm hung in a sling. He looked at me groggily through a new, shiny, visual band.

I marched right up to his bedside and threw a punch in his face. But, miraculously, he caught my fist in his palm, grasp surprisingly strong for someone still half-sedated.

"Inexor!" he cried, voice hoarse.

I wrenched my hand from his, socked him in the stomach, then kicked his broken leg. Swearing, he sat bolt upright, yanking out a couple IVs.

I drew my weapon and leveled it at his head.

"Inexor," he croaked again, florescent light flashing across his band, "what the hell is wrong with you!?"

"I could ask you the same, spineless traitor!" I screamed, digging my muzzle into his pale, hollow cheek.

"Stand down, now! You don't know what you're talking about."

"YOU COMMITTED TREASON AND BROKE THE EMOTIONAL PROTECTION LAWS!"

"Inexor, I did what had to be done. Scarlet is the Multi-Source Enchant, don't you get it? She's the only one in the world who can diffuse the spectrum. If she dies, that's it. It's all over. We'd have no way to end this war for good."

Right. Sure. As if *that* was why he did what he did. He was rationalizing. "You only spared her life because of your feelings for her. A true soldier would choose the crystal fragment over her life!"

"What good would that do? No matter where we'd hide the shard, the System would still eventually track it down. Mages can sense it through the spectral web, Inexor. It calls them to it. It wouldn't be long before we'd run out of places to stash it; Ichthyosis is small, and we don't have an ally anymore. The chase could last eras, but we'd only be prolonging the inevitable. Because, without Scarlet, the spectral web will *always* exist. She's it. The most important weapon in our arsenal."

He was right, of course. My hand trembled on the trigger. Everything he said made perfect sense. But, oh, how I wanted to keep hating him. How I wanted to blame someone, something, for the disaster the ninety-fourth age was already turning out to be. The blockade, the shortages, the fall of the alliance, the return of the System's control—it was all too much to bear.

I holstered my sidearm.

"You're a true patriot, Inexor," he said, touching the indentation on his cheek.

"Thank you, Cease."

SCARLET JULY

"Ma'am." A hand touched my shoulder. My eyes snapped open and landed on Raef's face. "You better get going; the officers' meeting is about to start. You fell asleep before Commander Lechatelierite issued the notice, last night. You've got ten minutes."

Cease issued the notice? "Did Cease overthrow Inexor Buird or what?" I blurted.

Raef's blonde brows disappeared beneath her wispy bangs. "*Commander Lechatelierite* did no such thing. He didn't have to." She handed me a glass of watered-down milk. "If you ask me, Buird seems quite relieved to have him back. As we all are."

So, Inexor stood down. Voluntarily. Wow. How on Second Earth did they manage to patch things up, so fast? After Inexor's behavior yesterday, I was positive someone wasn't waking up this morning.

"Mrs. Raef, I can't go to an officers' meeting," I piped, taking a tiny sip. I thought it rather ambitious that she and Dr. Calibre were starting me on diluted milk already. My stomach churned in protest to my single swallow.

"Why not?"

"I'm… not a diver, anymore. The only reason I'm even here, right now, is because I got stranded."

"Surely, you *want* to assist the Ichthyothian Resistance?" Well, *she* clearly did. Why else was she still here, after the alliance fell?

"Of course, I do. And, it's not like I have anywhere else to go."

"Then, what's the problem?"

I squirmed. "Um, well, even if I want to serve, that doesn't mean I can just barge into an officers' meeting."

"The Commander insists."

Did he, now? Well, there was no arguing with Cease. I swung my legs over the side of the bed, got to my unsteady feet and wobbled toward the door.

"Ma'am!" Raef called, sharply.

I turned.

"You can't go in *that*." She gestured to my baggy hospital gown.

I gnawed the inside of my cheek, irritated. It's not like I'd planned on an extended visit. Aside from a torn-up System diving suit, I didn't have any other clothing.

"Check your old locker," she went on, slyly. It's been... jammed... since you left."

I looked away. Jammed. Right. More like, wound shut with a strand of magical hair because it contained contraband in the form of old mage robes.

A shiver ran through me at the thought of putting on an Ichthyothian uniform again.

I nodded, turned on my heel and disappeared down the corridor. I easily found my unit in the locker-room, plucked off the protective strand and recalled my old combination. Sure enough, the contents were exactly as I left them. Digging past my diving suit, towels, undergarments, summer trainer and mage garb, I yanked out my ceremonial uniform.

There was just one little problem. On each sleeve were two cobalt-blue stripes. I chewed my lip. There was no way anybody here—especially Inexor—would be too pleased to see me flaunt a phony rank. But, what could I do? The meeting was in minutes. I stupidly tugged at the bands, but of course, they didn't come off that easily. There was no time to unstitch all four. And, if I tried to burn them off magically, that'd ruin the shirt. The Second Epoch of the Crystal-Land's End certainly wasn't the right time to damage precious textiles.

I stuffed the uniform back inside. Why did I have to wear it, anyway, when I wasn't officially a diver anymore? Why pretend to fit in when I obviously didn't? Attending an officers' meeting was already going to piss people off, no matter what I wore. I didn't need to make things worse.

I threw my Conflagrian robe over my hospital gown, tied the swathe tightly and hurried to the lecture hall. I arrived a split-second before Inexor snapped the door shut. Everyone at the long table looked up at me as I burst in, breathless and bed-haired. Their glassy eyes widened at the sight of my red robe, a sore thumb in the colorless room. I was sure everyone was secretly satisfied with my self-alienation.

Cease, sitting in a wheelchair up front, glared at me with fury that could freeze the entire Fire Pit in an instant. Apparently, he didn't approve of my choice of attire.

I exhaled as all eyes slowly traveled back to him. With a strange tightness in my chest, I watched the way they regarded his chair, IVs and digital casts. When I was new to the military world, I thought Ichthyothians were so hard to read. Their faces always seemed stoic. Now, however, I knew better. Now, I could detect the subtle emotions behind their stony gazes.

They were embarrassed for Cease. They could barely meet his silver stare.

Tincture, that made me so mad.

I remembered, about an age and a half ago, how hard the Trilateral Committee worked to keep Cease's paralysis hushed up, fearful it'd tarnish his perfect image. But, as far as I was concerned, it was an honor to bear a battle-wound. How could Ichthyosis be the so-called pinnacle of the 'civilized' world when it still looked down on a man who'd mar himself for his country? I made a special effort not to take my eyes off of Cease's face, as he spoke. At least, he'd know he had one person who wasn't ashamed. I'd bet, if the Trilateral Committee knew how brazen he was being with his injury now, they'd have his head.

Cease made no preamble; he launched directly into the meeting agenda. No doubt, that drove everyone nuts. They were probably hoping for some answers. Like, how he survived the battle on the seventh then showed up on base, about two weeks later, with me. But, Cease didn't explain a thing. Instead, he just asked us to brainstorm ways to break through the System blockade with six crystallines and one vitreous silica.

As Cease talked, Inexor seemed particularly uncomfortable. While most sat still, Inexor shifted about like a nervous Nurian. The moment Cease opened up the floor, Inexor popped from his seat.

"Sir, last night, I received a notice from the academy." I blinked. Academy? What academy? All the Nurian military academies were closed. I looked at the others. No one else seemed confused. "There's a class about to graduate. There aren't enough of them to fully replace the Nurians, but it's a start. And, they're bringing all their ships and weapons with them."

I gasped audibly as the truth hit me like a torch to the skull. Of course, the Childhood Program was still in the business of abducting kids and beating out their humanity.

It was time for the next batch of brainwashed victims to join us.

Something in Cease's eyes flickered. "When are they arriving?"

"February twenty-second, sir." That should give Cease's hardwired casts enough time to do their job.

"How many of them are there?"

"Three-hundred-fifty-seven, ranging in age from fifteen to seventeen."

My stomach flipped.

Cease kept his face almost still. Almost. His pointed nose twitched, ever-so-slightly. So, he was bothered. I wondered why this news would trouble him. He fiercely defended the Childhood Program when we talked about it, last summer. He was a product of it, after all. The masterpiece of it. And, we were finally getting more men and materiel. I'd expect this to make him happy.

But, somehow, it didn't. Why?

* * *

Barring miraculous recoveries, Dr. Calibre wanted Cease and I to spend at least the next couple weeks sleeping in the hospital. There was only one other longterm patient here: Tose Acci, who was in a coma. Poor Tose. I wondered what happened to him and how long he'd been under. Raef set me up by the south balcony, near Cease's curtained bed. Tose was by the far wall.

It was lights'-out. I curled up beneath my thin blanket, exhausted out of my mind. For once, sleep came easy.

Then, I got startled awake by the sound of my curtains being ripped right off their hooks. I leapt to my feet, hair poised defensively.

"Stand down!" Cease ordered in Nurian, aware that my stance was no different than if I'd drawn my sidearm. I sat, hair falling to my shoulders.

"Sir?" I peeped, in Ichthyothian.

"What the hell do you think you're doing, wearing your mage robe around base?" he demanded.

Really? Of all things to be upset about, right now. "Well, I–"

"I'm sure there's *something* in your locker that's more appropriate!"

"Sir, I didn't w-want to wear my uniform because—"

"Because you're trying to alienate yourself!"

"Well… yes, partially." Tincture, was he perceptive. "Sir, I can't pretend I'm still a part of this fleet. It's not last age, anymore—"

"Icicle can't afford to house refugees." Cease snatched off his visual band, eyes scouring me like I were an amoeba under a microscope. "If you're going to stay, you're going to earn your keep. Period."

I blinked. Of course, I had to stay. As long as the Core Crystal was intact, I had nowhere else to go.

"Okay. Yes."

"Yes, *sir*. You're a diver now, and you're expected to act like one—which means proper attire while on duty and addressing me with some respect, among other things."

I no longer felt like an amoeba—at least amoebas were autonomous organisms. I felt more like a dead cork cell in a catacomb of other dead cork cells.

"What's my unit assignment, sir?" I squeaked.

His gaze narrowed. What was his problem, *now?*

"Maybe, I could work with the new graduates, when they arrive," I suggested. "I *am* about their age, after all."

Were those tiny smile dimples on his cheeks?

"Give me your hand," he ordered.

Pulse hammering, I obeyed. He put his frigid fist overtop mine and, when he pulled away, there sat four, ragged-looking, v-shaped bands, in the center of my palm.

I felt like I swallowed a hunk of raw dragon meat.

"You demoted Inexor?"

Cease nodded. "He's the officer of unit five, now. He isn't upset."

We didn't have a unit five. Not yet, anyway. My lips parted. The new graduates. If Inexor couldn't stand the Nurians, how would he handle a unit of kids?

"Not upset? How's that possible? About thirty-six hours ago, he declared his intent to have your head. I think Inexor is capable of getting very, very upset."

"Well, he isn't, right now. I talked with him this morning and explained why I had to reassign him."

"Why did you have to reassign him, sir?" I whispered.

Cease looked me straight in the eye. "Because *you're* my Second, Scarlet."

There was a very loud silence.

"The rest of the fleet already knows," he went on, giving me a maddening look of approval that turned my cheeks hot. "I told them at breakfast." Breakfast. Which I didn't attend because I wasn't on solids, yet. Clever. "So, you could imagine their surprise when the Second-in-Command burst into the lecture hall dressed in a mage robe overtop a hospital gown."

"S-sir, why am I the last to know?"

"Because, now, it's too late for you to back out. Everyone's already counting on you."

My head spun. It made no sense for Cease to promote me to the top when I'd been out of the running for nearly half an age. Was Cease's judgment clouded by our relationship?

Cease, one step ahead of me, answered my silent question: "I'd never compromise the quality of my fleet for anyone or anything. I'm not making you my Second because of *feelings*, but because I trust you more than anyone else. Because I know what you're capable of and I believe in that. In *you*. If I died in combat, I'd want Ichthyosis left in your hands." Now, how could I respond to *that?* I was intimidated beyond belief. "I didn't make this decision lightly; I was sure to consider all my options, first. But, in any case, I knew I had to demote Inexor. I'm stunned Nurtic Leavesleft would reinstate him the minute I walked out the door."

Nurtic! Oh, poor Nurtic. Last I saw him, he was unconscious on the floor of Ambrek's scout. He was either dead or a POW, by now. I couldn't decide which fate was worse. Eyes burning, I swallowed a lump the size of a hobnail egg. Oh, Tincture, I needed to calm down. Couldn't think about Nurtic, right now. Couldn't show weakness in front of Cease, seconds after getting promoted.

"Illia Frappe has an edge," he went on. "He's strong-willed and authoritative. But, he's too impulsive and quick to distrust. I need creativity and loyalty, not recklessness and flightiness. Autoero Austere Jr. is detail-oriented and organized, but I need someone who can see the big picture a little better and not get so caught up in specifics. Quiesce Tacit has the analytical mind for the job, but he's too withdrawn and impatient—I need someone who'd engage better with others and hear out every unconventional idea." Cease's diamond eyes bored through me. "I don't praise often and I sure as hell don't flatter, so listen up: Scarlet, I chose you because you're the best I've got. The best I've ever had. My only regret regarding your prior service is that it lasted just two months. If your hands weren't tied by outside circumstances, I'd want you to stay and serve until your dying day."

"Th-thank you, sir," I breathed, dizzy. "But, if I could remind you of something," I swallowed, "I haven't really dived since the summer."

"Then, *practice*." He leaned forward. "Every free second you've got, hit the pool. Consider it part of your duty. Understood?" he barked, voice taking on a hard—almost cruel—edge.

"Yes, sir." I saluted, firmly.

"Good," he grunted. "Don't let me down."

"Of course, sir."

"I'm counting on you." He was sticking his neck out for me, he meant. It was a risk to promote me after such a long absence. A risk only a crazy person would take.

"I won't let you down, sir."

"You better not."

What more could I possibly say to reassure him?

"I promise I won't, sir."

"Not *won't*. *Can't*."

I couldn't take his eyes on me, anymore—the way they were piercing through me, sizing me up. I wanted him to look away. Just look away. Let me breathe, for a moment.

"You can't," he repeated. "Do I make myself perfectly clear?"

What was scarier, dueling with Principal Tincture or bearing the weight of Cease's full trust and faith?

The latter.

I spoke loudly, with confidence I didn't have: "Crystal."

He finally nodded and turned away. I exhaled.

He wheeled to his nightstand, covered in an assortment of medication bottles. He popped one open.

Something struck a chord in my mind. "Sir, is Mrs. Raef Nurian?" I asked.

"Yes," Cease answered through a gigantic tablet in his mouth. He took a swig of water. "I've been wondering why she's still here." He plunked down the glass. "But, I'm not going to make her leave. We need all the help we can get. I figured something must be up, like she has nowhere else to go, anymore. And, if you stay, you serve."

I thought of the conversation she and I had this morning. That's when I figured her pushy demeanor was probably a guise. She acted tough to fit in with the Ichthyothians, but in truth, it was likely just a mask concealing internal pain. Pain that compelled her to stay in a cold, foreign land instead of going home. Home to her family. She was married, after all. Perhaps, her husband was no longer around. Perhaps, she didn't leave Ichthyosis because she couldn't bear the prospect of returning to an empty house. But, no, that could only be part of the picture. Because, no one chose to stay at Icicle by default. If you could stand being here, it was only because you really cared about the war. I wondered why Raef still did and if there were other Nurians out there who shared her perspective rather than resenting the nation whose short-lived partnership turned their world upside-down.

Cease drew his privacy-curtains and, moments later, I heard the sound of furious typing. I stood up, reattached my own drapes and collapsed onto my bed.

Chest tight and breaths shallow, I couldn't relax. Not once since I left Icicle in August did I consider the possibility of being a part of the Ichthyothian Diving Fleet, again. And, now, I wasn't just a mere part of it, I was the Second Commander. Who turned back the clock?

CEASE LECHATELIERITE

January twenty-eighth.

Who turned back the clock? Because, I sure felt like I was reliving the Great Paralysis Fiasco of the Ninety-Second Age.

Except, this time, I was recovering fast. Too fast. The medical team was baffled.

"I didn't expect your nerve and tissue damage to heal *this* much until mid-February, at the earliest," Dr. Calibre gaped. "At this rate, you'll probably make a full recovery well before the arrival of the graduates, at the end of next month. It's almost… like magic."

Magic. Well, well, well. I figured Scarlet waited until I was asleep to lay her hair on me. My chest tightened a little at the thought. I'd long since accepted Scarlet for who and what she was, but that didn't mean I wasn't still a bit freaked out by the idea of her aura affecting the way my body functioned. All my life, I was taught to see magic as an attribute of the enemy. Evil. Repulsive. I still flinched internally whenever Scarlet touched me with her hair, though she only ever did so to help me. I had to actively fight the impulse to dodge her locks or strike her back.

Eighteen ages of habit sure died hard.

SCARLET JULY

February seventeenth. Cease's casts came off, earlier this evening. Because his nerve damage had already 'magically' healed weeks prior, Dr. Calibre gave him the green light to return to the water by tomorrow morning. He couldn't wait.

As promised, as soon as my own health allowed, I dedicated my every spare moment to independent diving practice... which, of course, was almost no time, at all. With the nation on high alert, nearly every minute of every day was occupied by drills, conferences, report-writing, more drills, more conferences and more report-writing. And, so, I took to practicing regularly after lights'-out.

Tonight was no exception. A little after thirty-six o'clock, I strapped on my diving suit and crept silently through the corridors, heading for the saltwater pool.

The pool was an amazing display of Ichthyothian technology. A mile deep and two miles wide, its walls were lined with wave-generators and its floor was carpeted with artificial coral. With the push of a button, automated cylinders darted about, simulating crystallines. A dial on the wall controlled the temperature, almost instantly mimicking the conditions of the frigid Septentrion Sea, the cool Briny Ocean or the warm Fervor Sea.

Some nights, I left the pool after only a few minutes, too exhausted or discouraged to press on. Other nights, I stayed in for an hour or two, using the first ten or so minutes to relax and unwind. I'd deactivate the wave-generators, hike the temperature all the way up, throw off my helmet, spread my arms wide and drift on my back in the middle of the liquid-blue oblivion, thoughts wandering as aimlessly as the water that filtered through my hair. Then, I'd descend a few feet, admiring the shimmering reflections dancing on the tie-dye surface. And, I'd slowly exhale, watching tiny bubbles issue from my lips like a string of lustrous pearls. At last, I'd surface, ready to start exercising, salt crystals clinging to my lashes.

Breathing slowly and deeply, I floated in the water now, back straight and arms perpendicular to my body. How exhausted I was. How my limbs ached. How badly I wanted to sleep.

As my muscles loosened, my lids drooped...

Something kicked me, fiercely. I tumbled toward the faux reef, inhaling a mouthful of saltwater. I felt a hand grab my collar from behind and forcefully drag me to the surface, at which I promptly erupted into coughs.

"What's this?" came an accented-Nurian voice in my ear. "A soldier caught off-guard?"

"Cease?" I gasped, cheeks flushing. Stupid, stupid! Why did Cease always catch me doing something stupid? "I could've drowned!"

"Your little nap was doing that without my help," he growled, shaking me. "Is *this* how you've been spending your practice-time?"

"N-no, sir." It wasn't how I spent *all* of it, anyway. "Today, I'm just so... tired." Way to go, Scarlet. Now, I looked stupid *and* weak.

Cease released me. It was oddly nice to be in the water with him, again—not trying to kill each other, this time. It'd been so long.

"Sir, what are you doing here?" I piped. "Your casts came off, what, three hours ago?"

"That's three hours I could've spent diving, if I weren't waiting for Calibre and Raef to clear off."

"Aren't you a bit... I don't know... stiff, or something?" Despite about six weeks of nonuse, Cease's right arm and leg were, miraculously, still the same thickness as his left.

"No atrophy, soreness or rigidity." He gave me a sly look. "It's like magic, isn't it?"

I averted his eyes.

Cease hopped out of the pool to turn on the wave-generators and significantly decrease the water-temperature. Then, he jumped back in and drifted like a raft caught in a storm, arms spread-eagled.

"I've really missed diving," he murmured, glassy eyes falling out of focus as they grazed the ceiling. "I feel more comfortable in the water than I ever did on land." His voice dropped a couple octaves when he added, almost embarrassingly, "I love the water."

I smiled to myself. How appropriate it was that an *Ichthyo*thian would love water more than land. The prefix 'Ichthyo-' meant 'of fish or sea creatures.' I was about to tell Cease this when he suddenly pulled his visual band from his utility belt, snapped it on and spurted—

"Let's practice the spin-toss maneuver." He grabbed my wrists and bodily pulled me toward him.

"B-but, we're not wearing helmets."

He gave a little chuckle—a sound my ears were so unaccustomed to, my heartrate jumped.

"Didn't stop you before."

And, before I could take a proper breath, he spun me around, thrust an arm across my ribcage, pressed my back to his chest and plunged us headfirst into the water. After descending about twenty feet, we boosted from a cylinder.

The glistening surface approached fast and, the next thing I knew, I was twirling through the crisp air, locks swinging. Cease caught me neatly from behind, then quickly resurfaced.

"I'm oriented, now," I said. "You can let go."

His arms didn't loosen. "Who said I want to?" he murmured, voice muffled by my hair.

That's when I noticed how hard his groin was pressed against my butt. Shivering, I tucked my knees and thrust my legs behind me, kicking him in the crotch and ripping myself from his grasp.

"Hey!" he called.

I swam for my life. Undaunted, he chased me down.

And, so began a rather long and intense spar. Intimately familiar with one another's fighting styles, we could practically anticipate each other's movements. Unfortunately, the whole ordeal reminded me of the *real* skirmish we had in the sea, in January.

Apparently, that battle was also on Cease's mind, because he decided to imitate the very move I'd made to pull off his helmet: he latched onto my back like a boa constrictor. No matter how hard I thrashed, I couldn't break free from his impervious hold. Lungs imploding, I struggled to bring the pair of us to the surface. I gulped the frigid air.

"Ha, now you know how I felt!" Cease cried, pure joy in his usually-stern voice. "Surrender, yet?"

"Never!"

He sighed, theatrically. "Very well, then." He pulled me under while my mouth was still wide open. When we came back up, I hacked like a thunderstorm.

"Y-you can't h-hold on forever!" I sputtered.

"That's what you think."

"I had a *reason* to do this to you, when I did! What's yours? We're not even wearing helmets!"

"I do have a reason."

"And, that would be…?"

Cease answered, but not at all how I expected. He pushed his face through my hair and kissed the back of my neck with his cold, wet lips, sending chills down my spine. Then, he whispered in my ear, "You win."

With that, he let go, scrambled out of the water and disappeared down the corridor, leaving me to float alone.

* * *

It was four-o'clock before I drifted off to sleep, serenaded by the creaking noise of Cease tossing and turning in his nearby bed. A series of odd dreams ensued. One entailed running barefoot across the Fervor beach during a snowstorm while sporting my diving helmet and brandishing a crossbow. Then, I heard a faint rustle.

Like any soldier trained by Ichthyothians, I slept alertly. At the sound of my drapes being drawn, I sat up like lightning, smacking hard into something small and white perched on the edge of my bed.

"Cease?" I panted. "What're you doing here?"

I only had my undergarments on. Cease never saw quite so much of me, before. Intensely self-conscious and embarrassed, I tried to cover up, but Cease was sitting on my blanket. Helpless, I crossed my arms, face burning.

Cease didn't even look at me. He strained forward, razor-sharp profile outlined against the window. A black mist seemed to hover around him. Omega's light filtered through the blinds and played on the angles of his pale face, giving it an eerie, milky glow. His messy, dark hair reflected strips of cobalt-blue and his fierce, glassy eyes were nearly white in the illumination.

That's when I noticed the tears glistening on his cheeks like flecks of ice on a layer of fresh snow. My breath caught in my chest. I'd never seen Cease cry, before. I could hardly digest the idea. Yet, here he was, not only crying but willingly leaving the privacy of his curtained bed to share his moment of vulnerability with someone else. With me.

His moist eyes met mine. And, somehow, I could instantly tell what was troubling him. His father's face just popped into my head. Perhaps, his mind sent me that image through the spectral web.

During our hike across sector seven, Cease only mentioned his father's death once. He seemed more upset over the impact the Centerscraper's destruction would have on the Ichthyothian Resistance. So, until now, I believed Cease wasn't really impacted by Finis's loss. After all, he never really knew his parents. He'd met them only once, briefly. And, from the little Finis had shared with me, that encounter didn't go too well.

"I made a promise to him," Cease whispered in his accented Nurian. He didn't bother to explain who he was talking about. He somehow knew that I knew. "To dismantle the Childhood Program." My heart soared. Cease, the masterpiece product of the Childhood Program himself, wanted to tear it down? I couldn't understand how he'd develop that desire in the first place, but it explained why news of the forthcoming graduates upset him. "That was back in August. I haven't lifted a finger in six months." He looked down at his balled fists. "I barely even thought about it." Startling me half to death, he sprung up and kicked my nightstand—medication bottles few everywhere, clattering noisily on the floor. "Now, it's too late! Even if I do it, he'll never know." He collapsed back down, head in his hands.

And, to my profound horror, he began to bawl at the top of his lungs. His loud sobs wrenched out my heart and left it bleeding on the sheets.

I sat there, terrified, gaping like an idiot. I had to say something. Do something. Cease needed help. Reassurance.

Comfort. He came to me in his time of need and I couldn't let him down.

"Cease," I finally squeaked, "it's not your fault Finis died before you could carry out your promise. The war took him from you, so suddenly."

"No, Scarlet." He shook his head vigorously, thick hair bouncing on his sweaty forehead. "It was *my* responsibility to protect the alliance, and I failed!"

"There's no way you could've stopped the System from firebombing the Centerscraper—you were locked up in Alcove City, at the time."

"And, why was I locked up then, hmm?" he heaved, right in my face. "Because I'm a war criminal!"

"Cease, the whole world has been spinning backward, since the summer. You've had too much on your plate. You wouldn't have had time for reform, even if you weren't dealing with legal issues. You weren't procrastinating, you were prioritizing. You've got a national emergency to deal with, right now."

Like a tire pierced by a nail, Cease deflated. "No," he whispered, scrunching his lids shut. "Even with all the time in the world, I'm still not sure I'd do it."

I froze. "What?"

"Scarlet, I need to tell you something," he said, switching to Ichthyothian. "I've been meaning to for a while, but I wasn't sure how or when to bring it up. Please don't misunderstand what I'm about to say; just hear me out."

My stomach jumped up my esophagus. "Wh-what is it, Cease?" I whimpered.

"I don't think you know how much you hurt me when you came here, last age. Or, how much your presence hurts me now, all over again." I felt like vomiting. What did he mean by that? "Toward the end of your service last summer, something happened to me. It was gradual. I don't really know how to explain it, but I'll try." His temples pulsed. "I started feeling like I was holding onto a live wire. All the time. Everything made me... react. I felt so helpless. So out-of-control. I'm not used to that. I had a hard time just doing my job. I felt guilty for things I needed to do—things my duty required. I couldn't think about the past without feeling sick inside. I mean, *sick*. Stomachaches, headaches, night-sweats, shaking, you name it. Because, I couldn't live with myself. I had to put up a front just to scrape by, day after day. It's like I had to pretend to be myself—my *real* self—just to keep from caving in."

"Your conscience was awakening," I breathed. "Cease, that's... great."

"I considered that. I figured, if most people live like this, I'll adapt. It's only a matter of time before I get used to it and be okay again, right?" he sighed. "But, as time passed, the pain didn't go away. It got worse." His voice dropped an octave: "I'm not used to wanting to be near someone. I'm not supposed to need anybody. It made me feel weak. Pathetic. The thought of never seeing you again, it was... unbearable. And, I couldn't fathom why. Your absence, Scarlet," he swallowed, "it really cut me."

I couldn't move or speak. I sat, dumbfounded, rooted to the spot.

"And, I worried a lot," he went on, "about you. I had no way of knowing how you were doing, which drove me up the wall. When I had a vision of you getting torched in combat, I went crazy. Not just because your death would impact the Red Revolution. The *old* me would've only cared about that. But, the new me... Scarlet, I was afraid for you. Afraid of losing you. Though you weren't mine, anymore. Never really were."

"Cease, these are all good things," I choked.

"That's what I kept telling myself. This was a positive change. I was becoming more like the person I admired most. You. I thought I wanted to be like you."

"Not just me, Cease, you were becoming," well, I couldn't say 'human' or 'normal' without offending, "like... most people. Like people who've never been subjected to the horrors of the Childhood Program."

"But, I'm not supposed to be like most people. The military didn't raise me up to be an average guy. They didn't make me the Leader of the Ichthyothian Resistance because I'm similar to everybody else. As long as I'm in this post, I'm supposed to be different. Stronger. Tougher. I was losing that, Scarlet. I was losing what makes me special. What makes me able to serve and fight as well as I do. What makes me a good commander. What my country needs me to be."

"Why not be both? Others have done it. Look at Nurtic Leavesleft."

"Leavesleft is dead."

"Look at *me*."

"That's different. You've always been the way you are. It wasn't a change for you. Or, for Leavesleft. You two know how to do it. I have no experience and no time to learn to be both. My country needs *me*—the old me. Now."

I shook my head. "Cease—"

"I can't afford to *feel* things, all the time. And, last fall, I slowly began to realize that. That it hurt too much to care. I didn't want to, anymore. I wanted to be myself. I needed to. I didn't have a choice. It was either act so-called 'human' and fail my country or let go of my new persona and become excellent again. I wanted to be excellent. That transition didn't happen overnight, though. And, it was agonizing, especially in the beginning. I had to fake it until I made it. Eventually, I relearned to feel... nothing. Almost all the time. Almost. Like, after battles. After insulting and tearing down my best friend. After invading the thoughts of Ambrek Coppertus and forcing him to slaughter *my own soldiers* without a weapon."

My lips parted as I remembered the night Ambrek came home from his 'captivity' with blood literally on his hands. I was disturbed he'd been able to kill like that. It reminded me of Cease's dark side. Now, I understood where—or from whom—the impulse had aroused. I placed my hands on my belly, suddenly nauseous.

"Part of me was sad to see that side of me leave—the side of me that was *you*. And, the reason I could even feel sad about that, in the first place, was because the Scarlet in me never fully went away. That's the only explanation. I can tell. I can tell there's something still here. But, most of me was—is—I don't know—glad to be free of the burden." He looked at the floor. "The only thing that didn't fade all this time is my attachment to you, Scarlet. And, since you came back last month, it's only been intensifying. But, in all other areas, I'm numb. Or, just mad. Really mad. Like, whenever I think about my promise—though, as I admitted earlier, that isn't too often. Why go through the trouble of reforming a system that works? Why fix what isn't broken? Just look at me; I'm proof it works. Why should I damage and weaken my own military?" Cease's eyes shot through mine. "That's right, Scarlet. I didn't neglect my promise because I had no time for it. I ignored it because I didn't—don't—*want* to do it. And, you know what? I hate myself for that."

He turned away, hunched his shoulders, gripped his hair and began to ugly-cry, all over again. It was hard enough to watch him fall apart the first time; I couldn't stomach more of it. I needed him to be okay, right now. And, I—almost—didn't care what it'd take to make that happen.

So, I reached up and touched his wet face, sliding my fingers across his painfully-protruding cheekbones. Then, I leaned in and hugged him. He buried his face in my hair and held onto me for dear life, frigid hands on my bare back. Goosebumps rose all over my skin.

I stroked his neck, damp with cold sweat. His salty scent filled my nostrils. I looked down at his shoulder and saw three cobalt-blue rank bands shining in Omega's light. Those stripes seemed to glare at me triumphantly, gloatingly, as if claiming ownership of Cease's life. The war had him completely in its power. Even if it ended tomorrow, Cease would inevitably continue living in its shadow. And, his new self was *just* alive enough to make coping with it excruciating. Worst of all, he'd have no choice but to handle everything alone. Because, once we managed to destroy the new Core Crystal, I'd have to leave Ichthyosis all over again, for round two of the Red Revolution. Becoming attached to him, and him to me, was pointless. Painful. Stupid. It didn't matter how much we wanted each other. Being together was wrong. I couldn't be selfish. If I really loved Cease, I wouldn't make a choice that'd destroy him.

My embrace was working; Cease was quickly calming down. His sobs quieted and his chest stopped quivering. Now, *I* was the one trembling, breaths shallow and rapid.

"You're shaking," he whispered. "Why?"

I didn't answer.

"Are you afraid," he asked, "of me?"

I knew I couldn't lie; he'd see right through it. Yes, I was afraid of him. Afraid of being with him. Afraid of holding him like this. Afraid of what it was doing to both of us.

"I-it's stupid of me," I babbled, "because I know you'd never hurt me."

Chuckling dryly, Cease pulled his face from my hair and touched his cold nose to mine. "Oh, Scarlet, can't you tell I already have?"

And, with that, he kissed me fiercely, powerful arms tightening around my waist. It was electrifying, terrifying and wonderful, all at once. I screamed silently in my head, even as I kissed him back. Why were we doing this? Why make our inevitable separation all the more agonizing? The kiss only served to torture me with a teasing taste of all the love from him I knew I could never have.

But, when Cease threw himself on top of me and we hit the mattress with a loud thud, I realized his plans for tonight involved giving me far more than just a taste. A mix of fear and desire shot through me.

He ran his frozen hands up and down my body. I found myself almost involuntarily unbuttoning and pulling off his shirt and undershirt. Soon, his firm, bare chest was pressed against mine. Oh, Tincture. What were we doing? Why was I egging him on and pushing things further? I loved him desperately and was turned-on like crazy, but I knew we needed to stop. Now. I turned my head, prying our lips apart. I struggled to slip through his grasp and sit up, shivering against the cold, metal headboard.

"C-cease, I think you sh-should go," I sputtered, trying to ignore the fierce pounding of my heart against my ribcage, as though in protest to my words.

Undeterred, Cease seized my hips and pulled me back down, under him.

"Is that what you really want?" his accented Nurian was thick in my ear. He kissed his way down my face and neck, lips like ice cubes.

I wasn't sure the answer was yes. Even as I was frightened out of my mind, a large part of me acknowledged how incredible it felt to be this close to him.

"The way you kissed me back and threw my clothes off," he hissed, "beg to differ." With that, he clamped his mouth over mine again, fingers probing my bra clasp.

He was used to being the one in charge. He wasn't accustomed to taking 'no' for an answer, ever. Well, I supposed, there was a first time for everything. I wound my hair around his wrists like handcuffs and bodily shoved him off of me.

"Scarlet?" he breathed, eyes wide.

Tears flooded my face.

"Scarlet, are you okay?"

I shook my head.

"Scarlet, I'm so sorry; I didn't mean to scare you!"

"I-I'm sorry for g-giving you th-the wrong idea," I blubbered, "but, I'm not g-going to s-sleep with you."

"And, I don't want us to do anything you're not totally alright with! I was only going to go further if you wanted to."

"I-I don't b-believe you."

Cease's jaw literally dropped. "What, you think I'm like Amok, or something?"

I didn't answer.

He turned his head suddenly, as though slapped. "Scarlet, I'm sorry." His tone was laden with anguish. "Please believe me. I wasn't trying to take advantage of you, I swear. I wouldn't do that to you. I love you."

Tincture. Those three words made me want to release his wrists, throw myself into his arms and take whatever consequences. I closed my eyes for a moment so he wouldn't see the weakness in them.

"Please," I whimpered, "be reasonable, Cease." I swallowed and spoke the horrible words we both needed to hear: "Be realistic. There's just no future for a Conflagrian and an Ichthyothian."

Cease didn't blink. "Why not?" His voice grasped me tighter than his arms ever did. "Once the state-of-emergency is lifted, I'm getting discharged from the fleet. After I serve my seven months in prison, I'll come for you. I'll leave Ichthyosis forever and move to Conflagria to join you in the Red Revolution. We'll be comrades, again. I'll be *your* second commander."

Holy Tincture. He didn't really mean that, did he? There was no way. It'd be a sacrifice of epic proportions.

"Y-you can't possibly promise something like that," I gasped.

"I can and I do," he declared.

"You do, *now*. But, people *change* over time. Just look at *yourself!* After only five months apart, I already don't even know who you are, anymore! *You* don't even know who you are or what you want; you're so confusing!"

"I do know what I want. Before I came over here to talk to you, I'd already decided." His voice was louder. Stronger. All the more hypnotic. "I tried to fight against it all these months but, by now, I realize this is one battle my old self can't win. I can't change my mind when it comes to you." He towered over me. "You. I want you, Scarlet. Not just tonight, but for the rest of my life. And, I don't care what it'll cost me."

I released him.

"Just go! Quit pouring salt on the wound and go! I can't do this, anymore."

I tried to push him with my hair but, with his amazing reflexes, he managed to catch a fistful.

"Why's there a wound, Scarlet? Because you know what you want, too. Deny it to my face, all you like—it won't change the truth. You want me. It doesn't happen often, but sometimes, surrender is the only viable option. Give in, Scarlet. Give in and give us a chance." His voice was so compelling. So commanding.

My lock snapped from his palm, cutting it deeply. But, he didn't even wince.

I threw his clothes at him, drew my privacy curtains and curled up beneath my covers, shuddering. Six ages ago, when I was deported, I swore I wouldn't let myself get weighed down by anything or anyone that could be taken from me. And, now, I'd foolishly let myself become attached to Cease. Of all people, I chose the one man all odds would be completely against. I buried my face in my pillow and wished Cease never accepted me into his fleet last summer and made me his right hand, allowing us to work closely enough to fall in love. Better yet, I wished I never became a diver, but got assigned to the Air Force or Ground Troops, instead. Moreover, I wished I'd never joined the military at all, but remained in Alcove City, far away from the Ichthyothian Resistance and the man leading it. Cease didn't deserve to be so hurt by me. A knot of guilt formed in my belly. I was weakening his militancy and causing him pain for no gain, whatsoever. He'd be better off if we never met.

Then, there came a small voice in the back of my mind, saying: but, what would've become of the northwestern hemisphere, if I didn't enlist? The first Core Crystal never would've ended and Ichthyosis would've lost to the System, ages ago. And, without me, Ichthyosis had no way to destroy the new Crystal. If I stayed in Nuria, Ichthyosis and Conflagria would both be condemned.

Several minutes passed before I heard Cease's footsteps travel to the balcony. He was finally gone.

But, I knew, he didn't become the Leader of the Ichthyothian Resistance by being the type to give up easily. There was no way this would be his last move on me. By rejecting him, I was just handing him a challenge. A fight. Cease loved a fight. And, when he fought, he almost always won.

Was I ready to go to war against the best fighter to walk Second Earth?

PART II
CRYSTAL'S END

The last trainees are climbing the diving tower
As slowly as they dare, their fingers trembling
On the wet rungs, bare feet reluctantly
Going one step higher, one more, too far
Above the water waiting to take them in…

They pause at the edge. Only one second away
From their unsupported arches, the surface glitters,
Looking too solid, too jagged and broken,
A place strictly for sinking, no place to go.
Each has his last split-second thoughts…

Upright, blue-lipped, no longer breathing, already
Drowned, they commit their bodies to the deep.

—David Wagoner, "The Naval Trainees
Learn How to Jump Overboard"

CEASE LECHATELIERITE

Before the Nurians left Icicle, they emptied out their lockers. But, because there were one-hundred-seventy Nurian casualties on the seventh, one-hundred-seventy scattered lockers were still unnecessarily occupied. They needed to be vacated to make room for the new graduates, arriving tomorrow morning.

Obviously, I could've gotten the maintenance crew to take care of things, but I decided to handle it myself, as a final goodbye to my lost comrades. Sentimental, yes. In other words, stupid. But, it was an experiment of sorts. I wanted to see if I could make myself feel something again, for anyone other than Scarlet, as I could back in August. I wanted to see if I could willingly switch between my militant self and the man Scarlet deserved. I wondered if it was remotely possible for someone like me to 'be both,' as she suggested.

Scarlet rejected me. It was infuriating, because I knew she actually wanted me. Badly. If she were genuinely disinterested, I'd accept that and let bygones be bygones. But, she burned for me. Consistently, her behavior and body language made that quite clear. She was always in tune to my moods, fluidly adapting to my every shift. She paid rapt attention to everything I said and did— every facial expression, word and gesture—no matter how subtle, immediately accommodating whatever she thought

I needed. She often looked at me with intense adoration in those laser-green eyes, as though hypnotized. And, last but not least, there was the way she kissed me back—desperately, passionately, lovingly.

Her rationale for why we shouldn't be together was based on speculation. But, who knew what the future held? How could we begin to guess? Yes, we'd probably face a lot of obstacles. So, what? Anything worth doing always had obstacles. The difficulty of a challenge shouldn't deter a diver.

Choosing to pursue Scarlet certainly was a path of heavy resistance, and not just from her or from our impractical circumstances. Every day, my mind warred with my heart. My draw to her was like a wound that wouldn't close. It made me feel weak and helpless. I was the Commander of the Diving Fleet, the Leader of the Ichthyothian Resistance—at least, for now. As long as I had this job, I couldn't afford to bleed. But, I didn't know how to cauterize the wound. I didn't know how to eradicate my fierce attachment to Scarlet and the pain it brought. Was love supposed to feel this awful? The more I thought about it, the more I believed the answer was probably no. The Nurians acted like love was the best thing life had to offer. Their world had stories and songs and movies about it. Their culture glorified it. They said it felt good. I didn't feel good. I felt pathetic, out-of-control and confused to death. Did this mean I wasn't really in love with Scarlet? Did I even understand the concept of love to begin with, to claim that was what I felt for her? Was I even capable of love—the same love the Nurians spoke of—in the first place?

I wasn't sure anymore.

I had a hunch normal people didn't need to try to trick themselves into feeling things. Well, here went nothing.

I worked my way down the hall, mind transforming the fourteen-dozen open lockers into fourteen-dozen plaques checkering the first Nurian War Memorial under construction in Alcove City. I willed myself to miss them. To grieve. To feel sad. To at least be impacted by the sheer *number* of casualties.

Nothing.

After thirty minutes of extracting smelly garments, dumping them into a wheeled hamper, I stopped hoping to find illegal trinkets. Bored and impatient, I was about to call in someone else to finish the chore when I came across a goldmine. Exactly what I was looking for. One Nurian's disregard for the possessions rule was particularly flagrant.

Every inch of his locker was occupied. I yanked out a wad of white cloth at the front, starting an avalanche. The last thing to hit the floor was a long, shapely, black case.

I jumped back, alarmed. Withdrawing my materials-detector from my utility belt, I approached it with caution. The machine chirped.

'**Outer structure:** *80% plastic, 10% various metal alloys, 10% synthetic fibers.*
Inner object #1: *75% wood, 15% plastic, 5% various metal alloys.*
Inner object #2: *65% wood, 30% synthetic fibers, 5% various metal alloys.*'

The list went on, but I got hung up on the first inner object. Seventy-five percent wood. That was astounding. Ichthyosis hardly had any trees. Clearly, this item was Nurian-made.

Drawing my weapon, I squatted beside the case, flicked its latches and opened the lid. I didn't understand what I saw inside. I'd never beheld anything like it before. A delicate item with abrupt, womanly curves sat in a blue velvet bed. My eyes traveled from its auburn body, to the semi-circular card on its face, to the four metal cords crossing its neck. I picked it up. It was light. Hollow. I peeked through one of the thin incisions on its front and read a rectangular sticker within: 'Imitation First-Earth Gasparo de Salo Viola.' I stared at the Nurian words, feeling as clueless as when I first laid eyes on Scarlet's pencil-sketches, last summer.

I put the wooden thing down and opened one of the case's little storage compartments. There, I found several more peculiar objects, like a hard, sticky, yellow-brown, translucent stone stuck inside a wooden frame, labeled in Nurian, 'rosin.' The next item was a black, rectangular device with a textured knob. All I did was pick it up when it started emitting a high-pitched squeal. Alarmed, I turned the dial, but instead of shutting off, a red light at the top-left corner began flashing in tandem with a clicking noise. I ran my hands along its side and thankfully found the power-switch.

Beneath the 'rosin' and the squeaky box was a familiar item, at last: an audio-player. I hadn't seen one of those since I was a student. Icicle Academy sometimes used them for instructional purposes. Why did this Nurian have one? Was it from his high school?

Beneath the audio-player was a book with gilded pages. A pocket bible. When I opened it, three photographs fell out.

Of course, this locker was Leavesleft's. I should've known.

In the first picture, the 'viola' was tucked oddly under his chin, its neck resting in his left hand. On the back were a couple lines sprawled in Nurian cursive:

To our little virtuoso: Congrats on your successful audition & Godspeed at the upcoming concert! Love, Mom & Dad

I looked up. Aha, the 'viola' was a *musical* tool! An instrument. I blinked. So, civilians actually put time and effort into learning how to operate these complex, wooden devices for the sheer purpose of producing interesting noises for entertainment? I was appalled. To me, music had to have a productive purpose, like instilling patriotism or providing rhythm for training exercises. The only other instruments I'd heard before were the drums and trumpet, used for wake-up calls, drills and the daily presentation of the national anthem.

I turned to the second photo, obviously much older than the last, judging from how young Leavesleft looked. His hair was platinum-blonde and his dimpled grin was nearly toothless. On either side of him sat a middle-aged man and woman who looked a lot like him. Their dark eyes and tan faces were radiant beneath mops of light hair. I was shocked to feel my chest tighten, a little. Was my experiment working, after all? I was both thrilled and horrified.

My fellow base-raised comrades never met their parents, excluding the likes of Autoero Austere Jr. I met mine last age, but I wasn't sure that sour, thirty-minute stint counted.

Attachment hurt. Look what it did to me and Scarlet. I was probably better off without it. I knew that. Then, why was I still jealous of Leavesleft?

Because, now, my eyes were opened. I was no longer ignorant of the way things were 'supposed' to be. I was aware that kids were meant to be raised in families, not armies. Which was why I knew, deep down, that I still needed to fulfill my promise to Finis. Even though he'd never know. Even though it was far too late for he or I to personally benefit. I couldn't, with a clear conscience, turn a blind eye to the systematic child-abuse my country facilitated.

The next photo was of Nurtic Leavesleft, Dither Maine and Arrhyth Link, sporting matching swimming trunks. They were soaked, like they'd just emerged from the shimmering pool behind them. It was strange to see water so bright. So turquoise. Around Leavesleft's neck was a gold medal suspended from a navy-blue ribbon. Around Link's neck was the bronze. I turned the picture over and read,

'High School Regional Racing Championship of the 92nd Age,' scribbled in Leavesleft's lefty handwriting. I couldn't imagine swimming for tokens that didn't mean anything. If we raced in the Childhood Program or at Icicle, it was to help determine grade-levels or rank. If the Trilateral Committee awarded medals, it was for life-saving valor or history-altering victory. To us, the water was a battleground, not a playground.

So, now, an entirely different emotion welled in my chest. Anger. The idea of competing for futile medals irritated me. It was so stupid. I almost dropped the pictures in the bin, right then and there.

But, despite myself, I turned to the last one.

Standing in front of a video-game console were the laughing faces of Ecivon Wen, Tnerruc Ruetama, Nurtic Leavesleft… and Scarlet July. Leavesleft's arm was casually draped around Scarlet's shoulders. I stared. I knew Scarlet and Leavesleft both lived in Alcove City before enlisting, but I never considered the possibility they'd have met before the academy—after all, the city was enormous, and Scarlet never attended public school. I looked at Scarlet's joyful face and felt a stab of envy. Around me, she was always tense. On guard. Even when kissing me and unbuttoning my shirt. She was never this relaxed in my presence. I'd never seen her smile quite like that. All four of them looked… happy. Carefree. The weight of the world didn't rest on their shoulders. Not yet, anyway.

They were all young adults, like me. But, I felt thousands of ages older. By the time I reached my teens, I'd already killed hundreds, fought in dozens of battles and brushed death countless times. I'd already felt pulses grow weak in my hands, heard the crunch of bones beneath my feet, felt warm blood trickle between my fingers…

I was never free. The Nurians were. Leavesleft, Link, Maine, Wen, Ruetama. Until I graced their shores and single-handedly turned their world upside-down.

But, for Scarlet, this picture recorded a lie. Maybe, Leavesleft gave her a reason to laugh, every now and then. But, she was never really free, either. Like me, she'd always been a prisoner of the war, even if she didn't know it, yet.

However, I couldn't say the war was solely a negative force in her life. It gave her purpose. It was a catalyst for her growth. For the development of her brilliance and creativity. It gave her an impetus to emerge from the city streets and live up to her true potential. It helped forge her into the person she was today. And, that person was truly remarkable, if you asked me. Sure, Scarlet's life wasn't 'fun' by Nurian standards. But, it was effective. Second Earth was different because of her.

I tucked the photos back into the bible, careful not to glance again at the arcade one.

Three of the four smiling kids in that shot were dead.

I noticed a couple lines sprawled on the book's inside cover: 'Fav. verse – Dec. '87: "Even though I walk through the valley of the shadow of death, I will fear no evil, for You are with me." –Psalm 23:4.' I frowned. Leavesleft was not yet a soldier, in December of the eighty-seventh age. Yet, the verse he chose sounded like something only a man who lived under the gun would wish for. Until Leavesleft enlisted, when had he ever 'walked in the valley of the shadow of death'? My forehead creased. Was this the Nurians' secret? Was this why Leavesleft was always so put-together?

It'd be nice, not to fear evil. I rarely showed my fear, but that didn't mean it wasn't always there, lying beneath the surface like a sleeping gelid.

Family, friends, music, religion—inside this case were all the things we base-raised divers were always deprived of.

It was a window into a world we never knew. Even if the war ended today, I knew we still wouldn't be liberated. Not really. For, memories made strong prison gates.

Oddly, I wasn't angry at Leavesleft for breaking the possessions rule. I did feel a little betrayed, though. Leavesleft was one of my most trusted subordinates. I promoted him in my place, before my arrest. Keeping this giant stash of contraband, right under my nose, was a brazen show of disrespect. It made me feel unobservant, incompetent and outsmarted.

I'd never heard non-military music before. I looked down at the audio-player and, before I could talk myself out of it, thrust the buds into my ears and turned it on. An overwhelming, chaotic swell of sound cascaded into my head. It was nothing like drill music or the national anthem. No wonder the Nurians were always so sloppy and distracted, if they were liable to have noise like *this* running through their minds at any time!

I stuck the audio-player in my pocket, packed up the rest of Leavesleft's things, marked his unit 'still in use' on my clipboard, then silently proceeded down the row of open locker doors.

SCARLET JULY

We stood at attention, before the entrance. The silence in the room was thick enough to slice with a glacier-thawing lance. I wondered if anyone could hear my heart pound.

It was the morning of February twenty-second. In minutes, three-hundred-fifty-seven graduates from Icicle Academy would arrive. Three-hundred-fifty-seven brainwashed children would enter the war like the men they weren't. And, the worst part was, Cease and I were the only ones here who thought there may be something wrong with that.

Slowly, the door swung open and a straight line of white suits poured into the hall. They marched in perfect unison, faces blank and eyes forward. Of course, none of them were decorated. The uninterrupted whiteness of their suits and the fluidity of their movements made them blend all the more into the monochromatic surroundings.

Each kid that paraded before us was a living, breathing reminder to Cease of his failure to fulfill his promise to Finis. I could see the anguish in Cease's stare. Oh, yes, it was subtle. I doubted anyone else would pick up on it.

As the grads lined up, I felt a twinge of déjà-vu. I remembered when the Nurians and I were the newbies, watching Cease's forty veterans emerge from the horizon. We were all intimidated out of our minds. Now, I was on the other side of the fence. I wondered, were these kids feeling as scared as I did, back then?

They looked so small. So vulnerable.

What an absurd thought for a sub-five-foot, eighty-pound sixteen-age-old to have. They were still larger and taller than both Cease and I. But, size wasn't what made them seem small and vulnerable, to me. It was their faces. Their immature, smooth, unscarred faces. However intelligent and well-trained they might have been, nothing could mask the fact that they were only fifteen to seventeen.

Except one.

I noticed him as soon as he strode in—the boy whose frame was dwarfed by the rest, but only because he was even younger. By a lot.

Cease barked for attention. He was answered with a single salute performed by three-hundred-fifty-seven white gloves.

"Congratulations, soldiers." Cease paced, hands clasped behind his back. "That's what you are, now. Soldiers. Not students. But, if you think that means you're through with learning, you just wrote your death sentence. I don't care if you were the academy hotshot—if you believe you've got nothing left to learn from me, or your unit leader, or the veterans, or the Conflagrians, or the lowest-ranking piece of dragon dung in this lineup, you're wasting your time, here. And, believe me, the mages won't hesitate to trim the fat." A fiery intensity ignited his words. "In this fleet, you *will* keep your eyes and ears open at all times and you *will* abruptly adapt to whatever's thrown in your path, or you *will* get slaughtered. Do I make myself clear?"

A chorus of voices cried, "Sir, yes, sir!"

"In battle, if you didn't think of something, the Conflagrians probably already did. No idea is too outrageous or terrible, anymore. The era of respectful warfare ended the second the System firebombed a skyscraper full of civilians.

And, if the enemy doesn't play fair, what do you do? You don't play fair. Because, the enemy's the best teacher you've got." Cease stalked past the small one, whose liquid-blue eyes carried a hint of arrogant revulsion. Cease picked up on it and turned on his heel. "And, if need be, I won't hesitate to be your enemy, too. Understood?"

"Sir, yes, sir!" everyone shouted, again.

Except the little guy.

Cease advanced on him. Besides me, he was the only subordinate Cease could tower over. But, the height difference wasn't much—maybe, three inches. And, the boy didn't seem intimidated in the least. In fact, did his eyes just narrow, ever-so-slightly? Oh, Tincture, was he asking for it.

"I see one of you has already decided to waste his time here," Cease said in a low voice. Neither of them blinked. "When I ask if I'm understood, I expect an immediate reply. Understood?"

"Yes."

"Yes, *what?*"

"Yes… sir."

"Name, soldier?"

"Krustallos Finire the Seventh," he answered, tossing back his stringy, chin-length brown hair.

"I'm keeping an eye on you, Seven."

"That's not my name, sir. It's Krustallos Finire the Seventh," the runt insisted, obnoxiously loudly.

Cease folded his arms across his chest. "I'll call you whatever the hell I want."

If Finire had any survival instinct at all, he'd shut up, right now.

The twerp took a step forward. "I prefer my real name. Sir."

Oh, Tincture.

"Get back in line, Seven," Cease ordered, coldly.

Finire didn't budge. "Don't call me that, sir."

Cease looked like he wanted to drop-kick the kid. "Get back in line *now*, Seven. My patience is wearing thin."

And, that's when I understood why Krustallos Finire VII unsettled Cease so much. He was ages younger than his comrades. He was daring and had an edge. He didn't hesitate to publicly defy authority. With his pale skin, glassy gaze and slight build, the two even shared a number of physical characteristics. Cease couldn't stand Finire because he reminded him too much of himself. And, Cease wasn't known for his self-love.

"Why don't you like my name, sir? Because it means the same thing as yours? Is that it, Commander Crystal's End?"

Cease's lips went tight. "Nonsense. Mage names have meaning. Nordic names don't." I couldn't believe he was actually engaging Finire's question! "Now, get back in line!"

Finire finally obeyed. I exhaled.

But, Cease didn't let anyone off that easy. "Seven, report to the pool at dinnertime to face the repercussions of your insubordination. Don't bother to change into your diving suit beforehand. Do I make myself clear?"

There was a pause.

"Yes, sir. As crystal."

I looked at Finire's smug face, disgusted. I may've felt sorry for him and his comrades for being victims of the Childhood Program, but nothing gave any soldier the right to disrespect Cease.

Krustallos Finire VII didn't know who he was messing with.

* * *

"My Second and I will have all unit assignments ready by the end of the week," Cease announced as we changed in the locker room. The new graduates strapped numbered vests overtop their diving suits. "As always, each unit will be led by one principal leader and one sub-leader. This means promotions for many of you."

The Nurians always got nervous at the prospect of promotion. But, the atmosphere in a room of young Ichthyothians was entirely different: I could practically feel their ruthless ambition effervesce.

"I expect most ranks to get filled by veterans," Cease went on. "However, if any of the newbies outperform the vets this week, I won't hesitate to adjust my decisions accordingly. I've been known to do that in the past, even with non-Ichthyothians." His eyes flickered to me. "So, I advise the current officers not to get comfortable. All your positions are now in jeopardy."

It was as though Cease tossed an unpinned grenade into the crowd. I was positive the room-temperature actually rose a few degrees. Cease sure knew how to motivate.

Finire's locker was only a couple doors from mine. He walked up to me now and blurted, without so much as a greeting, "Crystal's End implied you're not Ichthyothian." His gaze grazed my stripes. "If you're Nurian, why are you still here?"

And, good day to you, too. "Ma'am," I reminded him.

He paused. "Unless, you're not Nurian, either? Ma'am." He squinted his strikingly-Cease-ish aquamarine eyes at me. "If I didn't know better, I'd say from your coloring that you're Conflagrian."

Holy Tincture. Not even Colonel Austere could figure that out by just looking at me. Until now, Cease was the only one who did. Well, there was no point in hiding my heritage; all the veterans already knew, anyway. It was only a matter of time before the new grads would find out. Better to hear it from me.

Those within earshot looked scandalized by Finire's words. No doubt, his comment sounded like a serious accusation to them.

"Yes, Finire," I answered, loudly. "I'm Conflagrian. I'm just toning down my blinding, red aura to spare you the offense."

Every new grad within a ten-foot radius of us froze.

"You're *her*, aren't you?" Finire breathed. "The one whose mind can resist the System? Magical eyes and hair?"

"Red Leader in the flesh."

And, now, all eyes went wide.

"So, the *Ichthyothian* Diving Fleet is co-commanded by the *Conflagrian* Multi-Source Enchant. Anybody else think that's a little odd?" He cocked his head. "Should I call you multi-sourced, though, when you only have two sources? Doesn't 'multi' mean three or more? You're just a dual-source." Fear prickled my chest. "And, you're no 'Red Leader,' either. The Red Revolution is dead, as long as the Core Crystal's intact." He smirked. "Isn't it funny that a man named Crystal's End would help end the Core Crystal? Well, temporarily, anyways."

This punk sure knew how to get under the skin of authority. "You know, you really shouldn't call him that," I shot. "He's your Commander; you owe him respect." Cease got offended when I used his first name, without invitation. So, a nickname? Finire was flirting with death.

"The media hasn't been respecting him for months. They were nice only when they thought he was dead."

My hair twitched on my shoulders. "Keep talking and I'll give everyone a couple reasons to think *you're* dead. Now, put on your number!"

"Crystal's End gave me this one on purpose," he whined, holding up his vest, emblazoned with a great, big, cobalt-blue '7'. Finire was probably right. I suppressed a smile. I loved it when Cease's sense of humor kicked in, however rarely.

"It's not your place to question his orders. Put it on, now," I snapped. "And, may I remind you, I'll be assisting the Commander with choosing the promotions, so you may want to watch your attitude around me."

His eyes traveled up and down my body, like an elevator. "How did you become his Second, anyway? I mean, you're young enough to be in my class, and you're a *girl*."

"And, you're a whiny, egotistical, prepubescent dragon turd," I spat. "Shut up and get your vest on, *Seven*." I was appalled by the words escaping my own lips. Yes, Finire was insufferable, but that didn't give me the right to bully him. His lack of discipline didn't excuse mine; I shouldn't stoop to his level. I was behaving like Amok Kempt. I vowed not to judge Finire any more until I saw him in action.

He was amazing. His diving skills were comparable to Cease's, his tactical genius would give Amok Kempt a run for his money, and his lightning-quick reflexes coupled with his incredible eye-hand-coordination would make him a formidable piloting competitor to Nurtic Leavesleft and Tose Acci. He was observant, curious and unafraid to voice his out-of-box ideas.

The only problem was his attitude. He didn't like it when others interfered with his plans and typically insisted on his own way... which was usually better, anyway. Not to mention, attitude wasn't exactly a unique problem in the military. It wasn't enough to make me write him off. I was impressed with the brave, flawless, fluid way he led his comrades. If he didn't take orders well, yet everything ran smoothly when he *issued* them, then he should get a unit. If he got placed under someone else, he'd undoubtedly drive the poor officer mad. If all he could do was lead, he should lead. Simple logic.

Krustallos Finire VII wasn't the only grad whose performance was of note, today. I was floored by the discernment, responsiveness and precision of several of the newbies. My fellow veterans didn't seem as impressed, though. Apparently, my standards were too low... perhaps because I was automatically inclined to compare them to the Nurians. These teen Ichthyothians were far better trained, disciplined and skilled at the art of war than the Nurians, several ages their senior. It freaked me out. They were *children!*

No. Not children. Young soldiers. There was nothing childlike about their lives. There was nothing childlike about the way they carried themselves, or the orders they followed, or the deadly weapons in their holsters. In a better world—one in which justice prevailed—the administrators of the Childhood Program would face severe repercussions for their crime against humanity.

But, this wasn't a better world. This was a world in which the ends justified the means. And, this merciless child-abuse filled a desperate need of ours: we had an army.

SCARLET JULY

I buzzed Cease's intercom. The week was over; it was time to decide on unit assignments. The ceremony was set for tomorrow morning. I was now heading into my first private, one-on-one encounter with Cease since the night he tried to seduce me.

So, yes, I was nervous as hell.

"Enter," came his terse voice.

I took a deep breath and stepped inside.

"Sir." I saluted. I didn't dare call him by his first name since that night, either. Not out loud, anyway.

Cease nodded curtly, adjusting his visual band. "I told you to come prepared," he shot, looking at my empty hands.

"I did." I touched the side of my head.

"Fine." He stalked behind me and threw the door shut with a threatening bang. "But, *I* can't read your mind, contrary to what you may think, so you better be ready to speak up." He shoved a handwritten page in my hands, giving my right palm a lengthy papercut I had to spectrally heal. "My officer list. Read and respond."

My insides squirmed as I sat in his desk chair and he perched at the foot of his bed. He sure was being short with me.

"So?" he snapped, the second I was done.

"I agree with almost everything you wrote, Commander," I answered, honestly.

He cocked his head. "Almost?"

I nodded. "I don't see Finire's name on here."

His nose twitched. "That's because it doesn't deserve to be."

I leaned forward. "Why not? The kid is a born leader. His task forces complete every assignment without a hitch. People listen to him. No matter who we put him with, he manages to work with them and make things happen."

"No," Cease objected, "Seven doesn't work *with* anyone. I define working *with* others as listening to and refining their ideas, ultimately incorporating the ones of merit into your master plan. Seven has no patience for anyone's thoughts but his own, which is why he'd be an ineffective officer."

"Sir, I don't think he can handle being second to anyone. Whoever we put above him will become his target. They'll be in constant conflict. If we don't *give* him authority, he'll want to *take* it."

"Let him try, then!" Cease growled. "Before he can issue orders, he needs to learn to follow them!"

"Do we really have time for that, though?" I asked, thinking of the Conflagrian blockade and the fact that Icicle could no longer afford to serve its soldiers lunch on a regular basis. "Under normal circumstances, sir, I'd agree with you. But, this is an emergency. Do we really have the time or resources to let Finire learn things the hard way? Can we really afford to let him cause chaos, just so we can try to eventually fix or rescue him? He may be damaged beyond repair, who knows." And, before I could think the better of it, I added: "I suspect a lot of these men are."

Cease sat stone still. It was particularly difficult to try to guess what was on his mind whenever he wore his band, since his eyes were the most emotive part of his default-deadpan face.

"Why are they damaged beyond repair, Scarlet?" he asked, quietly.

My voice went small. "You know what I'm going to say, sir."

"I asked you a question, soldier."

I looked at my boots. "Because they're a product of the Childhood Program, sir."

Cease continue to stare at me for what felt like eras. My face burned hotter than a dragon's throat. I didn't want to know what his eyes looked like behind the band. I didn't want to see the fury.

"I'm a product of the Childhood Program," he finally said. But, to my surprise, he didn't sound angry. Just...disappointed.

And, not with me.

"I was talking about Finire and his fellow grads," I piped, feebly. Cease wasn't just a product of the Childhood Program, he was the pinnacle of it. Their most prized result. Everything it was meant to achieve. "At least, *you* see the flaws in the system. You have an awareness that no one else here does. And, you tried to do something about it—"

"Thinking about it isn't trying," he said in the same deflated tone.

"You still think about it?" I dared to ask. The last time we talked about it, Cease admitted he tended to put it out of his mind.

"Yes." He hesitated. "It got harder not to, since three-hundred-fifty-seven living, breathing reminders arrived at the start of the week. I could ignore things more easily when it was just us veterans. Having the new graduates around makes it all seem so...real. I look at them and think, 'none of them have ever heard a viola.' Isn't that ridiculous? Isn't that the stupidest thing you've ever heard me say? Our nation is in crisis and, here I am, fretting over the fact these kids will probably die in combat before ever getting the chance to listen to anything but drill-tones and the national anthem." He put his head in his hands. "Oh, Scarlet, I'm going crazy."

My heart swelled. That wasn't the stupidest thing I ever heard him say, it was one of the most beautiful. He wasn't 'numb to the world,' as he thought. I was elated.

Viola. He mentioned the viola, specifically.

"Sir, have *you* ever heard a viola?" I squeaked.

He stayed silent. Which meant—

"You have! But, when? How?"

He still didn't speak.

"So, you knew," I said, slowly, "about Nurtic Leavesleft."

"No, I didn't. Not when he was here, anyway. And, then, the night before the grads arrived, I opened his locker."

"Ah." I goggled at him. "You're not angry?"

His face darkened for just a moment. "Not really."

Was that so? "Well, sir… he didn't just keep it stowed away… he, um, sometimes used to play for us in the barracks, right before lights-out. Until I got my own quarters, I'd hear it with everyone. The Nurians and I enjoyed it a lot. But, I think it actually disturbed the base-raised, quite a bit. I guess they didn't know what to make of it. Anyway, Nurtic got away with it for so long, we couldn't tell if you really didn't know what he was doing, or if you knew but chose to turn a blind eye."

"I guess you have your answer."

I cringed internally, feeling like I betrayed his trust.

"If I knew back then, I would've been mad," he added, thoughtfully. "Real mad. I would've smashed his viola to splinters and made him wish he never learned to play the damn thing in the first place." He exhaled. "Too late for that, now."

Now, he miraculously wasn't upset. Now, he wished the new grads could hear it, too. Incredible.

"So, you listened to his recordings," I breathed.

"One of them, yes."

"What did you think?"

He pursed his lips. "It was… strange. It's not like the anthem. It's more… I don't know… disorganized."

"Did you like it?" I heard myself croak.

He went quiet. Perhaps, I pushed the envelope too far. I didn't want him to get irritated and shut me out. But, then—

"No. Yes. I'm not sure. I found it intriguing but off-putting. Like you said, I didn't know what to make of it. I was entering uncharted territory. But, I guess it wouldn't be fair to say I hated it, if there's still a part of me that wants to hear more."

Wow.

"Well, sir, if you didn't discard the audio-player, you could always—"

Suddenly, he snatched the rank list from my lap and abruptly brought the discussion back on track: "I'm glad we're mostly in agreement about the officer assignments; that makes things easier. But, I'm sorry, Scarlet; I'm not promoting Seven," he said, flatly. "I refuse to feed his ego. I'm placing him in your unit because I think you've got the best chance of getting through to him. My one condition is that you don't make him your sub-leader. Agreed?"

Krustallos Finire VII in *my* unit? Was I ready for that? Cease was planting a ticking time-bomb beneath me.

"Agreed, sir," I responded, as if I had a choice.

"Good," he grunted, grabbing something off his desk. "Now, *this* is the list of which soldiers should go in which unit. What do you think?"

I frowned. "I thought we're supposed to make these lists together, sir."

He shrugged. "Something's got to fill the hours between dusk and dawn. Now that I've got a speed-writer like you helping me with the weekly status reports, I've had a drought of nighttime activities. I considered waking you up one evening to collaborate… but, well…"

"Why don't you *sleep* at night, for a change?" I laughed, taking the pages from him. "It's perfect," I said, once finished. "It's exactly what I would've drawn up, with the exception of Seven's placement."

"Which I'm not changing."

"It's handwritten," I observed. "You usually type everything. I'm used to hearing your keyboard click, all night."

"Well, lately, I've been abstaining from the keyboard as much as possible."

"Why?"

"Carpal Tunnel." He grimaced, raising his left hand.

"You could've asked me to type for you."

He shrugged again.

Without asking, I brazenly sat beside Cease on his bed, reached for his hand and slowly began massaging his wrist and palm. At first, he tensed up at my touch. A moment later, however, he relaxed, closing his eyes behind his visual band. It was strange and wonderful to see him unwind a bit. I unbuttoned his cuff, ready to sooth the inflammation with spectrum, when—

"What's this?" I gasped.

"What?"

"*This!*"

On Cease's forearm was a barcode, captioned by a string of tiny, black numbers: '12-22-75-72587.' I recognized the format: it was his military serial-number. The first six digits were his birthday and the last four comprised his random identification-code. What I wanted to know was what it was doing on his skin.

"That's just my serial-number, Scarlet."

I stared.

He cocked a brow. "What's wrong? *You* have a number. We all do."

"Yeah, on my dog-tags and ID card, not my body!"

"The Childhood Program brands its students," he said, calmly.

Holy Tincture. "That's so *dehumanizing!* What are you, a farm animal?"

He smirked. "More like a piece of merchandise."

"I can't believe this!"

"Nothing about the CP should surprise you, by now," he said, irritably. "If I remember correctly, you're the one who called us 'factory-produced'?"

"I didn't mean it literally!"

He shifted his wrist from side to side as though noticing his mark for the first time. "It tickled."

Tickled? "You remember getting it?"

"Yes. I was promoted early, but not *that* early."

"They don't brand you upon arrival, as a baby?"

"No, not until graduation—which, as you know, usually happens between fifteen and seventeen. I got mine at ten."

A thought occurred to me. "Commander, are there more kids at the academy, right now?"

"Another class of three-to-four-hundred graduates every few ages." Suddenly, he sat up straighter, snatching off his band. "We could send them home!" he exclaimed, echoing my thoughts.

I nodded, vigorously.

"But, Scarlet, how'd we actually go about making that happen?"

We. My heart leapt. But, there was still a hint of resentment in his voice. Just enough to make me uncomfortable.

I looked him in the eye. "Sir, are you sure you want to?"

"Well, of course."

Of course, nothing!

He read my face. "I swear, I do. And, I'd like you to help me. Will you do this with me, Scarlet?"

I beamed. "Yes, sir."

"So, where to begin?" he jumped right to business.

"I suppose the first step would be to write to the commodores and admirals who run the system."

"The Trilateral Committee, you mean." His voice dropped an octave: "I was a part of the TC for a few months, when I was an admiral. But, once I was demoted, I got kicked off."

Great.

"Well, you're still the Leader of the Ichthyothian Resistance. We'll write them a letter, invoking the power of your office to request a formal meeting."

He chortled, "That's got to be one hell of a convincing letter."

"Language arts?" I gave him a smile, which he returned with his eyes. "My specialty."

CEASE LECHATELIERITE

*To the Diving Commander Cease Terminus
Lechatelierite,*

*We hope this letter finds you well. The Trilateral
Committee has considered your perspectives regarding
the Childhood Training Program and thanks you for
your interest and concern.*

*The Childhood Program has proved successful
throughout the ages in its endeavor to discipline,
nurture, educate and prepare capable and promising
individuals for the service of our country. We are very
proud of our military academies and the outstanding
results they produce. The Trilateral Committee
unanimously considers its youth program an authentic
way-of-life without which the Ichthyothian Resistance
would perish.*

*As a top graduate of Icicle Academy and the grandson
of the honored Diving Captain Terminus Expiri
Lechatelierite, we hope you share the same pride in our
nation's legacy of education. The Trilateral Committee
offers its sincerest regrets for rejecting your meeting
request and kindly asks you not to issue any further
communications regarding the matter. Thank you.*

We respectfully remain,

Trilateral Committee Chair, Admiral Oppre Sive
Trilateral Committee Secondary Director, Commodore
Rettahs Slous

"That's sort of what I expected, the first time around," Scarlet said, reading beside me at the breakfast table. "I notice they conveniently didn't address you as the Leader of the Ichthyothian Resistance. Makes you easier to brush off, I guess?"

I nodded, dropping the page by my plate of salmon paste and half-cooked green beans that tasted like it came from an era-old bag accidentally discovered in the back of a freezer. By now, the cafeteria had run out of crackers to accompany the fish spread. The fishy goo was hardly edible without it. This morning, Scarlet didn't bother retrieving a trey from the food-line at all, and I was beginning to see her point.

But, Dr. Calibre strictly forbade me from doing the same. Since returning from our seventy-seven-mile trek, he'd been on my case about unhealthy weight-loss. I fared worse than Scarlet on that trip because she could feed off her aura. So, at least twice a day now, I forced myself to eat something. I could never finish a standard portion, though. Which was a bit of a problem since the Ichthyothian government made it illegal to throw away food without 'legitimate reason,' like spoiling. And, I strongly despised using the Recycling Center.

The Recycling Center was a new addition to our cafeteria, established in response to the siege. Its purpose was to sort and extract 'sanitary' leftovers from plates, for incorporation into future meals. Yes, everyone found the entire concept utterly revolting.

Anyway, Scarlet now picked up my fork and began making grooves in the salmon slush on my plate. "The Trilateral Committee *'kindly asks you not to issue any further communications regarding the matter,'*" she recited from memory, in a mocking tone. "As if." She looked up at me, cutely cocking her rosy lips to one side. "Of course, we're going to reply. And, this time, we're really going to rub your rank in their faces and *make* them listen." She dropped my utensil and sprang to her feet, hair autonomously flying over her shoulders. She was all the more attractive to me, when set off like this. "Come on, let's go write this thing, now!" Her intensity caught the attention of a few new graduates, sitting nearby. They seemed startled and maybe a bit offended by her improper address. "Sir," she added feebly, I sensed more for their sake than mine. I should've been bothered by the way she talked to me but, oddly enough, I wasn't.

"We've got class with Colonel Austere until fourteen o'clock," I reminded her.

She rolled her enormous, green eyes. "This is more important." From a few seats away, Seven watched us, suspicion in his liquid gaze.

"Fine," I said. "But, first, what should I do with this food?"

Scarlet blinked. "Eat it."

"I can't."

"Then, why did you take it out of the line?"

"I don't know."

"Just drop it off at the Recycling Center."

"Mmm, doesn't this look too good to waste?" I murmured jokingly, glancing down at the contents of my plate, which Scarlet had transformed into what appeared to be a lumpy pile of vomit.

"Here." She grabbed my fork again, poised it gracefully and smoothed the top of the paste. Then, she drew what looked like two lopsided ovals connected by a canopy.

"What's that?"

"Music notes. But, of course, you wouldn't know that. May the food-sorters be entertained. Now, come on."

I peered over my shoulder. Seven and his band of followers were still sneaking critical peeks at us.

"Will you keep it down?" I hissed at Scarlet.

I left my trey at the RC and followed her out, feeling several pairs of eyes on our backs.

"Your position *does* permit you to request a meeting," she muttered furiously as we walked to my room. "They have no right to shut you up like that!" She shot a lock of hair around my doorknob.

"There's really no need to break in," I said mildly, strangely aroused by her anger. "I *do* know the key-code for my own quarters, thanks."

She bolted to my computer and began pounding the keyboard. In minutes, she produced and printed an eloquent yet fiery reply, quoting all the right statutes.

"What do you think, sir?"

"I think you should quit the military, take a time-machine to First Earth and become a lawyer."

She smiled her painfully-beautiful smile.

"It's just missing one thing," I added, slyly.

"What's that?"

"Your signature under mine."

Her hair squirmed like snakes. "Sir, we're banking on your authority here, not mine. Moreover, they know I'm Conflagrian. I'm the biggest scandal of the Ichthyothian military world. The last thing we need to do is remind them of my presence."

"I don't care," I insisted. "You wrote the letter; your signature's going on it. If you don't add it, I will. I'll forge."

She folded her arms.

"This is a direct order from your Commander: sign it. Now."

Flushing crimson, she picked up my pen. "I hate it when you pull rank on me."

"Hey, if I'm going to do it to men three times my age, why shouldn't I to a lowly subordinate like you?" I teased.

She stood and hollered directly in my face, "Well, you better show this 'lowly subordinate' some respect, or else you'll have to write your own letter!" She waved the sheet before my eyes.

So, I caught both her wrists, forced her arms behind her back and bodily pushed her up against the wall. Then, I towered over her in a mock-threatening way, nose nearly touching hers.

I wanted so badly to kiss her.

"Or, I could just take it from you, by force," I whispered.

And, there it was, again—that familiar look of burning adoration and desire, in Scarlet's gaze. The gravity was too strong; I decided to go ahead and take my chances. I sank my lips into hers, her wood-smoke scent filling my nose. Sure enough, she scrunched her lids and reciprocated, eagerly.

My door burst open.

"Sir, Colonel Austere sent me to request your attendance at the—" the voice fell silent.

Horrified, Scarlet and I jumped apart, looked to the doorway and saw none other than Krustallos Finire VII, crystal-blue eyes like shuttle-lights. Of all people to barge in, at a time like this! For a moment, I wondered how he was able to enter, in the first place. Oh, yes, because a certain Conflagrian mage broke my lock with her hair.

Seven's face took on a maddeningly superior look. He had a big advantage over us, now. Serious blackmail material.

"The Commander and I were just working on a letter to the Trilateral Committee," Scarlet babbled to her boots, feebly holding out the wrinkled page.

"Yeah, I saw you two *working*, alright." He smirked. "I think the Colonel would be very interested to hear all about it."

I rounded on him. "I thought I made it perfectly clear that you're no longer a little student at the academy, Seven. Your days of sucking up to authority are over."

"Funny you should mention sucking up to authority." His amused gaze shifted to Scarlet.

"Protocol mandates that you knock and request permission to enter an officer's room," she mumbled.

"You're not to speak a word of this to anyone, Seven. Understood?" I barked, knowing I actually had no right to give such an order.

He didn't answer.

I advanced on him. "Understood?" I yelled again, grabbing his collar.

Several agonizing seconds of unblinking silence passed before he grumbled, "Sir, yes, sir."

I threw him into the wall. "Dismissed!"

He gave me one last scathing glower before brushing himself off and disappearing down the corridor. He left the door wide open.

Scarlet still stared at her feet, face blood-red, eyes moist.

"Let's go," I said.

She bit her lip. "I-I'm sorry, sir."

"That's enough. Move it."

She nodded, took a deep breath and fled down the hall, hair flying behind her like a torch. I followed from a short distance.

The lesson was well underway. Scarlet situated herself in the seventh row, between Illia and Inexor. I sat in the very last row, among a group of new grads who looked rather frightened at the prospect of having their Commander's critical eyes on them for the next several hours.

Seven was up front, surrounded by his loyal band of followers. He took no notes. As I watched the back of his shaggy, long-haired head, my chest tightened. The Leader of the Ichthyothian Resistance and his Second were now at the mercy of an eleven-age-old egomaniac.

* * *

It was four o'clock on February twenty-eighth and every soldier not on night-watch was asleep in the barracks. It was the perfect time for Scarlet and I to continue working on our secret plan to dismantle the Childhood Program.

"Scarlet," I hissed as I tapped her door, lightly. The buzz of the intercom would be too noisy at this hour. "Scarlet, wake up."

I heard the creak of mattress springs. The door yanked open and she looked at me with surprise in her half-closed eyes. Her hair was a mess. Messier than usual, anyway. She clutched her red robe around her tiny body. The exposed skin of her collarbone, usually concealed by her uniform, was rather distracting.

"Cease?" she mumbled, drowsily. "It's four o'clock." She blinked. "Is something wrong?"

"Yes. I received another letter from the Trilateral Committee, late this evening, after you went to sleep." Her eyes instantly snapped wide open. "I want to work with you on a reply, before morning, if now's a good time."

"It already *is* morning," she retorted dryly. "But, of course, now's a good time," she quickly added in response to my dangerous glower. I ushered her into my room and handed her the page.

FEBRUARY 27TH OF THE 94TH AGE

*To the Diving Commander Cease Terminus
Lechatelierite,*

*The Trilateral Committee wishes to express its
disappointment in you for failing to honor our
previous request. Any further inquiry regarding the
Childhood Training Program, whether from you or
your subordinates, is prohibited.*

*The TC would like to kindly remind you that,
on January 7th of the 94th age, you were convicted by
the Alcove City Military Court and discharged from
duty. Your permit to continue serving as Commander
of the Diving Fleet will terminate upon the conclusion
of the nationwide state-of-emergency, currently in
effect. At that time, you will be expected to fulfill
the sentence issued to you by the Nurro-Ichthyothian
Alliance. Your status as 'Leader of the Ichthyothian
Resistance' therefore no longer legally permits you to
exercise authority over anyone beyond the soldiers of
the Diving Fleet.*

*Your meeting request is hereby formally declined. We do
not wish to discuss this matter with you again.*

We respectfully remain,

*Trilateral Committee Chair, Admiral Oppre Sive
Trilateral Committee Secondary Director,
Commodore Rettahs Slous*

"The alliance no longer stands," Scarlet breathed. "The
'Nurro-Ichthyothian Alliance' and the 'Alcove City Military Court' have no authority over anyone, anymore."

"It did when I was court-martialed."

"A sentence wasn't even properly *made* because Nurtic Leavesleft objected and pulled you out. Your trial never really wrapped up. You should demand a do-over. It's kind of like diplomatic immunity—you can request to be retried in your own country, by your own people."

"The judge was Ichthyothian-born."

"Doesn't matter. Nurian court, Nurian jury. The trial never concluded and Nuria has no jurisdiction over you, anymore."

"But, Scarlet, I'm guilty. Any jury will reach the same conclusion. I'll just end up being convicted, all over again."

She waved her hand. "That's not the point. The point is to expunge this fiasco from your record *for now* so you can temporarily resume the full powers of the office of the Leader of the Ichthyothian Resistance. Innocent until proven guilty, right? During the space of time between the expungement and your new court date, you'll have a clean slate and thus a green light to go ahead with your reformation plan. So, before we tell the Trilateral Committee anything else, we need to request a retrial."

I gaped at her. "So, you're saying, *if* the Ichthyothian military court system accepts my appeal, *then* I can use my rank to request a meeting with the Trilateral Committee so we can *then* attempt to convince them to shut down the Childhood Program?"

She nodded.

Wasn't her out-of-box thinking the foremost reason I promoted her? But, this wasn't just off-the-wall, it was off her rocker.

I shook my head. "That's a whole lot of 'if's, Scarlet. And, if I remember correctly, the courts were able to set my first trial within seven days of my arrest. What if something like that happens, again? There's no way I could get the Trilateral Committee to meet with me in a week!"

"Cease, why weren't you tried on Ichthyothian soil, in the first place?"

Of course. "Because all the Ichthyothian military courts were booked until May."

"Exactly! And, this time, they won't be able to expedite things by shipping you off to Nuria. We'll have more than enough time, trust me."

I trusted her. "Okay."

"We can't bother the Trilateral Committee again until we get a response from the justice system," she plowed on, businesslike. "And, that means, we should contact them ASAP."

The chair creaked as Scarlet swiveled back around, pawed my laptop and churned out another letter. Then, she got up and let me sit in her place, to read it. She stood over my shoulder.

"You're amazing," I said the moment I was finished, feeling heat radiate from her flushing cheek. "I approve." I turned and impulsively grasped her forearm. "Thank you, Scarlet. You've done more than enough. You can return to your quarters, now," I said, though without letting go. "Get some rest."

"Finire's on watch in this wing until six," she answered uneasily, glancing at my clock. "I don't know what he'll think if he sees me leaving your quarters at this hour, especially after…"

"Well, why don't you just wait here until then? I got my lock fixed," I said, bodily pulling her onto my lap. I noticed that, oddly, she didn't seem very hot to the touch. Hm. Her temperature was supposed to be at least a dozen or so degrees higher than mine. Was I feverish? I certainly didn't feel sick.

"Cease," she squeaked, looking down at me, hair hanging over half her face. "What are you doing?"

What was I doing? Just giving her yet another opportunity to realize how badly she wanted me. Just reminding her how intense our chemistry was. Just showing her how pointless it was to resist me. To resist us.

I reached up and stroked her wiry hair, tucking it behind her ears. "This," I answered softly.

Scarlet stayed silent and frozen in place. If she didn't like what was going on, sitting still and taking it without a peep wasn't really getting the message across. She had ample opportunity to object and get up. But, she didn't do or say anything to discourage me. She seemed to be waiting to see what move I'd pull next.

"And, this," I whispered.

Cupping her rosy cheeks in my palms, I leaned in and pressed my lips against hers, gently at first. Kiss steadily intensifying, I seized her waist. Like a switch got flipped, she suddenly came alive in my arms, reciprocating fiercely. Her tiny hands found their way into my hair; she ran her fingers through it.

We went on for several crazy minutes. When we came up for air, Scarlet gasped, "Cease, what are we doing?" Not, 'what are you doing' but 'what are *we* doing.' Good. At least, she acknowledged her active participation.

I nuzzled her. "What does it look like?"

Her nose twitched, cutely. "I'm n-not sure."

"Come on, you're smart; figure it out."

"Y-you're trying to… to lure me in, again."

I narrowed my eyes. "Nice try, but you can't pin this all on me. You sure as hell kiss like you're in love."

She clung to me as though her life depended on it. "I-I am."

"Then, what's the problem?" I hissed, nibbling her earlobe.

I slid my hands down her back and untied her swathe; it fluttered to the floor. Then, I started pulling off her robe. She only wore a loose, airy nightgown underneath.

"Cease—"

My lips interrupted her. She moved her mouth with mine eagerly, desperately, squirming in my lap. Soon, her robe was nothing but a red puddle at our feet.

"Take off my shirt," I ordered.

She promptly obeyed, wide eyes exuding both fear and desire. It was incredible how quickly she managed to unfasten every button.

"Now, my undershirt."

"I just d-don't know about this," she piped, even as she diligently and rapidly obliged.

"If you don't want to go on, don't. Hand over my clothes and leave. I won't be mad and I won't try to stop you. It's okay."

She didn't hand over my clothes. Instead, she dropped them on the floor.

I smiled and, instantly, her face turned redder. "That's what I thought," I said.

Her wood-smoke scent filled my nostrils as I pulled her in and sucked the freckled nape of her neck. She trembled.

"You're manipulating me," she murmured, lids fluttering shut. "Making it hard to go."

"I know how much you enjoy a challenge." I made my way up her chin and cheek. "I'd like to take off your gown, now; is that alright?"

She moaned as we kissed yet again, placing her hands on my bare chest, squeezing my pecs a little bit.

And, she shoved me away, hard, prying our lips apart.

"No," she choked, eyes popping open. "No, it's not!" She wrenched herself from my arms, leapt off my lap, stooped to the floor, grabbed her robe and hastily pulled it on.

I stood. "Fine." We didn't need to keep going, anyway; my point was made. The damage was done. Burned in Scarlet's perfect memory was exactly how good it felt to be this close to me and how passionately she responded to my advances. I knew it'd serve to erode her resolve to stay away. It'd haunt her until she finally gave in. I was one step closer to winning her over. One step closer to making her mine.

"I'm going to write our next letter to the Trilateral Committee," she croaked as I put my shirt back on. Then, she walked around me and toward the desk, loop comically large, as though afraid she'd get sucked into my gravitational field if she came any nearer.

"I thought we can't do that until we hear back from the court?" I rolled my desk chair toward her.

"I'm going to write what we'll send the TC if and when the court accepts." She sat down, hands groping for my computer. "That way, we'll be ready, immediately. Not a second wasted!"

And, she was off… but, this time, her concentration was shot. The same person who churned out a perfect letter just minutes ago was now unable to string two words together. Whenever I tried to get close enough to read and help out, she went rigid and scooted away from me. This fiasco went on for nearly an hour.

"That's it!" I finally burst. "This isn't going to work! Let's just stop." I pointed to my clock. "There's only fifteen minutes until six."

"I can finish by then!"

"No, you can't!"

"*Yes, I can!*"

"Quiet!" Did she want Seven to hear?

"I'm going to finish the letter!"

And, so, she did. In fourteen minutes, flat.

"Told you I could do it." She stuck her chin out at me. I fought the urge to grab it, pull her in and thank her in a very personal way.

"Amazing." My eyes raced down the screen. "Scarlet, what'll I do without you?"

"You're going to have to figure that out, like, right now," she murmured as she opened my door and fled.

SCARLET JULY

Barely three weeks remained until March twenty-fifth—
the deadline the Trilateral Committee gave us, to strike the
Conflagrian blockade line. My appetite for a breakfast of
recycled salmon paste and slimy oatmeal dissolved at the
mere thought.

Cease sat down directly beside me at the table, trigger-
ing an analytical stare from Finire.

"Ignore Seven," Cease hissed.

"Must you sit here, sir?" I asked in a small voice.

"Yes," he pressed. "I need to talk to you, now. It's important."

"What about?" I asked, lifting my ice-water to my lips.

"July twenty-fifth."

I nearly choked.

"Of *next age,* Scarlet. That's my new court date."

I plunked down my glass. It took all the self-restraint I
had not to throw my arms around him and squeak with glee.

"They accepted our request?"

I settled for merely grasping his arm. Finire noticed. I
quickly let go and grabbed my spoon, instead.

"Keep it down," Cease snapped. "Yes, they did. I got the
email, an hour ago. I'm cleared of all charges, until then.
Sixteen months of freedom. Or, longer, if the state-of-
emergency lasts beyond then." He smiled with—I couldn't
believe it—his eyes *and* lips. His enthusiasm was so
infectious, I couldn't help but grin back. Which, of course,

warranted a brow-raise from Finire. "I took the liberty of sending off your latest letter to the Trilateral Committee, along with the court's email," Cease went on. "There's no way the TC can refuse my request now that I've got a clean slate until at least July twenty-fifth of the ninety-fifth age."

"Some date, huh? That can't be a good omen!" I laughed.

"I added just one little thing to your letter," he said, still giving me that maddening smile that made it hard to listen and breathe at the same time.

"What's that?" I took another sip, just to give my hands something to do, so I wouldn't give into the dangerous, growing impulse to hug Cease right here, right now, in front of the entire fleet.

"I asked them to meet on March seventh."

This time I actually *did* choke. I coughed, really loudly. Of course, *that* got the attention of everyone on our side of the mess hall.

"Sir," I gasped, once all eyes—finally—turned back away, "that's in just a few days!"

"As I recall, *you* were the one who said something like, 'we don't have a second to waste!'" he mimicked my high-pitched plea so well, my cheeks burned. "The Trilateral Committee meets at the Trigon Center in Glass City, central Ichthyosis. That's roughly five hours northwest of here, when traveling by train… which we're, unfortunately, going to have to do, since the TC claims it can't afford to spare us a government semivowel due to the shortages." He rolled his silver eyes. "And, we can't use any of our own crafts to fly there directly ourselves because—get this—Trigon doesn't have a runway! No joke. So, we'll need to leave very early that morning to catch a—"

"Wait a minute," I blurted. "I'm going with you?"

He blinked. "Of course."

"Did you mention that in the letter? When Fair Gabardine and I wanted to meet with your dad, security didn't let Fair past the Centerscraper's front desk because—"

"Yes, I put it in the letter," Cease cut me off. "You're coming with me and that's final."

My breakfast squirmed inside my stomach like live worms. A Conflagrian mage—just the kind of person the TC would love to see. *Hello, Mr. Nordic Admiral, sir,* I imagined myself saying to Sive. *I come from the land of the magically oppressed. Now, let* me *tell* you *what's wrong with* your *system!*

"Sir, I don't think—"

He held up his hand. "Nothing you say will change my mind." And, with that, he got up and left me to my cold, sticky meal.

SCARLET JULY

March seventh.

"Come on, we're going to be late!" Cease growled through my door. He didn't bother with the intercom—he was louder than it. "What the hell are you still doing in there?"

"Just tweaking our notes and printing them out!"

"Tweaking, *now?* Get out here before I break your door down!"

"You don't have to," I babbled, trying to buy time as my printer took *its* sweet time. "You know the key-code!" I heard the clicking sound of buttons being punched. "Hey, that wasn't an invitation to actually use it!"

The door swung open and Cease came barging in. I managed to snag the last sheet a split-second before he grabbed my wrist and bodily ushered me out.

"You're such a bully, you know?" I laughed, but when I looked at his face, I saw he was in no joking mood. His eyes were venomous.

"The train isn't going to wait for us," he grunted. "Back when civility existed, the Trilateral Committee would've sent a semivowel."

"Hey, you can use your left hand again! Carpal Tunnel healing up like magic, huh?"

"Cut the small talk and pick up the pace. I'm practically dragging you," he muttered, snapping on his visual band.

"Well, then, quit wringing my wrist. I might need it, thanks," I retorted, prying myself from him.

"The station is in Nox City. We're taking a snowmobile there. Helmet on!"

"Yes, sir."

We dashed out into the hangar and hopped onto our snowmobile. Cease gripped the handlebars, I gripped his waist and, the next thing I knew, we were plowing straight through a snowstorm at three-hundred miles per hour. Though I surface-rode on crystallines, dove from vitreous silicas and flew dragons overseas, nothing prepared me for the stomach-swooping sensation of scaling the blinding Ichthyothian horizon on a snowmobile while flakes polka-dotted our visors.

The further north we traveled, the denser civilization became. As we entered Nox City, I burned with the curiosity of a tourist. I'd never seen civilian Ichthyosis before. I doubted Cease got to come out here all that often either. Roads were crammed with silver semivowels. Pedestrians darted up and down the sidewalks on skis. Of course, no one else wore heated scuba-suits, so they were all bundled like First Earth Eskimos in coats, hats, hoods, earmuffs, scarves, gloves—you named it, they piled it on. Tinted goggles shielded their eyes from the fierce wind.

Why was the city bustling at four o'clock? Why were there children wearing backpacks, skiing around well before dawn?

"Cease, why are the streets so packed at this hour?"

"Why do you think this city is called 'Nox'?" he answered. "It's so full, its set up so fifty percent of the population go about their daily lives at night while the rest sleep, and vice-versa. It's a 'nocturnatown.'"

Half the people around here were forced to be *nocturnal?*

"Wow."

"I was born a few blocks from here, at Krustallos Finire Hospital. My parents were part of the night-shift." He paused. "I guess that explains my insomnia," he added, dryly. I loved it when he attempted a joke.

It was incredible, how Ichthyosis managed to cope with its terrible weather and irregular landscape without a photon of magic. They had technological or organizational solutions for every possible obstacle. For example, countless colossal mountains obstructed the skyline, but of course, Ichthyothians wouldn't let ten-thousand-foot rocks get in their way! Each slope, no matter how steep, was cluttered with shops, malls, schools, residences, businesses and so forth. And, unlike Nuria's Alcove City, there were no overturned trashcans in the allies, nor graffiti sprawled on the walls of buildings, nor stench of urine nor rotting garbage. The town was dazzling.

I tried to imagine Cease adapting to civilian life, here in Nox City. I tried to picture him blending in with the masses, sporting a puffy coat and knitted scarf rather than a sleek diving suit or crisp uniform. I pictured him driving a semivowel up a mountain to an office-building for a day-job, rather than sailing the Septentrion Sea into battle. How ridiculous. The only idea *more* ridiculous than Cease living in civilian Ichthyosis would be Cease living in primitive, hot-weathered Conflagria, with me. Cease wearing robes and riding scabrouses and fetching well-water and using outhouses and fighting System soldiers with swords and bows and arrows. Absurd.

I pushed the thought to the back of my mind. Now was *not* the time to dwell on all the reasons a future with Cease was impossible.

We finally arrived at the station.

"You okay?" Cease asked, sweeping me off my seat and onto my wobbly feet.

"Yes, of course," I answered, though dizzy. "Why wouldn't I be?"

"Well, you squeezed my waist so hard the whole ride, I can barely feel my legs."

I was glad he couldn't see me blush through my reflective visor. "I'm sorry, sir."

He waved his hand. "Come on, let's go."

We scurried inside, yanked off our helmets and stood in line for a direct train to Glass City. As we waited, we received a lot of stares from passerby. Some even pointed openly, whispering behind their gloves. In the sea of bulky, fur-clad civilians, Cease and I surely stuck out in our skin-tight, white-and-blue diving suits.

We finally boarded the train, which resembled a massive, silver caterpillar. Each car seated roughly seventy passengers. Which meant Cease and I faced hours of being eye-groped by about seventy curious civilians. It didn't help that Cease had been on the news so frequently, since his arrest. People seemed both intrigued and intimidated.

Once everyone seemed to get enough of gawking at Cease (which took a while), they began to notice the person traveling with him. The image the Trilateral Committee put out for the Ichthyothian military didn't exactly include small females, so the general public didn't know a thing about me. Until now.

"I can't believe there's a *girl* in our military!"

"Look how little she is."

"She's even smaller than him!"

"Hold on, she's got stuff on her sleeves. What rank is that?"

"There's no way she could be a fighter; she's too tiny and delicate."

"She's cute."

"Shut up; you've got a girlfriend."

"Look at that hair!"

"Are they husband and wife?"

"No, silly, soldiers aren't allowed to marry!"

Cease and I ignored them. He spent most of the trip with his visual band on, studying our notes. Review would be pointless for me, so I had nothing better to do than to window-stare and people-watch. Maybe, I should take a nap; I was exhausted. Not to mention, I really needed to be on my A-game, today. I slid in my seat, tipped my head back and scrunched my lids shut.

Red and orange light flashed before me. The ground beneath my body was hot, too hot, like a stove. The air was thick and smoky and suffocating. I tried to throw my hair forward, but it wouldn't move. My own screams terrified me to the core; I'd never heard myself sound like that before, even when I watched my own family get slaughtered—

"Scarlet!" Something cold tapped my cheek.

My eyes fluttered open. "Sir?" I murmured.

Cease, visual band pushed up to his bangs, stared at me with concern. "You were calling out in your sleep."

I blinked. "I-I was?"

He leaned in and whispered, "If you had a vision, I need to hear about it. Speak to me quietly, in Nurian."

"I-I'm not sure what I saw." How come!?

"Scarlet, you can tell *me*," he insisted, breath tickling my ear.

"I honestly don't remember!"

"Since when are *you* forgetful?"

"I swear I'm telling the truth. I can't recall a thing, except that... I was afraid." Afraid? Tincture, what an understatement.

"Aw, will you look at that! He's comforting the little girl after her nightmare!" an elderly woman cooed to her companion. Cease and I looked at her, and a pink twinge touched her wrinkly face.

"We'll talk later, when we don't have an audience," Cease muttered to me.

I nodded, relieved the subject was dropped. For now.

"You okay?"

"Yes, sir."

"Good. We should be arriving soon."

"Are you Nurian, ma'am?" spouted a pimply teenager from a couple seats away.

Taken aback, I blurted, "Um, no."

"You definitely don't look native. Where are you from?"

I folded my arms and gave him my best impersonation of a Cease-glare. "The Ichthyothian military," I answered crisply, turning away.

And, I thought I saw tiny smile dimples appear on Cease's cheeks.

CEASE LECHATELIERITE

Scarlet was really impressed with Nox City. But, Nox paled in comparison to Glass, the nation's capital.

The Glass Train Station was seven blocks from the Trigon Center.

"We have ten minutes," I told Scarlet as we strapped on our helmets. "Let's move."

"Yes, sir."

In the soles of our boots were protractible skis. Deactivated, extended glacier-thawing lances made suitable poles. Heads turned and fingers pointed as Scarlet and I zipped down the sidewalk, weaving our way through the herd. I found nothing amazing about what we were doing. I wasn't used to being in a place where soldier status made you different or special. It was weird.

At last, we arrived. I yanked off my helmet, wind stinging my nose and whipping my hair into a frenzy. I slapped the intercom on the tall, iron fence and spoke through the howl, "This is Diving Commander Cease Lechatelierite and Second Commander Scarlet July, reporting for a meeting with the Trilateral Committee."

Slowly, the gate opened. Scarlet and I skied up to the entrance.

"Combat equipment isn't permitted inside." The guard stared at our diving suits with a cross between awe and confusion. "Please leave your utility belts and helmets here. They will be returned to you upon your departure."

As Scarlet and I unloaded, the guard continued to gape. I wondered what he found so interesting. Being military wasn't supposed to be special *here*.

"Sir, ma'am, we need to scan your barcodes, please."

"My ID is in my utility belt," Scarlet answered, making a movement toward the bin. The guard stepped forward, blocking her way. "It's in my utility belt," she repeated. "May I, sir?"

"I have no need to see your ID, ma'am, only your barcode."

Scarlet blinked. "My barcode is on my card."

The guard sighed and turned to me. "Sir?"

I took off my gloves and offered him my branded wrist.

"Thank you." His scanner beeped and the tiny console displayed my basic information, outlined in green.

"My Second-in-Command is unmarked," I said.

"Unmarked?"

"If you'd like to confirm her, she'll need her ID."

The guard nodded, turned to Scarlet and gestured to the tub. "My sincerest apologies, ma'am."

Scarlet looked taken aback by his sudden courtesy. "Thank you," she murmured as she dug out her card.

He scanned it. The screen flashed red.

"I'm sorry, ma'am, but it says here your ID expired on January seventh." He squinted at her info, brows shooting to his hairline. "You're from Alcove City, Nuria? Why haven't you returned home?"

I folded my arms. We were already late; we didn't need this buffoon making things worse. "My Second had to remain active-duty for classified reasons."

He glanced at me, clearly intimidated. It was convenient to have that effect on people. "Very well, then. Please proceed through the metal detector and spectrometer."

Spectrometer. Great. I guessed the guard was going to learn all about Scarlet's true heritage, after all. Clearly, the Trilateral Committee failed to warn him in advance. No surprise there. Of course, Sive and Slous would want to make our morning extra exciting.

"A note about my Second Commander," I said, stepping through the machines first. "The TC is aware that she's the Multi—"

My words got interrupted by a blaring siren as overhead monitors flashed:

'ELECTROMAGNETIC-FIELD ANALYSIS: BLACK
Wavelength Interval: 300 nm
Frequency Interval: 1,000 THz.'

What? Why wasn't I infrared? My heart hammered in my throat. Was my black aura really that strong? Strong enough for a spectrometer to think I was a mage!?

Immediately, security staff surrounded us, leveling weapons at our heads.

"Freeze, mages!"

"Hands up!"

"Sir, I can explain," Scarlet piped, raising her arms. "The Trilateral Committee already knows everything," she spoke quickly. "I'm Scarlet July, the Conflagrian Multi-Source Enchant; I'm immune to the mind-control of the System. Please, alert Admiral Sive or Commodore Slous—they can verify everything I'm saying. It's all documented."

"Yeah, but what about *him?*" one of the officers yelled, brandishing his sidearm at me. "Explain *his* readings!"

"Spectral twining is a known phenomenon," Scarlet breathed. "Apparently, it can effect anyone's electromagnetic field, not just those who are already in the visible range."

"The Trilateral Committee knows all this," I growled. And, they didn't give you a head's up because they wanted this fiasco to happen. They wanted to shake us up before the showdown. "Get Admiral Sive or Commodore Slous. They'll back us up."

As if on cue, the Commodore began approaching from across the hall. I never thought I'd be glad to see him.

He had a hint of a smile on his face. Bastard.

"Stand down, stand down," he said jovially to the guards, waving his hands. "Let them through."

Almost reluctantly, the security personnel lowered their weapons and stepped back. We followed Slous down the corridor, leaving slushy tracks all over the velvety, blue carpeting. As we entered the conference room, sixteen heads looked up in perfect unison.

Scarlet and I greeted the men with a salute. They all looked rather prim and proper in their ceremonial uniforms.

Admiral Sive, the Chairman of the Committee, rose to his feet but didn't return the gesture.

"Decided to show up after all, Commander?" He smirked. "You're late."

"We had some trouble up front, sir," I responded.

"Ah." Sive's eyes met Scarlet's, but only for a moment. "I see." He didn't even attempt to conceal his disgust. Anger prickled my chest. I took a deep breath. It was way too early to start getting mad.

I didn't bother to fill him in that it was actually *my* spectral readings that stirred the pot.

I offered him my hand. After a pronounced hesitation, he took it.

"You have a strong grip, Commander." He raised a trimmed brow. "I see you've recovered very well since your... return from the dead, I daresay."

I didn't blink. "Yes, sir."

"You were incapacitated for at least a month this time, correct?" He cocked his head and tutted. He actually *tutted.* I didn't think people really did that. "Keep at it and we may have to rethink that Silver Triangle we naively gave you," he said with a revolting wink, referring to my most prized possession, the medal I got in August. It was the highest honor a diver could receive. "Silly us; we thought you would've had your fill of needing our damage-control by now," he chuckled, "you know, especially after *that battle…*" his voice tapered.

"There was nothing to cover up." Just how long would this handshake go on? The awkwardness seemed to increase by the second. "This time, I worked directly with my men during my recovery."

The Admiral's temples pulsed. "Did you, now?"

"Yes, sir. And, previously, it was wrong of me to hide from my men and my country like a coward, as though it's a disgrace rather than an honor to be a wounded veteran."

His face contorted. "Very well, Commander." He dropped my hand as though it suddenly transformed into a poisonous spider.

Scarlet held out her little hand next, but Sive ignored it. Instead, his gaze traveled up and down our sopping-wet suits and lingered on the snow in my hair. Scarlet's magical hair, of course, was dry. "Just come from battle?" he jeered, puffing his chest as to show off his own perfectly-ironed, heavily-decorated ceremonial uniform.

"No, sir."

"Then, why the diving suits?"

"They're good for cross-country travel in a snowstorm, especially since we had to take public transit," I said, becoming all the more aware of the great puddle forming at our feet.

"Very well," he grumbled as he plopped down. "Please, take a seat. Your lateness has already wasted enough of our time."

But, there was only one empty chair at the table.

I didn't budge. "I believe you've been informed that both my Second and I would be in attendance today, Admiral?"

Sive glanced at Scarlet again, disdain in his beady stare. "As the topic of today's meeting isn't of consequence to her, we—"

"You fixed the computer system so her ID would scan 'expired,' despite the fact I personally reactivated it upon her return to Icicle in January," I shot, "and you neglected to warn security of her expected spectral readings!"

Sive was silent.

"Commander Lechatelierite," Slous interjected, glowering at Scarlet's vividly-red hair, to which he seemed to take personal offense, "how could Second Commander *July* here speak against the Childhood Program when she never experienced—"

"We'll proceed with this discussion *after* we've all been seated," I interrupted.

Scarlet looked at me with cautious eyes that demanded I cool down before I blew all chances of a civilized debate.

Sive tapped his earpiece. "Tye, can we get another chair in the conference hall? Thank you."

Moments later, an attendant came in with a chair. Scarlet, cheeks burning deeper than blood, silently took it from him and squeezed it beside mine—a difficult feat, considering the table really wasn't meant to accommodate nineteen. We were crammed, armrest to armrest.

"Well, now that we're all comfortable," Sive said acidly, "shall we get started, Commander?"

"Actually, I'd like to begin, Mr. Admiral, sir," Scarlet spoke perfect Ichthyothian, tone firm and polite.

Sive visibly jolted, as though expecting Scarlet to stay mute the entire morning. "Proceed." His knuckles grew white on his glass of ice-water.

Scarlet took a deep breath, stood and faced seventeen men who'd been taught all their lives to hate people like her. "Commodore Slous is right," she said bluntly, bringing triumphant smiles to the faces of the elderly generals who hadn't been to battle in so long, they forgot what it looked like to have a trap laid out before them. "I didn't graduate from the Childhood Program. I wasn't raised on a military base. I wasn't armed by the age of three, taught to kill by the age of six, or branded with a barcode by the age of fifteen." She rolled up her cuff, revealing her bare wrist. "But, I serve alongside those who were," she gestured to me, "my life in their hands and theirs in mine. As the Second Commander, it's my duty to understand how my soldiers think. Which is how I've come to see the extensive psychological damage they've all sustained—"

"How *dare* you!" erupted a captain sitting right across from us, as though it were outrageous to say something negative about the program we came to dismantle. He was probably hankering to blow up at the first possible opportunity, and would've done so no matter what we opened with. "How dare you wear our colors and masquerade as one of us, then stand before this council and insult the very system that led this country to greatness! Moreover, the Childhood Program wouldn't even exist if it weren't for Conflagria! Ichthyosis's hand was forced—extreme measures had to be taken—because of the threat *your* people pose to the entire northwestern hemisphere!" He leapt to his feet. "*This* is what I think of you and your kind, you barbaric fire-savage!" And, he leaned over the table and spat directly on Scarlet's face.

Oh, no, he didn't. I jumped up, knocking my chair over, ready to tear the bastard, limb from limb. But, before I could give him what he deserved, Scarlet gently touched my arm.

"It's okay, Commander," she told me quietly, eyes still on the man. She didn't wipe the bubbly saliva trickling down her pink cheek. "Thank you, sir," she calmly said to him, "for helping prove my point." She turned back to Sive. "May I proceed with our presentation, Admiral?"

Sive nodded, wordlessly.

I set my chair back on its legs and sat down, chest heaving.

"Sir, I joined the Ichthyothian Resistance because I believe wholeheartedly in its mission. As an adult enlistee, I had the freedom to make that choice. I decided I wanted to serve your county. Because, like you said, the Conflagrian System is a threat to international security. The System should be eliminated. But, at what cost? The cost of abusing thousands of Ichthyothian children? The cost of forcibly confiscating newborns from their parents and depriving them of their youth, throwing them into a world that wounds even the strongest of adults? Not to mention, how can they fight for a society to whom they bear no connection? Defend a country they never had a chance to be a part of? Die for a people they don't know? They are never given the opportunity to see art, hear music, know love, enjoy friends and family, have a hobby—live like those they're supposed to protect. My Commander, at eighteen, just heard string music for the first time in his life and told me what an impact it had on him. He wishes all his comrades had that chance."

Every eye was on me, now. An intense wave of embarrassment zipped through my body like an electrical current. That wasn't in the notes. I shot Scarlet a dangerous look and she returned it with one that pleaded for me to trust her.

I trusted her.

"These soldiers don't know who or what they're protecting because they've never been a part of their own culture," she went on. "They've been deprived of almost everything that makes life worth living."

"You don't believe a life of defending your country is one worth living?" asked an admiral at the other end of the table.

"Of course, it's a beautiful thing for a man to serve his nation, but wouldn't that sacrifice mean more if he knows what he's fighting for? If he could *decide*, himself, to leave it all behind so he can preserve it for everyone else?" she asked. "I made that decision and I'm glad I did. It fulfills me, every day. It gives my life purpose. But, my Commander never made that choice. And, neither did any of you."

I cleared my throat. "We're asking you to make the class of the ninety-fourth age the last to be thrown into combat before they're old enough to opt for that sacrifice themselves. No more children should be broken down and beaten into compliance in *my* Resistance."

"When a soldier lays dying on the battlefield, his thoughts should turn to the family he loves and the childhood he spent at home," Scarlet interjected.

"As you're all well aware, I got seriously injured during the battle in which the Conflagrian System introduced the Underwater Fire," I said. Several brows rose at the fact I'd elected to bring up the topic myself. "When I fell off my crystalline, suit scorched, I thought that was the end for me. But, the only thing I felt in that moment was guilt. Guilt for failing to uphold my responsibility to my fleet. Guilt for not winning, as I'm supposed to. Nothing else came to mind before I lost consciousness. And, *you know why?*" I erupted, and everyone sat up a little straighter. I knew how to control my tone to really strike and convict. Even if my words were nothing special, my voice was like a bullet in the ear. I had my inflections down to a science. Scarlet looked at me now as though hypnotized. She'd gazed at me with that kind of captivated adoration several times before, energizing and invigorating me. I felt like I could conquer the world, whenever she regarded me that way. "Because, all my life, I've had nothing and no one to live for besides the war. All my life, the only thoughts I've had are ones put in my head by the Childhood Program." I looked each man in the eye. "I've been *brainwashed*. And, what does that make the CP no different than? The Conflagrian System," I boomed. "Yes, the very same oppressive, totalitarian regime we're so dedicated to destroying."

My words seemed to suck all the oxygen from the air.

"As the Multi-Source Enchant," Scarlet chimed, "I'm the only mage who can independently resist the mental pull of the Core Crystal. But, I haven't always been able to. Until age ten, I was nothing more than Principal Tiki Tincture's puppet. My every thought was directed by the Crystal until July twenty-fifth of the eighty-seventh age— the day the System declared me a waste of island resources, killed my family, attempted to execute me and wound up deporting me to Nuria. I know what it's like to be controlled. I was born into cerebral enslavement. I was raised to heed every order given to me, without question. This experience taught me to detect the same sort of subjugation in the behavior of others. I've been on both sides of the fence; I know what to look for. I can tell when a person is being manipulated. I can tell when I'm dealing with a man who's been brainwashed. And, I can see it, right now," she swallowed, "not just in my Commander, but in each and every man sitting before me, at this table."

There was a long silence.

"What's been done to these generations—to you and me—is a crime against humanity," I declared fiercely, and Scarlet gave me that enraptured gaze, yet again. I ripped my eyes from her magnetic face and forced myself to focus on Sive. "It's *child-abuse* and we're prepared to support that claim with plenty of research." I tapped our notes.

"We've come to you today with a complaint but also a proposition," Scarlet said. "We would like for you to send home the remaining classes of the three childhood academies, redirecting the CP's resources into adult recruitment and training."

"Most of the work to establish this replacement structure has already been done," I said, "when the academies of northern Nuria were erected. All adult recruits can be educated just as the Nurians were, using similar curriculum."

"And, this new system will be far less expensive because the adults would only spend seven months in training, as opposed to the fifteen to seventeen ages that the Childhood Program requires," Scarlet added.

For the next three hours, Scarlet and I faced a continuous barrage of questions, comments, suggestions and oppositions. We stood before the men, a Conflagrian united with an Ichthyothian toward a common goal, tackling their every concern. If there was a question Scarlet didn't know how to answer, I typically could, and vice versa. Whenever we both knew how to respond, our words seemed to perfectly complement one another. Occasionally, I'd say something aggressive that'd shock Scarlet, or Scarlet would say something sentimental that'd unsettle me (like the viola comment... I mean, really) but, in the end, we trusted each other and pressed on, knitting a tapestry of resistance stronger than either of us could've woven on our own.

And, at long last, we won.

Every child-soldier at Icicle Diving Academy, Windy's Air Force Academy and Rink's Ground Troop Academy would be sent home by July.

Scarlet and I left Trigon, walking on air. I smiled up at the blinding-white sky, snow salting my lashes.

For you, father.

SCARLET JULY

Cease and I ran through the streets of Glass City, giddy with glee. It was the first time I ever enjoyed a snowfall. Behaving like the child he never had a chance to be, Cease hooked his helmet to his utility belt, flashed me an eye-smile that made my pulse skyrocket, and took off down the sidewalk hollering, "Try and catch me!"

I scrambled after him, weaving through the crowd, my own helmet bouncing on my thigh. He abandoned the walkway, detouring into Middle Glass City Park, where Ichthyosis's only trees lived.

Suddenly, Cease stopped and turned on his heel. I didn't expect it, at all—I skidded and rammed into him, hard.

"Ha!" His triumphant voice rang in my ear as he scooped me up and slung me over his shoulder.

Laughing, I thrashed and kicked. He toppled backward and we landed in a tanged heap, right by a stone monument. All around us, alarmed civilians backed away, probably thinking we were fighting.

"Gotcha!" I breathed, sticking out my tongue like a little kid.

In a flash, Cease rolled over so he was on top. I smelled his salty sent, even in the frigid wind. "Damn right, you got me," he hissed, kissing my nose.

"There's people everywhere," I warned, "gawking at us."

"Well, then, let's give them a *real* reason to stare," he murmured, thickly. And, with that, he clamped his jaw over mine. I thought I could taste his black aura in my mouth. I felt my own frequency quiver, as though plucked by his. An image spontaneously popped in my mind, then—red and black lifelines encircling one another, weaving together. Goosebumps rose on my skin, beneath my diving suit.

"Cease, no," I whimpered, the moment he relented. "How many times do we have to go over this?"

"If you don't want me, why do you always kiss back?" he asked, voice slick and compelling as ever.

I gnawed the inside of my cheek.

"Stumped you, didn't I?" he asked, not just smiling, but grinning. With teeth. I couldn't believe it. The sight wrenched out my heart and left it bleeding on the snow, beside us.

I had to escape. His draw was too strong. It was as though threads of the spectral web were tying me up, binding me to him, paralyzing me. I had to put some physical distance between us right now, before I succumbed to the ever-growing impulse to blow off our train home in favor of frantically making out with him right here on the ground for the next several hours without pause.

With one hand, I seized a fistful of snow. With the other, I grabbed Cease's jaw, as though initiating another kiss. Eager to oblige, Cease shut his lids and let me pull him in. That's when I wrenched open his mouth and stuffed it.

That ended things, quickly enough. Cease sat up, shocked, allowing me enough room to slip out. He spat a giant wad of slush. And, when he looked back at me, the all-too-familiar hardness had returned to his face. It was terrifying.

I got to my feet, leaning on the base of the monument. My eyes automatically slid through the engraved paragraph:

Many historians believe Ichthyosis would not have survived the 7-month "Epoch of the Crystal-Land's End" without the brilliant leadership of a man whose true first and last name evaded history books in favor of a nickname. As Ichthyosis is often called the "Ice-Crystal Island," the Ichthyothian people fondly christened their leader after the archaic Nurian word for "crystal": "Lechatelierite." Lechatelierite, who established the first colony back in the 17th age of the 2nd era, was 77 by the time Ichthyosis was granted independence from the Democratic-Republic of Nuria. Despite his old age, he fulfilled his post masterfully, using his remarkable intelligence, charisma and resourcefulness to help sustain the struggling land until the day he died, February 7th of the 71st age.'

I blinked. Cease stood beside me, stupefied, melted snow trickling from the corners of his mouth. I peered up at the stone statue. The man's face was narrow, his brows were furrowed and his hands were clasped behind his back.

'Lechatelierite' wasn't exactly a common name.

"Cease," I breathed, "why didn't you tell me you're the descendant of your nation's Founding Father?"

"I didn't even know my own parents' names until August, Scarlet."

I stared at him in wonder. "You've never studied the history of your own country?" For Tincture's sake, the Mage Castle taught its students to recite all Conflagrian System principals in chronological order. I remembered nine-age-old Fair pacing my bedroom, chanting it over and over, in preparation for an exam.

"No, Icicle Academy doesn't teach non-military history," he answered, hotly. "I can give you a biography of every important officer to serve in the First and Second Wars. But, we don't waste our time with the colonial period. That's for civilians."

I turned my head so fast, my hair flew over my shoulder by sheer momentum, not spectrum. "It's not a waste of time to care about the origins of your own nation! Do you even hear yourself? You're listening to your," I threw my hands up, "your *programming*, again!"

"Hey," he shot, "just because I don't agree with child-abuse doesn't mean I'm suddenly going to start caring about irrelevant matters!"

I couldn't believe my ears. "And, what does *that* mean? What do you consider 'irrelevant,' Cease? Anything outside the military world you're so mercilessly locked into?"

"I'm not 'mercilessly locked' into *anything!*" he erupted, voice slicing through the frosty air like a glacier-thawing lance on high. "The Childhood Program may've picked me for the Diving Fleet, but *I'm* the one choosing to stay in it, because I want to! Because the war is the only reason I get out of bed in the morning!"

A hobnail egg involuntarily formed in my throat. "You're no different than when we first met," I whimpered.

He kicked the monument's base, causing those nearby to jump. Tincture, civilians were so easily startled.

"How could you say that after what we *just* did at Trigon?" he yelled. "That isn't enough to prove I've changed? And, why the hell do you care if I change, anyway? What do you even want from me? I've told you many times that I value *you* above all else—including the war—and you rejected me! If you did that because you're actually uninterested, I'd understand and let it go. But, the infuriating thing is, I *know* you love me. And, I fought tooth-and-nail to mold myself into someone you could be with. Why'd you push for that painful transformation, then shut me out once I accomplished it? I've tried my best for you, Scarlet, but now, the war is all I've got left to live for. You've left me no other choice!"

Cease was so loud, everyone on our side of the park seemed to hold their breath; it was like a giant spotlight ignited above our heads. At the very least, they couldn't understand him since he was speaking—or, rather, screaming—in Nurian.

"To think, he was just kissing her, a moment ago," an old woman sighed to her friend.

Wind howled in our ears. I studied the triangular emblem on Cease's chest, unable to meet his eye any longer.

He turned away, rubbed his temples and stormed around the statue five times before coming back.

"I'm sorry, Scarlet," he said, quietly. "I'm really tense, right now; I think I'm a little shell-shocked from having abolished the Childhood Program less than an hour ago. Don't get me wrong—I'm happy about it. But, as you can imagine, it still isn't easy for me to digest." A shadow drifted across his face. "Anyway, I'm sorry for shouting and for blaming you for the way I am. That wasn't fair of me."

Yes, it was fair. He was right: what *did* I want from him? What business did I have, trying to soften him, if I knew we couldn't be together, no matter what?

"Let's head back to the station," was all I said.

When I took a single step, he caught my shoulder, roughly.

"Do you forgive me?" he demanded, commanding tone overtaking me.

"Y-yes, of course, sir," I found myself saying.

"Good." He released me.

There was a pause.

He glanced back at the monument. "The Epoch of the Crystal-Land's End, huh? Who knew we'd come full circle, five eras later? Except, this time, the Order won't save us."

That was it! Cease was a genius! (Well, duh).

"Why not?" I spouted.

He blinked. "Well, Scarlet, because we're at war."

"Yes, but, blacklisting would only make sense if we were on the offense. We didn't start this war; we're just guarding ourselves from invasion. If we didn't, we'd be conquered by now. How could self-defense be illegal?"

He shrugged. "Don't ask me where the Order gets its policies."

"You know what I think? I think the Order is unaware of the specifics of the war. I think they don't even know who started it or what it's about. I think the only thing they know is that Ichthyosis and Conflagria are involved, so they just blacklisted *both*. Maybe, if we made the details clear, they might be willing to help us out."

"Help us out?" His dark brows crept beneath his thick bangs. "Countries don't lend each other helping hands, Scarlet. Not on this earth. What do you expect the Order to do, grant us a war waiver and let us rejoin?"

"Yes."

He stared at me like I'd spontaneously sprouted wings.

"Just now, we were able to convince the Trilateral Committee to overturn a major policy," I pressed on. "We won over the best military minds. So, we're obviously one hell of a persuasive team. I'd say, the TC was good practice for facing off the Second Earth Order. Let's send a letter, requesting to meet with them."

His face was blank. He didn't speak for what seemed like eras. I wanted him to say something, *anything*, even if it was just, 'that's the dumbest thing I've ever heard, Scarlet.'

Finally, he said, "The Trilateral Committee had a legal obligation to accept my meeting request: we proved I should still possess the full range of power attributed to the office of the 'Leader of the Ichthyothian Resistance.' But, who am

I to the Order? A symbol of war. A paradigm of anti-isola-tionism. The mascot of an evil, blacklisted nation who tem-porarily led a member superpower astray. They're more like-ly to open their doors to System Principal Tiki Tincture."

"Cease, Arrhyth Link's *father* is the Chairman. If Arnold was willing to hand his son over to you, surely he'd let you into the Sequest Center! He's like a closet globalist, or something."

His eyes turned to large, silver coins. "Hold on. Arrhyth Link's *father* is the *Chairman* of the world government? How come Arrhyth never said anything about that when he was at Icicle?"

"Because everyone's already supposed to know!" I ex-claimed, in awe once again of Cease's ignorance of the non-military world.

"Ichthyosis isn't a member; I doubt even the civilians here know or care who runs the Order." He paused. "Wait, isn't the Chairman supposed to be from the Authority Nation?"

"Arnold's Orion; his wife's Nurian."

His thin lips parted. "I should've known Arrhyth had some Orion blood in him! That curly hair was a dead give-away. Wow, he must be one of the *only* mixed people on this *entire planet!*"

For Tincture's sake, I was anxiously awaiting Cease's reaction to my insane suggestion to face-off the con -gress of the world… and, here he was, musing about Arrhyth's ethnicity!

"So, do you want to do it, sir?" I squeaked.

He started walking. "It really depends, Scarlet. Is Arnold Link still there? By now, the Order probably knows about his son's participation in the Nurro-Ichthyothian conspir-acy. What if they impeached him?"

"That's very possible." I chewed the inside of my cheek. "We could look it up on the internet?"

"We can try, but I don't think the Ichthyothian media will have that kind of info, and we don't have access to foreign networks. The Order blocks all blacklisted nations, and Nuria cut us off, too."

I moaned. "When will the world stop misinterpreting the reason for the fall of First Earth and realize *isolationism isn't the answer?* What does any country gain from closing itself off? Every problem isolationism was instituted to prevent still wound up happening, anyway: there's war, crime, revolution and tons of unrest on Second Earth, and it's not going away just because we turn a blind eye to it and make decency illegal!"

"Now, Scarlet," Cease's voice was heavy, "we aren't meeting with the Order to take on isolationism. We aren't going to attack the philosophy on which the planet is run. That won't get us anywhere—but, kicked out. We're going in, focused on one goal: to convince them to let Ichthyosis rejoin since defending ourselves from imperialism doesn't, in fact, violate the spirit of their absurd laws. You'll just have to save your dream of rescuing Second Earth for later, alright?"

"So, you want to do it," I breathed.

He snickered. "You always know how to sweep me up into your crazy ideas. I wouldn't be *here*, right now—leaving Trigon with my promise to my father fulfilled—if you didn't make it happen."

I beamed. "How will we find out about Arnold Link if we can't just search-engine it?"

"Simple. We go ahead and send the Order a letter. If we're rejected, it's because Arnold's probably gone. If we're accepted, we know we'll see him there."

"Great," I grunted. "I hate not having any control over the outcome!"

Cease cocked his lips to one side—I tried to ignore how cute that was. "We must be spending way too much time together; you're beginning to sound like me!"

We plodded on in silence for a while after that, the thrill of today's victory already wearing off as we pondered the next daunting task.

Then, Cease touched my elbow and said in a serious tone, "Scarlet, I know you're the Multi-Source Enchant and all, but that doesn't mean *every* problem in the universe is yours to tackle. You know that, right?"

What? "Cease, where's this coming from?"

His face was set. "From what you said, just now, about isolationism."

He was so perceptive. Almost instantly, he cut to the root of the turmoil in my heart. Not a single day passed without my dwelling on the heavy weight of the prophecy. I didn't even know what it meant, yet I was supposed to fulfill it.

"There's just... so much I need to do..."

"Why do *you* need to do it? Because some old manuscript says so?"

Partly. But, that wasn't all. I *wanted* to save the world from itself. I burned for it.

"I want to do it," I said.

"What exactly is it?"

"I don't know for sure, but I have some ideas: ending this war, dethroning the System in favor of democracy and, most importantly of all, repealing and replacing isolationism with a system of moderate globalism. Why stop at rescuing Ichthyosis and Conflagria when all of Second Earth is in shambles?"

He folded his arms. "That's too much for one person. There's no way you can do half of that."

"But, I-I'm supposed to," I stammered.

"Are you? If you don't understand the prophecy, maybe it wasn't meant for you."

How could I respond to that? I knew he didn't intend to discourage me; he only wanted to relieve me. To take the weight of the world from my shoulders.

"If the Multi-Source Enchant doesn't fulfill it, who will?"

He didn't answer.

"I thought we already did," I croaked, "last July, when we diffused the spectral web. But, now, I see we must've misinterpreted the prophecy, because everything we worked to accomplish wound up falling apart, mere months later." I took a deep breath, but the vitreous silica sitting on my chest didn't take off. "Cease, my life's work has been undone!"

To my surprise, he suddenly stopped and pulled me into a tight embrace, leaning my head against his chest.

"Scarlet, listen to yourself." He stroked my hair and the strands on the back of my neck stood at attention—not from spectrum. "Life's work? You're sixteen."

"You should talk," I retorted. "Ichthyosis has been expecting you—our five-foot-two, one-hundred-pound, eighteen-age-old Commander—to complete *your* life's work, any day now."

"That's because everyone already knows what that's supposed to be. My purpose has always been cut out for me—I never had to figure a thing. My job is to win this war. Do whatever it takes. That's it."

I wiped my eyes in his diving suit. "Do you think we'll live to see everything we want come to fruition?"

"Nah," Cease chuckled. "I'm career military; I'm going to die young."

SCARLET JULY

As soon as Cease and I arrived home, we got to work. We grabbed our laptops and holed up in his quarters. The Trilateral Committee tasked him with breaking the news about the Childhood Program to the rest of the military. While he slumped on the floor and worked on drafting that notice, I sat at his desk and began composing our meeting request to the Second Earth Order. But, I knew, no matter how well-written, we only stood a chance if Arnold Link was still there.

I stopped typing and turned in my seat. "Cease," I peered down at him, leaning against the side of the desk, computer on his knees, "when does the Order meet?"

He pried off his visual band and blinked his tired, red eyes. "Why would I know that, Scarlet?"

"I remember Arrhyth saying something about his dad traveling at least once a month, but he didn't specify when *in* the month..."

"Well, unless this month's meeting is *after* the twenty-fifth, we'll have to wait until April."

Due to the dismal economic climate, March twenty-fifth was the deadline the Trilateral Committee gave us, to penetrate the Conflagrian blockade. And, we had to get the System Water Forces out of the way if we wanted to travel to and from Oriya in one piece.

Cease yawned, put his laptop on the floor, folded his legs to his chest and rested his forehead on his knees. He looked so small and vulnerable, curled up like that. The sight made me want to put my arms around his tiny frame, like that would shield him from all the crazy horrors of the world, and tell him everything was going to be okay.

How silly. *Me* protect *him*. Right. Sure. The strongest and most brilliant man to walk Second Earth was the last one to need anyone's guard. I turned away, afraid that if I beheld his balled figure any longer, I wouldn't be able to resist the urge to hold him.

My work got interrupted a couple minutes later by the sound of his head banging against the desk's edge. He sat up straight, bloodshot eyes wide.

"I fell asleep," he breathed.

I snapped my laptop shut. "Alright, I'll finish in my quarters. You need to go to bed."

"No, no, it's okay." He got to his feet, wobbling a little. "Stay where you are; I don't want to disturb you when you're doing so well. There's no need to kick yourself out."

"No need? You just fell over from exhaustion. Literally. I'll show you my draft tomorrow."

"How come *you're* not tired?" he asked, face slack.

Who said I wasn't? "Because I actually *sleep* at night."

"No, you don't. I see light beneath your door until two, sometimes three o'clock."

"I didn't say the *whole* night," I answered, alarmed Cease would be aware of something as insignificant as when my lamp was on or off. "But, I still get more rest than you."

"What do you do when you're up? Besides work, I mean."

I swallowed.

"Anything that'd explain the pencil shavings in your trash?" he asked with a smirk.

Heat coursed through my scalp. "What?"

"A few days ago, I overheard a couple janitors talking about it. You wouldn't believe how surprised they were to find pencil shavings on this base."

Ichthyosis had no expendable trees. So, finding shavings from an old-fashioned wooden pencil at Icicle was like unearthing ancient artifacts. Even the paper products made in this country were petroleum-based, which explained their weird, waxy texture. Cease stared at me, expectantly.

I studied my boots. "Nurtic Leavesleft gave me a wooden pencil, last age. I once made an offhand comment about how I didn't like mechanicals for shading, and how the *real* pencils we had back home were so much better... and, the next thing I knew, he conjured one up. Just one. Number two, HB—exactly the kind I said I liked. These days, I save it carefully, using it only for sketching."

Cease bit his lip. "I'd like to see what you've drawn with it," he said, to my great surprise. "The only other art I've seen before are those pieces you did in class, last summer. I still have them." He glanced away, as though ashamed. "And... I flip through them... a lot. Especially while you were away. I look at the seascapes. So peaceful. It's hard to imagine water without war. And, I look at all your battle diagrams." He hesitated. "Especially the Fervor Sea Base one." His face scrunched. "But, most of all, I look at the unfinished piece of us practicing the spin-toss. I always thought the Nurians were stupid for keeping photos of their family and friends in their lockers, but then," his voice jumped an octave, "when I found myself reaching for that picture, almost every night while you were gone, I realized I was behaving no differently." He turned his back on me and faced the door, chest heaving.

I stood, rooted to the spot, hugging my laptop. What I really wanted to do was throw the thing to the floor and take his trembling figure in my arms, squeezing the stress out of him.

"Cease," I piped, "you're so tired, you aren't thinking straight. Go to sleep. I'm leaving, now. I'll show you my draft, tomorrow."

He unbuttoned his collar, seized a folder from his desk and started fanning himself with it. Sweat beads trickled down his forehead. "I'm going for a walk," he spouted, pushing past me and opening the door.

"Now? To where?"

He waved his hand. "Around." And, he was gone.

* * *

It didn't take me much longer to complete the letter. I was already nearly done when Cease flopped over. I printed it out now, setting it on my desk. Then, I sprawled in bed with the lights on, still in full uniform, staring at the ceiling, thoughts running rampant. An hour passed and I was yet to hear Cease return to his quarters. Usually, when he couldn't sleep, he went to the hospital wing balconies, to stare at the sea. But, today, I had a hunch he was elsewhere. I got up, tucked the letter in my utility belt and slipped into the dark hall.

I made my way to the locker-room. And, sure enough, there sat Cease on the floor, beside Nurtic Leavesleft's old unit, opened. He was holding Nurtic's viola awkwardly in his hands. His button-down shirt lay crumpled beside him; he only wore his sleeveless undershirt. Marbles of perspiration dotted his messy hair. I wondered how anyone could overheat in forty degrees.

Cease didn't speak a word. His dark-circled eyes followed me as I sat down next to him.

"I knew I'd find you here," I said, quietly.

"So, my tactics have become predictable. Not good," he joked feebly, plucking one of the instrument's out-of-tune strings.

"I knew I'd find you here because you've been in one of your rare sentimental moods, all evening."

"You can thank yourself for that. That mood setting was not part of my original programming, you know." He gave a lifeless chuckle, the corners of his lips drooping. "The real Cease would kill me if he were here." His old self. He saw that man as his *real* self.

As his hands slid down the viola's fingerboard, I found my eyes traveling up his white arms. So smooth. Like fresh snow, but creamier. Like milk. Except, he had some scars and even a few burns, interrupting what was otherwise white perfection. I also noticed that, though Cease was still too thin, he no longer gave off the frighteningly-emaciated impression I got when I took off his shirt in February. Now, he was lean in more of an even, toned way. His arms had some definition. His muscles weren't the bulgy, rippling kind like Ambrek's, but dense and tight. I resisted the strong urge to touch them, to run my hands over the silky, pale slopes.

Cease noticed me staring. Heat rushed to my cheeks.

"It's freezing in here. I'm, uh, just surprised to see you without sleeves," I babbled, stupidly. "I mean, I'm wearing my robe over my uniform and I'm *still* shivering. There's a limit to how much spectrum I can use to heat myself, around-the-clock. How do you stand it?"

He blinked. "I'm cold-blooded."

What a creepy answer. Yet, I dared to give him a small, mischievous smile as I thought of his 'electromagnetic-field analysis' from earlier today. "Well, clearly, you aren't..."

He closed his lids. "I'm not a mage, Scarlet. I don't know what happened with that scan."

Yes, he did. The results were pretty straightforward. "Your magnetic field isn't infrared anymore, Cease. Your wavelength is in the visible portion of the spectrum. You have an aura."

"I'm not a mage," he repeated. "I'm not Conflagrian."

"The two aren't a packaged deal. We all have magnetic fields—wavelength interval is the only thing that sets apart the magical from the non. Mages have visible fields—or, colored auras—while everyone else doesn't. You weren't born with a visible aura, but by twining to me, your wavelength interval changed from infrared to black. That makes you a mage. There's nothing more to it. It doesn't matter if you're Conflagrian, Ichthyothian, Nurian, Orion, Anichian, whatever. If your frequency is setting off spectrometers, you're a mage."

Cease's brows disappeared beneath his bangs. "Really? If I'm a mage, what's my 'source'? I can't move my hair, or punch holes through metal walls, or run hundreds of miles per hour, or any of those crazy things your people do."

"That's because you haven't been trained. Mages in Conflagria go to school to learn how to do that stuff; they don't just wake up one day, wielding their powers."

"Unless they're you," he added, dryly.

"You're probably predisposed to a particular source; we just can't be sure what it is, yet, because you haven't been tested or trained. I do have a hunch, though. I think it'd be your throat."

At this, he looked a little offended. "You've said that before, but I still don't get it. Don't throat mages just yell really loud?"

"My dad could pop eardrums and break glass with a single shout, sure. But, no, that's not the extent of throat magic. They have the gift of perfect vocal control. That's what really makes them dangerous, in my opinion. It's almost like their words can hypnotize. I've never met a Nordic who can do the things you can, with your voice. I think it's one of the reasons you're such an effective leader. And, if you're *this* good without any help, imagine what you could accomplish if you did get some instruction." I inhaled. "Cease, I'm no throat mage, but I *am* good at figuring out how to manipulate the spectral web."

"I admire your ingenuity and spectral prowess, Scarlet, but if you think I'm going to let you 'train' me, the answer is: hell no."

What? "Why not?"

He didn't answer. My stomach somersaulted. Cease was supposed to be the one Nordic *not* repulsed by magic. Despite the Childhood Program, he accepted me, a mage, into his fleet—and, moreover, into his inner circle of confidence. He trusted me more readily than any of our comrades did. He was supposed to be different than them. What was his problem, now? It was almost like he wanted to do away with his aura. The aura that I gave him. The aura that grew from our closeness.

"Cease, your wavelength changed because of me. Because of our… interactions. You don't want to be like me?"

"I didn't say that. Don't put words in my mouth."

"You're the only Nordic on the planet with an aura and an opportunity to learn to use it. How could you turn a blind eye to that? Why'd you want to?"

He exhaled through gritted teeth.

"You already have the electromagnetic field of a mage, whether or not you acknowledge it. Ignoring it doesn't make the photons disappear. It just lets them go to waste. Imagine what we can unlock! Don't you want to be stronger and more powerful?" What soldier *didn't* want that?

"I'm not interested, Scarlet."

"Why? Are you afraid?"

He didn't speak. Which meant: yes.

"Cease, there's nothing to be scared of. Your aura can't hurt you. It's only ever helped you, in the past. It saved your life on more than one occasion. Nothing but good can come from cultivating it."

Silence. What was his problem? Why wouldn't Cease jump at the chance to increase his repertoire of talents? Unless—

"Are you nervous about failing?"

With language-arts as a glaring exception, Cease typically mastered whatever he attempted. He didn't do anything halfway and took a lot of pride in his vast arsenal of stellar skills. So, perhaps, he didn't want to try magic because the perfect Commander didn't want to voyage into the realm of the unknown-to-all-Nordic-kind and uncover a potential shortcoming.

"No, that's not it."

He had me stumped. "Then, what is it?"

"Scarlet, this is just... really weird, you know? I accept you for who and what you are, but... this is just a lot for me to take in, okay?"

I wasn't used to seeing Cease so shaken up. Especially over something positive. You'd think I were diagnosing him with a terminal disease, not telling him he had supernatural gifts.

He sighed. "Try to see things from my perspective, Scarlet. I met you less than an age ago. Until the spring of just *last age,* I believed everything the Childhood Program said about your kind: you're all nothing but evil, barbaric fire-savages. Knowing you has changed my perspective. It eroded my 'us-versus-them' mentality." He put Nurtic's viola down on his lap, learned forward and grabbed a large fistful of my hair. "I learned to do *this.* To be close to a mage. To touch spectrum. Without flinching. Without giving into destructive instincts. Before you, Scarlet, I only ever got *this* close to a mage to kill or exploit." He let go of my hair; it fell heavily onto my shoulder. "That transition wasn't easy for me." His gaze pierced mine. "You're the person I'm closest to in this world, Scarlet. You. A mage. The strongest bond I've ever formed in my life is with a mage. And, not just any mage, but the Conflagrian Multi-Source Enchant. The pinnacle of the spectral web. The mage of all mages. That defies everything I've been taught. Just being emotionally and physically near to a mage has been hard for me to wrap my mind around. So, what about *becoming* one? After eighteen ages of fighting and killing mages, I'm told *I'm* one, myself? That I have an aura I should learn to use?" He scrunched his lids. "Scarlet, I'm just not ready. I can't do this, right now. You've swooped into my life and turned everything upside-down, so quickly. And, you know what? That's hard for me. Sometimes, I feel a little push-back from you and everything you've done to me. So, just give me some time to process, okay?"

I was taken about fifty steps aback. "But, Cease, I—"

"You really don't get it, do you?" His eyes popped open. "Scarlet, I'm asking you to drop the subject and back the hell off. Hopefully, soon, all this will be moot anyway because, the second we're able, we're going to end the damn Crystal. Again. We just need to take care of the blockade, first. So, please, shut up."

"O-of course, sir," I breathed. "I'm sorry; I didn't mean to push. I won't bring up the topic again. I promise."

He turned away. I stared at his angular profile for what felt like eras.

"Well, anyway," I finally piped, "*this* is the real reason I came looking for you tonight, before we got sidetracked." I fished my draft from my utility belt and held it out to him. "If we go over it now, we can send it, first thing in the morning. Not a minute wasted."

Cease didn't even look at it. Instead, he just yanked the viola's highest string—the 'A,' which was so flat by now, it sounded more like an 'F.'

"I'll check it out tomorrow. I'm not in the mood, now."

What? Was Cease Lechatelierite actually putting off an important task because he didn't *feel* like it? My breath caught in my chest. Oh, Tincture. What did I do to him? Yes, I wanted to soften his militant character, but only enough to reverse the dehumanization he suffered at the hand of the Childhood Program. I didn't want him to fall apart.

"Okay, what's going on, Cease?"

"The draft can wait until tomorrow," he insisted.

"Since when do *you* procrastinate on serious business because you're 'not in the mood'?"

He cast me a sidelong glance in which I saw a scary flicker of his old self. "I'm a little bit angry, right now."

"Over what?" What *new*, anyway. Ichthyosis faced many daunting challenges, but none of them were a surprise, anymore. Considering how disastrous the ninety-fourth age had been so far, things were finally starting to look up, relatively speaking. We tore down the Childhood Program and had a real chance to get through to the Order. "Cease, you just fulfilled your promise to Finis and saved countless lives from oppression. Today's a good day."

"Is it?"

I almost fell through the floor. "You're not sure?"

"There's a lot to be unsure about, Scarlet. Ichthyosis is small; with neither Nuria nor the Childhood Program, we probably won't get enough manpower, from here on out."

I shook my head. "We can't possibly begin to guess how many adults will volunteer. There could be hundreds or thousands of willing men out there, for all we know. People really believe in the Ichthyothian Resistance, Cease. They believe in *you*."

He squared his jaw. Tincture, that was a bad sign.

"I destroyed a way-of-life. *My* way-of-life." His nose twitched in sync with his temples—which I would've found cute, if I weren't so frightened by what it meant. "I destroyed the infrastructure that made me who I am. If it weren't for the Childhood Program, Ichthyosis wouldn't have *me*, right now—the one leader who's been keeping us from defeat, all this time." His chest rose and fell. "By sending home those kids, I may've just let go of my country's next hope. The next *me*. I won't be around forever, you know. We have to think about that. What if I destroyed the future of my nation?"

"You didn't." I touched his upper arm, which I couldn't help but notice, even at a time like this, was just as firm and silky as I'd imagined. "There'll be others—other *adults*—who can fight for Ichthyosis and lead the Resistance, when you're gone. We don't need to resort to child-abuse to find them. And, just think about your father, Cease—"

"My father?" he heaved. "He's dead. He died thinking the worst of me, and nothing I do now will ever change that." His powerful muscles tensed beneath my fingers. "I betrayed my people." Waves of acherontic stress undulated through the spectral web. "I pushed the Trilateral Committee to trash the system I owe my excellence to. The system that raised my grandfather, who won the First War. The system that gave me my top-notch fleet. I tricked them into tearing down my own military!"

"You didn't *trick* anyone." How his body shook! Fear thundered through me as I realized I was about to witness a full-on Cease Lechatelierite panic-attack. How could I stop it? What could I say or do to calm him down? I couldn't stand to watch him suffer like this. I had to make it all better, somehow. I had to help him see what a heroic thing he did, today. He made history. "You argued, fair and square, and won. You didn't trick anyone," I repeated, loudly. "You did the right thing."

He glared at me with hatred I'd never seen from him before—not when he looked at me, anyway. It struck the root of my being. "It was *you* who forced my hand," he rumbled. "You manipulated me into betraying my country!"

I forced myself to stroke his shoulders, though what I really wanted to do was get up and run far, far away. "Cease, I asked if you really wanted to do this and you said yes."

Suddenly, he threw me off of him with violent force. Gasping, I rolled backward on the floor.

"Cease, please listen!" My voice came out thin and high. "Y-you did the right thing! And, you did it b-because you wanted to!" I sat up. "I'd never manipulate you, Cease—I-I love you."

"LIAR!" Holding Nurtic's viola by the neck, he slammed it into the lockers. Wood and strings flew everywhere. "YOU COULDN'T POSSIBLY LOVE ME AND MAKE ME DESTROY MY MILITARY!" He got to his feet and towered over me, black aura radiating thicker than ever before. He dropped the remains of the instrument with a loud clatter. "You've tried to tell me something many times, Scarlet, but I never listened." He took a step forward and I instinctively cowered. "You're right, about everything. Our relationship—if you could even call this fiasco that—is a dead end." I knew his words were true, but the blunt, unregretful way he spat them ripped my heart into a thousand shreds. And, then, he dropped the real bomb: "I don't love you, Scarlet. You're my closest bond, but it's not love."

"That's not true," I gasped, tears racing down my cheeks. "Y-you said—"

"I didn't know what I was saying. I'm not like you or the Nurians; I'm an Ichthyothian soldier, and that's all I'll ever know how to be. I tried to be someone else, someone who can love you, but I can't do it. And, I can't bear to try, anymore. It's not worth it. It hurts like hell and doesn't get me anywhere. I don't love you, Scarlet, because I *can't!*"

With that, he slammed Nurtic's locker shut and stormed out, leaving me alone on the cold metal floor, crying amongst shreds of splintered wood.

CEASE LECHATELIERITE

The next two weeks were a blur. Every morning, when the trumpet sounded, I awoke having momentarily forgotten why I hated myself so much. Then, my chest tightened as I remembered, all over again.

The Nurians said love was a good thing. It didn't take a military genius to see this hell wasn't good. The feeling of holding onto a live wire—the ache that ravaged my insides, rendering me weak and helpless—was anything but good. If love, as the Nurians claimed, brought clarity and security, yet all I felt was turmoil and confusion in my relationship with Scarlet, then I wasn't in love with her. Simple logic. Someone like Nurtic Leavesleft—with his futile music, faith in the invisible and willingness to let others take limitless advantage of him—could experience love. He was a paradigm of this irrational phenomenon. But, I couldn't be like him. By now, I figured I'd never understand love nor get it right, no matter how hard I tried. I couldn't analyze and assimilate it the way I could an enemy's battle-tactics. There was nothing mathematical, concrete or sensible in it. How could I comprehend something like that? Why should I want to? I had better things to do with my time and energy. I had real responsibilities. Like trying to defend the northwestern hemisphere from imperialism.

But, as the days flew by, I discovered this decision didn't actually vanquish the pain. Which made me real mad. So, trying to love Scarlet hurt. Trying *not* to love Scarlet hurt. I was trapped. What could I do? Was there no escape? Moreover, how did I get myself into this mess, in the first place? If I had any *real* discipline, I never would've approached her to begin with, last age. I never would've acted on my intellectual and physical attraction to her. How did that attraction get so strong, anyway? Why did it only intensify as time went on, against my better judgment and despite her numerous rejections? How did I let this happen? Was I really that stupid?

* * *

It was ten o'clock on March twenty-second—time for my officers to appoint their sub-leaders.

The ceremony was short and simple: each unit leader stood up, announced their choice and handed out rank-bands. As the morning progressed, I found myself approving, or at least accepting, each assignment.

Until Scarlet's turn.

"The sub-leader of unit one is Krustallos Finire the Seventh," she declared, to the applause of Seven's cronies. The runt rose with haughty eyes, stringy hair swinging. My blood boiled as he shook Scarlet's hand and accepted the stripes.

The hall emptied. Soon, there was no one left but Scarlet and me. I caught her shoulder, roughly.

"Sir," she breathed, eyes like crystalline-headlights.

I made no preamble. "How dare you defy my orders," I barked, fingers digging into her delicate collarbone. "We'll all pay for your insubordination!"

Face redder than usual, she spoke to the floor, "Commander, he's the best I've got, by a longshot. I made the right decision."

I snorted. "Like hell you did."

"Sir, have you heard back from the Order, yet?" she attempted to change the subject.

"Yes. We're welcome to attend their meeting on April seventh. They'll be sending us a plane."

"April seventh," she echoed, lifting her head. "This is great news!"

"You do know that we won't be able to get there safely unless we break through the blockade, first?"

"Um… yes, sir, I know."

"But, Seven will likely shoot our chances of doing that straight to hell!"

Scarlet's red brows constricted. "Sir, you're leaping to unjust conclusions!"

"What must happen for my suspicions to seem 'just' to you, hmm? A battle loss on the twenty-fifth?"

"Sir—"

"You told the Trilateral Committee that your job is to know your soldiers well. You claimed to understand the mind of a base-raised diver. But, the truth is, Scarlet, you don't know the first thing about what's going on in Seven's head. *I* do. And, I'm telling you, he's not ready for this position!"

"Sir, why don't we watch how he handles sub-leadership for the next couple days before making that call? If he can't do it, I'll demote him and install someone else, right away, I promise," Scarlet said. "Either way, I'm still the officer in charge of unit one, not him. And, you happened to trust me."

"Fine," I spat. "But, I'm expecting detailed reports on his performance, each night!"

"My pleasure," she responded, tartly.

"Dismissed!"

SCARLET JULY

By the end of my very first day with Krustallos Finire VII as my sub-leader, I'd already figured out the secret to handling him. It was quite simple: as long as I gave him the most complex assignments, he was perfectly happy to perform them without question. And, he was so talented and brilliant, he really was a good choice for those tasks anyway, regardless of the needs of his ego. Everybody won.

Nonetheless, I was nervous to tell Cease the good news, mainly because it'd involve talking with him in private. As I buzzed his intercom now, I thought about how his screams resounded from the locker-room walls, how it felt to be shoved by his cold hands, how Nurtic's viola looked when it split apart...

Why did I still love him, again?

Cease's door yanked open.

"Sir," I said, saluting. "I'm here to report on Finire's performance today, as requested."

Wordlessly, he nodded and stepped aside to let me in. My stomach knotted as he closed the door behind me. Without sitting down and with no further preamble, I launched into my analysis. Also standing, he listened with an expressionless face and folded arms. Was it just me or did his cheeks seem a little hollower than usual?

"Giving him the *illusion* he's in control?" he echoed, cocking a dark brow. "So, what happens when he realizes he isn't?"

"He won't, sir. The toughest assignments give him a sense of fulfillment, rendering him as obedient as ever. Not to mention, he does them so well, he'd be the best person to give them to, anyway."

"The role of a leader isn't always to do the hardest assignments," Cease rounded on me. "A leader is supposed to oversee and orchestrate the big picture, delegating tasks."

"Sir—"

He held up his hand. "And, you're not helping him in the long run, either. You're feeding his ego. To truly progress as a soldier, he needs to understand he's *not* always in control. He needs to be aware of how much authority he *really* has—or, doesn't have. Because, one day, God forbid, he'll disagree with your orders. And, then, he'll take you by surprise and wreck your entire strategy, leaving the rest of us to clean up his ugly mess."

Spectrum flared to my scalp. "Honestly, Commander? I think you're blowing things way out of proportion."

"Am I?" he growled. "How many military power-struggles have you witnessed in your lifetime? How many strategies have you had to salvage because of the self-promoting idiocy of a subordinate? How many people have you seen die because of someone's inflated head? I've been in the military longer than you've been on this earth, Scarlet; I've witnessed my fair share of Krustallos Finires. So, *you* don't tell *me* what to expect from a cocky bastard trained by the Childhood Program!"

Of course.

"You were one of them, weren't you?" I asked, quietly.

Cease didn't answer. His silvery eyes continued to blaze through me like cold fire.

I swallowed. "You were one of those 'Krustallos Finires,' right, sir?"

There was a tense silence. He pulled on his visual band, as though trying to hide behind it.

"The worst," he finally admitted.

There was another pause. I looked at him, expectantly. He plunked onto his bed and, to my surprise, patted the spot beside him. Nervously, I sat down and waited for him to elaborate.

"Since as far back as I can remember, all I've ever wanted was the best for Ichthyosis," he began, "and, by the time I graduated into the fleet, I was convinced I was it. After all, I could see things others didn't. I could draw successful conclusions, faster. I could solve every problem that stumped those above me. So, I craved the freedom to do whatever I wanted. I didn't understand why I had to take orders when I obviously knew better. I couldn't stand stupidity. Couldn't tolerate it. Nothing made me angrier. So, I steamrollered everyone in my path, on my way to the top. Soon, I found myself the Second-in-Command to Ecrof Ecreoc. Ecreoc was a tactical genius and a skilled fighter, but he was also abusive. His authority relied on force and threats. He wasn't the sort of leader you'd take a bullet for. We only followed him because we were afraid of him. Everyone was." Cease's face darkened. "Except me. I didn't fear him and I sure as hell didn't respect him. One day, I decided I'd had enough, so I pushed him right out of his place." *Pushed* him? What exactly did that mean? "And, I saw nothing wrong with my behavior. I thought I was doing Ichthyosis a favor. I wasn't stepping out of line, I was doing my nation a service. The results were tangible, too—we stopped losing battles, our strategies were more efficient, my comrades were happier. I considered myself innocent of all mal-intent because I saw it as: they *need* me." Cease sighed. "The line between confidence and delusion is thin. It's a dangerous thing, for a man to believe he can do no wrong." Cease took off his visual band and finally met my gaze. "So what if Inexor Buird nagged me for weeks on end about the possibility of a dangerous spectral advancement? If *I* don't think the System's likely to burn the sea, they obviously won't, right?"

I instinctively touched his hand, clenched around his band. "Sir, you're not still on about the Underwater Fire thing, are you? I mean, it was *one* battle, and it's been quite a while since—"

"No, Scarlet," he pulled his hand away, "I'm not 'still on' about that battle. I'm pissed about everything that's happened since. That battle's like a metaphor for my whole life, for this entire war."

Huh? I wasn't sure what he meant by that. He did tend to get lost in his own head, sometimes. I probably understood him better than anyone else, but that didn't mean we always saw eye-to-eye.

"How so, sir?"

"Well, sometimes, when we try hard to prevent something, we wind up actually *causing* it."

"Like Oedipus," I observed.

"I have no idea who that is. But, just look at our track record, you and me. You went after the crystal shard in the sea so the System wouldn't find it… and the System wound up finding it *because* you did. I decided Ichthyosis needed manpower, so I won us an ally, only to wound them until they had no choice but to leave us, higher and drier than ever before."

"Sir, I don't think—"

"Scarlet, no matter what you say, the bottom line is, we're back to square one. No, we're not even on square one. We're further behind than that. We're in the red. Why?

How? With all our logic and reasoning and careful planning, where did we go wrong?"

The heated question hung in the frigid air.

* * *

All Order representatives were required to be proficient in both Orion—or, 'Star,' the language of the current Authority Nation—and Nurian, the closest thing to an international tongue that Second Earth had. Oriya was famous for its phenomenal observatories and legacy of astronomy. So, just as First Earth Latin was the language of music and French was the language of love, Orion was considered the 'language of the stars.'

Star was only a slight variant of Nurian: the accent was different, as were a handful of terms and idiomatic expressions, but everything else was pretty much the same. Yet, I knew these minor distinctions would still pose an obstacle to someone like Cease. While the reps would talk *to* us in Star, we received special permission to reply in Nurian. That was nice of them, but not nice enough, if you asked me. I didn't understand why we couldn't *all* use Nurian, for Tincture's sake. They just *had* to make things difficult for us. It figured.

Upon accepting our meeting request, the Order emailed us a digital Orion-Nurian dictionary and some basic grammar guides. Tonight, Cease and I were having our first, joint study-session. While simply getting the gist was the furthest Cease would set his goal, I went the whole nine yards and became fluent.

"How about I say some things in Star for you to translate into Ichthyothian?" I asked him, now.

"Okay."

"*I wish to dissent that statement, Mr. Chairman.*"

"I want to… oppose… what… the leader… said."

"Good. *My apologies, sir, but I cannot process your request at the current time*," I enunciated slowly and clearly.

He hesitated. "Sorry, but... you... can't do that... at the moment?"

"Close enough. Here's another one: *please describe exactly why you support such an outrageous claim*."

"Explain to me how—I mean, why—you think what you do... because it's really odd?"

I was impressed. I never thought I'd see the day Cease would do decently at a linguistic exercise. There was a first for everything, I supposed. "A little twisted, but not bad, at all!"

He was elated. "Give me another one," he demanded, eagerly. "And, make it hard." Getting cocky, was he? "Come on. Say something, anything."

I grinned. "Anything?" I cleared my throat. "Alright, then. *I'm a soulless, cold-blooded war-machine who was built in a factory, stamped with a barcode and labeled with a price-tag*."

His face hardened. Oh, Tincture, I crossed a line.

"It was a joke," I squeaked. "I'm sorry."

"I'm sorry, *sir!*"

"Sir!" I shrank in my seat. "Hey, at least, you understood me!"

At that, I thought I saw his lips become slightly less thin. "You should be glad I only got a bit of it. Something about a factory."

SCARLET JULY

March twenty-fifth, two-thirty. Time for dispatch.

He paced up and down our line, a dangerous glint in his glassy eyes. I stood beside him, facing our men, as he spoke with exuberance and ferocity.

No, I wasn't talking about Cease, but Krustallos Finire VII, my sub-leader.

"Thank you, Finire," I said, upon the conclusion of his fiery pep-talk. "Let's go, soldiers!"

"Ma'am, yes, ma'am!"

For the new graduates, this was the inaugural fight of their lives. They marched to their shuttles with enthusiasm, but I knew better. Only a fool wouldn't be nervous at a time like this.

I certainly was. This was my first real sea battle since July of last age—not counting my brief stint on January seventh that ended quite miserably.

My unit would be surface-riding, today. They divided themselves between my hull and Finire's. Finire swaggered to his crystalline, sweeping his brown hair into a small ponytail before plunking on his helmet. I settled in my own cockpit, checking all my instruments twice and trying not to hyperventilate. Here went nothing.

All too soon, we arrived at the blockade. The wind leaked from my lungs as I drank in the horribly-impressive sight of a barrier hundreds of crafts strong, with a spectral presence formidable enough to literally send ripples through my hair.

Those at the forefront wasted no time; the moment we were within firing range, their turrets erupted like a thunderstorm. From below me, I saw Finire dart about, nothing but a grey blur, distributing surface-riders and gunning down ships.

"Good work, Finire," I informed him, privately.

"Why, thank you, Miss Dual-Source."

"Scarlet, get crystallines two through seven into cylindrical formation, for the primary strike," Cease commanded from the vitreous silica above, "and deploy diversion immediately."

"Yes, sir." I bit my mouthpiece. "Unit leaders two through seven, pass your surface-riders to your sub-leaders and begin arrow formation seven-two-five, behind me." I chomped my mouthpiece, again. "Finire, I'm going to need you to provide a diversion so my group can attempt stage one of penetration," I told him, knowing that, of anyone in this fleet, he had the dexterity and foresight to single-handedly preoccupy the entire enemy frontline without getting blown to pieces.

"You mean, like a sideshow?"

"July, seven System surface-riders are heading for you at eight-o-clock!" Inexor's voice rang in my helmet, stealing my attention away from Finire. "My spectrometer detects high concentrations of magic in each of their lower extremities."

It didn't take much brain-fluid to discern the objective of an entire team of leg mages making a beeline for my crystalline.

"Thank you, Buird!"

I glanced at my radar. Judging from their rate of approach, I figured I had eight seconds before they'd arrive and literally kick me apart. So, for seven of those seconds, I stayed straight, as though oblivious. Then, right before they could land, I dropped sharply. They hurtled past, on a pointless tangent into the cobalt-blue oblivion. I spun around and shot them down, one by one. Their orange-suited bodies bobbed to the surface.

"July, I'm waiting for an answer!" Finire called from somewhere.

"What?" I blurted. "Finire, I told you to get on with the diversion!"

"Scarlet, *where is the diversion?*" Cease rumbled.

"I'm on it, sir!" I squeaked to him. Then, to Finire, I said, "Sub-leader, deploy *now*, before we get too close!"

"July, I need reinforcement in sector seven-eight-seven. Who can help me? I've got three dragon ships on my tail!" Tacit cried.

I swiveled in my seat and peered through my rear window, zooming out my eyes.

"Crystallines eleven and sixteen, pass your surface-riders to nine and seventeen and approach Tacit's dragons at twenty-five and eighty-seven degrees, respectively," I ordered.

"Ma'am, yes, ma'am!" two voices chimed.

My arrow was behind me, all ready to pierce. Except—

"Scarlet, if Seven doesn't grab their attention *now*, your task force stands no chance! Where the hell is your sub-leader?" Cease boomed.

"I said, I'm on it, sir!" I gasped, gnawing my bit. "Finire, report!"

"All three of Tacit's tailgaters have been dealt with," he replied, sounding rather pleased with himself.

"You took them out?"

"Yes, ma'am."

Hot magic welled in my scalp. "Finire, I ordered eleven and sixteen to help Tacit!"

"I reassigned them to your cylinder. Think about it, Dual-Source: without them, you don't actually have enough support, now do you?"

I stared over my shoulder at the new additions to my arrow, dangling clumsily at the rear.

"Finire, it's not your place to modify my instructions without approval!"

"We have to move quickly, here. This is battle, not practice. I can't stop to ask permission before every blink."

"When I give an order, I expect it to be followed!"

He really didn't get how crucial the diversion was? Without it, my task force couldn't infiltrate and those aboard the vitreous silica couldn't dive!

"What, you mean the *sideshow?*"

"Finire, do it, now! Before it's too late!"

We were dangerously close! What was Finire's problem? I was giving him what he always wanted: the most difficult, complicated role. Why wasn't he doing it?

He finally jumped forward. For Tincture's sake, it was about time.

I addressed my group: "Alright, men. On my mark, let's—" I fell silent as I watched my cylinder break apart and zip past me, following Finire into the heart of the blockade, plunging like kamikazes. "What are you doing? Stop!" I yelled. "Our diversion isn't out, yet; it isn't safe to deploy!"

No one responded. A red light flashed at the corner of my visor, indicating my communications were severed. What? How? I hadn't sustained any damage, yet. Why wasn't my intercom working? Unless…

It was no secret that Finire was a genius at computer programming. He must've hacked the system to disable my link. Then, he ordered my arrow to follow him, instead of me. Without a diversion, the move was suicide. He was leading them to their doom.

Sure enough, his stunt caught the attention of, well, everyone. Crystallines dropped from his cylinder like hail. I had no choice but to try to be the diversion myself, ASAP. Better late than never. With dazzling, showy twirls, I weaved through the chaos, firing away. Some abandoned their pursuit of Finire's group in favor of chasing me… but, not enough. Men began to dive from the vitreous silica, though the groundwork wasn't laid out for them as it was supposed to be, by now. Our strategy was completely derailed. At this point, I was no longer worried about winning. I was worried about how badly we'd lose. This was a disaster worse than I ever imagined. And, so much depended on this battle. So much!

At last, the red light on my visor vanished.

"Attention!" I hollered universally, pulling out of a triple barrel-roll. "All units, retreat! I repeat: all units, retreat!"

"Commander Lechatelierite already called off this fiasco, five minutes ago, July," Inexor coldly informed me. "He wants you to retrieve all the surface-riders Finire left helpless in sector oh-eight-seven." *All* of them? "The vitreous silica is entering the water at seven-two-five to pick up the surviving crystallines."

Tincture, that was some assignment. How would I enter the enemy line, gather all the surface-riders and break back through without being overtaken? And, could my shuttle really carry so many?

I analyzed the flight-patterns of the System ships surrounding me, predicted their movements for the next minute or so, plotted my course accordingly and informed the stranded of my trajectory so they could position themselves in my path. It operated like clockwork. Finally, *something* went right, today. I sighed with relief as I swooped out, surface-riders all over me. My crystalline never felt so heavy. I stomped on the accelerator, chugging along at half-speed. Just a few more miles…

Then, my right wing got nicked.

Gyrating wildly, I headed for the seafloor, ears ringing with the squeaky sound of divers sliding across my hull. Framed in my left window was the terrifying sight of Cease hanging from a rung with only one hand, supporting a string of five men clinging to each other for dear life. They began dispensing deadline as a means to reinforce their chain and climb back up.

As if that weren't bad enough, a dragon ship was hot on my tail, firing like mad. But, my crazy spiral had one advantage: it made me hard to aim at. I could feel the System pilot's anxiety undulate through the spectral web as he struggled to get a target-lock. Why could I sense him so clearly? My heart hammered against my ribcage as I deciphered his wave frequencies. There were two of them— amber and copper.

Oh, Tincture.

"We're coming for you, July," Austere Jr. called, from the vitreous silica.

Suddenly, screams filled my helmet. Daring to take my eyes off my windshield and instruments, I peered to the left and beheld the most grotesque sight of my military career, to date. Like a flivver-wreck, I couldn't look away.

The torso of unit seven surface-rider Ecils Flah, one of the new grads, dangled at the end of Cease's chain, arms bound up with deadline, intestines trailing in the murky, bloody water. Ambrek literally blew the man in half.

"Scarlet, watch out!" Cease yelled.

I wrenched my stupefied gaze from the window and realized I was barreling toward the vitreous silica's belly rather than its open ventral hatch. Swerving sharply, I barely made it in, with a sloppy, much-too-fast landing. I was the last crystalline to arrive.

I yanked off my helmet, opened my cockpit and vomited right over the side of my shuttle. Then, I climbed out, shaking from head to toe. I watched Finire emerge from his own heavily-damaged craft, panting like a scabrous on a hot summer day, face as pale as a glacier. Blood pounded in my ears. I'd completely misunderstood him. It wasn't the most complicated tasks he desired, but the most glorious. He wanted to be the center of attention. He didn't understand the importance of a diversion. Disdainfully, he'd called it a 'sideshow.' Cease was right. Oh, Cease was right about everything. He saw straight through Finire from the start and I ignored all his warnings.

This battle loss was all my fault.

Cease and what was left of his chain of surface-riders lay in a crumpled heap on the floor, hacking away at their tangled cables. The moment Cease cut himself free, he stomped toward me, silver-grey gaze ablaze.

"YOU NAIVE FOOL!" he exploded, face red. "I'VE BEEN IN THE MILITARY LONGER THAN YOU'VE WALKED THIS EARTH!" He pointed at Finire. "I WARNED YOU NOT TO PROMOTE THAT ARROGANT, INSUBORDINATE BASTARD!"

Cease's whole body shuddered. I trembled too, but in fear. I didn't dare speak a word.

"Please, Commander, it's my fault, not hers—" Finire piped.

Cease rounded on Finire. "DON'T YOU DARE TALK TO ME!" He marched up to the boy, grabbed his collar and screamed directly in his face, spit flying: "YOUR IDIOCY COST US THIS BATTLE AND POSSIBLY THE ENTIRE WAR! YOU'RE A DISGRACE TO THE NAME OF SOLDIER!" With that, Cease tore the stripes right off the kid's sleeves with inhuman strength and bodily threw him into the side of my crystalline.

Cease turned back to me and I visibly flinched. "Scarlet, since I can no longer trust you to make appointments, I'm replacing Seven with Elpmi Pleh, as your sub-leader. Understood?"

"Yes, sir," I whispered.

At that moment, the vitreous silica docked. Cease spun about, threw open the door and stormed out.

The rest of us remained frozen in place for a few more seconds, looking anywhere but at each other. Finire didn't even get up from the floor. He'd finally learned his place. And, he did it the hard way. The cost of his education was his comrades' lives.

CEASE LECHATELIERITE

I called for a conference at nightfall. The newbies needed to take something more from our battle disaster than guilt or shame. Mistakes had to be studied, not just dwelt upon. Improvement came not only from experience, but analysis. Otherwise, a man could suffer a thousand traumas and still learn nothing.

Two-hundred-eighty-three soldiers filed into the lecture hall. Those were all the subordinates I had left. A hundred lives were lost today.

I stood before them with my hands clasped behind my back.

"Welcome," I began, "to the truth of war. Feels different than practice, doesn't it? Not quite as exhilarating. Not quite as fun. Pretty terrifying, actually," I started pacing, "because, now, there's something at stake. Now, your actions have real consequences. Now, your mistakes don't merely give you a poor mark in the grade-book. They cost lives. They alter the future of your country. They mean the difference between saving your people from poverty or plunging them further into it. So, what's next, now?" I raised my voice. "We sulk? Feel guilty? Walk around for the rest of our lives with our eyes on our boots? No. We bounce back. Immediately. We have the courage to act like the soldiers we're supposed to be, taking responsibility for our screw-ups. We analyze our errors from every possible angle, learning *never* to repeat them again." I turned on my heel and walked the other way. "So, what are our problems? Arrogance. Insubordination. Malicious trickery for personal gain. Believing ourselves to be invincible because we're just so damn smart." My eyes scoured Seven's. "Well, if you still don't understand the price of your idiocy, all you have to do is look around the room." I paused, then barked, "Go on. Look!"

Hesitantly, two-hundred-eighty-three heads turned a few measly degrees to the left or right.

"What do you see?"

Silence.

"Pleh," I called on the sixteen-age-old, pimple-faced, newly-installed sub-leader of unit one. "What do you see?"

The kid, undoubtedly feeling a little victimized, swallowed and croaked, "One-hundred of us are missing, sir."

"Not *missing*, soldier," I snapped. "*Dead*. One-hundred of us have been *killed*."

No one dared to breathe.

"Hard to hear it out loud like that, isn't it?" I folded my arms. "Which brings me to my main point: this war isn't about you or me. This fleet isn't about you or me. While you're here, the concept of the self is dead. This isn't the academy anymore, where grades and scores are the only things in jeopardy. This is about Ichthyosis. This is about doing everything and anything you can to bring about our fleet's success, *as a whole*. Even if that means doing the most demeaning dirty-work of your life. Because, if it weren't important, you wouldn't have been asked to do it, in the first place. We don't dish out useless assignments, around here. In battle, every move made could mean the difference between life and death, for dozens. So, if an officer took the time to open his or her mouth to give you an order, then that means you damn well better follow through if it's the last thing you ever do. Understood?"

Two-hundred-eighty-three hands saluted to the sound of, "Sir, yes, sir!"

"Congratulations," I declared. "Now, you're all veterans."

CEASE LECHATELIERITE

April sixth, thirty-five o'clock. The eve of the Second Earth Order meeting.

Our fleet was, once again, too small to take on the blockade. It wasn't a question of skill or strategy, anymore. Talent was useless without the resources to act on it. We needed more men. Period.

I spent the last couple hours trying to draw up a plan that'd only require two-hundred-eighty-four divers. But, no matter how I rearranged things, there were always too many points of exposure. So, I opened a new window on my computer screen and devised an ideal plan instead—what I'd do if I had as many soldiers as I wanted.

Seven-hundred.

I slammed my laptop shut and crawled into bed.

Hours passed. I lay like a board, lactic acid burning my muscles.

Ichthyosis once had an ally willing to provide everything we needed. In fact, our ally routinely gave us so many divers at a time, I actually had the nerve to complain of being overwhelmed. If only, back then, I could see the drought that awaited us. My face pressed into my foam pillow, visual band slicing into its stiff layers.

Sweat slithered down my forehead. I kicked my sheets to the floor, mind obsessing over Ichthyosis's bleak future. I needed to bounce my thoughts off of someone else. I couldn't stay stuck in my own head, despairing, until the trumpet sounded.

Through the wall, I heard dull scratching. Scarlet's pencil sharpener. Irritation whipped through me. Drawing, again! It was beyond me, why anyone would spend so much time scribbling pretty doodles on scraps of paper when there were more important things to do.

I jumped from bed and pulled on my uniform. If Scarlet had creative energy to spare, I figured I might as well put it to good use.

I rapped on her door. She opened and stared at me with cautious eyes, protectively clutching a fresh stack of drawings to her chest. She was dressed in her Conflagrian robe—a sight that still took me by surprise, no matter how many times I saw it.

"Commander?" she squeaked.

Of course, she wouldn't be enthusiastic to see me in private, late at night. I noticed the remnants of Leavesleft's viola gathered at the corner of her desk.

I had to choose my next words wisely. Being 'easygoing' was a conversational tactic I only had to learn since the arrival of the Nurians, who were sensitive and prone to taking everything personally. While we Ichthyothians tended to be direct when we needed something, Nurians often preferred to beat around the bush, acting differently than they felt. Playing these games made them *more* comfortable. I didn't get it. It was annoying, confusing and time-consuming. But, if it got me what I needed, I had no choice but to play along sometimes. Like, right now. I had to feign casual comfort with Scarlet; she was tensing up when I needed her creative juices to flow freely.

"I've been thinking about Ichthyosis's next step, and I noticed you're still awake, so I was wondering if we could brainstorm together, now," I worded carefully.

"You were *wondering?*" she echoed, blinking. "Um, yes, of course, sir. I'll come right over. Just one sec."

She scuttled to her desk, opened the seventh drawer and gently placed all her drawings face-down.

"Wait, let me see those," I blurted.

She brazenly snapped the drawer shut. "No."

I was taken aback. "Excuse me?"

She turned, laser-green eyes narrowed. "No, *sir*, you can't order me to do that because this is my private business, conducted off-duty. When I was sketching in class last age, you had every right to seize my notebook, but not this time. And, last I checked, paper doesn't violate the possessions rule, so there's no reasonable doubt of lawbreaking here, which means it's totally unjustified for you to request to search and seize my—"

I held up my hands. "Whoa, whoa, back up, Miss Esquire! I'm not *ordering* you and this isn't a formal *seizure*; I'm just a curious comrade asking to see your sketches for fun."

She blinked. "Fun. You."

"Yes, me."

"Really?"

Cocking a brow, I looked pointedly at her lips. "*You* of all people should know that I'm capable of occasionally taking pleasure in non-work-related things."

Her face reddened.

"Anyway," I plowed on, "what's the point of art if not to be appreciated, right?"

She frowned. "You don't even know what you're saying, sir. You're just quoting the Nurians like a parrot!"

What's a parrot? "I can *too* appreciate art," I countered, fully aware of how childish I sounded. Scarlet and I certainly brought out interesting things in each other. "I still have the sketch you did of us doing the spin-toss; I appreciate it!"

She stood akimbo. "Yeah, like a photograph," she snorted, "because it's *realistic* and you don't have a shot of us, otherwise. You don't see anything beyond that; it's not really art to you."

Wasn't the point of art to imitate reality? "*Is* there something beyond that?"

She threw her hands up. "Exactly!"

With that, she plucked a single strand from her scalp and wound it around the handlebar.

"Fine," I folded my arms, "keep them locked up. No one else will ever see them."

There was a peculiar look in her enormous eyes now, almost like she abruptly drifted into a trance. "Someone will."

"Oh? Who?"

The odd gaze vanished as quickly as it came. "I don't know," she breathed. "I have no idea what I'm saying." Her nose twitched. "Let's go to your quarters and get to work."

About time.

We walked over and she helped herself to my desk chair. "Okay, what's been on your mind, sir?" she prompted.

I didn't sit. "I was thinking about how small our fleet is, even with the new graduates." What was left of them, anyway. "I don't think we have the manpower to break through the blockade, anymore. That's why I came to talk to you. We need to figure out a way to get more soldiers."

"Isn't the Trilateral Committee working on recruiting adults?" A lock of Scarlet's hair spontaneously twisted around her finger. Sometimes, I wished she'd cool it with the casual displays of magic, around me.

"Yes, but, even if classes start tomorrow, they still wouldn't be ready to join the fleet until next age. Ichthyosis will likely starve to death, before then."

"What are you suggesting, retrieving the kids dismissed from the Childhood Program?" She sat up, straight as a lance. "Because that'd take even longer, and even if it didn't, there's no way—"

"Scarlet," I cut across her, "we need Nuria back. There are over five-hundred, fully-trained divers living there, right now. A few hours ago, I drew up a battle plan I think would work—but, it requires seven-hundred men. Nuria could give us just enough."

There was a pause.

"Um," she piped, "of course, getting the Nurians back would be ideal, but... how?"

"I was hoping you'd have some crazy ideas up your floppy, red sleeve."

She pensively perused her sock-feet. "Well, when we go to Oriya in the morning, we could convince the Order not only to let us rejoin, but to allow the alliance to reform."

That was ridiculous. I smiled, internally. "I knew you'd have an instant, insane suggestion. Elaborate."

"We'll be arguing the necessity of our self-defense, right? If we manage to convince the Order of *that*, it shouldn't be too hard to get them to see that our defense is totally inadequate without our old ally."

I nodded. It was a good point. But—"Even if Nuria is allowed to come back to us, will they *want* to? I mean, after what happened to the Centerscraper..."

"Are you kidding? I lived in Nuria for five ages before enlisting, and let me tell you, they aren't the type to swallow crap and stay quiet about it. They're a lot like the First Earth Americans, actually. Chances are, they're hankering to get back at the System. They only left us because the Order forced them to, not because they wanted to. What they really want is to fight. That's why they signed the pact, in the first place. And, they didn't even have their own bone to pick with the System back then, while they sure as hell do, now."

I felt a rush of gratitude toward Scarlet. "I knew it was a good idea to wake you up."

Her pink cheeks turned even pinker. So cute. "Yeah, well, let's just hope the Order will be as easy to win over as the Trilateral Committee." Easy. Right. The Trilateral Committee was no walk in a flurry. I didn't want to imagine the kind of welcome we'd receive from a huge board of politicians who all wholeheartedly believed in the inherent evilness of any warring nation.

"If Arnold Link is still there, I'm sure we'll be fine," I answered.

She ogled me in disbelief. Then, she beamed. It was painful, how beautiful her grin was. Her lips looked so kissable. "The New and Improved Optimistic Commander Lechatelierite," she laughed.

"I said, *if* he's there. That's a pretty big 'if.' So, sorry to freeze your fire, but I'm not actually being all that cheery." I adjusted my visual band, slipping down my nose. "Not to mention, we didn't exactly accomplish our meeting prerequisite: we were supposed to take out the blockade before attempting to traverse the sea to Oriya. It's going to be a rough ride."

Her face turned from rosy-pink to bloodclot-red. "Commander, I'm so sorry for promoting Finire—"

I put up a hand. "Don't get me started on Seven. Not now. I'm trying to keep my anger down, tonight. Talking about him is quick way to really piss me off."

"I'm sorry, sir," she whispered to the floor.

But, alas, I was already set off: "He's a kink in this entire fleet. He's the reason Ichthyosis is still under siege. And, if it weren't for his arrogance and stupidity, my unit would still be alive!"

She blinked. "Your unit?"

"The one-hundred graduates," I quickly corrected.

She stared at me, expectantly. "Now, I think we're getting somewhere!"

"No." I set my jaw. "Absolutely not. I'm not opening that can of abalone, now. That battle was ages ago, when I was in your rank. It has nothing to do with Seven."

"Doesn't it, though?" She stuck her chin out at me and I fought the urge to grab it. "Because, if you ask me, sir, I'd say you're using him as a scapegoat for your anger at *yourself.*"

I exhaled through my nostrils. "I already told you: I acted just like him when I was his age. That's it. We don't need to go into detail."

Scarlet's hair autonomously jumped over her shoulder. "How slow do you think I am, Commander? Don't you think I can piece together what must've transpired from all the clues you've already dropped?"

Frustrated, I peeled off my band and sat heavily on my bed.

"I'm not going to let this go," she pressed, "because you clearly won't, as long as Finire's around. And… I want to help you work through things." She deflated. "I just want to see you feel better."

She sounded so earnest. So sincere. She wanted to help me help myself. And, not because I was her military superior but because I was someone she cared about. Personally. Someone she loved. Even now. How did she do it? Why didn't she hate me?

Against my better judgement, I spilled: "Aright, fine. It was the winter of the ninetieth age and I was almost fifteen. I was Second-in-Command to Ecrof Ecreoc," I spoke quickly. "I'd already been his Second for a few ages, by then. It was the longest I ever spent in a single position without upward mobility. One day, we headed out to battle—I won't bore you with strategy specifics—with a so-so plan of his. Irritated by the glaring flaws, I told Ecreoc what I thought we should do instead but, because my ideas were unconventional, he wouldn't listen. I was bursting with self-righteous anger as we deployed, Ecreoc and I each piloting a crystalline. I was supposed to cover him as he and his surface-riders—my unit—made the primary strike. I wanted to prevent his stupid strike from happening and do things my way, instead. He was going to go about it all wrong, without substantial reinforcements. So, when the time was right, I simply… took the lead. I didn't go as far as to sever Ecreoc's communications or anything like that. Rather, the others chose to follow me because, once I told them what I had up my sleeve, they *wanted* to. My plan made more sense to them. With units two and five gathered on my rungs, I forcefully took over Ecreoc's role in the battle. And, my strike turned out to be a huge success. But, doing it meant abandoning my assigned post at Ecreoc's tail. Because I left him exposed, his crystalline got shot down. He and every surface-rider on his hull—all of unit one—got killed. I may've saved the battle overall, but my insubordination directly caused the deaths of ten of my comrades, including Ecreoc himself. When we returned to base, I knew I deserved to have my ass handed to me. But, what happened, instead? I got promoted. Not only did the Trilateral Committee give me Ecreoc's job, they created a new title for me: 'Leader of the Ichthyothian Resistance.' And, now, here I am, three ages later, still in command, still the Leader of the Resistance. But, every day, I remember I only have it all because I stole it right out of the hands of my predecessor."

Scarlet claimed she'd already figured out what went down but, judging from the scandalized look on her face now, she obviously wasn't prepared for all *that*. Several seconds of stunned silence passed.

"Now, do you understand why I can't stand to watch Seven make my mistakes, *right under my nose?*" I raged. "He'll always have those hundred lives hanging over him. I've handled my fair share of insubordinate idiots during my service but, until Seven came along, I didn't know what it'd be like to deal with… well, myself. From the moment I first laid eyes on the runt, I knew I'd met my first real challenger. I saw too much of young Cease in him. The good *and* the bad."

Scarlet gently stroked my wrist. Her touch was warm and soft. "Commander," she breathed, "have you forgiven yourself for what happened?"

I didn't answer. Which gave her my answer.

"Once you do, sir, you'll find that you've simultaneously forgiven Finire, too."

Her words swam in my mind. I knew I couldn't do it. Where would I even begin?

"It's a decision you'll just have to make," she continued. "Just decide to move on. Decide to stop tormenting yourself for the past. I've forgiven Finire. While that doesn't bring back those hundred lives, it does lift a huge burden from my shoulders—and Finire's, too."

Impossible. "How do you manage it, Scarlet?"

"Manage what?"

I waved my hands. "Being the way you are! Sure, you get mad, but it never lasts. Never turns into a grudge. I bet you don't even hate," I thought of the vilest name I knew, "Ambrek Coppertus, do you?"

She shook her head. "I still hurt over what happened with him, of course. But, no, I don't hate him. I actually wish I could understand why he did the things he did, when he's obviously capable of better."

She wished she could *understand* him? She genuinely believed he was *capable of better?* Unbelievable. How could she even think about him without her hair spontaneously igniting?

She always tried to understand me. She always saw the best in me. Despite everything I put her through.

"I can't believe you don't hate Ambrek Coppertus," I said. "I can't even believe you're sitting here with me, right now, trying to help me with my personal problems. If I were you, I wouldn't want to look me in the face."

"It's April, Cease," she said quietly, calling me by my first name for the first time since that terrible night in the locker-room. "I've long since forgiven you. I just never found the courage to tell you, until now."

My eyes actually stung. I was floored. "Come here," I croaked, getting to my feet. "Come here, *now*."

She stood and nervously took a couple steps my way. I put my arms around her, as tightly as possible without actually crushing her ribcage.

"I know you've already forgiven me, but I need to say this," the words poured from my mouth. "I'm sorry. I'm so sorry, Scarlet, for everything," I spoke into her hair, inhaling her intoxicating, wood-smoke scent. "Nothing excuses the way I've treated you. Even if I can't love you, I can acknowledge how wrong it was for me to—"

"It's okay, it's okay," she cut me off, though without sounding relieved in the slightest. "Please, Cease, just calm down."

She let me hold her as long as I needed to. It was a while before I finally withdrew. Was it just me or did she seem reluctant to pull away, herself?

"Are you wearing your mage robe *over* your uniform, again?" I asked, suddenly very aware that her top two buttons were undone.

"Yes. I'm cold."

"The base is heated."

"Yeah, 'heated' to forty degrees. It's cold as hell in here!"

"Wouldn't hell be hot and fiery, like Conflagria?" I asked, deviously.

She gave me a playful scowl that hurt my chest for some reason. "In *Dante's Inferno*, the lowest circle of hell is a lake of ice!"

"Who's Dante?"

She blinked. "Never mind; I keep forgetting how ignorant you are."

Thanks. "Well, anyway, your outfit is such a contradiction." I looked at her white and blue cuffs, emerging from her floppy, red sleeves. Her paradoxical ensemble perfectly represented her role in life. "I like it when you wear your mage garb." I touched her elbow. "Not while on duty, of course." I gently ran my fingers up her arm and onto her breakable shoulder. She froze. "But, just when we're alone together." She trembled slightly as my path traversed her delicate collarbone, freckled neck, pointy chin and pink lips.

"Cease," she whispered, breath tickling my hand. That's when I realized what I was doing. I pulled away, biting down on my tongue. But, it was too late; she was already triggered. "Why do you think you can't love?" she asked the very last question I wanted to answer. "How can you just decide, one day, to lock yourself out like that?"

I was silent. Scarlet's enormous eyes grew sad, stirring in me an irrational impulse to comfort her—to tell her things I'd already decided never to utter again, like how I felt there were outside forces pulling us together, no matter how hard we resisted. Or, how devastated I was when she left in August. Or, how I never wanted her to leave Icicle again, though I knew she had to. Or, how difficult it was to stand this close to her and *not* touch her.

But, there was so much more to it than that. There was pain. There was a horrible ache that consumed me, weakened me. This desperate attachment I felt was worse than a battle-wound. It wasn't good. It was a knife in my gut. I couldn't have it. I didn't want it. There was no way love should feel like that.

She deserved to hear the truth, no matter how harsh. But, all I could bring myself to say was: "I tried, Scarlet. I just don't feel it. Honestly, I don't think I can."

"Love isn't a feeling," she said, taking me by surprise. "Feelings can go along with love, sure, but they're just sprinkles on the sundae." Why would Sunday—or any day of the week, for that matter—be sprinkled? And, with what exactly? Rain? Hmm, maybe this was a foreign idiomatic expression. Scarlet and the Nurians tended to use a lot of those. The Nurian language had so many, it was ridiculous. I wondered if Conflagrian did, too. Probably. "Love is a decision," she went on, "to put someone else's needs above yours, above anything or anyone else. To commit to them. To be willing to do whatever it takes to preserve their well-being, even to your own detriment."

A decision. Hadn't I made that decision, already? Last July, I decided I'd rather leave the Core Crystal intact than see Scarlet fall into the Pit. In January, I decided to give Ambrek the shard so he wouldn't kill her. Without realizing it, I'd been putting Scarlet above all else for quite some time now, even the war. And, I didn't know why I did that. There was no logical explanation. I just felt like I had to. I still felt that way, even now. Was this really love?

"Love is a choice," she insisted, "and the way it *feels* is just a garnish. Decorations. Feelings aren't the foundation of love, they just make love enjoyable."

No. I didn't enjoy what I felt. Not one bit. It scared me half to death, how my strange attachment to Scarlet impacted my decisions.

"I'm not enjoying myself," I said, flatly. "This can't be what love feels like."

"What exactly *are* you feeling?"

Pain. Terrible pain. But, looking into her moist eyes, catching the fluorescent light, I couldn't say it.

She misunderstood my silence. "Nothing? How's that even possible? Do you really feel *nothing?*"

I wished. "I used to."

"What about now?" How many minutes passed since her last blink? "What about when you told me you loved me, in August?"

I looked away, unable to stand her intense gaze, any longer. I had to be honest. Maybe, then, she'd finally leave me be.

"Scarlet, I do feel the same way I did in August." But, it wasn't pretty and it wasn't love.

Her lips parted.

I took a deep breath. I knew if anyone overheard us, we could get court-martialed. "It built up gradually, since we met. The first time I noticed something was after our first real conversation, right after you graduated into the fleet— when I called you in to discuss how to make strategic use of your magic and you wound up spilling your life story and asking about *my* upbringing. As the Nurians would say, you really 'stirred the pot' and caught me off-guard, that night. Of course, I'm interested in all my soldiers, so I can figure how to use them best. But, when I listened to you... I don't know... it was just... different. I was *really* interested. In you. I wanted to know *you.* You fascinated me. Not just your military prowess, but who you are as a person. And, those thoughts I had about you, they scared me. I knew I wasn't supposed to think that way, about anyone. So, I avoided you for six weeks. Because I was frightened of my draw to you and wanted to put an end to it. I thought I could, if I just stayed away long enough. But, then, the war took precedence. I realized, to do what's best for Ichthyosis, I needed you in a leadership position, working closely with me, because you were simply the best soldier I had. So, I decided to try to push aside my attraction to you and go through with the promotion. But, just as I feared, the more we interacted, the more my infatuation with you intensified. By the end of July, I thought that meant I loved you." I inhaled. Here went nothing. "Scarlet, I do feel the same… things… now. It hasn't gone away. It actually got a lot worse since you came back into my life, in January. But, I know it's not love because it isn't good. It's… agitation. Fear. Bitter longing. Helplessness. Weakness," my voice fell an octave, "and pain. Not physical pain, like a battle-wound. A different kind. One that's internal. Mental. I don't really know how to describe it. So, to answer your question: yes, I used to feel next to nothing, before you came along. Nothing but anger and urgency, usually related to whatever's going on in the war at the time. But, now, there's this horrible pain, nonstop, no matter what. I can't stand it."

"Maybe, that's just how love feels to you."

Impossible. "That makes no sense. Love's supposed to be good. And, this mishmash of emotions is anything but."

"But… you said you decided…?"

I shrugged. "Apparently, I've made the decision, over and over, to put you first. I always do. I don't know why and I don't know how to stop. But, doing that hurts me. Badly. I'm ashamed of it." Scarlet opened her mouth, but I quickly steamrollered her: "Look, Scarlet, we've saved future generations from the Childhood Program, but it's too late for me. I think of the Nurians—I look at *you*—and know I can't be like that. I can't do it. I can't make myself feel good.

I wouldn't know where to begin. It's beyond me. I can't love you. Accept it."

"But, Cease—"

"That's enough!" I erupted and she actually took a step back. "I'm done discussing this! I explained everything as best I can! This conversation is a waste of time and energy. We should be focusing on the enormous national crisis we're facing, not this stupidity! Scarlet, you need to back off. That's an order!"

Her upper lip quivered. Great. She was going to cry. I couldn't take that. Even if I didn't love her, it was still excruciating to see her suffer. But, I couldn't comfort her. From now on, I couldn't do anything that'd give her hope.

"Damn you and your stupid war!" Angry tears streamed down her flushed cheeks at an astonishing rate. "I knew all along that the odds are against us, I *know* we can't have a future together, *I'm* the one who told you that over and over, yet I still keep crawling back to you, disregarding my own words and I don't know why, I don't know why you have this *hold* on me," she rambled, throwing a couple punches. I noticed she didn't use any magic against me. She settled for gentle swings of her tiny fists. So, she wasn't actually trying to inflict real harm.

Nonetheless, I wouldn't stand for it. I grabbed both of her hands, thrust them behind her back and bodily pushed her up against the wall.

"I'm going to try and follow your orders, sir." She sniffled and hiccupped. "You're dead to me, Cease. Happy, now? Cease Lechatelierite is DEAD!"

She scrunched her lids shut, probably so she wouldn't actually roast me with eye-fire. Her whole body shook.

I didn't move or speak until she was completely silent and still. Which took a while.

"Scarlet," I finally whispered, still pinning her down. I had a hunch, if I let go, her knees would buckle. "It's late. Early, actually."

She nodded. "I should leave."

"Yes, you should."

There was a pause.

"Um, sir?"

"Yes?"

"I can't go if you keep holding me here, like this."

"Right," I answered, slowly. Why were my hands and feet frozen in place?

At last, I released her.

"Goodnight, sir." She unstuck herself from the wall.

"Good morning, actually." I opened my door.

And, with that, she ran like enemy ships were on her tail.

CEASE LECHATELIERITE

I threw the door shut behind Scarlet, sighed through gritted teeth and collapsed onto my bed. It was three-thirty—we'd leave for the Sequest Center in only four hours. Great. Exhaustion was *just* what we needed to kick-start a day of facing off the world government.

How, Scarlet? How did a tactical brainstorming session turn into a stupid fight? It seemed like our private meetings always either ended in kissing or shouting. What the hell. I rolled over, burying my face in my pillow. That was the problem with you, Scarlet—you were crazy, and you were driving *me* crazy, derailing me from my duty, wrecking my concentration and subjecting me to a bazaar trauma no base-raised soldier was meant to endure.

All my life, I'd only had to deal with two types of relationships: us-versus-them and superior-subordinate. That was it. Yes, Inexor and I called ourselves 'friends,' but our rapport sailed on rough seas the moment Fair and Scarlet entered the picture. By now, it was clear to me that I simply wasn't meant to get close to others because, in the end, I inevitably screwed everything up.

Until Scarlet came along, no one ever loved me. Not like that. Many loved what I did for them—defending Ichthyosis, instructing, leading and so forth—but, Scarlet was the first person to ever love me for me, God only knew why. I didn't deserve someone like that. I was ticked at myself for ever saying those three stupid words that started this whole fiasco. Because, the bottom line was, I didn't love her and she was just going to have to get over it.

"I don't love you, Scarlet," I murmured into my pillow.

It was really hot in here. My clothes and sheets were moist with sweat. I sat up, unbuttoned my uniform and tossed it to the floor. Why was it so stuffy? I pulled off my undershirt and dabbed my forehead with it. I pictured the way Scarlet's face looked when she yelled, "You're dead to me, Cease. Happy, now?" No, not at all, I thought savagely, so get the hell away from me before I make you wish you never enlisted.

I punched the white metal wall, sick inside. Love was supposed to feel good. I was miserable. So, I clearly wasn't in love.

Then, why couldn't I stop thinking about Scarlet?

Because I was mad at her. Because she shattered my focus on the eve of a really important mission.

At last, my lids grew heavy...

"You're dead to me, Cease. Happy, now? Cease Lechat-elierite is DEAD!"

My stomach swooped—I was falling, falling, falling! Then, without warning, I smacked hard into a protruding cliff. The rock beneath my body was hot, so hot! Like a ship engine. The sweltering, smoky air clogged my lungs. I coughed and gagged but couldn't even hear myself over the deafening crackles. Shuddering, I rolled over and vomited, the scent of burnt plastic filling my nostrils. Then, I looked up and there she was, staring at me with wide, scared eyes, sobbing with an open mouth. I wished she'd stop. Stop screaming, stop crying. I couldn't stand to see her like that. How could I make her calm down?

Her face morphed into a different one. Grey-green eyes scowled at me from beneath a wild mop of auburn hair.

He looked so familiar. Where did I see him, before? You'd think I'd remember this face. He was the memorable type. The young man—just a boy, really—turned and walked away from me, robe blowing in the furious wind. It was suddenly very important for me to know who he was. I tried to call out to him, but my voice died in my throat—

The trumpet pierced my consciousness. In half an hour, the Order's plane would be here. I jumped out of bed as though electrocuted.

SCARLET JULY

April seventh, seven-twenty-five.

"The Order's plane will be here in five minutes!" Cease's voice growled. "Ready?"

I yanked open my door. "Yes, sir."

"Got our notes?"

"Yes, sir."

"And, the Orion-Nurian dictionary?"

"I've already memorized it but, yes, sir."

"Well, *I* still need it," Cease shot, acidly. "Contrary to what you may think, I can't read your mind."

Ugh, Tincture. Were things already souring between Cease and I, this morning? We couldn't afford to be at each other's throats, today. We needed to be on our A-game, cooperating as never before. It was literally us against the world. We had to push aside last night's fiasco, for now.

"You come close, though," I said, daring to smile.

Dressed in full ceremonial uniform—pins, cords, medals and all—we trekked through the thick snow to the runway. Of course, it'd be far more practical to travel in diving suits, considering the nasty weather, but we'd learned our lesson from our encounter with the Trilateral Committee: what we wore impacted the amount of respect we got.

Bouncing on Cease's chest was his Silver Triangle, gleaming in the white light. I resisted the urge to touch it. He looked even more handsome with all his decorations on.

Decorations. Each one represented another harrowing trial in his life, many of which I hadn't a clue about.

"Poor visibility," he mumbled, sleeve-wiping his visual band, "which is both good and bad."

It was easy to forget the limitations of average sight. Even blizzards made no difference to me; I could see between snowflakes.

"How so, sir?"

"It's good because it'll make it hard for the blockade ships to aim. But, it's bad because our pilot has to navigate through it. He's already late. I wonder if he's okay."

I moaned. The last thing we needed was to get Order personnel killed.

At last, I saw a sliver of silver emerge from the skyline.

"Here he comes!" I breathed, tremendously relieved.

Cease stared in the direction of my gaze, nonplused. Apparently, even with his band, he couldn't see it, yet.

"Are you going to wear your visual band to the meeting, sir?" I asked.

"While it'd be nice to see who I'm talking to, no, for dignity's sake, I'm not."

"Oh. Well, I think you should. The conference hall seats fourteen-hundred—that's a lot to keep an eye on."

"You can just record everything with your photographic memory and play it back for me later," he said. Tincture, I loved it when he attempted to be funny. "I can gather enough from their vocal inflections," he added, seriously. "I don't need to see expressions."

I never disagreed more. Cease was excellent at deciphering faces; it'd be a shame to let that skill go to waste, today.

"I think you should wear it, sir," I repeated. He wasn't shy to appear before his fleet in a wheelchair. What was his problem, now?

"We'll see about that when we get there."

The plane made a sloppy skid-landing on the ice. It slipped so far, in fact, that it nearly cleared the shore. My pulse hammered as the little craft halted only a couple yards from the water.

"Wheels?" Cease gaped. "They sent a plane to an *ice* land with *wheels* instead of skis? Isn't Oriya in the tundra region? I'd expect them to know how to handle winter weather!"

"It's April," I said. "It isn't still 'winter' for anyone but us."

He mumbled something else, but the wind swallowed his voice.

The plane laboriously taxied back to us and dropped a ramp. I greeted the pilot, a relatively elderly man, with a handshake and a sentence of fluent Orion, warranting an astonished stare from him.

"You speak Star, ma'am?" he croaked.

"Yes, sir."

"What about the language of your old, illegal ally, ma'am?" he asked, making a less-than-kind reference to Nuria. "You speak that, too?"

"Yes, sir."

"And, of course, you speak your ice-dialect," he added.

Cease looked a little offended by that. Ichthyothians were quite adamant about the fact their tongue was *not* a dialect... though, if you asked me, it pretty much was. It sounded like a warped version of Nurian with random, extra consonants.

"Three languages!" the pilot whistled as we took off. "You could work as a translator for the Order. Good pay." I actually spoke four, not three, but I certainly wasn't inclined to share my Conflagrian heritage with him. "I'll put in a good word for you?" He winked.

"No, thank you. I like my job."

"You like war?" he asked, voice suddenly turning sharp.

"Not at all, sir. My job isn't to pick fights, but to defend Ichthyosis from unwarranted attack."

"Say what you like, ma'am; you can't change the fact your job is to kill."

I glanced at Cease, peeling off his visual band and rubbing it on the front of his uniform. This man had the typical, closed-minded mentality of an isolationist... which was no surprise, coming from someone employed by the Order.

"Don't waste your breath on him," Cease muttered. "Save your steam for the conference. He's not flying too well, either; let him concentrate."

A long while later, the pilot started swearing in Star. "Conflagrian fire-savages!" he cried, slamming his joystick to the left. The plane lurched. "I don't know how to play their war-games!"

In a flash, Cease snapped on his band, sprung to his feet and jumped onto the flight deck. "Where's the weapons panel? I'll take care of them."

"Weapons?" he hollered. "Oriya follows the law!"

Cease blinked. "The Order sent you into a *warzone* totally *unarmed?*"

We swerved sharply, narrowly evading a stream of fire. I had a strong suspicion it was chance, not skill, keeping us alive so far.

"Stand aside," Cease commanded. "I'm taking over."

"I won't let you make war with my plane!"

"Move before I make you!"

The pilot wrenched his scandalized eyes from his windshield and instruments. "Are you threatening me, warrior?"

Cease seized him by the collar and quite literally threw him out of his seat. Then, he dove for the unfamiliar controls. Seconds later, the plane stabilized.

"Scarlet, I'm going to need you to—"

"I'm on it, sir!"

I darted to the emergency exit, anchored myself with a length of deadline and yanked open the door. I was surprised to see only one craft attacking us. The rest sat still as stones. Why?

"What are you doing?" the pilot cried to me.

"Buckle up and shut up," Cease snapped.

I willed my every photon to surge into my eyes. Then, I shot the furthest-reaching flames I'd ever dispensed in my life. Orange anacondas erupted from my pupils, snaking their way to the sea.

"*M-mage!*" a voice squeaked, as something poked my cheek.

It was the muzzle of my own sidearm. In the pilot's hands. He must have nabbed it from my holster while I was preoccupied. Bold move.

Sweat speckled his curly hair and now-colorless face. "Infiltrator! Enemy of the free peoples of Second Earth!"

In a flash, my hair knocked the gun clean out of his hand. Along with a finger.

He staggered back, screaming at the top of his lungs, blood everywhere.

"Tincture!" I exclaimed, slamming the door shut.

I picked up the pilot's finger, which made his eyes boggle all the more. He scampered to the tail. The plane suddenly tilted to the right, sending us both to the floor. I rolled toward him, grabbed his wrist, pressed his digit against his bloody stump and delivered a dose of flesh-healing and anesthetic spectrum.

For some reason, this only freaked him out more. He screeched like I just threw his finger out the window.

"Look, it's reattached!" I piped. "You're going to be okay! I just need to—"

"GET AWAY FROM ME, MAGE!"

He scrambled to his feet, but I lassoed him with a lock. Then, against his will, I held him down and set a splint with deadline.

Cease was prepping for landing. I left the traumatized pilot alone to join Cease on the flight deck.

"The plane is at eighty-seven percent damage," he informed me, grimly. "Not how I hoped to return the Order's property."

"The pilot just tried to kill me with my own sidearm, so I sliced off his index finger with my hair," I said. "I stuck it back on and set the bone, but I think he'll probably be needing trauma therapy, or something."

Cease drank in my words without expression. "What a way to start the day. How on earth are we going to explain all this to the Order?"

I shrugged. "Maybe, this story will help prove our point: we need their cooperation because the System is a hazard not just to us but to the entire northwestern hemisphere— the Water Forces just attacked an *Orion* plane, after all."

Cease shook his head. "Only because it departed from Ichthyosis."

"Oriya isn't even a thousand miles from Ichthyosis. It's only a matter of time before the warzone grows too close to them for comfort."

"Hold your thoughts for a moment; I need to land."

A couple minutes later, we came in clean.

Cease stood. "All ready for a nice, long day of bickering?" he asked dryly, sifting his hands through his crazy hair. I loved it when he did that—it was so sexy. He removed his band, surveying the blood sprinkled across the front of my uniform. "So much for looking neat. Come on, let's go."

"What about the pilot?" I peeked into the passenger cabin. "Oh, he already left." Not that I blamed him.

"Scarlet, let's move." He ushered me out the door. "We don't need to add tardiness to our already-lengthy list of offenses against the Order."

Dashing through the sixty-degree breeze, I looked up at the brilliant sunlight. Though still dull compared to the orange-red fury of the Conflagrian sky, it was the first time I'd seen a clear day in months. It was beautiful.

We entered the Sequest Center. The lobby furniture was a deep, cherry wood. The floor was a rich, royal purple that reminded me of my father's aura and the drapes were a luxurious, burgundy velvet. A massive crystal chandelier hung from the cathedral ceiling. One wall was adorned with countless plaques, engraved with the names and nations of every Order rep to have ever served, written both in Star and in their respective, native languages. Which was how I discovered that every country but Oriya, Nuria and Ichthyosis all used different alphabets. I almost drooled. This display was a linguist's dream. I wondered if I could get my hands on the materials to learn—

"Scarlet!"

I sheepishly ripped my gaze from the wall and looked at Cease, much farther down the corridor.

"What're you doing?" he demanded.

"I'm sorry, sir, I was just—"

"Stay with me!" he growled.

We hurried to the entrance of the colossal conference hall. To my surprise, there were neither metal-detectors nor spectrometers. I supposed, as an organization that believed in its façade of peace, the possibility of someone bringing dangerous equipment inside hadn't even been considered.

Until now.

I heard an audible gasp to our left. I turned and saw a young, uniformed, curly-haired doorman staring at my utility belt with shuttle-light-eyes. There was something familiar about him. But, I'd never been here before.

"I-I'm sorry, sir, ma'am," he stuttered, hand flying to his pimpled, peach-fuzz chin, "b-but, *those* aren't allowed in here." He took a few steps back, as though hurt by the mere sight of our guns.

"I'm sorry about that, sir. We'll dispense of these, right away." I responded kindly, unbuckling my utility belt.

Cease didn't take my lead. He gave the purple-vested, bow-tied, black-collared, acne-ridden teenager a look of scathing distrust. The poor kid met Cease's stern, silvery stare for less than a second before glancing away in fright.

"S-sir? Y-your belt, please?" he spoke to his polished shoes.

"Should we trust him?" Cease asked me in Ichthyothian.

I was a bit disgusted by Cease's paranoia. "Come on, sir," I muttered, resisting the urge to roll my eyes. It was either obey or not enter. What choice did we have?

"I'm uncomfortable with the idea of going anywhere un-armed," Cease insisted.

"Commander," I tucked my hair behind my ears, hoping he'd understand the gesture, "do you think we're ever *really* unarmed?"

The boy shifted from foot to foot, growing all the more nervous at the sight of us whispering in our strange, foreign tongue. "I'm just doing my job, sir, ma'am," he piped.

"Alright, fine." Cease finally un-holstered his weapon, leaving his belt on. "But, you're returning everything to us when it's time to go," he ordered sternly, in Nurian.

"O-of course, sir." It obviously took him a whole lot of self-control not to run from the room, calling for his mom-my. For Tincture's sake, Cease needed to watch his effect on people, a little bit.

At last, we proceeded, pausing to take in the jaw-dropping sight of a chamber designed to seat fourteen-hundred—two delegates from each nation, arranged in alphabetical order by country name, except for Oriya, who had the privilege of front-row seats. I noticed two empty flag-posts and four vacant chairs—no doubt, where Conflagria and Ichthyosis used to sit.

At the center of the stage was a massive throne and podium, for the Chairman. A vast, digital screen filled the wall behind his station. The doorman settled behind a control panel at the far right of the room, strapping on headphones and pushing buttons. Apparently, he was a technician, too.

All the reps were already seated. Cease and I stood, frozen, like a pair of lost children.

"Come on," I said, eyeing the two abandoned spots all the way at the left end of the third row, next to the nation of 'Ibid.' We made the long, intimidating trek across the room and settled behind our plaque that read:

'Guests:
Commander Cease Terminus Lechatelierite
Second Commander Scarlet Carmine July
North Ichthyosis Island'

"The meeting will begin in five minutes," said a voice in Star, over the PA system.

"At least, we're not late," Cease said as an attendant came by and handed us tiny microphones for our collars. "We may've bashed up their plane and injured their staff, but hey, we're not late."

I looked around, listening to the bizarre, beautiful, multilingual hum, all around me. In the first row sat a pair from the Socialist Republic of Anich, a small Septentrion-coastal nation. Their eyes were dark and braided and their silky, black hair reminded me of my mother's. Their language sounded fluid and sweet. I peered at their notepads, at the intricate characters in vertical columns. Each letter was like a piece of artwork unto itself, with its dashes, dots, curls and crosses. It was language as I'd never seen before.

"Wow," I breathed.

Cease wasn't looking around, but rather paging desperately through the Orion-Nurian dictionary. Already?

"What, Scarlet?" he snapped.

"Just listen to those two, speaking Anichian!" I sighed. "And, get a load of the beautiful writing on their notepads!"

"I can't see it from here."

"It's stunning," I cooed. "Cease, do you think Anichian would be difficult to learn?"

"Was that an attempt at humor, or are you trying to spite me?" he shot.

"Sorry." I bit my lip. "What are you trying to look up, anyway?"

"The words up front."

The giant screen read:

'April 7ᵗʰ of the 94ᵗʰ Age, 7ᵗʰ Era
Second Earth Order
Session #787
Sequest Center
Constellation City, Oriya'

I gasped. These Star words were almost identical to Nurian. "Cease, you can't understand *that?*" From our study sessions, I was under the impression that he was a little more advanced.

His fingers drummed against the wooden desk. "I can understand verbal Orion far better than I can read it!"

"Okay," I whimpered, intensely unsettled. The thought of facing off the Order without Cease's full support filled me with dread. I couldn't stand against them alone. We'd won over the Trilateral Committee because of our teamwork.

"Presenting, the Second Earth Order Chairman, Mr. Kaerb Breach of the Free Peoples of Oriya," the PA sounded, bringing all conversation to a halt. All thirteen-hundred-ninety-six representatives applauded as a curly-haired man in black judge-robes marched in.

Icy fear shot through me.

"W-where's Arnold Link?" I choked. If Link wasn't here, who accepted our meeting request?

Beside me, an Ibidian rep spoke up, "You mean, the ex-chairman?"

"Ex?" Cease croaked.

"Oh, yes. Impeachment proceedings began in January. March twenty-seventh was his last day." She seemed rather satisfied with our distress. "The lame duck extended your invitation just before getting ousted."

Cease and I looked at each other. Without Link, did we stand a chance?

"It's okay," Cease whispered to me. I tried not to stare at the sweat-pearls, already breaking out on his forehead. Who was he trying to reassure, here? "We can do this, Scarlet. We handled the Trilateral Committee just fine and these aren't even military minds."

I nodded, swallowing. It was us against thirteen-hundred-ninety-six. So much of our hope was hinged on Link. I closed my eyes, trying not to hyperventilate.

"Please welcome Diving Commander Cease Terminus Lechatelierite and Second Commander Scarlet Carmine July of the North Ichthyosis Island Military," Kaerb Breach declared, spitting the word 'military' as though it tasted foul.

The screen up front displayed a gigantic, live video of Cease and me. The blood on my uniform seemed accentuated by the much-too-bright spotlights.

We were greeted by stifled, scattered applause. Bad sign.

"At the conclusion of today's session," Breach continued, his image thankfully replacing ours, "we will hold a majority vote for the inquiry posed by our visitors: should the Order reaccept the North Ichthyosis Island, a blacklisted nation currently at war with the South Conflagrablaze Captive?"

A wave of appalled murmurs swept through the crowd. Bad sign the second.

The screen depicted Cease and I, once again. Cease's face was paper-white, shiny and fixed in a tight contortion. But, nonetheless, he managed to give off an authoritative aura. Next to him, I looked like a little, blushing girl.

"Our guests will have the floor for an uninterrupted seven minutes. A thirty-second warning will be given. Upon the conclusion of their introduction, we will hold a twenty-five-minute question-and-answer session followed by an eighty-seven-minute period of free-discourse."

Wait, what? Only seven minutes to pose our main argument? I looked at the stack of notes on our desk and felt a wave of nausea. There was no way we'd get through half of it. We'd have to whittle things down to the bare essentials, on the fly.

The feed was meant to be live, but it had a slight delay to it, so Cease and I got to watch ourselves exchange surprised glances, on the big screen. Laughter rippled through the chamber. A slight pink twinge touched Cease's cheeks—which the hypersensitive recording equipment delineated, all too well.

"*Seven minutes?*" he hissed at me. "Why didn't they tell us about the meeting protocol, before now?"

"Commander Cease Lechatelierite and Second Commander Scarlet July have the floor," Breach announced. "Sir, ma'am," he nodded at each of us, "your time begins, now."

Now, now! Not a moment to waste!

We activated our microphones and got to our feet. In the process, my crimson-speckled uniform got fully exposed to the cameras. Gasps surrounded us.

"Did they just come out of *battle*, or what?"

"How *dare* she enter an assembly of peace looking like she's fresh from a kill!"

"Hostile, warlike appearances, both of them."

"Will you look at all those medals and cords on the man-boy's costume?"

"Those shameful tokens of death and destruction!"

"What do they represent, the number of lives he's taken?"

I inhaled, forcing myself to tune out their words. It was too early to get unnerved.

For the sake of courtesy, Cease sacrificed a few seconds to greet and thank the congregation. I wasn't prepared for the array of confused facial expressions that'd follow. Of course, his heavy Ichthyothian accent would throw them off. Why didn't I see this coming? My face burned. His mage-like mastery of tone wouldn't do squat if he were incomprehensible.

"Ichthyosis's hand was forced," he was now saying. "The South Conflagrablaze Captive has been attacking us for seventeen ages and counting, with imperialism as the ultimate goal."

"We neither wanted nor initiated this war," I intervened in perfect Star. Thirteen-hundred-ninety-six pairs of eyes turned to me. "We only engaged in it, in self-defense."

"Surely, we had no choice but to *defend* ourselves from an evil dictatorship?" Cease growled a little too aggressively. "As an innocent victim, Ichthyosis should've received support from all of Second Earth, to put an end to the hostilities. But, instead of uniting to achieve the Order's self-proclaimed goal of worldwide peace, what did you do?" *Uniting?* Tincture, did he really just use that word before an assembly of isolationists? "You turned your back on us," he half-yelled. "Blacklisted us. Treated us like criminals. When the only thing we're guilty of is guarding the ideal of liberty from those who hate it!" Cease exhaled into the microphone and I could feel the room collectively cringe. "You charged us for repeating the mistakes of First Earth when it's *Conflagria* who's the culprit, not Ichthyosis."

And, now, I was starting to boil. Besides using our precious time to beat a dead scabrous, his wording placed the blame where it didn't belong. How dare he villainize Conflagria!

"Thirty-second warning."

Uh oh. "Ichthyosis came close to ending the war, several times," I spoke up. "Standing on the border between war and peace, all we needed was a slight push over the edge. Yet, remaining unfortified, we always fell back into desperation. And, so, the war has dragged on. Since the seventy-seventh age, our security and livelihood has been threatened by an oppressive dictatorship. With the System sea-blockade in full swing, the innocent citizens of Ichthyosis have been left to starve. The only natural resources we have are salmon and petroleum, which we'd gladly offer to you in exchange for rations that would literally save our lives."

"Your introductory time is up. A seven-minute recess will precede the twenty-five-minute question-and-answer session," Breach announced.

The spotlight over our heads extinguished and a buzz of conversation slowly overtook the assembly. Cease pulled a little towel from his utility belt and mopped his forehead.

"Cease," I piped.

He lifted his face from the cloth and started fanning himself with our notes. "Yes?"

"Why did you say that when you know it's not true?" I murmured, in Ichthyothian to deter eavesdroppers.

"What are you talking about?"

"You said the war is Conflagria's fault."

He blinked. "It is."

I felt slapped. "You *know* it isn't. Conflagria and the System are distinct!"

"Of course, *I* know that, but *they* surely won't understand. Do you think we had time to go over that, anyway? We don't need to complicate things, right now. All the Order needs to know at the moment is: Ichthyosis is innocent, Conflagria is guilty. Help the innocent. Clear and simple."

I looked away.

He grunted. "Scarlet, look at it from their point-of-view. Conflagria was once the tyrannical Authority Nation whom the whole world despised and ousted. How'd it look if I started defending it?"

"I didn't say you should defend anyone! All I'm saying is, you shouldn't have even mentioned Conflagria, at all! Say, 'the System' instead! Is that so hard?"

He slammed his fist on the table, causing the Ibidians beside us to jolt. "Why does it matter? No one would notice or care!"

"It matters because you're making Conflagria look bad. You're undermining Conflagria's chances of ever negotiating with the world, in the ages to come! That's one of my goals after the Red Revolution—"

He threw his hands up, knocking our name-stand to the floor with a clatter. "Why are you even thinking about *after* the revolution when there isn't even a revolution in the first place because the damn *Ichthyo-Conflagrian War is still on?*"

"Because I think ahead!" I cried. "I plan for the future! I look farther than the next stage of this stupid war!"

His silver eyes flashed. "You know how ridiculous you sound? If we don't take care of this 'stupid war' first, none of us will have any future!"

"Choosing our words carefully is *not* ridiculous! You're being nearsighted!"

He snorted. "What's next on your agenda, huh? Single-handedly overthrowing world isolationism?"

"Yes, as a matter-of-fact, fighting isolationism is a goal of mine! But, I never wanted to do it alone—I was actually hoping *you'd* help me!"

From over my shoulder, I heard a whistle. "Just listen to those two!" the Ibidian woman exclaimed. "I don't understand a word of their harsh-sounding, consonant language—that bastard dialect of Nurian—but, they're sure having at it! Bickering like an old married couple!"

"Figures they'd be *fighting*," her colleague retorted. "They're people of war."

Cease and I closed our mouths.

"May I have your attention, please," Breach's voice sounded. "Recess has come to a close and the twenty-five-minute question-and-answer session will begin momentarily."

Great. Cease and I just spent our break in the most counterproductive way imaginable. I shut my lids and took a deep breath while Cease wiped his face, again.

"Questions may be answered by any one of our visitors, at a time," Breach said.

My eyes popped open. Cease and I weren't allowed to collaborate?

"Our first inquiry comes from Representative Eil Etalosi of the Socialist Republic of Anich."

The woman with the long, shiny, black hair stood and turned. "Commanders, if the Order makes an exception for

Ichthyosis and allows you to continue your war while enjoying membership, wouldn't that open the door for other such conflicts in the future?"

"No, ma'am." Cease stood up, rendering me silent for the duration. "If Ichthyosis is reaccepted, then Conflagria—the only nation in the world interested in disturbing the peace—would be the only one shut out from the Order," he spoke so quickly and fiercely, his words came out a little slurred. Heat whipped through my hair. He was antagonizing my people, yet again!

Etalosi blinked. "I'm sorry, sir, but could you please repeat that? I'm having a hard time understanding you. It was also difficult to discern your introduction but, due to protocol, we couldn't ask you to clarify, at the time."

To my horror, her remark was followed by a widespread murmur of agreement.

A very flustered Cease attempted to reiterate not only his answer to Etalosi's inquiry, but the brunt of our opening, as well. Frustrated and rushed, he began randomly inserting Ichthyothian terms in the middle of his sentences. It was torture to watch him struggle when I could easily translate everything he wanted to say, directly into Star. I felt a surge of anger toward the Order for their stupid policies. Why isolate Cease and I from one other? Didn't they know that the most progressive and refined thoughts were always the result of collaboration?

Well, of course, not. That was the problem with the whole world-system.

Etalosi wrinkled her nose. "My apologies, sir," she simpered after Cease finished regurgitating his speech-soup, "but, I still don't understand. Are you saying the planet should collectively restrain Conflagria?" She cocked a brow.

"No," Cease strained forward, "I'm thinking—saying—Conflagria wouldn't even attempt to—to wage war again if—"

"Permission to interject on my Commander's behalf, Chairman Breach!" I finally burst in Star. The entire hall seemed to stop breathing, in surprise.

"I'm sorry, but that's against protocol, ma'am." He adjusted his cap and stroked his curly, white beard. "You're not permitted to talk out-of-turn. I believe your partner has the floor?" He cast Cease an amused glance.

"I can translate his argument into Star for the council, sir."

Breach sighed, theatrically. "Very well, you may proceed for the sake of time." He gave Cease a scathing look. "But, only this once."

I noticed from the corner of my eye that Cease's face was red.

I cleared my throat. "What my Commander is saying, Representative Etalosi, is that, if Ichthyosis is reaccepted, the Conflagrian System—the sole entity in the world with an interest in starting wars and imperializing—would be the only one left out of the Order." I revised Cease's words to take the blame off of Conflagria and put it where it belonged. "And, it follows that the System wouldn't dare attempt international hostilities again, if they knew their targets wouldn't be blacklisted, but rather supported by all of Second Earth."

Breach's nostrils flared. "If that is indeed what you believe, Ichthyothians, then you don't understand the first thing about this hallowed organization whose membership you carelessly seek! You imply that we'd function as a *war*-alliance. No, ma'am! No, sir! That would open up the possibility of world war! We don't exist to bolster your might and scare off your enemies, as you attempt to do with all those ridiculous cords, medals and ornate symbols of violence on your military costumes!"

Cease's scandalized eyes raked my face. I doubted he understood a word either of us said, considering how fast we spoke, but it didn't take a military genius to gather things were going south, very quickly.

Cease flicked off his microphone and I followed his lead.

"Scarlet, what did you say?"

"Exactly what you said!"

"Really?"

"Yes!"

I glanced forward and my heart nearly stopped. "Oh no, the camera's been on us, this whole time. Everyone can see us talking, now!"

"Then, shut up!"

"Our second question comes from Representative Kink Gyre of the Free Peoples of Oriya," Breach proceeded.

Gyre addressed Cease directly, "Commander Lechatelierite, did you not travel to northern Nuria in the fall of the ninety-second age with the intent to forge an illegal war alliance?"

Cease stood, re-activating his microphone. "The documented motive behind the meeting was to increase the volume of Nurian exports—"

"The *documented* motive, by which you mean your cover-story?" Gyre cut across him. "Don't try to bend the truth, Commander Lechatelierite; your cheap tactics won't work here. This is an arena of justice, not a battlefield. Did you or did you not travel to Nuria under the *pretense* of discussing trade-relations while furtively planning on persuading Nuria to become your illegal ally?"

Cease was trapped. "I did, sir."

Gyre turned to the assembly, arms extended, palms up. "And, we see the outcome of this deceitful manipulation!" He gestured to the Nurian reps, several rows up. "We see the grievous consequences of the malicious trickery and scare-tactics Commander Lechatelierite employed to lure a loyal member-nation from the ways of peace and righteousness into the abyss of violence and war! In the end, Nuria paid dearly for their dangerous partnership, with the lives of thousands of innocent civilians employed by the Vessel Trading Company in Alcove Ci—"

"Excuse me, sir," Cease shot, "this is a 'Q-and-A' session, not free discourse. Is there a question for me buried in that little speech?"

"Yes, as a matter of fact, there is." Gyre adjusted his microphone. "Why should the Order trust you now, Ichthyosis?" he boomed. "Why should we aid those who knowingly snuck around behind our backs?"

Cease, face as fierce as ever, opened his mouth, but Breach cut him off.

"I'm sorry, sirs, but only one question per nation." It figured that Breach would only mention that *after* Gyre got to finish vocalizing all his hostile thoughts. "Our next inquiry comes from Representative Oc Etarepo of the Democratic-Republic of Nuria."

Nuria! What sort of query would we get from our former affiliate whom we so deeply wronged?

A light-haired, tan-faced, dark-eyed man stood and addressed us from five arcs back. "Commanders, could either of you kindly remind the assembly of the reasons for your nation's involvement in the war and our consequent alliance?" My heart soared; for once, we were being asked something constructive. I didn't detect a hint of antagonism in his voice.

Cease flicked off his microphone. "He's asking for a description?" he whispered before the delayed feed could switch back to us. "Please, take it."

I nodded, rising to my feet. "Sir, the goal of the Conflagrian System in this war is to absorb the North Ichthyosis Island into its empire. Think of System Principal Tiki Tincture as the Napoleon of Second Earth. How could we ignore such a threat? As the Order knows from experience, spectrum makes the System a dangerous and formidable opponent. Ichthyosis only engaged in combat to protect its liberty and the welfare of the *entire northwestern hemisphere.*" I turned to the technician sitting behind the control panel at the far right of the room. "Sir, could you please pull up a map of the northwestern hemisphere?"

It took the pimple-faced, curly-haired, young man a few moments to realize I was actually talking to him. When he noticed over a thousand heads turning his way, he visibly jolted from his stupor.

"Right away, ma'am!" he squeaked, head buried in his terminal.

I pulled a laser-pointer from Cease's utility belt—thank Tincture he kept his on—and delineated the ice and fire islands, respectively. "If Ichthyosis is captured by the System of the South Conflagrablaze Captive, the System's domain will extend both north and south, making it the furthest-reaching empire in the history of Second Earth. The land-hungry dictatorship will thus have the remainder of the northwestern hemisphere *completely surrounded.* Their next target would undoubtedly be the Democratic-Republic of Nuria," my red beam slid across the sandwiched continent, "followed by the Free Peoples of Oriya and the Socialist Republic of Anich. With the Ichthyothian military sustaining heavy losses on a regular basis and Nuria lacking a military infrastructure of its own to protect itself, our old ally felt the moral and ethical obligation to heed our desperate plea for help." I flicked off the laser. "The danger is real. Ichthyosis is fighting to defend not only itself, but a quarter of the planet. Because the System *will not* stop at taking one nation captive. With the Core Crystal, their magic is far less exhaustible than any of our resources. They won't rest until Second Earth has reverted back to the early

days of the Order, when everyone was under their tyrannical control." I looked at the Nurian rep. "Have I answered
your question adequately, sir?"

"Very well, ma'am. Thank you." Oc Etarepo and his wife
barely suppressed their smiles.

I sat down, pleased yet perplexed by their behavior. Sure,
I figured Nuria would detest the System and thirst for revenge against it, but I didn't expect the wounded superpower to rally to Ichthyosis so readily—not when thousands of civilians were still fresh in their coffins.

"The twenty-five-minute question-and-answer session
has concluded," Breach declared. "The protocol regarding the eighty-seven-minute free-discourse period is as
follows: inquiries by members are made on a first-come-
first-serve basis. Questions can be posed by one or both
delegates of a single nation or, if similar enough, co-posed
by multiple nations at a time. Each will be answered by
one or both of our guests. Should anyone make a statement deemed inappropriate by the Chairman, the Order
reserves the right to expel the speaker from the conference
hall, immediately. Free discourse will now begin."

The second those words left Breach's lips, it seemed as
though the entire assembly pushed their request-buttons,
like a coordinated task-force of dragon ships. Rapidly,
country names began populating the screen. I noticed four
nations all received the same '1-A' call-number.

"Cease, what does that mean?" I whispered. "Those four
all have the same designation."

He swallowed. "Breach said countries are allowed to col-
laboratively pose questions. Those guys probably all have
similar ones, so they'll be allowed to attack us, at once."

"It's not four anymore." The list grew to seven.

"But, we can team up now, too." He reached for my hand
under the table. "We'll fight them off, together."

I only nodded.

"Would '1-A' please rise?" Breach ordered.

Fourteen stood.

Everything went fairly smoothly for the first few minutes. Cease and I could handle a delegation of fourteen, well enough. We'd faced off seventeen at the Trigon Center, after all. The opposition posed by '1-A' wasn't the problem. The problems began when '1-B' and '1-C' began interjecting before '1-A' even sat down.

When the first '1-B' rep spoke up, I expected Breach to call him out for talking out-of-turn. But, it wasn't long before I figured how the system *really* worked. Despite different *letters*, all nations with the same *number* were considered part of a single argument.

There were seven letters in category '1.' It went all the way to '1-G.' Goosebumps rose on my skin, as though submerged in the Septentrion Sea without a diving suit. Judging from the epic sweat-monsoon pouring down Cease's face, he probably felt as though tossed into the Conflagrian Fire Pit. It was truly thirteen-hundred-ninety-six against two. It didn't take a military genius to see those weren't great odds.

For several endless minutes, Cease and I were verbally assaulted from all angles. Some reps even stooped so low as to use nasty ad-homonym attacks, recanting and embellishing Cease's war crimes.

"Excuse me!" a voice now called from the seventh row. It was Oc Etarepo of Nuria. "Representative Etalosi, I don't believe the details of Commander Lechatelierite's court-martial are relevant to the issue at hand," he cried, eyes impassioned. "Not to mention, Lechatelierite was never even sentenced. Commander Nurtic Leavesleft withdrew him from trial!"

Breach banged his gavel. "Excuse me, Nuria, you aren't permitted to speak, yet. We're currently addressing the delegation of category '7-A' through '7-I.' The assembly will respectfully disregard your statement."

My scalp prickled. Nuria's call-number was '87-__.' I doubted we'd make it anywhere near '87' before time ran out.

The council abruptly returned to ripping Cease's head off. The entire category-'7' argument came to a close only half an hour before free discourse was scheduled to end. By now, Cease was completely discredited. I doubted his word was worth a grain of Conflagrian sand in the eyes of the assembly, anymore. That team sure did their homework, digging up every exaggerated, defacing rumor they could find.

Twenty-six delegates from category '8' now rose, and the topic switched from Cease-bashing to reiterating every anti-isolationist act Ichthyosis committed since the establishment of the first Nurian colony. For Tincture's sake, how could Cease or I answer to things that happened eras before we were born? And, what did they have to do with anything, anyway?

As free discourse wore on, it was becoming increasingly difficult not to attack isolationism directly. Cease and I were trying to act like we agreed with the general principle, yet believed self-defense didn't violate the spirit of the laws. However, I was beginning to find it impossible not to scream, "For Tincture's sake, the reason you find so many anti-isolationist offenses in our nation's history is because all your laws make no sense and hamper the progress of civilization as a whole! It's what caused these problems in the first place, you idiots! ISOLATIONISM IS NOT THE ANSWER!"

I noticed that the hall was dead silent, every eye on me. Cease's face lost what little color it had.

"You didn't," he gasped.

"D-didn't what?" I sputtered, heart stirring an eight-Richter earthquake in my chest.

"And, so, your true motives are revealed, Ichthyothians," Breach jeered, triumphantly. "What you said, Second Commander July, goes against everything this assembly stands for. No, we won't welcome a nation who follows in the footsteps of First Earth! Ichthyosis has no place in the Second Earth Order!" The timer beeped, signaling the end of free discourse. Breach snapped it off. "All in favor of reaccepting Ichthyosis into the Order?"

From the seventh row, a single name-stand lit up. Nuria.

"All in favor of rejecting Ichthyosis and escorting the Commanders from the conference hall, immediately?"

Every other name-stand glowed.

Something seized my upper arm. "Come along, miss," a guard ordered. "Your plane is waiting."

Another guard approached Cease. "Don't you dare touch me," Cease growled at him.

From across the hall, the young technician watched us anxiously. He pulled off his headphones, abandoned his terminal, disappeared into a backroom for a moment, then emerged with my utility belt, Cease's gun and a white envelope. He ran to catch up with us.

"Here you are, sir, ma'am," he chirped. Waving the envelope, he added, "This is an invoice for the plane damages and the injured pilot's medical care."

"Great," I grunted.

"My name is Kaew Link, ma'am. I work here, part-time. I'm student at the Little Dipper School of Government."

He was a Link? Huh. I knew his features seemed familiar.

"I'm Arrhyth's cousin," he answered my thoughts. "Arrhyth and Uncle Arnold keep me posted on everything going on back in Nuria, you know, after January seventh and all…"

I nodded, letting the guard drag me outside. Normally, I'd be very interested to meet my friend's family but, right now, I didn't have the heart for it.

"Hold on, I need to tell you something," Kaew persisted, tailing us. "The Order's got Nuria's hands tied right now, but you still haven't seen the last of them."

Wait. "What?" I croaked.

"The veterans will find a way. Do you really think *five-hundred military geniuses* won't figure something out?"

With that, the guards bodily ushered Cease and I aboard our plane and snapped the door shut. We slipped into the sky, Kaew's figure dwindling with distance. Cease strained in his seat, face in his towel. With one swift motion, he flung it across the cabin. It smacked a window and slid to the floor.

"We weren't supposed to attack isolationism!" he screamed at me, cheeks red. "Save your damn plans to rescue the world until *after* the war takes my life, will you?"

"Cease, don't talk like that," I breathed, horrified.

"You're smarter than this, Scarlet!" he heaved. "We had an agenda, for goodness' sakes, you *wrote* the effing agenda!"

"I know, I know!" My throat tightened. "I'm so sorry, sir!"

He held up his hand. "Please, don't start crying and apologizing—I don't think I can take that on top of everything, right now!"

"S-sir, I-I just—"

"Please, Scarlet, for once in your life, just shut up and leave me the hell alone!"

I closed my mouth. An excruciating hour of silence passed.

"We weren't going to make it, anyway," Cease finally broke the ice. "I realized that about halfway through free discourse, when an Ibidian rep called me an 'ignorant Spartan.'"

"I can't believe Breach let so much mud fly. I thought the Order's supposed to have rules about inappropriate speech."

"You called everyone idiots."

"I didn't mean to say that aloud."

"Well, if you ask me, 'idiot' is far too gentle a word." He exhaled. "Scarlet, what are we going to do, now?"

I looked out the window, watching the glistening sea speed beneath our wings. I didn't give Cease an answer.

But, my thoughts always came circling right back to Nuria.

ARNOLD LINK

Throwing off my suit-jacket and tie, I plopped onto the living-room couch and flicked on the TV. Boy, did I need a distraction after the rough day I had.

"Nationwide approval ratings for the Second Earth Order has reached an all-time low," said Claver Causerie, a blonde Channel Seven anchorwoman. "Public opinion has only plummeted since our newly-installed Secretary of State, Arnold Link, was impeached from his office of Chairman. News of the Order's aggression toward two Ichthyothian visitors at their April meeting has triggered yet another upsurge of anti-Order demonstrations. As we speak, hundreds from a new political action committee, the 'Veterans and Families of Nuria,' are rallying outside the Sequest Center in Constellation City, Oriya. Channel Seven is live at the scene."

The screen displayed a chanting and sign-waving crowd outside the Order Headquarters. The camera zoomed in on a young man flanked by a brunette reporter in a pencil-skirt, holding a comically-large microphone. The man carried a poster with the words, 'Support Our Brothers of the North' sprawled in blue marker and he had a white snowflake painted on his tan cheek.

"Why are you here today, sir?" prompted the reporter, Rethy Swa.

"Because the Order doesn't understand the necessity of self-defense," he answered. "The people of Ichthyosis didn't want war; they were forced into it to protect their sovereignty. And, now, the Order is turning a blind eye to a threat endangering all of us!"

Another man standing nearby leaned into the microphone. "But, most of all, we're here because *isolationism is not the answer!*" he cried, brandishing his poster, which bore the same slogan. The cluster behind him suddenly noticed they were on camera and began to cheer with renewed enthusiasm.

"I notice that line is also printed on the back of your shirt," Swa commented. "Straight from the horse's mouth?"

"Yes, Second Commander Scarlet July is right!"

Swa walked over to a platinum-haired, middle-aged woman wearing a sweater depicting the Ichthyothian and Nurian flags, posts crossed.

"And, what about you, ma'am? I understand you're the one who organized this protest?"

"That's right."

"Please introduce yourself for our viewers."

"My name is Diana Maine and I'm the president of the Nurian Veterans and Families PAC. The globalist sentiment has really taken hold of Nuria since Arnold Link's impeachment. And, no doubt, the Order's blatant injustice toward their Ichthyothian guests at their most recent meeting only added fuel to the fire."

"Would you mind sharing which division of the Nurro-Ichthyothian military your son served in?"

"Dither was in the Diving Fleet," she replied, proudly.

"Ah, so he worked with the Leader of the Ichthyothian Resistance, himself?"

"Yes, he did." She smiled. "Commander Cease Lechatelierite is a brilliant man whom we all wholeheartedly support."

"Is your son here, today?"

"Of course. Most of the Nurian vets from the Diving Fleet are, as well as a few hundred from the Air Force and Ground Troops."

"We'd very much like to meet your son."

"I'm here," a voice said from off-camera. The picture blurred for a moment before fixing on Dither Maine and my boy, Arrhyth, standing on opposite ends of an enormous banner bearing Scarlet July's slogan.

"What a privilege it is to speak with you both," Swa greeted them. "Would you mind explaining to our viewers why you're here, today?"

"We're here in support of Ichthyosis and all our former military leaders—Cease Lechatelierite, Scarlet July and the late Nurtic Leavesleft," Dither recited. "My fellow Nurian comrades and I were unjustly forced to leave the Diving Fleet during this critical stage of the war."

"Without us, there are only twenty-seven soldiers left at Icicle," my son interjected. "*Twenty-seven.* Their situation is desperate; they need us. And, a lot of us are determined to return, regardless of the consequences or obstacles."

"With or without the Order, Nuria's taking action. Our goal is to be back by the twenty-fifth, no matter what," Dither said. "Ichthyosis is literally starving. There's no time to waste."

"Channel Seven thanks you for your time," the reporter said, turning back to Diana. "I just have one more question for you, ma'am, if you don't mind?"

Diana nodded. "Sure."

"How do you feel about your son possibly returning to the frontlines?"

"Of course, I'm scared," she said. "But, I believe it's the right thing to do. I certainly wouldn't call myself or this committee 'pro-war.' We believe war should only be a last resort. But, I'm afraid that's the point we've reached already—we can either defend ourselves from the threat posed by the Conflagrian System or submit the western world to tyranny. What the Order doesn't realize is that several nations are endangered by the mage empire, not just Ichthyosis. We can't afford to abandon our northern brothers in their fight to contain imperialism. I see no difference between this and the need to contain communism during the Cold War of First Earth. If Nuria and Ichthyosis go down, there'll be a domino effect. Oriya would probably be next. So, we're here today because we want the Order to authorize the reestablishment of the Nurro-Ichthyothian Alliance. And, if they don't, we think Nuria should secede and do it, anyway."

"A bold statement. Channel Seven thanks you for your time, Mrs. Maine."

"My pleasure."

Causerie returned to the screen. "Indeed, that is the sentiment endorsed by quite a bipartisan assortment of political authorities across the country: the Briggesh administration, our Secretary-of-State Arnold Link, our House Speaker Ecivon Wen Senior, and our delegation to the Order, Mr. and Mrs. Oc Etarepo."

Channel Seven then cut to an old clip of the infamous meeting on April seventh. Lechatelierite's pale forehead glistened with sweat and July's cheeks matched her red hair. They both looked beyond exhausted.

"Excuse me!" Oc's voice called. The camera zipped up to where he and his wife sat. "Mrs. Etalosi, I don't believe the details of Commander Lechatelierite's court-martial are relevant to the issue at hand. Not to mention, Lechatelierite was never even sentenced. Commander Nurtic Leavesleft withdrew him from trial!"

Breach banged his gavel. "Excuse me, Nuria, you aren't permitted to talk out-of-turn. We're currently addressing the delegation of category '7-A' through '7-I.' The assembly will respectfully disregard your statement."

The screen switched back to the anchorwoman. "Regarding Nuria's next course of action, a vote will be taken in both houses of congress on April twenty-second. The proposal on the table? Whether or not Nuria should issue an ultimatum to the Second Earth Order threatening secession unless it permits the reinstatement of the Nurro-Ichthyothian Alliance. Earlier today, a heated debate took place in congress on the topic of this prospective foreign-policy change. Channel Seven offers an exclusive peek into the senatorial session."

My impassioned face filled the screen with *'Channel Seven Exclusive!'* flashing at the corner.

"As the Diving Fleet's Second Commander so brazenly announced to the Order on April seventh, *isolationism is not the answer!*" I cried. "We have a right to defend ourselves from terrorism. We have a moral obligation to the western world to protect democracy and practice containment. We will not submit to the ethical vacuum known as the doctrine of isolationism and turn our backs on our brothers when they need us most!"

A combination of jeers, cheers, boos and applause erupted from the crowd. A senator who had no particular love for Ichthyothians since the day Lechatelierite first graced our shores in ninety-two, War Pact draft in hand, stood and shouted, "Mr. Secretary, your proposition will have serious consequences for every Nurian man, woman and child. By demanding secession, you're asking this country to forgo the vast majority of its international trade-relations and put itself under siege! Our economy will crumble! We'll all end up starving, like Ichthyosis!"

"No, senator, that's only what the isolationist doctrine wants you to think," I argued. "The Order wants you to live in fear, believing there's no other way to survive but within the confines of its narrow, dictatorial policies. But, Nuria is a world superpower. Economic theory holds that we bear the resources and industrial fortitude to press on without the Order for seventeen more ages before falling into a depression. The only natural resource we sorely lack is oil, which Ichthyosis has in abundance. No, I'm not daring to claim that our economy won't suffer. Secession will be a blow, indeed. But, we will survive. And, we'll be doing the right thing that'll save us all, in the end."

"You wear the façade of globalism, Mr. Link, when in truth, what you propose is far more isolationistic than any policy ever forged by the Order! You want to *separate* Nuria from the rest of the world and limit our trade-relations to one weak, warring power!"

"Our goal is long-term, not immediate, senator. We must have patience—"

"A revolution against the *world*, Secretary? Is *that* your ultimate goal for this country?"

And, with that, Causerie returned to the screen. Apparently, Channel Seven liked suspenseful, theatrical cliffhangers.

"Nationwide opinion polls reflect that an astounding eighty-seven percent of the population support Mr. Link's proposition. Evidenced by today's senatorial debate, however, our legislators remain far more divided—"

I turned off the TV. So much for taking my mind off of work.

ARRHYTH LINK

I inhaled the warm air with an open mouth.

One last time.

Yellow light filtered through the lush foliage of the Alcove City Park. I admired the bold beauty of the tall oaks.

One last time.

My eyes traced the glittering skyline.

One last time.

Who knew when I'd get another chance to feel sunshine on my skin, stand beneath a green tree, breathe air above thirty-two degrees, experience four distinct seasons, embrace my family, eat a hot meal, sleep in a soft bed...

It was April twenty-fifth. Three days ago, the Nurian congress ruled in favor of my dad's proposition. One of our SEO reps, Oc Etarepo, relayed Nuria's intentions to the Order, who promptly denied his request to maintain membership while resurrecting the alliance. And, so, Nuria was seceding.

Ichthyosis was a dark and dreary land. I disliked it from the moment I first tread upon the icy shore of Aventurine City, back in the summer of ninety-three. I felt trapped by the uninterrupted monochrome of my surroundings—from the buried ground to the white-capped mountains to the cloudy sky liable to spit golfball-sized flakes. Ichthyosis even made snow look ugly. And, then, as if all that weren't bad enough, there were our Ichthyothian comrades, whose temperaments were no less frosty than the environment.

Yet, Ichthyosis was where I wanted to be. It was where duty called. It was Nuria's one true ally in this cold, isolated world. It was the nation I decided I could die for, upon enrolling in the Diving Academy back in the fall of the ninety-second age.

I spotted a cherry-blossom tree nearby. I looked away, as though stabbed by the very sight.

"Dither," I murmured, "I'm going to miss having four seasons. Now, there'll only be one. And, I never really liked winter."

"Yeah, we're giving up a lot," he said. "Home, family, friends, normalcy. But, that's why we have to go. To protect all that. To make sure our loved ones still have a home, in the ages to come. And, Icicle isn't all bad. I mean, how many people can say they've served with the world's best military leaders?"

I grinned, thinking of Lechatelierite and Scarlet. I looked forward to seeing them again, especially Scarlet. For the last couple of weeks, it felt so surreal to watch re-running clips of the two of them, together, on TV.

Getting steamrollered by the Order.

I didn't know how or when Scarlet turned back up in Ichthyosis, but it made sense she'd rejoin the fleet after the Red Revolution went under. With the Core Crystal reinstated, there wasn't much she could do by herself in Conflagria. I figured Lechatelierite sent for her. He'd think to do that.

Lechatelierite. I hadn't a clue how he managed to survive January seventh, but everyone was relieved he did. Not long after Dither and I informed his mom that he went MIA, the news reported that he randomly turned up on base and resumed his post. No details were given. Why didn't Nurtic make it, too?

"There's just one thing the fleet will still be missing," I said.

"What's that?"

"The world's best pilot."

We were quiet.

"You can fly nearly as good as him," Dither finally broke the silence. "The lessons he gave you have paid off, bigtime. You just never really got the chance to show Lechatelierite what you can do because he almost always made you surface-ride instead of pilot."

"That's not the point."

Dither sighed. "I know. And, I hate to sound like a cardboard Ichthyothian, but we have to accept he'll never be back." He gave me a sad smile. "But, in a way, he's still with us, right?"

"Right."

"So, we're not just doing this for the alliance, but for Nurtic."

"Yes, for Nurtic."

Another pause.

"The System blockade is still out there," he added, ominously. "It'll be a rough flight."

Because of the blockade, we'd travel today by air rather than sea—with yours truly on the flight deck.

I shrugged. "I'm up for it. Nurtic taught me some pretty good tricks."

"Pretty good? You have his style nailed."

"Not quite *nailed*, but I'll accept the flattery," I chuckled. In my opinion, being compared to Nurtic was the greatest compliment a pilot could receive. "The trip will be a good warm-up for our return to military life."

Dither snorted. "Warm-up. Right. More like, the biggest challenge of your life."

"Shut up; you're making me nervous!"

"Well, you should be!"

I laughed. "Come on, let's go. We've got a train to catch."

We were bound for the abandoned Nurian Diving Academy, where we'd meet up with the five-hundred-one other veteran divers for the flight to Aventurine City, hauling as many supplies as we could fit onboard with us. Cameras from every news channel imaginable would capture everything and broadcast it live. The entire nation would watch us make history. The vets of the Air Force and Ground Troops would deploy a couple days thereafter, for their respective bases.

Communications severed after the alliance fell, we now had no means to warn Ichthyosis of our approach. I smiled to myself. I had a feeling this was an ambush Lechatelierite wouldn't mind.

ANAPES PATRICI

Ambrek Coppertus, the leader of Flame Team Seven, was a magnificent pilot and a fast learner. It was hard to believe that his first sea battle was only about four months ago. His previous proximity to the Multi-Source Enchant gave him a lot of invaluable insight on the strategies, tactics and interworkings of the Ichthyothian Diving Fleet.

But, recently, he'd been having difficulty concentrating on his assignments. He was always tense, and not in a productive, battle-ready way. He used to be the most even-keel man I knew. His temperament was the primary reason he got picked to go undercover, in the first place; how else could a man stand to live in the enemy camp, around the sundial? I couldn't do it. Ambrek's cool, level head made him the perfect candidate for the job. And, indeed, he pulled it off masterfully, accomplishing more in a mere five months than anyone anticipated.

But, oddly enough, it seemed that the moment Ambrek had to abandon his double-life, he started to self-destruct. I thought he'd be relieved not to have to sleep with the enemy, anymore. What on Tincture's island was wrong with him? I had to get to the bottom of things before his behavior caused collateral damage. Maybe, he was developing post-traumatic stress disorder? That wouldn't be too surprising, considering all he'd been through in such a short space of time. I myself was immune. As an internal-organ mage, illnesses of the mind and body weren't things I had to worry too much about.

Today, I decided to confront him.

"You wanted to speak with me, Captain Patrici, sir?" Ambrek now stood in my doorframe.

"Yes. Close the door and sit down."

He obeyed.

I leaned forward. "Officer, I wanted to ask if there's anything troubling you? Anything you'd like to tell me in confidence?"

His answer was immediate: "No, sir."

"There's nothing I can help you with?"

"No, sir."

My fingers drummed the desk. "I'm going to ask you one last time, soldier."

He squared his jaw and folded his massive arms.

"You've been calling out in your sleep," I pressed. "Your bunkmates have been complaining."

He raised a copper brow. "I wasn't aware, sir."

"Really?"

He shrugged, though a pink twinge touched his bronze cheeks. "It's just dreams, sir."

"Recurring?"

"If it matters, yes, sir."

"Of course, it matters. Coppertus, in the spectral world, dreams can be visions. Especially if they're recurring."

"These aren't visions, sir. When I wake up, I can hardly remember a thing. Visions are clear. Lifelike. All I can remember about these nightmares is how they made me feel and who was with me."

"How did they make you feel and who was with you?"

Ambrek squirmed. "Captain, is this really necessary?"

"Yes."

"Why, sir?"

"Because, if you're not having visions, recurring nightmares may indicate PTSD."

"I don't have PTSD!" he growled. "You're not a medicine man. I'm just stressed. That doesn't mean I have some mental illness!"

"Watch your tone when addressing your superior," I snapped. "We need to get to the bottom of this because, whatever's going on with you, it's impacting your performance at sea. I'm not dismissing you until you answer me."

"Fine." He inhaled. "I felt… confused."

"By what?"

"Like I said, sir, I can't recall any detail. Just… anger. Rage, even. Then, fear. I was both terrified and glad, at the same time. The pleasure was sickening, really, so I hated myself. I grew guilty. Couldn't stand it. Then, I woke up."

"Who was with you?"

"What?"

"You said you remember who you were with."

He shifted. "Only her face. Nothing else. Not where we were or what we were doing."

Her. Of course. There was only one 'her' who could have such an impact on Ambrek. His late sister.

"Was it Crimson?" I asked, voice gentler. Ambrek and his sister were very close. He took her death badly.

He looked away.

"Coppertus?"

He didn't speak. That's when the truth hit me like an Ichthyothian glacier.

"Not that Nordic tool, the Multi-Source Enchant?" I seethed.

His face purpled.

"How many times have you have this 'dream'?" I demanded.

He shrugged, again. "I'm not sure, exactly. A lot."

"How old are you?" I asked.

"Twenty, sir."

Pieces fell into place. He was having premonitions, a rare type of vision. Women developed the ability in their teens while men did in their early twenties. Most mages lived their entire lives without enduring a single one. While regular visions were crisper than any dream, clear as life itself, premonitions were always blurry and tough to recollect because the future was uncertain and subject to change.

"Coppertus, I think you had your first premonition."

He slowly absorbed my words, terror crystallizing in his golden eyes.

"Is-is it… inevitable, sir?" he stammered. "The content of my premonition, I mean. Can I prevent it from happening?"

"Nothing about the future is set in stone—that's why it's fuzzy. So, no, it's not inevitable, just likely."

"Likely," he echoed, trembling. "Sir, if you were in my sandals, you'd want to do anything to stop it. Anything." He gnawed his lip. "But… how can I look out for something if I don't even know what it is?"

"I wish I had an answer for you."

"Have you ever had a premonition, sir?"

I shook my head. "Most mages never do."

He gripped his armrests so tightly, the wood actually cracked. "Captain," he choked, "is there something I can do, spectrally?"

"I'm no spectroscoper, but I doubt there's anything that can be done from a magical standpoint. The future is an obscure realm and our science there is barely more than guesswork. But, that doesn't mean you're totally helpless, Coppertus. You control your own actions, after all. So, from now on, make a special effort not to do anything rash. Think before you act. Contain your anger. Don't let it have the upper hand."

He nodded and jumped to his feet. The nerve!

"I haven't dismissed you, yet."

He turned on his heel. "Sir?"

"You said you were with the Multi-Source Enchant," I looked him in the eye, "in your premonition?"

"Yes, sir."

"Then, maybe, it wouldn't be so bad if you *did* let 'it' happen."

He froze.

"Do you understand me, soldier?"

There was another lengthy pause. Then, he quietly mumbled, "Yes, sir."

I smiled. "*Now*, you're dismissed."

* * *

I scanned my instruments. I was at the bridge of the mothership, overseeing the blockade.

It'd been exactly one month since our last sea battle with the Ichthyothians. Since their hilariously ineffective attempt to penetrate our line on March twenty-fifth, the Diving Fleet didn't dare strike again. They were seriously outnumbered.

Indeed, our blockade appeared vast and mighty. All our ships were *there*, stationed in the Septentrion, scaring off potential threats with sheer, visible bulk. But, what Ichthyosis didn't know was how severely strained the spectral web was, right now. The System was currently investing the vast majority of the Crystal's emissions into implementing our latest endeavor—the project both created and destroyed by Fair Gabardine, later salvaged by a few of our other fine spectroscopers. So, only one of our sea crafts had some—but, not a lot—of usable spectrum. If the Nordics attacked the blockade today, we'd be screwed.

My unit leaders took turns manning the single operational sub-plane. Today, Ambrek Coppertus was in the cockpit.

Ever since Ambrek learned his 'dreams' were likely grounded in reality, he got consumed by figuring out what they meant. When not at sea, he spent his time at the Castle library, hunched over ancient spectroscopy texts, reading about the ethereal topic of divination. Desperate for advice, he asked every one of his comrades if they'd seen a premonition before. None of them had.

A green dot now blinked at the top-right corner of my spectroscope, rapidly approaching from the southwest. Tincture.

"Coppertus," I called, "incoming Nurian craft, sector eighty-seven, twenty-five-thousand feet above sea-level!"

"I'm on it, sir!"

"Hurry! It's heading for Ichthyosis!"

AMBREK COPPERTUS

I ascended into the cool, blue sky. The Nurian plane twirled and spun, dodging my fire, leaving a corkscrew contrail behind its grey shape. It executed feint after feint, confusing and frustrating me beyond measure as I only managed to nick its wings and singe its hull. With dozens of dizzying loops and lightning-quick rolls, this pilot was about as predictable as a dragonfly.

Hold the torch.

Did Nurtic Leavesleft and Fair Gabardine escape from Conflagria, after all? Was I facing Leavesleft, right now? Fear thundered through me. Of course, I was. Who else could fly like that?

At long last, I got a solid target-lock. I slammed the emerald-green button at the top of my joystick. But, nothing happened. My engine went quiet.

Oh, Tincture. My craft was out of spectrum!

As if on cue, I began a stomach-swooping tailspin, the cobalt sea rapidly exchanging places with the sky. I crashed into the icy waves and stupidly ejected while belly-up. I struggled against the incredible downward momentum, flailing my numb limbs, screaming in my helmet—

CEASE LECHATELIERITE

I pushed the salmon slush around my plate with a fork, surrounded by two-hundred-eighty-some other soldiers eating lunch in near-silence. This afternoon, I'd receive the weekly status report from the Air Force and Ground Troops. Any minute now, Illia Frappe would come up to me with a fat envelope in his hands. A fat envelope filled with miserable news.

"Commander, sir?" came his voice from behind me, as if on cue.

"Thank you, Frappe." Without looking at him, I held out my hand.

But, he didn't give me anything.

"Sir, an unidentified plane is circling the facility with its landing-gear down." Well, that'd sure be an odd method of attack. "Tacit just manned the south turret. He's keeping it in his crosshairs, at all times."

"Tell him to hold fire," I grunted, "until I attempt communication."

I marched to the terminal at the front of the mess hall. Every pair of eyes watched in suspense as I put on the headset. To my surprise, I was greeted by a loud hiss of static. Why was the connection poor?

"Identify yourself, immediately!" I called into the microphone.

"This—Ar—ink—nd—Nur—v—rans—r—questing—perm—ion—land!"

"Repeat!" I demanded.

"Is—th—you—Com—ander—Lech—rite?"

Anticipation shot through me. "I said, identify yourself!"

"This—s—Arrh—ink—an—N—ian—vet—ans—requ——ing—pe—ssion—land!"

No way. "Arrhyth Link? Arrhyth Link and the Nurian veterans, requesting permission to land?" I echoed, and every diver in the room sat up straighter.

"Yes, C—ander! Ship—ritical—dition—can't—circ—m—ch—longer!"

"Permission granted!" I flicked a switch to redirect my transmission. "Tacit, let them land!"

"Yes, sir." There was a pause. "Who is it?"

"The Nurians."

"*What?*"

"Clear the runway, officer!" I snapped. "Their plane is in critical condition; they can't circle, much longer!"

"Right away, sir!"

I yanked off the headset and surveyed my men, white-faced and murmuring to one another.

"How's this possible, sir?" Seven gasped. "Is Nuria leaving the Order?"

Lost for words, I didn't answer.

Scarlet was looking at me and smiling. Smiling broadly and beautifully, with more life in those giant green eyes than I'd ever seen.

At last, Illia and Quiesce opened the door. Arrhyth Link and Dither Maine were at the forefront of a pack of about five-hundred, all sporting matching blue shirts emblazoned with the Ichthyothian and Nurian flags, posts crossed. A lot of them carried boxes, undoubtedly full of supplies and foodstuffs. My comrades watched in stunned silence as they entered… until Scarlet leapt to her feet, lifted her hands and began clapping. From the other end of her table, Seven chimed in. The rest of unit one followed suit, in seconds. Soon, the entire mess hall was engaged in a standing ovation.

At the center of it all, I just stood and stared.

"What, Commander, aren't you happy to see us?" Link asked with a grin.

I blinked. And, slowly, I uncrossed my arms and joined the applause.

* * *

"The Order denied our request to legally reinstate the alliance, so Nuria is seceding," Arrhyth Link was explaining to everyone. The Nurians were dispersed throughout the mess hall; spots of blue were scattered in the sea of white. The cheerful atmosphere had long since given way to cold, fearful silence. Not a single man touched his lunch. "As of May seventh, Nuria's Order membership and access to the worldwide rationing network will cease. But, economic theorists estimate the alliance could self-sustain for about seventeen more ages before our economies plunge into a full-scale 'Great Depression' like the '1930s' of First Earth. So, we still have some time…" Link noticed me, shaking my head vigorously. "Commander?"

"That estimate is obviously incorrect," I voiced, bluntly. "It doesn't take a university scholar to figure those numbers are totally unrealistic. There's just no way a nation with a high consumption rate like Nuria could last nearly two decades *without* international trade *while* at war *and* while supporting Ichthyosis's deadweight, I'm sorry."

"I wasn't finished, sir." Link took a deep breath, yanking a curl. "Yes, if the alliance persists in a state of full-scale war for the duration, we wouldn't last. We only would if the war gets… contained… within a certain, earlier timeframe."

"Define 'contained' and 'timeframe,'" I demanded.

He swallowed. "We have three months to destroy the Crystal, sir."

The shock in the air was as thick as the spectral smoke undulating from the Fire Pit.

"Three *months?*" I echoed. I expected our deadline to be measured in ages, not months. We only had until the end of July?

He shifted on his feet. "It's proportional: the longer we take to end the Crystal, the less time we have to resolve our differences with the Order. Three months to end the Crystal and seventeen ages to reconcile with the world would be ideal. The shorter or less intense the war, the longer we can last without global trade. And, vice versa."

No one dared to breathe or blink.

"Alright, then." I clasped my hands behind my back. "I'm allotting no more than two weeks before we attack the blockade. In fourteen days, we need to have reorganized our units, restructured our officer hierarchy and developed a viable plan of attack." I looked at each diver's face, in turn. "From now on, soldiers, there's no such thing as Nurians or Ichthyothians, veterans or new grads. We're the Nurro-Ichthyothian Diving Fleet, and we have three months to get it together."

* * *

All seven-hundred-eighty-seven men—five-hundred-three of them sporting ridiculous t-shirts—began pouring out of the mess hall.

"Arrhyth Link!" I called. He withdrew from the blue and white crowd and came over to me, bushy curls bouncing.

"Yes, sir?" he piped.

"How did you make it here without getting shot down?" I cut to the chase. "You were outnumbered by hundreds."

He hesitated. "Commander, you won't believe my answer."

I cocked a brow. "Try me."

He wrung his hands. "Something really strange is going on. Only one ship attacked us. The rest stayed at or below sea-level, holding their fire. I have no idea why. But, if the System can't fight properly right now, we should take advantage of that, while we still can. We should strike, right away. We shouldn't wait two weeks, sir. We need to go, like, today or something."

I shook my head, disgusted. Typical Nurian impulsiveness. If we went in unprepared, we could lose the last manpower we'd get for who knew how long. Warm bodies weren't a readily-replenishing resource, anymore. If we failed—again—we wouldn't get another chance. I fought the urge to bite off his head and dismiss him without explanation. I had to remind myself that I was grateful he was here. He didn't have to be. He wasn't supposed to be.

"Link, we can't assume they didn't fight because they *can't*. We faced them in battle very recently and they killed a hundred of us." At that, Link visibly flinched. "They could be curious about your operation, deliberately letting you by for the purpose of espionage. Or, maybe, they're setting a trap, wanting us to come to the conclusion you did, luring us to strike on their schedule. I can't gamble with lives, Link. It'd be a suicide mission. We've got a lot of integration to do, over these next two weeks—a lot of trust to build in very small window of time. Your men are only familiar with a handful of us."

"Yeah, I was wondering about that, sir." Link's eyes lingered on Seven's retreating back. "We were only expecting to find the original crew here. Who're the other three-hundred?"

"Two-hundred-fifty-seven. They're new graduates from Icicle Academy. The class of the ninety-fourth age—or, what's left of it, anyway. They joined us in February."

Link stiffened for a moment then nodded, clearly downplaying his horror. "Sir, they look so *young*. Younger than you, even. Maybe, they're about Scarlet's age? And, one of them," his voice dropped to a whisper, as if relaying juicy gossip, "one of them is so little, he looks like he's only *ten*, or something!"

As if I weren't already aware of my own subordinates! "That's Krustallos Finire the Seventh, the former subleader of unit one," I spat, tartly. "The soldier single-handedly responsible for destroying our entire strategy, last battle. He's eleven. The rest of them are between the ages of fifteen and seventeen."

"Wow," he squeaked. "Are there any more of them, sir?"

"More of what?"

"Little kids at the academy?"

I looked away. "Normally, there would be. But, not anymore. I had them all sent home."

His jaw unhinged. "Really?"

For some reason, his surprise irritated me. "Yes, really."

"That's great, sir! But…"

"But, what?"

I could tell he didn't want to say it anymore, but it was too late: I'd backed him into a corner.

"But… I just… wouldn't expect y-you to do something like that. Sir."

I folded my arms. "And, why's that?"

Link looked as though he wished he could instantly evaporate. "I don't know."

"Yes, you do."

There was a silence. I didn't blink.

"I mean you're… you're *you*," he finally blurted.

I took a step forward. "What's *that* supposed to mean?"

"I mean, well, you sort of grew up on base yourself, d-didn't you, sir?" he stammered. "Did Scarlet suggest it, or something?"

"No, she didn't. While she helped me accomplish it, sending them home was my idea." Scarlet wasn't the only one around here with virtue!

He backed away a couple paces. "I'm sorry, sir, I just—"

I held up my hand. "I'll see you on deck in ten minutes with the others, Link. Go pick up your gear. Dismissed."

He saluted, breathed a sigh of relief and bolted out the door.

FAIR GABARDINE

"I hear voices!" Nurtic hissed. "Quick, get down!"

We dropped to the floor and rolled beneath a cupboard. Which, unfortunately, stirred up a lot of dust. Which was very, very bad because Nurtic was allergic. (Seriously. And, of all places for a person with a dust allergy to be stranded…!)

He sniffed, swallowed and blinked but, before he could literally blow our cover away with a sonic sneeze, I clamped my hands over his mouth and nose. His hair and lashes were matted grey. Dust also caked the blisters all over his chin and cheeks. He'd been shaving with my sword. No joke. When I asked him why on Tincture's island he'd want to shave when he apparently couldn't do it without literally skinning himself, he said he couldn't stand the thought of a beard in this heat. Apparently, he'd rather bleed.

The front door now banged open and two pairs of sandals came stomping in.

"Cuivre didn't give us enough fire," growled an angry female voice. "Look at this lousy torch! How'll it satisfy our whole tribe?"

"Well, what did you expect at a time like this?" a man's voice responded. "Almost all the spectrum is being redirected, in preparation for the project's launch. For the time being, they barely even left a photon for the blockade."

"No kidding. I can't believe they couldn't stop that Nurian boy from getting away in an enormous carrier. I know a couple little planes have squeaked past the blockade already, but a gigantic transporter? That's just embarrassing. Also, where on Tincture's island did the Nordic kid get his hands on a craft like that?"

"I suppose he took that white-haired traitor with him."

"No doubt."

Startled, my head hit the underside of the cupboard. Nurtic kicked me.

"No matter. It'll all be over, soon. The Water Forces are nearly ready for emission. Gearing up for it has been a real drain, but they've somehow worked it out so that, once the irradiation actually begins, the spectral shortage will be over for all of us. Their blockade ships will be fully functional and we'll go back to getting decent fire rations, among other things."

"Thank Tincture."

I wondered if they could hear my heart pound. Nurtic, who didn't understand a word, stared at me with fearful concern in his hazel eyes.

"You want us to move there, right?" the woman asked.

"It'll be a while until everything is ready, but yes, I'd like us to go, as soon as possible. I'm ready for a fresh start."

"Me too. The New Conflagria. It's about damn time."

And, with that, they went back outside, probably to share their fire with their tribe.

"Fair?" Nurtic whispered once the coast was clear. "What's going on? What were they saying?"

I looked at him and swallowed. "They think we've escaped."

His powdered brows furrowed. "What? Why?"

"Someone flew past the blockade in a big plane—not just a little scout, but a full-sized carrier—without getting shot down. They think it's you."

He shook his head, hair mopping the nasty floor. "Small crafts slipping by, I can believe, but a *carrier?* I'm flattered, but that'd be a stretch, even for me." He stopped for a moment to let out a whooping sneeze. "There are hundreds stationed in that blockade, and carriers sure offer a lot of surface-area to aim at."

"The enemy ships are weak, though; apparently the System can't afford to give them much spectrum."

"Fair, this is all good news. This means the manhunt for us will cool off, and the Diving Fleet may actually stand a chance of breaking through the blockade. Why are you so shaken up?"

I grabbed the front of his burlap robe. "Nurtic, the System can't properly outfit the Water Forces because all the spectrum's being redirected into 'the project.' *My* project! They figured it out without me!"

All color drained from his face. He looked like he couldn't decide whether to vomit or cry. The enemy was about to bombard Ichthyosis with magic, meteorologically preparing it for Conflagrian occupation. No doubt, the melting ice would cause tremendous tides, floods, storms and hurricanes, slaughtering countless civilians.

Apparently, the System decided it wouldn't even wait for Ichthyosis to wave the white flag before moving in.

CEASE LECHATELIERITE

Shipments of foodstuffs always came in on the last day of the month. Since the blockade began, salmon was the only grocery we received with any consistency. Upon delivery, the tubs of raw fish would be promptly whisked away to the kitchen for cleaning, cooking, mashing and freezing. Earlier this morning, it was Link's turn to help unload the cargo. That's how he discovered the salmon didn't arrive as paste, as he'd assumed, but whole and fresh. Which meant, he had a window.

By the time I entered the mess hall, he and Maine had already emerged from the serving line, plates filled with vivid, steaming, orange-pink strips.

"Nice work, Arrhyth!" Maine beamed at his trey, then looked up at me. "Oh, good morning, Commander," he picked up his fork, "did you see the nice surprise the chefs have for us, today?"

I blinked. "What's *that?*"

"Salmon," he answered simply, clearly enjoying every moment of my stupefaction. "Smoked salmon."

Seven emerged from behind a crowd of excited Nurians, giving his own plate an analytical glare. "It looks so… bright. I can hardly believe this is the same stuff the paste is made of."

Inexor appeared at my left shoulder, also inspecting his meal. I noticed he forgot to get utensils. "It's *hot*. I actually see *vapor*," he groaned. "I feel like I'm in Conflagria, again."

"Well, I like it," Scarlet voiced from my right, accompanied by several nodding Nurians. "It has a lot more flavor. Not to mention, it's nice to eat something that isn't still half-frozen, once in a while."

"Exactly," Maine pointed at Scarlet, "this has everything that typical base-food lacks: taste and temperature."

Link looked at me. "Well, aren't you going to get some, Commander?" The grin on his face was maddening—it was almost as if he were daring me to lose my cool.

I pursed my lips and stalked away without a word. Link technically didn't do anything wrong; there was no official rule forbidding soldiers from entering the kitchen or talking to the cooks. It just hadn't happened since he unearthed an ancient tank of ketchup from a storage cubby, last age.

I was the last to go through the serving line. When I came out, there was nowhere left to sit, but—

"Over here, sir!" Maine waved his arms, obnoxiously. Nurians often talked with an abundance of animated body language, even when near to one another. In my opinion, if you needed someone to flail for your attention, there was something very wrong with your sense of awareness and you probably shouldn't be a soldier. "We saved a seat for you." He gestured to the place across from himself and Link, right beside Scarlet.

I had half a mind to ignore him and take my meal to my quarters, but I thought the better of it; it wasn't the right time to act divisive. Not with mere days left to get this hodgepodge of base-raised veterans, new graduates and Nurians united and ready to take on the blockade. I had to set an example.

They watched as I placed my trey on the table, sat down, cut a small chunk of neon fish, put it in my mouth and chewed.

"Well, sir, what's the verdict?" Link asked.

There was a pause.

"I think it could use some ketchup," I finally said.

Everyone within a ten-foot radius of us abruptly turned and stared at me. I started slicing a second bite, pretending not to notice.

"Sir," Link breathed, "did–did you just make a joke?"

I met his gaze, nonchalant. "So, what if I did?"

He blinked, repeatedly. "I've just never seen you… *not* be serious, before."

"A person can't be serious, continually."

"*You* can," Maine insisted.

I didn't answer.

"Now, for real this time, sir; what do you think?" Link pressed.

After two bites, I decided I couldn't choke down another molecule of hot, sticky, rubbery salmon. The taste was so strong, my eyes stung.

"I think it's time for all of you to finish up and report to the south field for glacier-surface practice. Ten minutes."

With that, I stood and got in line for the Recycling Center.

"First, he sits with us, *then* he refuses to get provoked, *then* he tries to kid around with us!" I overhead Link whisper excitedly.

"The look on his face was deadly, when he first saw our plates," Maine's voice mused. "I didn't expect him to be in the mood to tolerate us, after that. And, to think, he actually cracked a joke!"

"You're not helping him, you know," Scarlet grumbled. "If he says something you honestly think is funny, then *laugh*. Ogling him like he just sprouted wings isn't encouraging him to loosen up and do it again."

"What, like *you* weren't surprised?"

"No, I wasn't," Scarlet responded, coolly.

I glanced back and saw both Link and Maine gape at her.

"Right, sure," Link said, dryly. "Have you ever seen him 'loosen up' before now? Have you ever heard him laugh?"

Scarlet stayed silent. But, I thought I saw her cheeks redden.

ARRHYTH LINK

Scarlet finished her meal before Dither and me. Okay, well, technically, she didn't *finish*—there was still food left on her plate when she got up. But, there always was, when Scarlet was 'done' eating. My eyes tailed her as she headed to the Recycling Center.

"You know," I said to Dither, sticking another delicious, flaky hunk in my mouth, "I think Scarlet and the Commander would make a good couple, don't you?"

Dither froze in mid-chew.

"I know it's against the rules and all that; I'm not accusing anyone of anything," I added quickly, suddenly aware that my words could involuntarily spark a rumor that'd ruin their lives. "They just seem to… I dunno, *match* each other, you know?"

"As much as a flame could ever match an ice-cube," Dither snorted.

"No, seriously, I think they'd be good together."

He started laughing into his water glass.

"Come on, opposites attract, right?" I insisted. "They'd, like, balance each other out, or something. And, I think they kinda match up physically, too. The first time I saw the Commander, I thought: damn, he's so short, he'll never find a girl tiny enough for him. And, then, I realized: hey, *Scarlet's* smaller!"

Dither gave me a sly smile. "There's just one little problem, Arrhyth. The idea of the Commander ever loving anybody is ridiculous. About as likely as an Ichthyothian spring rain."

I pulled my fork out of my mouth, cheeks full. "The Commander loves all his soldiers."

"You know what I mean—loving like *that*. Romantically. I just can't picture it. He's about as cuddly as a piranha."

"Soldiers *are* allowed to have relationships once retired, you know. Judging from the number of military brats we have around here—like the Colonel's son—it *does* happen."

"Yeah, but Commander *Lechatelierite?*" Dither chortled. "Can you imagine a little kid running up to Lechatelierite, throwing his arms around his neck, yelling 'daddy, daddy!'?"

I chuckled; the image really was hilarious. "No, I guess not. But, I can see Scarlet as a mom. She's very compassionate and nurturing."

Dither wiped his mouth. "Ooh, could you imagine if the two of them actually did have a kid—what he'd be like?"

There was a pause, then an explosion of:

"*Crazy* smart."

"A scientific *and* linguistic genius."

"Hyperactive. Terminally insomniac."

"A swimmer. Well, very athletic, all around."

"But, small enough to accidentally get sucked into a vacuum cleaner."

"Big, glassy eyes."

"Enough hair to carpet the whole base."

"*Magical* hair."

"Red hair, grey eyes."

"No, dark-brown hair, green eyes."

"How about auburn hair and grey-green eyes?"

We laughed.

"One thing's for certain," I said. "He'd totally *own* the military."

"If Scarlet ever lets him enlist, you mean."

"Her opinion wouldn't matter. Any kid of those two would do whatever the hell he wants."

"Except exist, in the first place."

Silence.

"Yeah," I murmured. "Well, come on, let's hit the locker-room."

CEASE LECHATELIERITE

My men marched down the corridors, sporting summer trainers. At the front of the crowd of blonde, black and brown heads was Scarlet's vividly-red one. I pulled her aside.

"Yes, sir?"

I looked at her wiry arms. "You have my permission to wear your regular trainer, or even your diving suit, if you like. Everyone here already knows you're a mage. There's no need to waste spectrum, heating yourself."

Her brows lifted. "Thank you, sir, but its okay. I'm not cold."

I narrowed my eyes. "Don't lie to me."

"No, really, sir," she insisted. "I almost feel like I'm right next to the Core Crystal or something. See?" She pressed a hand against my bare arm and it wasn't just warm, but scalding hot.

"Do you have a fever?" I asked anxiously, touching her forehead—which Seven noticed, of course. "Are you sick?"

"I actually feel great, sir. Better than usual."

Weird. "If you say so."

The south gate swung open. But, instead of enduring the usual snowy blast, the air was still. Still and… room temperature. Forty degrees.

I looked up at the sky, which was overcast, as always… but, not white. The clouds were a dark, dreary grey. I took a few steps, and the snow beneath my boots wasn't hard and packed, but soft and slushy.

What the hell was going on, here?

I faced my fleet. "Alright, men, today's practice will be a real exercise in cooperation," I spoke in Nurian. "No diving suits equals no intercoms, which means—"

Something wet touched my nose. I fell silent. Everyone watched me, tense. And, there it was again, slowly increasing in frequency—drops of lukewarm water dotted my skin. No, it couldn't be. I craned my neck.

It was raining.

* * *

The rain gained intensity until it became a thunderstorm that lasted well into the evening. The sky flashed, rumbles sounded and waterfalls smacked the snow-covered ground, shattering glaciers and sweeping ice-sheets out to sea. The sea itself no longer reflected a dazzling cobalt-blue, but a dismal grey-black, like a rippling expanse of oil.

I'd never seen rain on Ichthyothian soil, before. No one had. It was the first time in our nation's history the temperature broke freezing. The weather made the headlines, which greatly amused many of the Nurians.

"*Breaking news?*" Link stared at the TV in the rec room. "A little rain and thunder, seriously?"

Channel Seven dispatched a 'live reporter at the scene'— in other words, they made a man with an umbrella stand right outside the studio.

"I don't see what the big deal is." Maine rolled his eyes. "It's probably just global warming."

"And, this heatwave was completely unprecedented," the news reporter said. "The NISF ran tests today on the molecular composition of the atmosphere, revealing normal levels of greenhouse gases. Meteorologists everywhere are puzzled…"

"Okay, maybe not, then. But, still, everyone's making a big deal out of nothing," Maine said.

No one spoke. Maine probably didn't believe his own words. A foreboding air overcame the lounge. If the weather didn't return to normal very soon, the consequences for an ice-land would be drastic.

SCARLET JULY

By the morning of May first, the temperature hit seventy-seven degrees and the sun broke through the clouds over Aventurine City. By afternoon, the multi-foot snow-accumulations had melted to a mere handful of inches. By nightfall, the ground itself was visible.

The news showed footage of small children venturing outside, barefoot and in t-shirts rather than their usual coats, boots, scarves and goggles. The brilliant sunlight kissed their pale, grinning faces as they ran freely.

The news also showed the horrors of rising sea-levels, earthquakes, glacier-shifts, tsunamis, hurricanes, roofs torn off by crazy winds, submerged twenty-story apartments, dead bodies floating in floodwater, homes and semivowels swept into the Septentrion, gelids buried by avalanches, kids crying and mothers screaming...

In a single day, the civilian death-toll mounted higher than that of the Nurian Trade Centerscraper attack. The Ascet administration suggested the stranded write their social-security-numbers on their arms in permanent marker so their corpses could be more easily identified, later on.

By May third, the government issued an emergency evacuation notice to several coastal cities, including Aventurine. The problem was, all typical means of civilian transportation were now useless: snowmobiles and semivowels couldn't glide on surfaces void of snow or ice. So, almost everyone had to rely on commercial or military craft. The Diving Fleet transported as many as our vitreous silicas and crystallines allowed, making dozens of trips per ship per day, bringing people inland and to our base.

By the morning of the fourth, a quarter of the nation was submerged. Icicle was one of very few facilities in the country that could operate just fine underwater. Designed to withstand the beatings of war, it was an airtight, bomb-proof sanctuary. By the end of the week, thousands of civilians were either living on our base or aboard our ships. I wasn't sure exactly how many the Air Force and Ground Troops took in but, no doubt, they were also bursting at the seams.

Today, May fifth, seventeen of our crystallines and two of our vitreous silicas went on yet another rescue mission, scouring the submerged residential roads of Aventurine City. Cease and I were now aboard one of the manta rays alongside a couple units and a few dozen soaked, panicked civilians.

"I've detected three more on Debacle Street, sir!" Frappe reported from the helm. "We'll be there in a minute!"

As we arrived, Frappe ascended so our hull poked the surface. Helmet on, I opened the hatch to the sight of three sobbing, coughing, white-faced, trembling children holding onto a roof-beam for dear life—identical twin sisters who looked about nine or ten and a boy who looked no older than four. One of the girls had a bleeding gash across her cheek. The toddler sniffled into the blouse of a floating middle-aged woman whose pale blue eyes stared lifelessly at the grey sky.

Cease and I flipped open our visors.

"Where's the rest of your family?" Cease demanded, much too harshly.

The girl with the cut hiccupped. "Daddy went to the grocery store three days ago but never came back."

The other sister gave their brother an anxious stare. "I think Roop broke his leg when stuff fell from the house."

"Scarlet, get the twins inside. I'll handle the boy."

But, Roop refused to let go of his mother's body.

"Come on!" Cease barked, grabbing his arm.

For Tincture's sake! "Easy, sir; he's injured!"

Cease's eyes glinted dangerously. "Frappe spotted another group down the road; we don't have time to waste!" He turned back to the child. "I said, move it!"

Roop, unrelenting, screamed at the top of his lungs.

"Let go of that!" Cease demanded. "We can't take that along!"

Did Cease just call the kids' mother *that*?

"Whyyyy noooot?"

"We don't have room for corpses! We need to use our limited space for the living before we can even think of collecting the deceased!"

The toddler didn't get it. Words like 'corpse' and 'deceased' went right over his head. All he knew was, his mom was here now, but this harsh stranger was telling him he must abandon her.

"I can't leave mommy!"

"She's *dead*," Cease growled. "Now, come along!"

Roop emitted a series of earsplitting shrieks as Cease literally slung him over his shoulder, broken leg flapping.

"What are you doing?" I cried, horrified.

"Nothing! *He's* the one being irrational and stupid! We obviously can't take a dead body onboard!"

"Irrational and stupid? He's a *child*, for Tincture's sake!"

"Commanders, please hurry up," Frappe's tense voice sounded in our helmets. "One of the four I'm tracking at the next intersection isn't giving off as much of a heat-signature, anymore." Which meant he or she probably just died.

Cease and I quickly scrambled inside with the kids and shut the hatch.

I took Roop from Cease and held him protectively, stroking his wet hair. "It's okay," I said, softly. "We're bringing you and your sisters where it's safe and dry. I'm going to bind your leg so it'll heal up and all the pain will go away, okay?"

He nodded, wiped his tear-and-mucus-covered face across the front of my diving suit and threw both his arms around my neck.

I gave Cease an accusatory look over Roop's shoulder. "Some father *you'd* be," I hissed in Nurian, so none of the civilians would understand.

"Who said I'm ever going to be a father?" he spat, also in Nurian. "What's it to you, anyway? Aren't I dead to you?"

I didn't answer. Those words were like acid, burning holes through my ears.

I gently set the boy down on the floor and took off my helmet. His head flopped back and his chest slowly rose and fell.

Cease also removed his helmet. "He's asleep?" he gawked. "He was hysterical, a moment ago. How did you get him to relax?"

"Easy," I retorted. "Just don't manhandle him and bark in his face about his dead mom, and exhaustion takes care of the rest."

Cease pursed his lips and stalked away.

I turned back to Roop, rested a lock on his leg and fed him a steady stream of anesthetic spectrum. I wondered why the chore didn't drain my aura in the least. I worked on his splint to the sound of total chaos, all around me.

"We must find my son!" a woman screeched, grabbing Cease's shoulders. I knew how much Cease hated being touched without permission. It probably took all the self-control he had not to strike her to the floor. "We can't leave the area until you find him! Stop the ship!"

"I'm sorry, ma'am, but we've recovered every living person in this neighborhood," Cease said, tone flat. "He's either dead or not here."

I flinched at the awful bluntness of Cease's words. Cease stepped away from her, only to be assaulted by another townie, in seconds. A tall, burly teenager towered over his slight frame—a sight so absurd, I almost laughed. Cease's small stature sure made him look like an easy target, but anyone remotely aware of current events should've known better.

"You didn't let my girlfriend aboard!" he yelled.

Cease looked almost bored. "That's because she's dead."

"Says who?"

"She didn't have enough of a heat-signature, sorry."

"Just listen to him!" someone else interjected. "He feels nothing for our losses! For him, death is business!"

Grunting loudly, the teenager balled his fist and took a swing at Cease. In the blink of an eye, Cease dodged the blow and got him in a headlock. Everyone watched with bated breath as the bloke trembled in the Commander's grasp.

"I don't want to hurt you," Cease's quiet voice barely overpowered the guy's whimpers. "My job—and the job of every soldier aboard this ship—is to help you. To rescue the living. That's it. The only thing we ask of you in return is to stay out of our way and let us work. We've detected thousands of heat-signatures in this city, and every second we waste could cost a life." Cease released the poor man, who promptly ducked into the crowd, face red and eyes watery. Cease didn't give him a second glance. "I know how loss feels, believe me," he said to the entire cabin. "I've endured more variations of loss than any of you can imagine." He put his helmet back on, visor up. "Death isn't the business of the Nurro-Ichthyothian military. Stopping it, is."

SCARLET JULY

By the morning of the sixth, a state-of-emergency was also declared in each Nuria and Oriya. So much Ichthyothian ice had melted by now, the rising sea ravaged their northern shores. Southbound highways in Nuria were jammed with flivvers. Stuck on the road for hours on end, people began openly urinating and defecating in the street. Those not fortunate enough to possess a flivver of their own resorted to violence to force others from theirs. By now, the Nurian death-toll hit the hundred-thousands.

Oriya fared even worse. A mere bead on the Septentrion coast, Oriya wasn't large enough to have a dry inland. The population had nowhere to go. And, unlike Ichthyosis and Nuria, it had no military to mobilize for rescue operations. The nation was utterly helpless.

Although Nuria was literally drowning in its own problems, it still opened its borders to the very country that was forcing its hand to secede. Central and southern Nuria absorbed fleeing Orions and fellow citizens, alike.

"My husband passed away in the Centerscraper bombing on January seventh," a teary Alcove City resident said in a televised interview. "So, I have room in my house for those who've also lost everything. I'm now hosting an Orion family from Constellation City. The mother went missing, yesterday. I understand a lot of what they're going through."

"I took in a family from Notser, a small town near Nuria's northern shore," said another interviewee from Alcove City. "When Alcove was contending with the aftermath of January's terrorist attack, the whole country showed their love and support. So, now it's *our* turn to help everyone else. This is the least I could do."

In under a week, the capital alone adopted over seven-hundred-thousand Orions and nearly a million northern Nurians. Alas, the northwestern hemisphere defied the Isolationist Laws as never before, banding together during this time of crisis. Oriya swallowed its pride and agreed to receive aid from the very nation it forsook, demonstrating that isolationism truly wasn't the answer.

* * *

"Second Commander July," Frappe called from several yards away, "we need your help, over here!"

He gestured to Dr. Calibre, standing amongst a small group of surgeons and nurses. With the hospital wing at capacity, the medical staff resorted to treating several of the injured, right here in the barracks. I jogged over, pushing through the dense crowd of soldiers, healthcare personnel and civilians. I looked down at a small, pink-faced, dark-haired girl sprawled on a bed like a boneless sack of flesh. She looked maybe seven or eight.

"Her house literally imploded on her," Frappe explained. "Dr. Calibre's team is ready to operate, but we ran out of anesthetics. Could you…?"

"Of course." It was only about the hundredth time, today.

I knelt by the girl and she recoiled. "No," she whimpered. "No more pain!"

I touched her with my hair, anyway. She gasped, eyes wide, but learned very quickly that I didn't come to hurt her.

"You make the owie go bye-bye?" she breathed, relaxing. Smiling, I stroked her rosy cheek. "Yes."

"Your hair moves like a snake. And, it's as bright as fire." She swallowed. "Are you from the fire?"

"Yes, I'm a mage, if that's what you mean."

She inhaled sharply, her simple worldview instantly shaken. "But, how? I thought mages are mean. Mommy always says they are the ememy."

"Enemy," I automatically corrected her. "No, mages aren't the enemy. It's the System—Conflagria's government—that is. The System is an evil dictatorship. So, if Ichthyosis wins the war, Conflagria does too, because then all mages will be free. That's why I'm in your country's military. I'm a mage who supports the Ichthyothian Resistance."

"Oh, wow." She nodded. "That's cool. I like it better this way. I always thought fire and ice should be friends. Opposites are s'pposed to attract, you know?" And, with that, she closed her eyes and promptly fell asleep.

I got to my feet, a strange sensation building in my chest. A seven-age-old comprehended in seconds what the rest of the world still failed to grasp for eras.

Frappe peered at me. "Are you alright, ma'am?"

Ugh, why was my face always so readable? "Yes, why wouldn't I be?" I snapped.

"Well, you're three-thousand miles from the Crystal and we've been asking you to use your spectrum, all day."

"Oh." I shrugged. "I'm not drained in the least; it's okay."

"Are you sure? Because Commander Lechatelierite seems very concerned."

Was he, now? "If I weren't up to this, I wouldn't be doing it," I answered, coolly. Cease never babied me before. What was his deal, now?

"Well, he keeps saying things like, 'she shouldn't be able to keep up like this; something's wrong.' He walks around, mumbling it over and over."

Sometimes, I wondered if Cease really was mental. "Since when do we complain about being *too* strong?" I threw my hands up. "If I wasn't, half these people wouldn't have had their surgeries today. So—"That's when it hit me. I gasped. "Where's the Commander, now? I need to speak with him, immediately."

"Last I heard, he's in barrack eight with unit seven." He lowered his voice. "They're passing out dinner to the civilians lodging there. But, don't advertise that in *here*. The kitchen is so busy, the people in *this* barrack probably won't be getting any food for another hour or two."

Without pausing to thank Frappe, I sprinted down the hall and into barrack eight, slamming hard into someone.

"You have a bad habit of doing that, you know?" Arrhyth laughed, half a dozen plates of salmon miraculously still in his arms despite my impact. "For someone with magical eyes, you sure suck at watching where you're going."

"I need to see the Commander, this instant." I scrambled to my feet. "Frappe told me he's here." I scanned the bustling room. He was nowhere in sight.

"You just missed him. He was grumbling something about 'too much energy' when he just walked up to me, handed me these plates and left." The stack wobbled in Arrhyth's arms. "Speaking of which, do you mind helping out here, for a bit? At this rate, barrack ten won't be having dinner until midnight."

"Do you know where Lechatelierite went?"

"He didn't say."

Wordlessly, I spun around and ran all the way to Cease's quarters. Before I could press his intercom, the door swung open.

"Scarlet!" He looked at me through his visual band, surprised. "I was about to go find you. I need to talk to you about something." He ushered me inside.

"I know, Frappe told me," I choked. "My aura's extraordinary resilience while still three-thousand miles from the Crystal isn't normal."

"And, neither is this climate. There must be a correlation." Cease sat at his desk and pointed to the map on his computer screen. "The NISF has determined that the heatwaves are originating from hundreds of specific points in the Septentrion Sea. I had the computer plug them all in... Scarlet, they match the coordinates of the blockade ships."

Pieces fell into place. Oh, Tincture. "It isn't just heat they're emitting; it's pure spectrum. Sir, I think the System is trying to weave the magical web more strongly across Ichthyosis."

He turned, chair squeaking. "So, the heat is a side-effect of the web's fortified extension?"

No. The terrible truth was painfully clear, now. "Spectral emission is possible without so *much* heat."

He pulled off his band. "What are you saying, Scarlet?"

"It's deliberate." I swallowed. "Sir, the System is preparing Ichthyosis for Conflagrian occupation."

SCARLET JULY

May seventh.

A report from the Trilateral Committee arrived early this morning with bad news. As a result of the not-so-natural-disaster, the TC claimed the alliance's resources were now too depleted to sustain a full-scale war until July. Admiral Sive therefore requested we move up our infiltration date from July twenty-fifth to May twenty-fifth. Instead of two months, we now had barely more than two weeks.

Today, our goal was to take care of the System blockade. Our fleet was never readier for battle, and not because we had great numbers or abundant equipment. In fact, the opposite was true, as the rescue operation occupied most of our vitreous silicas and claimed the lives of seven divers. We were ready because the disaster was the best cohesion training we could've asked for. By now, the Nurians, new graduates and Ichthyothian veterans had all finally learned to trust one another, completely.

The battle started off alright. We seemed to pose a decent threat to the Water Forces. I felt pretty optimistic about our odds... until the System managed to gather enough magic to unleash their infamous Underwater Fire. With the water temperature already abnormally high, the fire spread more rapidly than ever before, as though the sea itself were composed of oil.

Today, I surface-rode. Over and over, I fumbled with my sidearm, feeling frustrated and handicapped. Our weapons were simply no match for UF. The only thing that was comparable was… well, more UF.

Wait, hold the torch. Why *not* fight fire with fire? What was the difference between the System's UF and the waterproof version of my eye-fire? Fair Gabardine was the original UF engineer, after all—it was obvious where she got the idea. She saw me defend myself on July twenty-fifth of the eighty-seventh age. She saw me set water ablaze.

"Link!" I called to the pilot of the crystalline on which I was currently perched. "Take me to the frontline. Stay near the surface. Don't let any of our comrades follow. In fact, order everyone to stay back at least three-hundred yards. We have to go in alone."

My orders must've sounded like suicide, but Arrhyth trusted me.

"Ma'am, yes, ma'am," he said, without hesitation.

When we arrived, dozens of dragon ships swarmed. I threw off my helmet and spun, flame-throwing in all directions, burning every System ship within a two-hundred-yard radius.

Snapping my helmet back on, Arrhyth and I descended.

"You produced UF?" he squeaked. "I didn't know you could do that."

"Neither did I." Not like *that*, anyway. "Now, we better hightail out of here. Come on!"

Arrhyth accelerated, but several ships still managed to converge upon us like flees to dragon dung. I grew a little dizzy as Arrhyth maneuvered evasively. Surface-riding with him was almost as bad as with Nurtic Leavesleft.

One pursuer was particularly persistent. Within fifteen or so minutes, Arrhyth managed to shake off everyone but him. One by one, the determined dragon ship nicked

Arrhyth's dorsal fin, left wing and tail. I held onto the gyrating crystalline for dear life. Finally, Arrhyth managed to take out the enemy's engine. A millisecond before exploding, I saw the orange-clad pilot eject. He plummeted toward the seafloor, pearly bubbles trailing behind him like a shooting star.

"Link, let's go back to the frontline," I ordered. "Alone."

"But, July, we just got away," he croaked, voice tense. "You want to do another UF raid or what?"

"No. I have a different idea. You won't have to stay with me, this time. Just drop me off and clear out." There was no time to explain. My stomach knotted.

"Ma'am, yes, ma'am."

THUD!

"Link, you've got a System surface-rider on your hull!" Dither's voice called from somewhere.

At that moment, I felt something seize my ankle. Before I knew it, I was being forcibly dragged to the shuttle's belly. It didn't take a military genius to figure my attacker was a hand mage. His tinted helmet reflected my own image, warped and small. Torn seat-straps dangled from his waist. This was no surface-rider; this was the ejected pilot. He survived.

Thankfully, his utility belt was missing. It must've ripped off during the ejection. But, that didn't mean I was safe. Up close and personal, his hands were the only weapons he'd need. I aimed my gun at his head, but he knocked it out of my grasp with one swift, powerful punch. It disappeared into the current. Then, he socked me hard in the stomach, my arrhythmic suit doing little to absorb his magical blow. I doubled over and vomited in my helmet. Lunging forward, he clutched my neck. But, before he could snap it in two, the sea disappeared from around us. I blinked repeatedly but couldn't see anymore. The air felt hot and humid, against my skin. And, there was pain, terrible pain, searing across my collarbone and stomach.

"Hurry!" I screamed. Why? Hurry what? What was going on? Where was I? Why was I yelling? Why did everything hurt?

The agony abruptly ceased and the dusty air was replaced, once again, by the oddly-lukewarm Septentrion Sea. My vision cleared. The System soldier backed away from me, trembling all over. Then, he boosted off the crystalline and swam away. I didn't try to stop him.

"We reached the central line, Second," Arrhyth's voice sounded. "I'm dropping you off."

CEASE LECHATELIERITE

What the hell was Scarlet doing? Was she suicidal?

I asked Link to take me in, after her. "Now!" I barked.

"But, sir, she said she wanted to go alone," he piped. "I just dropped her off."

"I don't care! I gave you an order, soldier!"

"Y-yes, Commander."

Rocketing to the frontline, I poked my head above water. There she was, treading in the thick of the chaos with her helmet off. To make matters even worse, her weapon was missing.

"Link, protective gyrate!" I ordered.

Eyes closed, Scarlet breathed with an open mouth, tiny frame bobbing. She looked like she was struggling just to stay conscious.

I flipped open my visor and called out to her, "Helmet on, now! We're coming to get you!" Then, to Link, I growled, "Link, let's move in!"

Except... we couldn't. We suddenly had no control over our trajectory. Because, at that moment, all air and water within a thousand-foot radius of Scarlet began to course around her with shocking momentum. Her hair lifted off her shoulders, billowing in the wind. What the hell? Scarlet couldn't control the weather. The vortex intensified until the current literally ripped me off of Link's hull. Colors flashed across the night sky. Call me crazy, but the sight of so much spectrum sizzling in the atmosphere reminded me a lot of last July's diffusion.

Oh.

Perhaps Scarlet was producing some sort of… magical vacuum? Like a human spectrometer, she indiscriminately drew in all nearby auras, tearing into the fabric of the spectral web itself, inducing a widespread diffusive state. I watched as her locks compacted everyone's spectrum into an enormous ball of fire.

She held it high above our heads.

SCARLET JULY

Shrieks and cries filled the inky sky. In my mind's eye, I could see and feel the splintering wavelengths of every mage in the vicinity. Their sources diffused but their mental enslavement remained—not quite what I was shooting for when I generated the vacuum. My hair held the molten sphere high above our heads. I'd initially intended on crushing it like the Core Crystal, but by now, I'd grown too weak to do it: like a sun with its own gravity, the fireball had begun to absorb my magic, too. Electric jolts zipped down my locks and into my scalp, as if urging me to let go. But, I couldn't drop it; what if it spurned a deadly shockwave upon contact with the water? My hair bent under its growing weight; it came dangerously near to the surface. I caught sight of Cease in the tide, visor up, struggling to swim to me, arms flailing, mouth shouting. I never even had the chance to make things right between us and now we were both going to die. My stupidity was literally about to wipe out our entire fleet.

At last, Cease made it to the eye of the whirlpool, beside me. But, he wasn't looking at me, anymore. Instead, he stared up at the orb, its reflection dancing across his visual band. Was he in shock?

"Sir," I whispered, "I'm s-so sorry."

At that moment, he raised his hands.

"No!" I cried, futilely attempting to jerk the thing away from him. I didn't need to spend my last seconds watching Cease roast. We needed to go at the same time, or me before him. He drew closer still, within my arms' reach. "Stay back!" I screeched. "Don't touch it!" I grabbed his shoulders, fighting hard to hold him in place. What on Tincture's island got into him? Yes, he was about to die anyway, but what was the point of hastening it, *right in front of me?*

"Scarlet, stand down," he instructed, tone eerily calm.

"No! YOU stand the hell down!"

"Let me do this, Scarlet. That's an order."

"Do what, kill yourself!?" I cried, hysterically.

The visual band slipped to the end of his nose and, for a moment, he regarded me with his own two beautiful silver eyes. The eyes that gripped my heart with ferocity, no matter what transpired between us.

"Yes, if that's what it takes," he said, monotonously, "to save you."

And, with that, he tore himself from my grasp and lunged for the flaming ball of death.

"NO!"

As his hands plunged into its lava surface, his gloves instantly burned off. And, he screamed the worst scream I ever heard from a human. He sounded like a scabrous at the slaughterhouse. The noise terrified me to the root of my being. I knew Cease could literally undergo an operation sans anesthetics without making a peep. So, to hear this same man call out like that—it was too much to bear.

The sphere of fire wasn't heavy, anymore. In fact, it wrenched itself from my hair and ascended higher and higher into the smoky sky, spinning like crazy. Cease dangled from it, nothing but a little, white blur. And, the fireball began to rip apart, showering the sea with color. The water temperature rose and rose until I felt like a lobster, boiling alive. At last, light engulfed my sight as a loud bang resounded.

The atmosphere darkened and I saw Cease's tiny figure drop through the air. I dove and caught him in my arms like a spin-toss flyer. I snapped his visor down, secured his limp frame on my back with deadline and swam to the nearest crystalline as quickly as possible.

"Maine, open up, I have the Commander!"

My aura was gone and I didn't know how long it'd take to recrystallize. Likewise magicless, the Water Forces had no means to sustain the siege or continue their spectral heating endeavor. The blockade was over. The terraforming was stopped in its tracks. The System wouldn't establish New Conflagria, quite yet. We had a clear shot to go ahead and traverse the sea for the next Fire Pit infiltration. We achieved everything we set out for, today. Whatever Cease did to the sphere of fire, it worked. Tincture only knew how.

But, as I climbed aboard Dither's crystalline, Cease's flaccid form tied to me, the victory tasted sour in my mouth.

SCARLET JULY

The hospital wing was a madhouse, due to the influx of injured civilians, but Nurse Raef managed to get Cease a room with just one other (also unconscious) roommate. Being the Leader of the Ichthyothian Resistance had its perks, I supposed. He lay before me now, incapacitated in a white bed, feet elevated, hands wrapped in gauze, an array of IVs and prongs protruding from his pale arms and chest, a feeding tube up his pinched nose and a cold pack strapped to his sweaty head. His diagnoses?

"Spectral overdose, hyperthermia and a whole lot of third-degree burns," Dr. Calibre said. "He was exposed to about four times the lethal dosage of spectrum for a non-magical being. He should've died the moment his flesh grazed the fireball. The fact he's still alive is a miracle. But, if he doesn't wake from his coma in a week…"

He didn't need to finish his sentence. I swallowed and nodded. And, with that, the doctor left me alone in the dimly-lit room with the flaccid form of my Commander. I stood and stared at his pointy profile. Normally, he was a very light, fitful sleeper. He looked deceptively peaceful as he lay perfectly still on what could become his deathbed.

How did he survive? How did he destroy the orb? I wished he would wake up so we could talk about it. The two of us could tackle any crazy puzzle when we put our heads together. We were a great team. The logical and the creative. The north and the south. The fire and the ice. If I lost him, I'd lose a part of myself.

I reached out and touched his face, tracing the razor-sharp edges of his jaw and cheekbones. His skin, already the color of death, was surprisingly soft. Scars and premature wrinkles were but mere ripples in a sea of white ivory. It wasn't the rough, ragged flesh of a man who spent his entire life on the frontlines; it was the tender skin of a boy barely beyond adolescence.

"Please don't die," I whispered.

I blinked back tears. Oh, Tincture. I couldn't cry. Not here, not now. The last thing this fleet needed was a dead Commander *and* an arrested Second. In fact, just staying in Cease's room for this long was probably a bad idea. Sticking around to hear his prognosis was understandable. Checking on him from time-to-time thereafter was also reasonable. But, standing solo by his bedside for an extended period, sulking and fretting? Definitely suspicious.

As if on cue, the door behind me creaked open.

"Ma'am? What're you still doing here?" It was Raef. Great.

"Um, I, uh, I was just…" The hobnail egg in my throat swelled as the stress of being caught red-handed piled atop my sorrow over Cease. This was it. I was going to break down in front of a witness. My emotions were about to bubble over before a third party. I gulped and blinked, frantically fighting to keep it all in. But, then—

"You're not trying to *heal* him, are you?"

Taken aback, surprise abruptly overcame my irrational desire to sob into Raef's scrubs. "W-what?" I blurted.

"Don't play stupid, ma'am, it's unrealistic!" she reeled. "I know how he recovered so quickly in January and February; you used your freakish sorcery to tamper with his metabolism!"

Now, it was my turn to get angry. "So, what if I did?" I shot. "Without me, he wouldn't have recovered in time for the graduates' arrival. What's wrong with that?"

"It's downright unnatural; that's what's wrong with it! Magic is the reason he's here in the first place!"

Wait, what exactly was *unnatural* about spectrum? I was pretty sure colored lifelines naturally occurred on this earth. I was reasonably certain I was a human being and not some space alien nor genetically-engineered monster nor factory-produced robot. I swore I could feel steam issue from my ears. But, right now, I didn't have the energy to engage Raef in a debate over her racially-charged statements and assumptions. Not when my nerves were already shot to hell over worrying about Cease's wellbeing.

"Mrs. Raef, I'm not trying to heal him. I can't; I lost my aura in the battle and I don't know when it'll come back."

She narrowed her eyes. "Well, then, what *are* you up to?"

I was silent. Tincture, why did I correct her? Her theory was far safer than the truth.

"Ma'am, he's under surveillance by medical professionals so, I assure you, your vigil is completely unnecessary."

This was my chance. "Yes, you're right; how silly of me." I turned toward the door. "In that case, I best be off—"

"Hold on, you weren't *visiting*, were you?"

Was that a barely-suppressed smile on her face? I saw nothing funny about the possibility of court-martial.

"N-no, of course not."

There was a pause.

"Oh. Well, I think it'd be nice if people did that sort of thing, around here," she said, to my great shock. Then again, she was Nurian. "No one ever bothers to visit *him*." She jerked her thumb at the curtain on the right side of the room.

I walked over, drew the drapes and looked down at the comatose form of Tose Acci, entangled in wires and tubes. There were so many things attached to his body—a feeding tube, respirator, pacemaker and catheter, to name a few—I almost didn't recognize him. He'd been hospitalized since before Cease and I arrived home from our trek across sector seven. I remembered him from my service, last age. What a loyal and sharp soldier he was. Not to mention, how uncharacteristically charismatic he was for a base-raised diver, able to hold pleasant, non-work-related conversations. He was one of Nurtic's piloting protégés, like Arrhyth. His exceptional flying skills made him an invaluable asset to the fleet. But, now, apparently, he was totally forgotten.

"Tose Acci was rushed here immediately following a battle in mid-January," Raef recounted. "His body was shutting down; half his organs were failing. We placed him on life-support, but everyone really expected him to die that day. Right before he fell into his coma, he looked up at me and said Nurtic Leavesleft's name, asking if we could bring him in. Of course, Leavesleft had been dead for over a week by then, and Illia Frappe wasn't shy to remind him of that, to his face. His last words before going under were, 'I really messed up, didn't I? But, Nurtic would be proud of me, anyway.' And, then, he closed his eyes."

I already was in a terrible mood, and Tose's tragic story didn't exactly help. I made a mental note to come back to the hospital as soon as my aura crystallized to give him a good dose of healing spectrum. I stole one last look at Cease and left.

If Cease didn't stir in seven days, he'd be lucky to end up like Tose.

SCARLET JULY

Minutes slipped into hours and hours slipped into days—it was all a blur to me. Just as the NISF predicted, Ichthyosis was rapidly refreezing, now that the blockade and its spectral emissions were gone. The tide receded, revealing horrific remains. Morning dew became frost glazing mountains of rubble and corpses. Tropical storms turned to blizzards that buried the dead and capped the damaged skyscrapers. For the first time in my life, I was actually relieved to see snow.

My men and I were mobilized in an ongoing mission unlike anything our military had seen before: rebuilding Ichthyosis and northern Nuria from ruin. Day and night, we worked on recovering bodies, clearing debris from the streets, helping displaced civilians relocate from our property, and so forth. And, as time passed, my aura slowly recrystallized.

Preoccupied all week with the op, I forced myself to abstain from visiting Cease. It was torture. I was worried sick, every minute. I mean, *sick*—I lost my appetite, suffered severe insomnia and cried nightly.

It was now the evening of the seventh day and I couldn't take it, anymore. I marched to Cease's bedside, yanked his curtains back and hissed in his ear, "Know what today is, sir? May fourteenth. Time's up!"

"He can't hear you, ma'am," Raef's exhausted voice sounded from the other side of the room, where she was busy swapping out one of Tose's IV pouches. "It's dinnertime; please, go be with your comrades. Your conscious comrades."

I ignored her. On the verge of hysterics, I shook Cease's shoulder. "I'm in charge of this fleet, now, sir," my voice came out much too high, "and that means you have to obey me. Wake up, now! That's an order!"

"Alright, alright, just give me a moment," he murmured, faintly.

Raef dropped Tose's bag on the floor. Cease's lids cracked open, revealing two diamond slits. The nurse and I stared in wordless shock as he struggled to pull himself upright, sweaty hair plopping onto his pale forehead.

"It's hot in here," he croaked.

"It only feels that way to you because your temperature's quickly dropping back to normal, sir." Raef peered at one of the many glowing monitors lining the wall.

"The temperature outside has also returned to normal," I told him with a grin I couldn't suppress. What I really wanted to do was throw my arms around him while shouting, 'THANK TINCTURE YOU'RE OKAY; I'M SO FREAKING HAPPY!' but, a witness stood right beside us.

He blinked, rapidly. "What did you say the date was?"

"May fourteenth."

He swore. "I've been here for a week?"

"Yes, sir."

He got to his feet, ripping prongs and needles from his chest and arms.

"We've got less than a fortnight until the infiltration." His voice was crisp and businesslike. "Come on, Scarlet; we've got work to do."

"Oh, no, you don't!" Raef stepped in front of him. "You're not going anywhere until Dr. Calibre discharges you!"

"Fine," he snapped, clearly uninterested in wasting even a single second on argument. "Scarlet, go get my laptop."

"Yes, sir!"

* * *

"This infiltration will be quite a bit different than the last," Cease said. "No cover identities—the System knows our faces, now. So, we'll have to stay cloaked until the deed is done." Since the ninety-third age, all vitreous silicas were shielded with diffusion technology, rendering them undetectable by spectrometer. But, my aura would still be needed to omit us from plain sight. "I think Arrhyth Link should be our pilot, since our better options obviously aren't available, anymore."

Our better options. Meaning Nurtic Leavesleft or Tose Acci.

"Hmm," I sighed, "Link is talented, sir, but… is he good enough for a mission as high-stakes as this?"

"What choice do we have? And, if you say Seven, my answer is, like hell would I ever trust him with a single flake of snow—"

"Commander, is that you?" a voice sounded from the other side of the room. A hand bearing two IV needles pushed the drapes back with a squeak. "I thought you went MIA on the seventh, sir." He didn't say of which month. "What a relief it is to see you. Does that mean Nurtic made it, too?" He stared down at his body. "Wow, I can't believe *I'm* alive! I could've sworn I was dead." His eyes fell on me. "*Scarlet?* What're *you* doing here?"

It was Tose Acci. Awake. Moving. Talking. I guessed the spectral healing really worked out for him.

Raef ogled. "Two in one day; it's a medical miracle! I must alert Dr. Calibre." And, she scrampered off.

"What's the date?" Tose asked with alarm, sounding a lot like Cease.

"May fourteenth," I answered, again.

His jaw literally dropped. "That means I've been dead—unconscious—for— for—four—"

"For four months, yes."

For a moment, he looked like he might pass out, again. Then, he thought the better of it.

"I have so many questions," he breathed. "Sir, ma'am, what's become of Ichthyosis since January?"

Cease and I exchanged bewildered glances.

"I wouldn't know where to begin," I chuckled.

"I do." Cease turned to Tose. "The Trilateral Committee has given us an ultimatum to destroy the Crystal by the end of May. We're infiltrating Conflagria in eleven days."

"Eleven days!" He sat bolt upright, face bright and alert. "What can I do to help? I can't believe I've done *nothing* for a third of an age!" He sounded so appalled at himself. So eager to pitch in. So enthusiastic to do his duty. He actually stood up then, yanking out prongs and wires without a flinch. "I feel fine. Great, actually. No stiffness nor soreness. Full of energy. Rehab and retraining will be a breeze. How may I be of service, sir?"

I smiled at Cease. "What do you think, Commander?"

With uncharacteristic joy in his eyes, Cease looked at Tose's erect frame, then at me. "Of course, we'll have to see how retraining goes, but I think we just might have our pilot, Scarlet."

CEASE LECHATELIERITE

Scarlet and I stood at the edge of the stone cliff, in the depths of the Fire Pit.

"Do it!" I shouted over the crackling flames. "Do it, now!"

"S-sir, I c-can't!" she sputtered. She wheeled around to face me, trembling from head to toe.

"Why not?" I demanded.

"Because it's *you*," she squeaked, voice high, cheeks crimson. "You're the Crystal. I can't destroy you!"

"No," I shook my head, "Scarlet, I'm not the Crystal." I inhaled the hot, smoky, spectral air. "I'm the Crystal's end."

And, that's when I woke up, tangled in my sheets and drenched in cold sweat. I breathed out. I knew that what I saw moments ago wasn't a vision; it lacked the sharpness and realism of my prior ones. It was only a dream. Random. Meaningless. Yet, it haunted me, just the same.

The Crystal's end. I thought of the spectral orb and what my touch did to it. I fell back onto my pillow, head throbbing, thoughts churning like molten lava.

CEASE LECHATELIERITE

On the eve of the infiltration, May twenty-fourth, Scarlet, Acci and I met in my quarters to review our plan, yet again. After going over all the piloting logistics, I dismissed Acci.

"Departure at seven-thirty sharp," I reminded him. "Now, go get some rest."

"Sir, yes, sir!" He saluted and headed for the barracks.

Scarlet and I spent an additional hour going over everything else. Not that Scarlet really needed to. Nor did I, by now. Everything had long since been burned in my brain. I was just being paranoid and obsessive. As usual.

At last, I stood and stretched. "Ready to be dismissed?" I asked Scarlet with a yawn. What a strange thing to say to a subordinate. Scarlet was the only one I'd ever deliver orders to like a suggestion. When she and I were alone, our professionalism tended to falter. To say the least.

She shrugged. "Guess so."

I nodded. "We're ready for tomorrow."

She didn't answer.

"At least, this plan doesn't require learning any foreign languages," I chuckled.

Whenever I smiled or laughed, Scarlet's whole face instantly illuminated. She always acted stoic enough around everybody else but, with me, her mask slipped and she became her real self. Animated. Emotive. Full of life. And, religiously attuned to my moods. The way I acted directly and immediately impacted her own temperament. It was like, she couldn't dare to be okay unless she knew I was, too. I should've been bothered by this—the Childhood Program taught me that such behavior was not only unprofessional but downright dangerous—but, I usually found myself enjoying how much Scarlet cared.

I guessed I wasn't dead to her, after all.

"I don't remember a single word of Conflagrian you taught me," I added, cheerily.

The corners of Scarlet's lips twitched. "Not even how to say 'fire'?"

I shook my head.

"*Pyro.* And, *pyro sphaira* is 'sphere of fire.'"

"Sphere of fire," I echoed. "That sounds very…" I paused to recall the unfamiliar word, "poetic. Where does it come from?" Unlike us base-raised, Scarlet was liable to spout pop-culture references, though not to the same extreme as the Nurians.

"I made it up. That's what I call the flaming mass of spectrum you inexplicably diffused, earlier this month."

I made a face. Handling the orb was the worst pain I ever experienced; I found myself longing for death just so the agony would cease…

"What made you do it?" Scarlet's voice pierced my thoughts. "How did you know you could destroy it, like that?"

"I didn't," I answered, honestly. "Not consciously, anyway. I just felt, I don't know, *compelled* to touch it." As the words left my lips, I realized how stupid I sounded. I'd never dare to say something so illogical in front of anyone but Scarlet, who typically took my hunches and feelings seriously. "It seemed like the right thing to do. I can't explain it. I don't understand it myself."

"You should've died."

"That nearly happened," I pointed out. "And, I didn't diffuse all of it, anyway. I'm not that good. Just got half."

She shook her head. "No, you've got it backwards. I only managed to *extract* half of everyone's auras, which you destroyed in entirety."

Wrong. "Nope, you tore out everything. *You* are that good. But, I wasn't strong enough to diffuse all of it. It was a fifty-fifty chance, whether I'd knock out their sources or the mind-control. I didn't know how to choose."

"They were cursing me like I killed their mothers," she squeaked. "My old Reds wouldn't treat me that way, during the brief window they were free of the mind-control."

"Really? If *I* suddenly started beating the crap out of you, you wouldn't get a little pissed at *me?*"

She blinked.

"You pulled out everyone's auras—*all* of everyone's auras—and compacted them into the sphere," I insisted, "but, I only had the strength to destroy part of it." Well, *temporarily* destroy, anyway: as long as the Core Crystal existed, mages would always, eventually recover their full auras, regardless of the severity of the sustained spectral injury. Ending the Crystal was the only way to strip mages of their auras for good. What Scarlet and I collectively accomplished in the *pyro sphaira* battle was mere, momentary disarmament.

"How do you know?"

I gnawed the inside of my cheek. "I could sort of... see their spectrum, in my mind. Well, it was more like a feeling, really. I could *feel* all the threads, in a way. I could tell there were two kinds of magic in each aura, but I couldn't discern which sustained the dominion of the System and which sustained their sources. It's like, in each hand, I held a different facet of every man's wavelength. I didn't have the capacity to destroy both, so I randomly chose; I curled my fingers around one and my mind extinguished it. That's when I passed out. Now, I know I messed up. But, if I could do it again... Scarlet, I can recognize the frequencies, now. I know the difference. I know what to look for."

"You're never going to do it again," she said, flatly.

There was a tense pause.

Should I say it? "Unless I fall into the Fire Pit."

"No!" She leapt to her feet, hair flying. "Don't even *say* such a stupid thing!"

"I'd know how to pick, this time. I could destroy the mind-control without eradicating the entire web. Conflagria would get to keep its magic *and* be free. It's everything your people need."

"No, no, NO!" Scarlet screamed so loudly, I wondered if the entire hall could hear. Sheesh, and she said *I* was the throat mage. "We don't even know how you diffused those frequencies in the first place—no one but the Multi-Source Enchant should've been able to! What happened is probably a non-repeatable freak accident! You'd just wind up killing yourself for nothing! Besides, the new Core Crystal is probably like a gazillion times larger than the sphere by now; there's no guarantee you'd be strong enough to take it on!"

I put up my hands. "Scarlet, I was just thinking aloud; I'm not serious."

"Damn right, you aren't!" she hollered.

"Hey," I snapped, "watch your tone when addressing me!"

She was breathless and ruby-faced, hair squirming like snakes. Riled up like this, she was all the more attractive to me.

I stood, towering over her. "You've given me so many reasons to demote you lately, you know," I said in a low tone, giving her a look that'd probably freeze her insides over.

"Then, why don't you do it?" She stepped forward, apparently undaunted. She was so close to me, now. I could feel her body heat.

"Hell, because you're just too good at your job! Who else would cope with me as much as you do?"

"*Cope* with you?" Scarlet was incredulous. "Everyone here loves you, Cease. You have our full trust and respect. We'd follow you into the Septentrion Sea without diving suits. We'd take a bullet for you, without hesitation. I know I would."

That wasn't what I meant and she knew it.

"Scarlet, who else in this fleet would have the wit to discern when I'm wrong, the courage to challenge my decisions and the persuasiveness to change my mind about things I've been taught since birth?" Moreover, who else could wreck my lifelong stoic-streak so all I could think about right now was how sexy she was, all worked up?

"Well, who else in this fleet would listen so attentively to every whacky suggestion made by a green subordinate like me?" she countered. "Anyone else would dismiss my unconventional ideas and stick me at the bottom of the totem-pole. But, you have patience. You value out-of-box thinking. You listen."

What's a totem-pole? "I didn't always listen, you know. I didn't listen to Inexor, back when he first suggested the possibility of the Underwater Fire. I thought he was being ridiculous. I thought I knew better."

"Cease," her voice was heavy, "you're not still on about that battle, are you? That was so long ago. So much has happened since then. You learned from your mistake. You listen, nowadays. You hear us out. You trust the instincts and intuitions of your soldiers."

"Some more than others." I didn't blink. "I trust you."

Her embarrassed gaze dropped to the floor as she sat down on my bed.

"We still haven't figured out why you could diffuse the sphere of fire," she murmured, changing the subject.

"We will." I took a deep breath. "But, I think, deep down, we both already know."

She froze.

"If your flesh came in contact with the Crystal, it would detonate, right?" I pressed on. "I touched the sphere with my hands," I swallowed, "and it makes sense my magic would have similar properties to yours since you're where my aura came from."

Her eyes grew wide at the fact I'd just voluntarily brought up the subject of my aura. The subject I'd previously insisted we never broach again.

"By this time tomorrow, the web will have diffused for good." I cleared my throat. "But, Scarlet, I just wanted to let you know," I hesitated, "I'm… glad I got to be a mage, if only for a little while. I'm incredibly lucky to have shared photons with the Multi-Source Enchant. With you."

At this, her lips parted.

"And, I'm sorry for getting upset whenever you tried to talk about this before," I blazed on. "All along, I should've been grateful for the gift—the honor—of twining to your frequency. So, this may be a little late but," I solemnly met her eye, "thank you, Scarlet."

A long, stunned silence ensued.

"You're welcome, Cease," she finally breathed.

Then, cheeks burning crimson, she looked away. A moment later, she scooted back, folded her legs and rested her face on her knees. She looked so small, curled up like that. Smaller than usual, anyway. I felt the irrational urge to scoop up her tiny, balled figure in my arms, like that'd shield her from all the craziness of this war and the impending Crystal's end.

Right. *Me* protect *her*. The Multi-Source Enchant—the strongest, bravest warrior I ever had the privilege of serving alongside—was the last person to need anyone's guard.

It took me a moment to realize she'd fallen asleep. She sat so still, the only indication I had was the sound of her deep, even breathing. I perched beside her and touched her warm, delicate shoulder.

"Scarlet," I said, quietly. "It's nearly midnight. You need to go to bed."

She sprang up, as though something poisonous slithered in my sheets.

"So do you."

"Don't tell me what to do."

"You need rest as much as anyone else!"

Forget rest, I was suddenly and inexplicably rather rest-*less*. I didn't know how much self-control I had left. And, I knew, if I made a move on her, she'd give in for about ten minutes or so, hungrily and passionately, before suddenly freaking out and running away, acting as though she never actively participated in the first place. I didn't want that painful pattern to repeat itself tonight. So, I needed her to scoot. Now.

"Leave!"

She went to my desk and started gathering our notes. "I'm leaving."

"Not fast enough."

"Hey, where are *you* going?" she chirped.

My hand was on the doorknob. "I never said *I'm* turning in, yet. I'm taking a walk."

Her red brows rose. "Now?"

"Why not?"

She smiled, and the beauty of it stabbed me in the chest. "Go to bed, Commander," she sang, teasingly. So, she thought we were still bantering.

"I will."

She walked right up to me, and I thought I might explode. "Sleep! Now!" Laughing, she put her hands on my chest and tried to push me in the direction of my bed.

That was it. She took things a step too far. I couldn't stand the feeling of her hands on my body, not now. Not when all I wanted to do was pull her in and let loose. Not when I knew how eagerly she'd reciprocate, at least in the beginning. I shoved her away, a little too hard. She wasn't expecting it; she staggered.

"You're dismissed!" I barked. "Move!"

She scampered out into the hall without so much as a 'yes, sir.' A second later, I heard her door snap shut.

I headed to the balconies. I needed to cool off.

CEASE LECHATELIERITE

Usually, the thick, pasty clouds were impervious. But, tonight, there was a small break in the haze, like a rip in a sheet of silvery fabric, barely wide enough for a sliver of the moon and a couple stars to peep through. I stood on the icy balcony, hands clasped behind my back, thawing in the subzero, late-May wind. The fate of three sovereign nations would be sealed within a mere thirty-six hours and all I could think about was Scarlet.

"The moons look orangey-red, back home," came a small voice. "Alpha is also visible there, as we're just above the equator."

A delicate figure crept into my peripheral vision. Omega's cobalt-blue light danced across her wiry hair and gave her eyes an aquamarine tint. She clutched her robe overtop her uniform—a feeble shield from the bitter, spring night.

"The dust also masks the stars and makes everything look muddy." She gazed dreamily at the dazzling horizon.

"Go inside," I ordered, stiffly. "Get some rest. We've got a big day ahead of us."

"Sir... is tomorrow really the right time?" she croaked.

At this, I snatched off my visual band and glowered at her. I needed her on her A-game, physically *and* mentally. I couldn't tolerate doubt. Not now.

Not if it was unfounded.

"Why wouldn't it be?" I shot.

She trembled. "I don't know... s-something just doesn't... feel right. I'm scared."

Scared. Now. "Of what?"

"I'm, um, not exactly sure."

I couldn't believe this. She was getting cold feet, mere hours from dispatch. She stared at me with pleading eyes, wringing her hands and quite literally shaking in her boots. She looked like a Childhood Program trainee about to take her first dive, not a seasoned veteran heading into the most important op in Ichthyothian military history.

I was seeing red.

"Snap out of it, Scarlet!"

"Sir—"

I raised my voice: "If you don't have a real, rational reason we shouldn't go tomorrow, we're going tomorrow, and I expect my Second-in-Command to do her damn job!"

"I-I'm sorry, I just—"

"We're destroying the Crystal. Got it? Failure isn't an option; it's *never* an option in my fleet!"

"I know, but—"

"This is the only thing that matters to me, understood? I don't care what it costs!" I yelled, though I knew I didn't believe that for a second. I'd care a whole lot if the Crystal's end cost Scarlet her life. "Go inside!"

Angry at both of us, I stalked to the other side of the balcony. Scarlet's emotional insecurity was always her greatest flaw. I stared off into the distance, watching the tide mercilessly crash into the shore. Several minutes passed.

From behind me, I heard a sniffle. What the hell was she still doing here?

"Why are you out here, sir?" she beat me to the punch.

Well, that was one question I couldn't answer truthfully. You see, Scarlet, I came out here to get away from you, not because I actually didn't want to be around you, but because

I couldn't bear to play it cool any longer, pretending I didn't feel like I was holding onto an electric fence.

Damn, this whole mess pissed me off so bad.

"I'm not tired," was all I said.

"Yes, you are." She walked up to me and gently stroked the back of my hand, which was gripping the rail so tightly, my veins protruded like wires. "You're so tense, all the time." She nimbly slid into the narrow gap between my body and the rail, winding her arms around my neck. I could smell her wood-smoke scent, even in the cold wind. "So agitated," she leaned her head against my collarbone, "like you're about to burst."

Confusion, anguish and desire welled in my chest, beneath Scarlet's cheek. She'd made it abundantly clear, time and time again, that she believed we'd never work. What changed, today? Our situation wasn't any different, was it? Why was she throwing herself at me? This was unusually aggressive of her. She never initiated anything physical between us before; that was always me. Was she just desperate for comfort, scared of tomorrow's mission? Or, was there more to it?

I peered down at her. "Scarlet, what are you d—"

Stealing my trick, her warm lips cut me off. Abandoning reason, I gave in, reciprocating hungrily, fiercely, for what felt like eras. Still kissing, her fingers crept beneath my shirt, tracing my abs and pecs. I followed her lead, loosening her swathe and grasping her slender, bare waist, beneath her robe and uniform. But, when her hand slid down to my belt buckle, tugging furiously, something in me snapped. Suddenly submerged in a fiery sea of enraged bewilderment, I withdrew sharply, backing several paces away.

"What the hell, Scarlet?" I erupted.

"S-sir!" she squeaked, clearly startled to the core.

"Explain to me what's going on, *right now*, before I lose my effing mind!"

"I'm s-so sorry!" Her eyes rapidly watered. "I didn't mean to overstep o-or upset you—"

"Is that so?" I shouted. "Please, do enlighten me," I threw my arms up and she visibly flinched, "what exactly *does* it mean when you coldly cast me off all age, then randomly decide one day to unfasten my belt while sticking your damn tongue down my throat? What the hell *am* I supposed to take away from that, hmm?"

"Cease," she whispered, horrified.

"You have some nerve, you know," I brutally plowed on, "to pull something like this without a word of explanation," I gave a dry, raucous chortle, "after stonewalling me every day for three months!"

"I said I'm sorry!" she cried. "I-I thought you were accepting my advances; I wouldn't have escalated things so much if I didn't get the sense you wanted to—"

"Oh, don't you *dare* use that excuse," I snorted, "you hypocrite."

"Cease, if I've been rejecting you," her quivering voice jumped an octave, "it's not because my feelings for you ever changed, but because I couldn't get past our circumstances. You know that. You know that's the only reason I'd dare turn you down. *I* never stopped loving you, not for a second."

It was as though she kicked me in the gut, with those words. Because *I* was the one who'd told her, out-of-the-blue one evening, that I'd had a change of heart—not just a problem with our circumstances, but an actual emotional shutdown. I'd said the most hurtful things imaginable. What I did to her was a hundred times worse than anything she ever did to me. I looked away.

She boldly strode forward and cupped my face in her minuscule hands, forcing me to meet her gaze, once more.

"But, to be honest, Cease, I've decided by now that I don't actually believe any of those awful things you said to me, that night in the locker-room. You said them in anger; you were in shock over the whole Childhood Program thing. I believe you do love me, every bit as much as I love you. And, by now, I've also realized I can't force myself to dismiss our relationship just because it's inconvenient or illegal." She swallowed. "So… if we both feel the same about each other *and* agree to simply screw our circumstances, then there's nothing standing in our way, anymore." She scrunched her lids, rivers streaming down her ruby face. "Let's go for it, Cease. Let's quit wasting the little time we have left."

At once, all my rage evaporated like a single snowflake under the powerful Conflagrian sun. Though, I didn't quite agree with her conclusions. Firstly, I didn't think I truly loved her, not like a civilian-raised man could anyway, because I was in pain and love was supposed to feel good. But, at the same time, I knew deep down that, no matter what, that pain was here to stay, because something in me changed forever, since she came along. I was desperately attached to her, helpless to fight against it. She haunted my mind more than the war.

Secondly, I disagreed with the idea of flippantly 'screwing our circumstances,' merely living for today and enjoying the scant 'time we had left' before she went home. I couldn't do that, not when there were clear ways to work *with* our circumstances. Yes, 'inconvenient and illegal' was putting it lightly. But, truthfully, since I was being discharged at some point anyway, what did I have to lose by leaving Ichthyosis for good, after my imprisonment? Joining Scarlet in the Red Revolution would even give me a new war to fight. I'd be a soldier, again. The more I thought about it, the more I liked the idea. Why be a lonely civilian here when I could be a warrior alongside the woman I cared about, somewhere else?

In the meantime, I needed us to solidify our relationship. I needed to know, beyond a shadow of a doubt, that we'd have something *real* to come back to, after our long separation. Something that'd justify leaving my country behind, forever. Something that'd justify the permanent anguish I'd suffered since she came along—the emotional hell of attachment.

In sum, I needed to make Scarlet mine. Mine, without question. Last age, our time apart was agonizing largely because I didn't know her whereabouts or if I'd ever see her again. I didn't know where we stood. Where her head was. Where her heart was. Who she was with. What she was doing. My vision of she and Ambrek kissing made my blood boil. I didn't want to have to worry about things like that. I needed reassurance that, despite the miles and ages, she still belonged to me, period.

I knew what had to be done. I put my lips to Scarlet's ear. "Marry me," I whispered, fiercely.

SCARLET JULY

Cease's words struck me like a surge of hot spectrum.

"I-I want to," I sputtered into his neck, "but—"

"But, what?" he snapped.

"But, I, um… I was only suggesting that we… i-ignore our circumstances until I go away—"

"No," he retorted, flatly. "I can't do that. I can't *not* think about the future. And, neither can you. I know you better than that. You won't be able to put it out of your mind for a second. The entire time we're together, you'll be dying inside."

"Yes, you're right," I admitted, extracting myself from his circulation-stunting embrace. "I absolutely hate the idea of only having you for now. But, that's still a hell of a lot better than not having you ever. Because, in reality, those are the only choices we've got. Either we consider the future and come to the obvious conclusion—that we can't do this at all—or, we *ignore* the future and casually enjoy ourselves until I leave."

"No," he repeated, crossly. "I can't just throw down these next few days then give it all up the moment you walk out the door. That isn't fair to either of us. I'm not going to do this at all unless we do it right. Because, the choices you spelled out *aren't* the only ones we've got. We can reconnect during the revolution."

"O-okay," I succumbed helplessly, "I guess we can try."

"No, we're not going to *try*." He folded his arms. "We're going to do it."

I couldn't believe how irrational and pushy Cease was being. Sure, good soldiers remained resolute in the face of terrible odds. But, good soldiers also knew how to analyze the terrain and adjust their plans and expectations accordingly. Cease wouldn't dare leap before looking in battle, so why was he so eager to in his personal life? Couldn't he see that stubborn determination without careful consideration was no way to tackle monumental challenges? That wanting and willing something to happen didn't actually guarantee its fruition? That we couldn't simply strongarm the future to fit our desires?

"That's not how life works," I objected.

"I don't care. You sought me out tonight with a proposition, so I'm telling you my conditions for acceptance. I need more than a 'maybe' from you. I need a definite, '*yes*, we *will* rendezvous during the revolution.'"

Panic bubbled in my gut. "I… I don't know how to promise that."

"Yes, you do." From his pocket, he retrieved his Silver Triangle, his most prized possession. "By taking this," he urged in his most compelling voice. The voice of a throat mage. The voice I was used to instantly answering with, 'yes, sir.'

"What? N-no," I choked, "I can't—"

"Just take it," he cried, "and say, right now, you'll marry me!"

I hesitated while his eyes shot through mine like silver arrows.

"Scarlet?" he pleaded.

Opening my palm, I accepted it. "Yes, sir." Could he hear the twinge of anguish in my voice?

He crushed me in his arms. "Call me Cease already, will you?" he hissed into my hair.

The two of us stood still for several minutes, icy wind pounding our frames.

"So, I was right?" I squeaked. "You do love me, after all?"

"Wait for me, right here," he whispered, nose brushing my ear. "I'm going to get the form. I'll be back in a moment; I just need to look around the Retirement Center."

I pulled away, stricken. "What form?"

He blinked. "For our marriage."

Wait. "What?"

"We could sign it, right now."

"Now?" I gaped, stupidly.

"Why not?"

"I don't know," I started hyperventilating, "maybe, because we'll be apart for Tincture knows how long."

"Exactly. Let's make this a done deal before we have to put three-thousand miles between us for an indefinite period. Let's have something *real* to come back to." His tone surrounded me, captured me, shackled me.

"A long-distance marriage?" He was crazy!

"How's a long-distance agreement-to-get-married any better?"

"There's a word for that: engagement."

"Whatever. A long-distance *engagement*. What kind of foundation is that? And, why would we be readier to commit after a long gap than we are today? Why wait to make this real *someday*, *somewhere* when we can do that right here, right now?"

"Because… active-duty military personnel aren't allowed to get married."

A smile touched the corners of his lips, but I was too freaked-out to enjoy the sight of it. "They aren't allowed to do this, either." He grabbed my head with both hands and kissed me, roughly. "Never stopped us before, has it? Until I leave these shores forever, no one has to know. We can keep it a secret. We've been breaking the Laws of Emotional Protection for some time now, anyway. And, we have a witness—Seven can speak up anytime, giving the courts a reason to extend my sentence. We're already putting everything on the line, as it is. Let's make it worth it. I'd get charged for kissing you, I'd get charged for marrying you, I'd get charged for anything in-between. If we're going to risk it all no matter what, we might as well finish the race." His voice pierced my soul, consuming me, drugging me: "Scarlet, before you go, I want you to be mine—*really* mine. And, I know that's what you want, too. Admit it."

He made so much sense. Why beat around the bush? I myself sought him out tonight, driven by a sense of urgency I couldn't really explain. Wasn't he trying to give me exactly what I truly wanted, deep down? An end to wondering what we were. A conclusion to this seemingly-eternal saga of taking turns chasing one another. A solution to this agonizing, confusing limbo. He was willing to give himself to me completely, right now. His moods oscillated so widely and rapidly, I wasn't sure what to expect tonight, when I went looking for him. A tearful argument? Yelling and pushing and shoving? Anxiety-ridden, reluctant acceptance of my love? A one-night stand? The start to a brief affair? A cold, crisp dismissal?

Certainly, not an immediate elopement.

But, in the end, I knew he was right: I wanted him, not just for now, but forever. More than anything. Then, why was I still so scared?

I closed my wet eyes and nodded.

He stroked my cheek. "Wait, right here," he ordered. "Don't move." He turned on his heel, slid open the door and disappeared down the dark corridors.

I stood, paralyzed, heart pounding and extremities prickling. He returned all too soon with the form. Wordlessly, he slapped it down on the frozen handrail, withdrew a pen from his utility belt and stared hard at me. I was positive I'd pass out, if my heartrate got any faster.

"Ready?" His voice was bland, as though merely asking if I were good to spin-toss.

No. "Yes."

With one swift motion, he sprawled his lengthy signature. Then, he thrust the pen at me. My numb fingers struggled to scribble my name beneath his. At last, he swept up the document, tucking it into his belt. That was it. He was my husband, now. I couldn't believe it. I almost never got what I wanted. Not without it getting quickly ruined, anyway.

His arms encircled me so firmly, I thought I might spontaneously splice in half. His salty scent filled my nostrils as he lifted my tear-soaked face from his chest and planted a kiss on my quivering mouth. His lips weren't cold, as they usually were. I kissed him back with urgency, feeling his acherontic aura wash over me. And, I saw, in my mind's eye, red and black lifelines lacing together, tighter than ever before.

"I love you," I breathed.

He took the Silver Triangle from my clenched fist and pulled its ribbon over my head. There was something frighteningly final about it hanging around my neck.

"Sooner or later, I'll be retried and discharged. After I serve my sentence, I'll leave Ichthyosis for good and follow you to Conflagria, where we'll begin a new life together. I'll be *your* Second Commander in the Red Revolution. I'll help you pursue all your crazy dreams of ending global isolationism. I'll start a family with you. We'll do whatever we want, together. From now on, you're never alone, even if you're half a world away. Because you'll still have me. Forever. Scarlet, you're more important to me than anyone or anything, even ending the Crystal. Even this war. Even Ichthyosis. I commit my life to you."

And, before I could answer his beautiful words, he scooped me up, put his face to mine and—as we were divers—had no need to come up for air for quite some time. Cradling me in his arms, he carried me inside, to his quarters.

Icebergs drifted in the Septentrion Sea. It was only a matter of time before they'd make their way across the Briny Ocean and to the Fervor Sea, where they'd dissolve in the fiery fury of the Conflagrian heat.

CEASE LECHATELIERITE

Scarlet lay her warm cheek on my chest, red hair spilling all over me. I could hardly see a thing in the darkness, but I could feel her frequency permeate the air. I'd sensed her wavelength several times before, of course, but not like this. Not so clearly. It was like, her aura wasn't just nearby, but rather it... washed over my consciousness, in a way. It was hard to describe. Her spectral presence was overwhelming, overpowering. Intoxicating. When I kissed her, I could almost taste the photons in my mouth.

After we destroyed the Crystal, it'd be all gone. Forever. I was surprised to actually find myself saddened by that. Never in a thousand ages did I think I'd come to miss the spectrum. Scarlet's spectrum.

"You know," she whispered, stroking my collarbone, "we may have to just give up and go to sleep soon because, despite our best efforts so far, I don't think it's physically possible for me to fully express how much I love you, all in one night."

I smirked. "So, you're a quitter? Huh. I thought I trained my soldiers better than that."

Laughing, she playfully punched my stomach. "I love it when you try to be funny."

Try? "Sorry, Red Leader, but I'm not going to let you forfeit this mission," I sighed.

"Is that so, Commander?"

I wrapped my arms around her waist. "I don't kid around when it comes to the success or failure of my ops."

She seemed to melt into me. "I'd say tonight's a success, wouldn't you?"

I smiled, knowing her extraordinary eyes would see it clearly, in the blackness. Bare chest pressed against my ribcage, I could feel her heartrate quicken. "We've always been a great team."

She giggled. "In all seriousness, though, we should get some rest."

I kissed her forehead. "In that case, I guess it's a very good thing we have the remainder of our lives to fully carry out our mission objective."

She was quiet. But, I could almost hear her think. Her whole body tensed; her lifeline quivered.

"You don't have to leave for the revolution immediately after we end the Crystal, you know," I said, heavily. "No one is expecting you to take off the day after tomorrow, or anything."

"It already *is* tomorrow."

"You know what I mean. Finish off the month of May, at least. Hell, stay all summer; I'm sure the Reds will be fine. I need you more than they do."

Silence.

"Last time you destroyed the Crystal, you practically left the same minute you regained consciousness. You can't do that, this time. We have a lot of… business to take care of, first."

"Business?" Her head shifted.

I threaded my fingers through her wiry hair. "If we're going to be apart for a long while, we need to make up for it in advance, right?"

"I love it when you talk logic to me," she chortled, kissing my neck, "it's so sexy."

SCARLET LECHATELIERITE

Cease wasn't around when the trumpet sounded at seven o'clock. I woke up in his bed alone, face-down in his salt-scented pillow, tangled up in his sheets, groggily wondering if we really did just elope hours prior and spend half the night releasing an entire age of pent-up passion, or if it was all a crazy dream. I sat up and felt his Silver Triangle slide across my collarbone. I traced the medallion's cold, hard edges with my fingertips. I looked down and saw it glint in the light filtering through the blinds. It was very real. As was our marriage. I swallowed.

Breakfast. The mess hall was silent for the first time in weeks. The entire fleet seemed to share my unease. Every eye evaded mine as I exited the line with my trey. I wanted to sit with Cease—perhaps, his presence would calm my anxiety—but, he was nowhere in sight. I plunked down beside Tose Acci, who gave me a small, Nurtic-esque smile I didn't return. I picked up my spoon and force-fed myself a mouthful of gooey salmon, though my stomach churned in protest. I took a sip of water and felt it slither down my esophagus like an icy snake. Even my lifeline quivered like a harp string. It was probably just nerves.

So, we'd end the Crystal, today. Again. I'd really miss my powers. I didn't look forward to feeling cold and sick, all the time. Mage bodies simply couldn't function at full capacity without spectrum. But, what choice did we have?

Relentless fatigue and weakness were better than endless war and mental oppression. Right?

"Acci, July," Illia Frappe's voice sounded from behind us. "The Commander requests your presence in his quarters, immediately."

Was it seven-thirty already? My heart pounded as I glanced at my wrist. Nope, only seven-fifteen. I guessed we wouldn't have time to eat much. Not that I could, anyway.

"Thank you, Frappe."

Tose and I left the mess hall, all eyes following our backs. The walk down the corridors seemed unusually long and agonizing.

Cease's door flew open before I could press the intercom. Without so much as a good morning, he waved us in and launched into a run-down of the day's itinerary. He dismissed Tose after reviewing the piloting logistics but held me longer to reiterate everything else. He knew I didn't need review, so clearly this was more for his benefit than mine. Fine by me. I answered all his questions without hesitation, even as my belly twisted as though digesting molten lava. I hoped he couldn't tell how nauseous I felt. He was clearly pretty strung-up, himself—he paced much too quickly, pale forehead shining with sweat. He looked so small and vulnerable as he practically ricocheted off the walls. I wanted to catch him and squeeze the tension from his tiny frame.

"Good," he grunted upon my completion of the drill, surveying me up and down. "Dismissed."

I stared.

"I said, dismissed!" he yelled. "Move!"

It was like anchors were strapped to my feet; I couldn't budge. I felt slapped by the curtness of his order.

The words rose from my throat involuntarily, like vomit: "Cease, do you love me?"

He froze.

"You didn't actually say it, last night." I looked down at my boots. "I asked, and you didn't answer."

Silence.

"Now isn't the time to discuss this," he finally replied, tone frosty.

I peered up at him in disbelief. "It's a yes-or-no question. Either you do or you don't. Which is it?"

He placed a hand on my collar and felt for the Silver Triangle, under my uniform. With a flick of his fingers, he pulled it out, pressing the medallion in his palm. "You're my *wife*," he declared, fiercely. "This here," he shook his fist, "means you're *mine*."

"Then, look me in the eye, right now," my voice trembled, "and tell me you love me."

He didn't speak. The silence was so loud and violent, it tore up my insides. He let go of the Triangle; it swung and hit me in the chest. The little medal suddenly felt like a tremendous, unbearable weight.

"How could you marry me if you don't love me?" I croaked. "I love *you*."

He blinked. "I know."

"You *know?* For Tincture's sake, is that the best response you can come up with?"

"Scarlet, we're about to go on the most important mission of our lives; this isn't the time!" he thundered.

"Well, when *will* it be time, Cease? When will I find out if my *husband* loves me?" I screamed.

He grabbed my upper arms and shook me hard. "Quiet! Do you want the whole base to hear?"

I trembled in his death-grip, feeling bruises form beneath his fingers. For some reason, my spectrum wouldn't heal them. It was hard to believe these were the same hands that gently held and comforted me, last night.

He saw my fear and let go. There was a pregnant pause. His chest rapidly rose and fell.

"We do have time, Scarlet," he finally said. "Like I said last night, you don't have to leave Icicle immediately after we end the Crystal. The Reds can get started without you; they'll be okay. You can stay here for the summer, so we can figure things out."

Figure things out. I couldn't believe my ears. "You were supposed to figure *that* out before marrying me. Was everything you told me, last night—e-everything we did—a lie?"

"No, of course, not."

A lump the size of a hobnail egg formed in my throat. "All that stuff you said about me being more important to you than the war, and moving to Conflagria to join me in the Red Revolution after you get out of prison, and starting a family together—did you mean any of it?"

"Yes. All of it."

"I don't get it. Why would you want to do any of that if you don't love me?"

More silence.

I couldn't take this. Nothing made sense. This was a nightmare, worse than I ever imagined. I put my hands over my face and felt hot tears tickle my palms.

"I don't believe this," I wailed. "You *tricked* me into marrying you."

He seized my wrists. "No, Scarlet. I want to be with you. For the rest of my life. I swear."

"I can't do this," I found myself saying. I wrenched myself from his grasp and whipped off the Silver Triangle. "I can't stay married to someone who doesn't love me."

His iron eyes flashed. "You're not backing out. You can't. Scarlet, you can't do that!" He sounded so frantic, so pleading. He clamped my fingers back around the medallion, squeezing so hard, the metal edges dug painfully into my skin. His stare was so intense, I fought the urge to look away. "Scarlet, I'm sorry." His hands shook on mine. "I'm sorry I'm so messed up. I don't know what's wrong with me, why I hurt all the time. But, I do know this: I can't handle losing you. I can't do it. You're mine. You're supposed to be mine, forever. I won't let you go home for the revolution without knowing for a fact that I have you. Please, give me a chance to figure things out."

I stared.

"Scarlet?"

Cease's intercom buzzed. "Commanders?" came Tose's voice.

It was seven-thirty. We hadn't even changed into our diving suits, yet.

Cease hesitated, then dashed over to slap the button on the wall. "Just a minute, Acci!" he growled. "Wait for us in the hangar!"

"Yes, sir." His footsteps disappeared down the hall.

Cease whirled around. "Scarlet, say you're not backing out. Say it. Now."

My lips parted but the words wouldn't come.

"You made a vow." He advanced on me like a predator to his prey, eyes damp and chest trembling. "A promise."

I looked down at the medal. Half of me wanted to hurl the thing at his face.

"Scarlet, if *you* love me, you won't do this to me!"

He swore I was more important to him than anything. Was it true? I thought back to July thirty-first of last age, when he proved he'd rather leave the Crystal intact than watch my life end along with it. I thought about January seventh, when he forked over the shard to Ambrek, to spare me. I thought of how he fearlessly lunged at the sphere of fire a couple weeks ago, readily willing to burn alive for me. I thought about the marriage form he so eagerly signed last night, despite how much he risked by doing so. He really was willing to throw away his whole world, just for me. He put me first, before everything, even his country, even this war, even his very survival. Despite the brainwashing of the Childhood Program. Despite the obvious fact he'd be totally miserable living in a primitive desert for the rest of his life. His actions reflected an insanely sacrificial love. Was it possible he did, in fact, love me, but was just too wounded to recognize it for what it was? Perhaps, he had a mental block against the four-letter word itself. He thought his pain meant he couldn't love. Maybe, all it really meant was that he was fighting against the shackles of his upbringing. Of course, that'd hurt like crazy.

I knew who he was before choosing to marry him. I knew all about his screwed-up past and how damaged he still was. I made the choice to love him anyway. I agreed to wear his medal, sign that form and commit my life to him. As much as this whole mess broke my heart, I had to give him a chance to figure things out. I had to try to help him understand the love that his choices expressed. If there was anyone who could do that, it was me. Leaving him now, so tormented and confused, would only wound and traumatize him more. Perhaps, beyond repair, this time. I couldn't do that to him if I really loved him. I took an oath to be there for him whether things were good or bad. And, they were very bad, now.

Cease was sweating profusely. I felt his wavelength shudder. That's when I noticed his frequency interval was too short for him. It wasn't purely black, anymore. There were distinct red photos in his acherontic light. It was as though the spectral web were reminding me of the finality of our union. Our auras were hopelessly blended. Our lifelines were more tightly twined than I thought possible.

"No," I finally breathed.

"No, *what?*" he boomed.

"No, I'm not backing out, Cease. I won't give up on you. I want to help you."

He pulled the ribbon back over my head so hard and fast, he gave my neck robe-burn my spectrum oddly couldn't heal. Then, he threw his arms around me, buried his face in my hair and let out a grunt that sounded like a hybrid of relief and anguish.

"Don't you dare scare me like that ever again, Scarlet," he cried. Then, he broke into noisy, un-soldier-like sobs, my locks absorbing his tears.

* * *

The flight over was long and nerve-wracking. Tose at the helm, it was just Cease and I in the passenger cabin, waiting, waiting, waiting.

"Some honeymoon, huh?" I smirked.

"Moon?" he echoed, looking out the window. "It's daytime."

"Never mind." I rolled my eyes. "I'm going to go refill my water canteen," I said, though I wasn't thirsty.

I got to my feet but, before I could take a step, he caught my arm and pulled me roughly onto his lap. He snatched the canteen from my hand and tossed it aside. It clattered loudly on the floor.

"Cease," I squirmed, "we're on duty."

"Never stopped us before," he chortled, winding his arms around my waist. "Got anything better to do until we arrive?"

"B-but, Acci—"

"Can't see or hear us." He nuzzled me. "How about a repeat of last night?"

Wait, what? Here? Now?

"I-I don't know—" His jaw interrupted my objection by clamping over mine.

Tincture, was he a roller-coaster. Earlier this morning, he coldly cast me aside, barking about how we needed to stay focused on nothing but work, today. Yet, now, he wanted to make love in the vitreous silica on the way to the most important operation of our lives!? What got into him?

He undid my collar and started sucking the nape of my neck. I sat stone still, arms at my sides, eyes open.

He took the hint and pulled away. "Scarlet, you okay?"

I didn't speak.

"Scarlet?"

I swallowed. "I'm sorry, sir." I didn't necessarily want the 'sir' to come out biting, but it did. "Cease," I quickly corrected.

In half a second, all the passion in his gaze evaporated. It was terrifying. "I guess I shouldn't be surprised you're not in the mood…"

I studied my boots. For several agonizing seconds, I felt his knifelike glare stab my burning face.

"Just don't change your mind about us," he finally said, tone dead. "Not until you've given me a fair shot."

I nodded.

He learned back. "I'm not holding you down. Go ahead and get up."

I didn't move. "Um, if it's okay with you, I'd like to stay," I squeaked, "for a little while."

His angular brows raised. "Fine." He folded his arms and stared out the window.

Five minutes passed. Ten. Fifteen. This was unbelievably awkward. This wasn't how it was supposed to be. I knew marriage wasn't a fairytale or anything, but something told me this wasn't how a husband and wife were meant to behave, mere hours after eloping. I sat on his lap, willing myself to relax. To feel comfortable and safe with him, again. To enjoy being this close to him. I scrunched my lids.

"Scarlet?" Cease touched my elbow.

"Yes?"

"You can trust me. You know that, right?"

Could I? I resisted the urge to snort. "You're the best military leader Second Earth has ever seen," I said, blandly. "I can't think of a better soldier to hold the fate of the alliance—"

He made a noise that sounded like a cross between an angry grunt and a sad sigh. "That's not what I meant. I'm not talking about trusting me with the *war*. I'm talking about trusting me with *you*."

My eyes cracked open a sliver. "Sir—"

"Don't call me that," he snapped. "Not when we're discussing personal stuff. When we're out on the battlefield, sure. But, right now, I'm not talking to you as your commander, but as your husband. Cease."

I chewed my lip. "I'm sorry... Cease."

"I meant everything I told you, yesterday. Every last word. And, spending the night together did mean something to me. I care about you, Scarlet. More than anything."

"You already reiterated all that, right before we left, earlier this morning."

"But, you don't believe me. I can tell."

My hair twitched on my shoulder. "I promised I'm not going to bail on you yet, okay? You don't have to worry." I jumped off his lap. "Now, we really should focus on the mission—"

"Scarlet, listen to me." He grabbed my wrists. Hard. "If I had to choose between you or ending the Crystal, between you or the war, between you or Ichthyosis... I'd choose you. Every time. I think I've already demonstrated that. I'd demonstrate it again today, if it comes down to that."

I held my breath.

"Please, try to understand how difficult this is for someone like me to say. How tough this conclusion was to reach. I'm not like you or the Nurians, Scarlet. Hell, I'm not even like the average base-raised soldier. The likes of Inexor and Tose are a lot more human than me," he said, miserably.

Did he really believe that? If so, that was downright heartbreaking. I felt my anger toward him begin to melt.

"That's not true, Cease."

He snorted, "Really?"

"Yes, really. Back in the ninety-second age, do you know why I wanted to be assigned to the Diving Fleet rather than the Air Force or Ground Troops? Not because it's the most prestigious branch. Not because I've always loved to swim. But, because of you. Because, even back then, I already trusted you—not just your reputation or your military prowess, but *you*, your person. I was drawn to what I'd seen of you. I believed you'd give me a chance, when anyone else in your position would kill me the second they uncovered my identity. I believed you'd see beyond the fact I'm a *fire-savage* and accept me into your confidence, despite everything you were taught about my kind. I believed you'd be able to understand the distinction between the dictatorial System and the innocent Conflagrian population. I believed you were different, despite your lifetime of intensive brainwashing. And, guess what? I was right, on every count. You met all my expectations. No, you exceeded them. Because, not only do you trust me with your men, you trust me with your future. I don't just mean the future of Ichthyosis. *Your* future. You're willing—no, *eager*— to leave your country behind forever and spend the rest of your life fighting a civil war in a hot, primitive, foreign desert, just to be with me." I touched his sharp cheekbone, throat tight. "For Tincture's sake, Cease, if all that doesn't make you 'human,' I don't know what would."

Cease stared at me for what felt like ages, face not quite deadpan. Then, he gently put his hand overtop mine, on his cheek.

"Scarlet?"

"Yeah?"

"Thank you," he choked, squinting, "for loving a screwed-up guy like me."

"You're welcome. Thank you for turning your whole world upside-down for me."

He shook his head. "Believe me, Scarlet, I'm getting the better end of the deal. I don't deserve you."

I chuckled, lightly. "Believe me, Cease, you deserve so much more than the life you've had, so far."

He pulled me back onto his lap and twined his arms around my body, eyes full of love he didn't know he was capable of. "Something tells me the rest of my life will be a whole lot better than the first eighteen ages. Something tells me it'll be really, really great."

I smiled, stroking the triangular emblem on his chest. "First, how about we work on making the rest of our flight really, really great?"

* * *

As soon as our mini vitreous silica came within eyeshot of the Conflagrian shore, I had to commit nearly my entire aura to editing it from sight. When we reached the outskirts of the tropical forest, Tose dropped a ladder. By then, my spectrum was so depleted, I could hardly stay awake. I couldn't understand why I was having such a tough time. I didn't remember this task being quite *so* difficult, last July.

Cease and I pulled on our helmets and began descending the ladder. When the two of us stepped out from the invisible shelter of the ship, I had to dedicate extra photons to cloaking our bodies.

"It's so disorienting," Cease mused through the intercom, "to be invisible."

I could see everything just fine myself but was far too strained to allow Cease that privilege. It was easier to blanket us from everyone, entirely.

"Mmm-hmm," I murmured, lids drooping. We winked in and out of sight as I teetered right off the rungs. A second before I would've hit the sand, Cease caught me.

"Scarlet?" He set me on my feet. "*You* slipped?"

"Y-you intercepted me?" I wheezed. "How? You can't see me."

"I was legally blind for a while, remember? You get pretty good at imagining where things ought to be, after an experience like that. I spotted you for a split-second, which was enough for me to guess where you were headed."

"Interesssting," I slurred. "I rely on vision mmmore than anything." And, with that, my world went black.

Sometime later, I came around, moaning, to the sight of Cease on his hands and knees.

"Scarlet, you passed out! What's wrong with you?" He flipped up his visor. His band slid to the end of his nose, revealing wide eyes. He stared where he imagined my face would be, which really wasn't too far off.

I removed my helmet, breathing with an open mouth and gazing hungrily at the sun. I flicked a knob on my suit, deactivating its forty-degree 'heater.' Why was my aura so weak?

"Cease," I groaned, "when I went under, did-did—?"

"You and I stayed invisible," he answered, "but, no, the ship didn't."

Oh, Tincture.

I rolled over and retched directly on his lap. I was too tired to concentrate on specific cloaking, at the moment—I masked general areas. So, he couldn't see the vomit, nor could he really feel its wetness through his diving suit, but he sure understood what those awful sounds were.

"Scarlet, did you just throw up on me?" he asked in a matter-of-fact tone.

"I'm sorry, sir," I whimpered.

"I hate to say this, but it really isn't a good time for you to be sick."

He probed around until he found my shoulders, pulling me upright. He waited patiently as I leaned against him for several minutes. Our op was off to a bad start.

"Alright, let's do this," I finally said, pulling my helmet on.

His visor snapped down. "You sure?"

"I feel better," I insisted. "And, I'll be stronger than ever, once we're in the Pit." I sounded quite convincing. Like I was trying to persuade myself as much as him.

We headed into the thick of the forest, searching for the passage Ambrek and I used in January to sneak into the Mage Castle. It was now painfully obvious why the tunnel was built, in the first place—to allow the double agent to sneak more easily between Red and System territories.

My hair sliced the lock off the door.

"Ladies first?" I asked Cease.

"Not today, Mrs. Lechatelierite," he answered, a protective note in his voice. Tincture, did that sound bizarre. It was odd and wonderful and terrifying, all at once. Conflagria didn't participate in the marital-name-changing tradition of the rest of the western world, so 'Scarlet Lechatelierite' seemed rather alien to my ears.

"Hey, I never said I was taking your name," I teased. I couldn't anytime soon, anyway. Our marriage would be confined to secrecy for who knew how long.

"Hmm, having an Ichthyothian name *will* make life in Conflagria really interesting, won't it?"

I laughed, though I felt woozy. "Attaching myself to an Ichthyothian will make *all* aspects of my existence really interesting from now on, no matter what."

"You must be one tough soldier, to take on such a mission."

And, with that, he tucked his chin, bent his knees and sprang into the pitch-black hole. Gnawing the inside of my cheek, I followed suit. As I landed, my aura instantly diffused. Luckily, our visors were equipped with night-vision. We proceeded through the winding tunnel, temperature rising with every step. When we reached a fork, we went left, following the glowing light. As we got closer to our destination, I felt my spectrum slowly crystallize. To our relief, our path thus far was unobstructed. No guards, no boulders, no riddles.

All too soon, we found ourselves on a narrow, crooked cliff, projecting over the molten core. We were miles beneath the crust of the earth, facing a fire that seemed to tickle the orange sky itself. Our ears were filled with crackles and roars. Rocks intermittently dislodged from the cavern walls and crashed into the massive pool of bubbling, steaming lava. Straining my eye magic, I peered into the blinding base of the inferno and looked directly at it—the scintillating Core Crystal, the weapon responsible for the enslavement of my nation. Though mere months old, it was already as immense as four vitreous silicas.

For a moment, the two of us stood, staring in awe. I peered at Cease and saw flames dance across his visor. Nodding, he firmly said, "Come on."

Déjà-vu accompanied me as he led the way, quickly yet carefully, chin up and back straight. His steps were graceful and fluid. I tailed him closely, eyes fixed on his back so I wouldn't look down. When we reached the edge, he lassoed half a dozen stalactites with deadline. I stood a foot in front of him. He shot two more cables around me, binding my waist to his. We were bolted to the spot.

"Secure," Cease said. "Now, do it, Scarlet."

"Yes, sir." I took off my helmet.

Suddenly, a rock came shooting from nowhere, spectacularly shattering Cease's visor, visual band and nose-bridge, in one go. Cease inhaled sharply and yanked off his helmet, glass and blood raining everywhere. I gasped.

But, apparently, he was only concerned with his sight, not his demolished nose. "My visual band!" he cried. "I can't see a thing in this glare without it." He dropped his helmet and growled, "Let's get on with this, Scarlet, now!"

My pulse hammered. "Cease, the rock," I breathed, "it flew diagonally. And, with enough force to break both your visor and your face. This can't just be a random accident. Something strange is going on."

He tried to reply but wound up coughing a disgusting crimson mess onto my shoulder instead. Fair enough—I hurled my breakfast on his lap; he spat blood all over me.

"Let me heal you. I can't mend bone, of course, but at least—"

"No, don't waste your magic! Ending the Crystal knocked you out for a week, last age, and your aura was a lot stronger, then." Yes, it was. Why? I felt perfectly fine, yesterday. But, since I woke up this morning, I felt half-diffused. The timing couldn't have been worse. "Just do it, Scarlet. Now!"

"Yes, sir."

I took a deep breath and leaned over the edge, Cease's wires fully supporting me. I channeled my aura into my scalp and—

All six of our cables snapped, in rapid succession. I screamed as we pitched off the cliff. Spinning wildly, Cease somehow roped the ledge. The whiplash was so strong, our backs probably would've snapped if it weren't for our diving suits. We hung, swinging, slamming into the side of the stone, flames licking our faces.

Cease managed to pull us upright, chest pressed hard against my back, arms looped tightly around my waist, gloved hands clutching the deadline. His breathing was loud and sticky in my ear. I laboriously used my hair to pull the two of us up to safety. After we severed the cables and untangled ourselves, I lay on my side, nauseous and spectrally-depleted beyond belief. Blood churned in my ears as my heart throbbed like a semi-automatic against my ribcage. What was left of my aura inexplicably drained from my sources, collecting into a blurry, blotchy, unusable mass in my gut. What was happening to me? Why was my aura clotting up in my belly? Why was I so wasted from such a simple spectral exertion? I should've been feeling on top of the world, this close to the Crystal. Moaning, I closed my eyes. My frequency was so weak, I couldn't even see through my lids, anymore.

"Cease," I panted, "I can't do it; I can't end the Crystal today. I don't know what's wrong with me. I'm sorry, I'm so sorry, please don't be mad—"

"Scarlet, to the hell with the Crystal; we need to get you out of here, now." His voice was tense and urgent. "Deadline doesn't break; it has to be cut. Scarlet, someone's here."

When I opened my eyes halfway, my vision was dimmed.

That's when something dark and green dropped from above and landed atop Cease; his tiny frame collapsed, face-down.

It was Ambrek Coppertus.

Feet on Cease's spine, Ambrek stooped and twisted Cease's arm right out of its socket, magical hands overcoming the arrhythmic suit. I groped my utility belt, only to find it gone—it must've fallen into the flames when we tumbled off the cliff.

A surge of adrenaline mixed with spectrum burned in my head, giving me the strength to knock Ambrek clean off of Cease with a swipe of hair. Cease sprang up into a somersault, dislocated arm flopping disturbingly, and landed catlike on Ambrek's back. I stood in combat stance with my locks poised, unsure what to do next. How could I attack Ambrek if Cease was all over him?

Cease, clinging to Ambrek with only his legs now, used his one good hand to draw his weapon and press it against Ambrek's ear. In a flash, Ambrek flipped Cease over his shoulder, slamming him into the ground. Then, he slapped Cease's sidearm out of his grasp; it disappeared into the fire. Ambrek ripped off Cease's utility belt and threw that overboard, too. Cease kicked Ambrek in the face then rolled away from him.

I finally had a clean shot at Ambrek. Squinting, I launched a fireball at his chest, but he ducked against the stone and it whizzed above him. I shot another, this time hitting his shoulder; his copper-green robe ignited. He swept it off; it fluttered into the Pit like a phoenix. He advanced on me, marbles of sweat trickling down his bare bronze chest, and grabbed my head with both hands, squeezing so hard, I was surprised my skull didn't implode. As though wedged in a vacuum-cleaner, my very last photons surged into his palms—obviously, my sphere of fire stunt was what must've inspired him to even attempt the rather difficult and convoluted art of spectral suction. And, to my horror, he was apparently very gifted at it: in seconds, I was as infrared as a Useless.

"Well, that was easy," he whispered, maliciously. "Something wrong with your lifeline today, mighty Multi-Source Enchant?"

To the sound of Cease shrieking obscenities in Ichthyothian from somewhere behind us, Ambrek kissed me violently on the mouth, his jaw gnashing mine, and tossed me to the stone like a sack of taro.

Then, he turned and dove for Cease—half-blind, weaponless and one-armed.

"Crimson says, hello," he growled.

And, with that, he hurled Cease right over the cliff.

Cease had no deadline. I had neither my utility belt nor my hair-magic. There was no way to save him.

The worst scream I ever screamed tore from my throat as I watched my husband's tiny, white body tumble toward the pool of hungry, blue-white flames and bubbling, crimson lava.

CEASE LECHATELIERITE

I dropped like an anchor through the smoky air, landing heavily on a narrow ledge below. Who was I kidding? I was done for. I wasn't safe up here; magical fire could catch onto rock. It was only a matter of time before the flames would reach me.

But, I wouldn't wait. I had work to do. If I was going to die, I'd take the System down with me.

Yet, I knew, ending the Crystal wouldn't necessarily end the war. I couldn't believe I'd never see the war resolve, after all. The purpose of my existence was to win for Ichthyosis. Period. That's why I was born. What would the alliance do without me?

Moreover, what would Scarlet do without me? I was abandoning her. Here. With Ambrek Coppertus. Diffused.

I prevented my life from flashing before my eyes. I didn't want to think about my cold, dark past. I only wanted one image to fill my mind, now. I lifted my gaze to Scarlet, screaming and crying as she peered over the cliff.

Was my life a waste?

No. Because I loved Scarlet. I finally understood, in this black moment, that my emotional pain didn't nullify that. It was probably just a byproduct of what Scarlet called my 'programming'—all the lies the Childhood Program fed me since infancy. Because of the few, precious months I spent in love with Scarlet, all eighteen ages of my life were worthwhile, even if I didn't win this war like I was raised to.

I loved Scarlet and she loved me, and that was enough of a victory for this soldier.

SCARLET LECHATELIERITE

Ambrek pinned me down with a knee to my back. His iron grip held my head over the cliff's edge, forcing me to watch the man I love face his imminent demise. From a ledge below, Cease looked at me one last time with those beautiful, silver-grey eyes. There was something different about them. They were neither piercing nor anguished nor icy, as they usually were. They didn't reveal any fear of death, either. They were gentle and warm. They seemed to reach out to me from his bloody face like two beacons of white light.

He neither screamed nor cried, so I did both for him, struggling to breathe beneath Ambrek's weight. The fire caught onto the soles of Cease's boots.

"NO!"

"Scarlet," Cease's throat-mage voice competed with the inferno's crackling, "listen to me!"

I gnawed my lip and strained to hear his final words.

"I get it now, Scarlet," he spoke fast. "I understand what's been going on with me, all this time. I'm able, I always have been, I just never realized it until now, that this pain is simply a part of what it means for someone like me to fall so hard, despite everything." The fire crept up to his knees. "What I'm trying to say is, I love you, Scarlet!" Flames licked his thighs. "I love you," he gagged, "and I'm so sorry!"

His arrhythmic suit curled off his blackening flesh. I shrieked, consumed by hysteria. Cease—who somehow managed to remain conscious and calm, whether by adrenaline or magic or Tincture knew what—smiled and silently delivered a complete sentence to my mind, through the spectral web: 'My love, I can't think of a better way to die than to free your—no, *our*—people.' And, with that, he tucked his chin and deliberately rolled right off the ledge. The blaze swallowed him whole.

A streak of acherontic light swooped up from the depths of the Pit—Cease's black aura was liberated. Rather than dispersing into the air as auras of the dead usually did, his struck me in the head. Glowing auburn, I jumped to my feet, shoving Ambrek away. He fell backward, gold eyes like crystalline headlights. I chucked fireballs at him but he deftly dodged them all, though not without singes. But, all too soon, I was wasted, yet again. Ambrek ran toward me and tackled me like a football player. Straddling me on the stone, he seized my neck.

"Goodbye, my betrothed," he hissed.

At that moment, our surroundings began violently vibrating. A deafening rumble sounded as the cavern walls began to break apart. Ambrek looked up, dumfounded, forgetting he was about to strangle someone.

Thinking of the sphere of fire, pieces fell into place.

"The joke's on you, Ambrek," I chortled. "It's no different than if you threw *me* overboard."

"What?" he demanded, shaking me hard.

"Cease can destroy the Crystal, you fool; his aura's born from mine!"

"N-no," Ambrek choked. "That's impossible. Nordics can't twine. They don't have a place in the spectral web."

"This one does."

The Crystal was going to explode, burying us in rubble. Fine by me. I didn't care for my life, anymore. I wouldn't try to save myself.

A length of diffusion rope swooped around Ambrek from somewhere behind him, yanking him off of me. He flailed on his back, like a netted fish out of water. A moment later, a hand grabbed mine. I looked up into the tan face and hazel-green eyes of... Nurtic Leavesleft.

What?

"*Nurtic?*"

His grasp felt quite solid, so he couldn't be a hallucination, could he?

"Scarlet, we've got to get out of here!"

He dragged me back across the cliff, dodging falling rocks and spurts of lava. The second we ducked into the tunnel, the Crystal detonated, emitting a spectral shockwave that would've swept me off my feet if Nurtic weren't literally holding me up.

The two of us ran. We ran and ran. We ran for hours, all the way through Crimson's passage, the tropical forest, the villages and into the Dunes. As the System's dominion lifted, we witnessed violent skirmishes pop up, here and there across the island, like scattered thundershowers. But, not a single aura diffused. So, Cease succeeded. He chose the right frequencies to extinguish.

Nurtic pulled me into an abandoned shack, somewhere in the southeastern Dunes.

"The mind-control's gone," I wheezed. "I don't have my helmet, so I can't call Tose Acci, but I'll tell you where he's waiting. Go home, Nurtic. He can drop you off in Alcove City, on his way to Icicle. Leave me here to restart the Red Revolution. I don't need to go back to Ichthyosis." I swallowed as fresh tears stung my lashes. "There's nothing there for me, anymore."

"Scarlet," Nurtic said, firmly, "you need to go to the hospital."

I pushed him away, suddenly furious. "So, I have some cuts and bruises; I'll heal them spectrally!" Whenever my aura came back, anyway.

Nurtic's eyes—all the more enormous-looking, now that his face was gaunt—bored through me. "You have to come with me to Ichthyosis; you need medical attention." He grabbed my shoulders. "You can always fly back here, afterward."

"Nurtic!"

"Scarlet, I won't leave you behind!" he yelled in a rather un-Nurtic-like manner.

I threw my hands up. "Fine. Let's rendezvous with Tose. He's not too far from here."

'Not too far' wound up meaning two solid hours of wading through knee-high sand. Nurtic coughed and sneezed and sputtered, the whole way. Even so, he never ceased to keep a close eye on me, as though worried I might kneel over, at any moment. But, I suspected I was still in better health than him. Starvation had ravaged his normally athletic figure, making him even longer and lankier than usual. His hair was bleached from the Conflagrian sun and unevenly shorn, as though he'd been hacking it off with a sword. His face was weather-worn, dry, and darker than Ambrek's. His chin and cheeks were cut in several places. Every movement of his bony limbs looked painstaking, like his skin was too tight for his joints. He wore a ragged burlap robe, swathe cinched snuggly around his much-too-narrow waist.

Four months. He'd been stranded here for four months.

How did he escape the System's clutches? Where did he hide out, all this time? How did he know I was coming, today? I didn't vocalize any of my questions. I was too upset to care for answers, now. All I could think about was Cease and the life we wouldn't have together.

At last, we arrived at the shore, to the horrifying sight of twisted, mangled, robed corpses floating in blood-tinted water. A powerful stench pervaded the air, causing Nurtic and I to dry-retch. Among the colorful bodies was a white suit. Tose Acci.

The ship apparently incurred only minor damage. The communication system was completely demolished—a smart move, on the System's part—rendering us unable to inform Icicle of the dramatic turn of events. But, the engine still ran, which was what mattered most.

Nurtic carried Tose's figure inside and lay him on the floor before settling in the pilot's seat. Nurtic talked a lot as he flew us to Icicle, answering all the questions I should've asked. Preoccupied with my misery, I only half-listened. He spoke of life as a POW. He told me how Ambrek Coppertus put him under Fair Gabardine's supervision and how he helped her break through the mind-suppression—using my aura—so they could go into hiding. He talked of how they traversed the island, spending each night in a different shack, cave or valley. He spoke of his dust allergy and how his body adapted to eating meager scraps. He told me about the endless, circular conversations he and Fair had and how they drove each other nuts.

I spoke only once the entire flight, when we were halfway across Nuria. "Where's Fair, now; is she okay?" I piped, voice dead.

"She had a vision, last night." Nurtic's knobby fingers drummed the joystick. "She saw you were planning on coming today. She told me, this was my opportunity to escape. She asked me to leave her behind if the Crystal gets destroyed, so she could help restart the Red Revolution."

I nodded. So, Fair was safe. She was fine.

Unlike my husband.

On top of my unbearable grief for Cease, I felt intensely guilty for Tose's death. It was obvious the System only noticed him because I fainted and failed to consistently cloak the vitreous silica. I curled my legs on the seat and held my aching stomach, silent tears streaming down my face.

Nurtic immediately put the craft on autopilot to rush to my side. I shrunk away.

"Just fly the ship, Nurtic," I snarled. "I don't need you to feel sorry for me. It's already my fault you've been marooned, all age."

"Not so, Scarlet," he objected, quietly. "If you hadn't rescued me in January, I would've died at sea."

Ugh, typical Nurtic. "I was the one who shot you down, in the first place!"

"Only because you had to."

I glared at him, unable to see clearly through my tears, without spectrum. "Quit trying to make me feel better, for Tincture's sake; that's impossible, right now!"

"I know nothing I could say or do would make any of this okay, Scarlet," he breathed, sadly.

I knew what Cease would say to me now, if he could say anything at all. I shut my lids and imagined him talking in his matter-of-fact tone: 'As unfortunate as it is for the Ichthyothian Resistance to lose its leader, Scarlet, you can't deny that my death accomplished what nothing else could. It freed your people from the System without diffusing the spectral web. Conflagria is liberated without facing total physical degeneration and economic ruin. It's everything your people need.'

I perused the floor. Cease's imaginary words made perfect sense. But, I wasn't in the mood for logic and reasoning. I just wanted to wallow until I didn't have the energy to, anymore. I wanted to cry until I was empty, until my well was dry.

I rested my face on my knees. Cease was gone. I couldn't digest it. He wouldn't be at breakfast in the morning, scowling over a bowl of oatmeal without touching a bite. He wouldn't head out to sea with us, shouting orders in his blaring, throat-mage voice. He wouldn't secretly pull me into his quarters after lights'-out so we could spend another night tangled up in each other's arms. Gone were the evenings of slaving over war reports and battle plans. Gone were our arguments, banter and endless language-games. Gone were our dreams of having a future together, fighting in the Red Revolution and raising Ichthyo-Conflagrian children and leading the world in a rebellion against isolationism. It was gone, gone, gone. Our marriage was over before it had a chance to really begin.

Nurtic put an arm around my shoulder and softly sang Psalm twenty-three in my ear. He didn't know how much that reminded me of my late brother, Caitiff Carpus, the 'partial-multi-sourced' musical prodigy who used to serenade me to sleep when I was really little. In many ways, Nurtic was like a big brother to me. Since the day we met, he was religiously protective and attentive. He fed me when I was literally starving to death on the streets, expecting nothing in return. He was the man who could've loved me without ever hurting me, but I never chose the path of least resistance, so I wanted Cease. Maybe, if Cease never existed, I would've fallen for Nurtic and been happy. But, life didn't work that way. Especially, if that life was mine.

I thought back to the nightmare I had while in transit to the Trigon Center, back in March. Only now did I understand what I saw. It was a premonition of the worst thing to ever happen to me.

I was furious at Ambrek. But, for some reason, I didn't want revenge. Rather, I wanted to… speak with him. Ask him why he did what he did. Figure out why he became the person he was, when he was obviously capable of better. I didn't believe anyone was one-hundred-percent bad. All people had to have some good in them. Even the man who pretended to be my best friend and trusted comrade for five months, only to stab me in the back and kill the love of my life, before my very eyes.

The Core Crystal wasn't inherently evil, either. Contrary to popular belief, *it* wasn't responsible for the enslavement of my people and it didn't perpetrate the war. It was simply a powerful tool that fell into the wrong hands—that of the System. But, now, Cease took it from them. Apparently, all the Crystal needed was another Crystal to facet it, to teach it to sparkle.

Two Crystals ended today, but neither were entirely gone. There wasn't enough of the Core Crystal left to fuel the mind-suppression of the System, but there was enough to sustain our sources. There wasn't enough of Cease Lechatelierite left to physically walk beside me, but his memory and aura would always live inside me.

Cease, a man of the ice, died in the fire. He died in a land where no Ichthyothian could possibly belong, no matter how willing he may've been to eventually relocate. He was three-thousand miles from his home—from the nation he loved with all his heart, though he never really got be a part of its society and would've voluntarily denied himself the opportunity to do so, post-incarceration. But, he died as he wanted to. He couldn't think of a better way to go than to free my—no, *our*—people.

All his life, Cease was nothing more than a thawing ice-crystal. He seemed as strong as a diamond at times, but in the end, he was as ethereal as a snowflake melting beneath the fiery fury of the Conflagrian sun.

ARRHYTH LINK

Scarlet, Lechatelierite and Acci were overdue and every-one was tense. Frappe and Tacit were on their way to Con-flagria with their units, but it'd be a while before they'd arrive. Dither sat across from me at the dining table, food untouched. I went through the motions of eating, but I wasn't hungry in the least. With every passing second, a thousand questions percolated my mind. Did Scarlet de-stroy the Crystal? Why didn't Acci respond to our multiple calls? Did the System find them? Did they get shot down? Were they caught up in battle?

Lechatelierite left Buird in charge, today. Never mind that Buird was the officer of unit five; he was still Lechat-elierite's go-to guy, in Scarlet's absence. Old habits died hard, I supposed. Once Scarlet left for the Red Revolution, I fully expected Buird to be reinstated as Second, largely bypassing the chain-of-command.

Buird came bounding into the mess hall now, announc-ing that the flight-control tower detected the vitreous sili-ca, approaching the shore. It'd land within the hour. Frappe and Tacit were ordered to turn around.

Dinnertime ended, but no one moved a muscle. We sat and waited with bated breath.

At long last, the door burst open. And, what I saw made me wonder if I'd gone crazy from stress.

Framed in the doorway was Nurtic Leavesleft, face a rictus of death, cradling Scarlet's limp form. He was battered, bruised, torn, tanned, bleached and emaciated all at once, as though someone made a clay figure of him and twisted it up.

"Scarlet needs to go to the hospital, now," Nurtic said, voice hoarse. "I don't think she's only sleeping, anymore. I pinched and shook her, but she didn't stir. She's breathing, but her pulse is very slow."

Before anyone could reply, Nurtic turned on his heel and disappeared down the corridors. Abandoning my seat, I took off, after him.

"Nurtic!" I breathed, catching up with him. "Nurtic, what's going on? Where are Lechatelierite and Acci? How are you alive? What happened to you? Where've you been, all this time?"

"Conflagria," he snapped, not looking at me. His long legs took big strides. "The System captured me on January seventh."

I goggled at him. "Everyone thought you died at sea, that day."

"I know. I could tell from the way you all *didn't* search for me, over the past four months."

Touché. "Did Scarlet find you?"

"More like, the other way around."

Fear prickled through me. "Why? What happened?" My heart hammered in the region of my Adam's apple. "Nurtic, where are Lechatelierite and Acci?" I repeated.

He didn't answer.

"Nurtic?"

His eyes finally flickered to mine. "I'd prefer to tell everyone at once, Arrhyth."

We reached the hospital wing. Nurtic kicked the door open, barged in and deposited Scarlet in a vacant bed before Raef, who ogled the pair of them as though they were ghosts.

"She's breathing but unconscious. She's likely very dehydrated. Her pulse is weak. Her aura has diffused. She needs a full-body scan," Nurtic ordered.

"Oh, dear." The nurse bent over Scarlet and touched her violently-flushed face. Then, she looked up at Nurtic. "Please," she gestured to the bed beside Scarlet's, "you look dreadful."

"No, I'm not staying. I need to speak with the fleet, first." He turned toward the door and sprinted back down the hall. With what energy, I hadn't a clue. I tailed him.

"Did Scarlet destroy the Crystal? Is that why she's passed out and her aura's gone?" I pressed. I understood he wanted to save all the gory details for the fleet, but at least he could give me a clue whether the op was a success or bust, overall.

He hesitated. "No." I stopped breathing until he added, "Lechatelierite did."

"What?" I almost tripped. "That makes no sense."

Nurtic glowered at me. I'd never seen him look at me, or anyone, that way before. "I said I want to tell everyone, all at once."

"Alright, alright." I paused. "It's really good to see you again, Nurtic."

"Same to you," he replied, brusquely.

We reentered the mess hall. Buird, forgetting that Nurtic was a commander and he, well, wasn't, began to interrogate the poor man before he could say a word.

"Leavesleft, where are Lechatelierite and Acci?" he growled angrily, as though Nurtic were somehow responsible for the catastrophe everyone sensed had happened. "Did July destroy the Crystal?"

"Sir, please, let me explain from the beginning—"

"Answer me!" he thundered.

"Lechatelierite and Acci are dead," Nurtic revealed, bluntly. "And, no, Scarlet didn't destroy the Crystal." It was as though Nurtic dumped buckets of ice on all our heads. The color drained from every face. "But, the mission wasn't a failure, sir." How absurd those words sounded! "Please, let me start from the beginning."

Nurtic's voice was so rough and quiet, we had to strain to listen. As he spoke, the room went silent enough to hear a single snowflake settle upon the white world outside.

* * *

After Nurtic finished his update, the Ichthyothians dispersed. We Nurians stayed behind to have a little reunion with our back-from-the-dead friend. We cried, hugged and laughed. The evening was joyful in one respect, sorrowful in another. We were happy because Nurtic was here. We were sad because Commander Lechatelierite was not.

SCARLET LECHATELIERITE

I fell asleep somewhere in Nurian airspace. Over and over, in my dreams, I watched Cease burn, his black aura snaking into the sky. Guilt and sorrow twisted my stomach; bitter acid burned my esophagus.

I came around to the sound of beeping machinery. I couldn't see through my lids. I felt a hand drift across my forehead, brushing aside a tuft of hair. My eyes popped open. I sat up, catching a wrist. A woman gasped.

It was Insouci Raef.

"I-I'm sorry," I sputtered, letting go.

"Believe me, ma'am, I'm used to it, by now. All my patients are soldiers—the most paranoid people on the planet." She walked around my bed. "And, technically, you count as two patients, so you get double paranoia points," she added, dryly.

It took a moment for her words to travel from my ears to my brain.

"What?"

She folded her arms. "Ma'am, when I gave you a medical scan, I detected two human lifeforms."

Was I still asleep? "I don't understand."

"July," she leaned forward, "you're pregnant."

I sat in stunned silence for what seemed like eras. How long was I unconscious, for something like that to be detectable already?

When I remembered how to operate my vocal cords, I managed to stammer, "W-what's today's date?"

"June first."

I married Cease on May twenty-fourth. "So, how could you possibly know, already...?"

"Ichthyothian technology never ceases to amaze me, either." She held up her scanner. "This here can detect pregnancy mere hours after blastocyst implantation." She put the device down. "It's a boy. Due February twenty-fifth of the ninety-fifth age."

I was shocked beyond belief. I sat there, blinking and gaping. So, that explained why I'd been so spectrally drained since the morning of the op; my aura was already channeling into my son!

Raef watched my silent reaction with concern in her sapphire-blue eyes. "As horrible as this sounds, ma'am," she began, stroking my arm, "I'm actually not surprised. With all these young, hormonal, sex-deprived men locked up here, I knew there's no way a pretty girl like you could go very long without being targeted."

Huh? "What?"

"Oh, please don't protect him, whoever he is!" she cried. "I've seen it before, when I worked in forensics in Alcove City—victims protecting their attackers!"

"What?" I breathed, yet again.

"I know the statistics," she went on, shaking her head. "You may be the first female diver to serve at Icicle but, back on First Earth where female soldiers weren't so uncommon, at least eighty percent of women in the American military claimed to suffer some sort of sexual harassment at one time or another—"

"Mrs. Raef, I wasn't raped," I interjected, solemnly. "It was consensual."

"You're sixteen. The guy you were with, is he one of the new grads?"

"N-no."

"So, a legal adult took advantage of a minor."

"Mrs. Raef—"

"You've got to pursue this and press charges."

"No!" I swallowed and added in a small voice, "I can't anyways, even if I wanted to."

"Why, did he threaten you? Is he blackmailing you?"

"Oh, no, nothing like that. It's because he's…" But, I couldn't bring myself to say it aloud.

Raef marched over to a cabinet and unearthed an orange bottle filled with large, olive-green pills. "These only work during the first eight weeks of pregnancy." She plunked the container on my nightstand. "One tablet would cause the embryo to detach from the uterine wall—a lot less hassle than a surgical termination down the line, believe me."

I stared. "You mean, you want me to kill my son?"

She winced at my word-choice. "No," she answered, slowly, "I want to spare a teenage girl from the tremendous burden of motherhood—or, a kid from winding up in an orphanage, since the adoption and foster-care system in this country is total garbage. Basically, I want to prevent a cluster of cells from becoming a potentially unwanted, unloved child."

My face grew hot. "He already *is* a loved, wanted child to me," I shot. "Maybe, the timing isn't great," to say the least, "but, I could never give up the legacy of the man I love!"

She frowned. "You're so naïve, confused and idealistic. You've got to face reality, ma'am: the father of your baby is an active-duty soldier who broke the Laws of Emotional Protection and you're carrying physical evidence of his crime. But, we have everyone's DNA on file, so whether you abort or carry to term, we'll do a paternity test to prove exactly which bastard deserves to be behind bars—"

"Mrs. Raef, please," I stopped her, giant marbles slipping down my cheeks. "I know who the father is and he can't possibly deny it."

Her blonde brows constricted. "Oh? And, why not?"

"Because he's dead." There it was. I put my chin to my chest and murmured, "My husband died in the infiltration."

There was a long, strained silence. That left her only two guesses. Tose Acci or—

"Commander Lechatelierite?" she gasped, stupefied. "*Commander Lechatelierite* is the father of your child?"

I nodded.

Her jaw literally dropped.

"Please don't tell anyone," I whimpered.

"Well, no matter what I do or don't say for the time being," she gave a wry chortle, "the truth will still be pretty damn obvious once the kid is bor—hold up, what do you mean, 'husband'?"

"I married Cease the night before the mission," I piped. "We signed a form he got from the Retirement Center."

She blinked. "Was a judge present? Did that judge sign it, too? Stamp it? File a copy with the state?"

I knew that was how marriage worked in civilian Nuria, according to Order statutes. But, Ichthyosis hadn't been an Order nation in quite a while, not to mention this wasn't civilian society. I assumed Cease knew how marriage worked in the Ichthyothian military. A no-nonsense, one-step process seemed fitting.

"N-no."

"Then, your union isn't legal," she said, flatly.

Terror shot through me. "No," I objected, numbly. "We signed the right paper. We're married."

"It's not that simple. Without a judge, *your* signatures carry no legal weight. That's the way the Order does it."

"Ichthyosis isn't a member."

"It was once the Order Authority. The convention stuck."

"And, marriage works the same way in the military as in civilian Ichthyosis?"

"Yes."

I felt like throwing up. "Cease brought me a document and said we'd be married if we signed it. I believed him. He didn't say there's more to it."

"He probably didn't *know* there's more to it. It's not like the Childhood Program teaches its students what the process looks like. Base-raised soldiers don't get the opportunity to learn that until discharge or retirement. I doubt Commander Lechatelierite set out to trick you, Scarlet; he was just ignorant."

"No, no, no." I put my head in my hands. This wasn't happening. I couldn't accept it. I wouldn't. "Is it possible to… to make it legal, now? Can a judge sign, stamp and file it, now?"

"*Until death do us part,*" she quoted. "You can't marry a dead man, I'm sorry."

"Please," I pleaded, as if she had the power to single-handedly and instantaneously amend the law, "is there anything we can do? Anything, at all? The certificate is proof we wanted to marry, before he died."

She gave me a thoughtful look. "Where is it?"

"Cease tucked it in his utility belt, right after we—" I felt as though a flaming sword pierced my gut. The form was probably still in his belt. In the Fire Pit.

I ripped out my IVs, leapt from bed and sprinted down the hall. I knocked Cease's door off its hinges with hair-spectrum I didn't know I already had, jumped inside and began tearing his quarters apart, yanking out drawers and dumping the contents of his closet. I searched every nook and cranny twice, despair escalading with every second. Obviously, the form wasn't here. The only proof of our attempted marriage was gone. At last, I dropped to the floor, sobbing loudly, surrounded by all of Cease's stuff. Burying my face in his summer trainer, still salty with his scent, the full blow of his loss finally came down on me. The white walls of his room—the very room in which we spent endless nights working, where we discussed everything from unit assignments to the meaning of art, and where we consummated our fake marriage—seemed to close in on me as I leaned against his metal desk, crying and shaking and screaming.

Raef stood in the doorway. She stepped over the unhinged door, took my hands, pulled me to my feet, put an arm around my shoulders and walked me back to the hospital where she had me lie beneath a heated towel. Eventually, my sobs faded to hiccups. After Raef re-stuck my IVs, she sat at my bedside.

"I'd love to give you tips on pregnancy and parenthood," she said with a small, sad smile, "but, I've never had a child, myself."

I was surprised—she wore a wedding band and looked well into her thirties. I unstuck my throat and croaked, "Are you planning to?"

She shook her head. "Maybe, if I remarry, one day. The war took my husband. Evael Raef used to work at Finis Lechatelierite's company. On January seventh, he was killed in the terrorist attack."

Everything made sense. "That's why you're still here, isn't it? Even after the alliance fell. Without your family, you felt you had nothing to go back to, in Alcove City. So, you stayed at Icicle, where your purpose is."

She nodded. "Most of all, I didn't want his death to be in vain. After packing my bags, I turned right around and unpacked, realizing the best thing I could do next was continue giving the war-effort everything I've got. Because, the more work we all put into it, the sooner we can make it stop."

INEXOR BUIRD

June seventh.

Today, I'd deliver the official State-of-the-War Address. Though Scarlet was technically the Leader of the Ichthyothian Resistance, I assumed the task because she clearly had no interest in it. Since waking up on the first of the month, she'd distanced herself from everyone, making it abundantly clear she no longer thought of herself as one of us. Once Dr. Calibre deemed her healthy and strong enough, she'd head back to Conflagria for the Red Revolution, for good this time.

The Trilateral Committee sent a camera crew to Icicle, now stationed at the rear of the lecture hall. Inhaling, I stood before all my fellow divers, not to mention the millions watching on TV. I wasn't a master linguist like Scarlet, nor an emotionally-charged orator like Leavesleft, nor an electrifying master of tone like Cease. I planned on keeping things plain and simple. I didn't devise a clichéd preamble, either. No litany of thank-you's nor I'm-honored-to-speak-to-all-of-you's. I wasn't in the mood, and I suspected neither was anyone else. So, I cut to the chase.

"On May twenty-fifth of the ninety-fourth age, the magical 'mind-control' sustained by the totalitarian System of the South Conflagrablaze Captive was diffused via the partial destruction of the Core Crystal." I didn't bother to explain how such a phenomenon was possible. I wasn't sure I totally understood it, myself. Whenever I tried to ask Scarlet about it, she clammed up. Any mention of Cease or the incident responsible for his death made her completely wall off. "However, the spectral web remains, allowing mage civilization to progress with minimal disruption. The masses are free to think their own thoughts and collectively work toward establishing a peaceful democracy." I averted Scarlet's stare, knowing there was no guarantee the Red Revolution would ever yield republican democracy, especially since the alliance had no intention to provide any aid. After barging in and turning their world upside-down, we simply swooped out, with no plan to help clean up the mess we made. We would leave it all to Scarlet and her Reds. Which didn't go over too well for them, last time.

"The Conflagrian System has refused negotiation and does not wish to forge a peace treaty with the alliance. Eliminating the System's spectral dominion is a great step in history, no doubt, but it doesn't mean the war is over. We learned that lesson the hard way, last age. All three branches of the Nurro-Ichthyothian military therefore intend to remain battle-ready, with the academies functioning at full capacity. Economic theorists predict the alliance could survive without Second Earth Order rations for approximately seventeen more ages. And, so, we will do everything in our power to finish this war by the eleventh age of the eighth era. Nurian veterans, to accomplish this goal, I ask that you please stay at your respective bases as long as you are able."

As those words left my lips, my eyes drifted across the faces of Nurtic Leavesleft, Arrhyth Link and Dither Maine. They watched me with a somber intensity that made my chest ache. Before I met Fair, I didn't react emotionally to things like that. Before Fair, I hardly gave a damn if my decisions and demands impacted others on a personal level; all I cared about was achieving my ends, no matter the cost. Now, I could appreciate the fact that I was asking the Nurians to make a sacrifice of epic proportions. I could share in their grief and pain.

"The System continued to fight after we destroyed the Core Crystal last July, despite total diffusion," I went on. "This time around, their sources are intact, so the threat of spectral attack remains." I looked at Illia Frappe and Quiesce Tacit. "This is not the end of the war, Ichthyosis." My gaze shifted back to Leavesleft and his friends. "This is not the end of the war, Nuria." I took a deep breath and stared solemnly at the camera. "A new chapter has just begun: the Magic Wars."

And, with that, my speech was over. I just had one last announcement to make: "Comrades, I invite you to attend the memorial for the Ex-Leader of the Nurro-Ichthyothian Resistance, Diving Fleet Commander Cease Terminus Lechatelierite, who died in combat on Conflagrian soil on May twenty-fifth, at the age of eighteen." Everyone sat up a little straighter; this would be the first memorial for a base-raised solder in Ichthyothian military history. "The ceremony will be held on June seventeenth at seven-thirty, here at the Icicle Diving Base. Thank you. Dismissed."

Everyone silently filed out of the lecture hall, except Krustallos Finire VII.

"Well done, sir," he said, strolling toward me.

I cast the kid a sideways glance. I doubted he really had anything of substance to say; he just wanted attention. Which I sure didn't feel like giving to him.

"Thank you, Finire," I answered through tight lips, turning toward the door.

"Call me Seven."

That stopped me in my tracks. I swiveled back around. "What?"

"That's the nickname the Commander gave me," he said, as though everyone didn't already know.

"Yeah, but I thought you hated it."

"I did." Seven shrugged. "But, not anymore."

"Oh." Wow.

"You know, I really liked him. I think that's why I never said anything about his breach of the Emotional Protection Laws."

My lips parted. "You knew about that?"

He nodded, not asking how *I* knew. "One day, back in February, Colonel Austere asked me to deliver a message to the Commander, in his quarters. So, I walked in on him… and Scarlet… all over each other. Lechatelierite got real upset and yelled at me, while Scarlet turned redder and wouldn't meet my eye. I saw them going at it again, very late at night, right before the op. I was on watch in their wing when I spotted him carrying her down the hall to his room, kissing. They didn't see me, though."

Fraternizing in the middle of the night, on the eve of the infiltration? I knew Cease and Scarlet had some sort of strange, dysfunctional, on-and-off relationship since last age, but I hadn't a clue how far they actually took things. I guessed, mere hours before the most dangerous mission of their lives, they figured they might as well throw down because it was now or never.

They were right.

"I could've had them both court-martialed, but I didn't want to," Seven paused, "because I really liked Lechatelierite. Yet, I never told him that. And, now, I can't."

I always thought Seven hated Cease's guts. No doubt, the feeling was mutual. But, of course, I couldn't exactly point that out now, when Seven was clearly hurting over how things ended between them. My time with Fair taught me to be more considerate of others' heartache.

"Well, we soldiers don't exactly talk about things like that," I said. "But, if that's the way you really felt, I'm sure he could tell."

Seven shook his head. "No, I don't think so. I thought so highly of him, I made a special effort to make his life a living hell. Looking back now, that seems so twisted and backward." His crystal-blue eyes bored right through mine. "I think, in war, when there's a constant danger of coming home in a body-bag, soldiers should be able to tell each other how they feel."

SCARLET JULY

June seventeenth.

We hadn't gone out to sea since the Crystal's end. Like last summer, the System was taking a moment to regroup. All quiet on the battlefront for the time-being, the fleet put all its energy into the ongoing spectral-hurricane relief effort. This morning, however, we'd stay at Icicle for Cease's memorial. The first memorial ever held for a base-raised soldier.

It'd take place in the lecture hall. Without a body to bury, there was no point in holding it outside. Last week, an engraved plaque was donated by the Trilateral Committee in Cease's honor. But, mere minutes after it was installed, it got buried by snow. The flag beside it was still at half-mast, until today.

At dawn, a couple hundred soldiers from the other two branches arrived at Icicle. We all assembled in the lecture hall, now—blue-suits to the left, black-suits to the right and white-suits in the center. Every man wore a black scarf around his collar as a symbol of mourning.

I wore the scarf, but not the uniform. Instead, I sported my mage robe, overtop my summer trainer. I stood out like a flame in a snowstorm, attracting offended stares from just about every non-diver to look my way, but I didn't care. This outfit meant far more to Cease and me than my ceremonial dress ever did. This was what I wore on our 'wedding' day.

Not to mention, Cease expressed to me, on more than one occasion, how much he liked my native garb—a sentiment that ran contrary to the traditional Ichthyothian hatred of all things Conflagrian. Forget protocol; today, I wore red for Cease.

I sat by Nurtic, Arrhyth and Dither. Nurtic gave me a small, dimpled smile I didn't return. His clothes swam on his emaciated body.

Of all people, the Trilateral Committee chose Commodore Rettahs Slous to give Cease's eulogy. For Tincture's sake. He stood before us and reiterated, in a monotonous voice, a string of empty details about Cease's service. He rattled off a list of battle-stats and rambled about how quickly he'd sped through the Childhood Program and the chain-of-command. The longer Slous spoke, the more irritated and disgusted I became. Was that all anyone had to say about such an incredible, multi-faceted man—a bunch of dry, two-dimensional, history-book facts? Cease deserved to be commemorated in a personal way. Slous hardly even knew Cease. Then again, I suspected that Inexor and I were the only ones here who really did.

So, after Slous finished his vacuum-cleaner droning, I brazenly marched up to the podium and took the microphone off its stand.

His eyes raked me. "Excuse me, ma'am—"

"Thank you, Commodore, for allowing me the privilege of providing the closing comments, today." I saluted him, firmly. Not wanting to cause a scene in front of literally the entire military, he reluctantly left the stage, face purple.

Every eye in the lecture hall watched me with far more interest than Slous ever got. I inhaled and began: "No Ichthyothian civilian passes through the public-school system without memorizing the name and basic bio of their nation's greatest military leader, Cease Terminus Lechatelierite.

But, there's a lot more to Lechatelierite than the fact he was a diver who got promoted young and won lots of battles. While statistics may be interesting, they belong in a classroom, not at a memorial service. History books won't tell you that Cease Lechatelierite made his first friend at the age of seven with his lab-partner in physics class." I glanced at Inexor. "Or, that he was an insomniac who typed every night until he got Carpal Tunnel. Or, that he cried over his father's death, despite having never known him. Or, that he liked to spend his evenings on the balcony outside the hospital wing, gazing at the sea. Or, that when he found an illegal audio-player in the locker of an MIA subordinate, he chose to listen to the viola-music on it rather than discard it." I looked at Nurtic, whose sandy brows disappeared beneath his bangs.

I said nothing about our breach of the Laws of Emotional Protection.

"If we're going to talk statistics, allow me to bring up a few particularly-interesting ones," I pressed on. "Fifty-five divers were killed in combat on May seventh. Seven more perished in the spectral-disaster relief effort. One other soldier besides Commander Lechatelierite died during the infiltration on May twenty-fifth. Are these just numbers on a page? Or, are they lives who also deserve to be remembered? Why are we only honoring the Commander? Because he has rank and reputation?"

Not a single soul in the audience moved nor blinked.

I spoke for thirty more minutes, recognizing all sixty-three men who died in May, starting with Tose Acci. When I left the stage, the hall emptied quickly. Divers headed for the barracks and those from the Air Force and Ground Troops boarded their respective carriers.

I sat alone for a few minutes before venturing outside and kneeling by Cease's plaque. So, this little thing was all

Ichthyosis could give to commemorate the greatest military leader to walk Second Earth? With my hair, I melted the snow from his last name—the name I'd never get to take as my own, after all.

"Regardless of legalities, Cease, I'll always think of you as my husband," I whispered, breath curling around my face. I reached into the folds of my robe and touched the medallion, resting on my chest. "I've been wearing your Silver Triangle against my skin, right by my heart, since you gave it to me. I always will. And, I'll be sure to pass it onto our—" I hadn't cried since the day I awoke from my coma. But, now, right here on Icicle's south lawn, I broke my military discipline. Tears froze halfway down my cheeks, falling to the ground like sleet. "To our son!" I sobbed. "Cease, I'm carrying your child. I'm so sorry you'll never know that or get to meet him." I blew my nose in my sleeve. "I can feel his aura, already. He's iridescent. Red and black. A blend of us both. I'll always see you when I look into his eyes. You were my crystal, my energy-source, my fire. I loved you, love you and will always love you until the day I join you. Goodbye, my crystal, goodbye."

NURTIC LEAVESLEFT

June twenty-first. The longest day of the age. The summer solstice.

It was a Conflagrian holiday. Not a bad day for Scarlet's return, I supposed. I'd leave Icicle today, too. The Second War Pact of the Ninety-Second Age contained a provision awarding recovered Nurian POWs honorable discharge and safe transport home. Also, to my great shock, the Briggesh administration pushed the Trilateral Committee to award me a Silver Triangle on my way out the door.

Before the trumpet sounded, I sat up, hunching so I wouldn't bump my head and wake Frappe in the bunk above me. I glanced down the rows, taking in the peaceful sight of everyone still sound asleep. Two bunks away, Arrhyth unconsciously yanked one of his brown curls. In the bed below him, Dither lay on his stomach, face planted in his pillow, legs tangled in his sheets. My chest tightened as I wondered how long it'd be until I'd see them again. Seventeen ages, if all went well. I couldn't believe it.

Seven o'clock. At the sound of the obnoxious brass blare, everyone jumped up and headed for the showers. In the locker-room, I shamelessly pulled out my viola case, right there in the open. I hadn't played a note since before my captivity. It'd been nearly six months. The case felt curiously light. I opened it and saw that my viola and audio-player were missing. A small smile touched the corners of my lips;

I knew where—or, with whom—the audio-player spent its last days, and that was fine by me. It was the best gift I could've given Lechatelierite, before he passed away. I pictured him sitting on this bench, straining forward, brows furrowed, as non-military music filled his unsuspecting ears.

The grin slid off my face as I wondered what in the world happened to my instrument itself.

Something warm gently touched my shoulder. When I turned, there stood Scarlet in her deep-red robe, holding my large viola in her tiny hands.

"It's not perfect, but I tried my best." She held it out to me. "Fully reassembled. I reattached all the old strings too, but they'll probably still need to be replaced, anyway. And, the bridge is warped. Badly. I'm sorry."

I took it from her. "Thank you, Scarlet," I breathed, confused. "What happened?"

"The, um… the Commander…" she fumbled with something at her neckline, "well… one time, when he got real mad at me, he sort of… took your viola a-and—"

I held my hand up. "It's okay." I didn't want her to relive a rough time she had with Lechatelierite, on account of me. "That's just fine, Scarlet. I understand." Actually, I really didn't understand how my viola got involved in a fight between the two of them. Whatever went down was obviously violent. I clenched my jaw as I imagined Lechatelierite striking her with it, or something. The thought made me so angry. It wouldn't be the first time Lechatelierite manhandled Scarlet, either. Last summer, upon returning from his brief imprisonment, he threw her to the floor, in front of the whole fleet, when she tried to embrace him. True, her behavior was unprofessional, but nothing excused his aggression. He could've stepped aside or ordered her to back away. She would've obeyed. Yes, Scarlet was a soldier, but you don't just hit an eighty-pound girl who meant no harm. Especially if she's your trusted comrade. Your Second Commander. Your right-hand woman. Your secret significant other. Whose only crime was being happy to see you come home alive.

And, yet, he was the one she cared about. Last August, I saw the two of them kissing passionately. I hadn't a clue what happened to their illegal romance since then but, apparently, it was the kind of relationship where Lechatelierite pushed her around and yelled and smashed things.

"I didn't really have the proper tools to reconstruct it," she went on, nervously, "but, I hope you—"

"It's perfect," I said, smiling at her. "If you didn't mention something happened, I wouldn't have been able to tell, just by looking at it." Except that, from now on, every time I *did* look at it, I'd remember how my former Commander abused one of my best friends. I wondered what else he did to her while she was under his thumb. "You did a wonderful job; you truly are an artist."

She looked as though I lifted a vitreous silica from her shoulders. She stood there for a while, then swallowed. "I searched for your audio-player, but Cea—Lechatelierite's quarters have been completely cleaned out. Everything's gone—laptop, books, clothes. His closet and drawers are all empty."

"That's fine. I don't need it back. I'm glad he found it. I can't think of a better use for it."

She nodded, a distant look on her flushed face, and drifted out the door.

Needless to say, she and I were the center of attention, at breakfast. We each shook hundreds of hands. Even the new graduates bid me farewell, though we hardly knew each other; we'd never gone to battle together.

"On the news back home, I saw clips of you and Commander Lechatelierite taking on the Second Earth

Order," Arrhyth said to Scarlet. "That was *some* Star you were speaking! I had no idea you knew Orion!"

"I didn't, until the weekend before," Scarlet answered. "I taught myself, just for the meeting."

He whistled. "For goodness' sakes, I liked being on even footing with you in *something!* We were both trilingual— until you just *had* to go and break the tie. Now, you speak everything I do, and more."

She chuckled. "Yeah, well, you're still far ahead of the average, monolingual Second Earthling."

He grinned. "Teach me Conflagrian sometime, okay? I want to catch up with you." Like they'd ever see each other again.

She smiled a sad smile. "Sure."

With that, he stepped aside to let someone else have a turn.

He and Dither were the very last to come to me.

"Seventeen ages," Arrhyth said. "That's how much time we've got to polish off this war, before a great depression strikes. In the meantime, we're in for a major recession."

"The war could end before then," I said with all the cheeriness I could muster. "You never know."

"You never know," Dither echoed, "it could never end."

"Well, maybe, the Order will reaccept Ichthyosis and Nuria, lifting the deadline," I said.

"That's already been tried."

"It can be tried again. Or, maybe isolationism can get overthrown, entirely."

"That's what we love about you most," Arrhyth laughed. "You're so optimistic, you're delusional."

I laughed too, though it made me sick to hear it was delusional to dream of a united world.

"We wouldn't have you any other way," Dither agreed.

They punched my belly until some salmon and oatmeal came up in my throat and I returned the favor with a couple back-thumps and shoulder-whacks. Then, the three of us cried for a moment before regaining composure and saluting one another properly.

"Man, things are going to be different around here," Arrhyth sighed, wiping his forehead in his sleeve. "No Lechatelierite, no Scarlet, no you. That's quite an ending."

"Don't think of it as an ending," I said, foot in the doorway. "Think of it as a new beginning."

* * *

Scarlet and I boarded a small plane and departed Ichthyosis for the last time in our lives. We soared above the shimmering, cobalt-blue Septentrion Sea, the island quickly diminishing to a tiny white fleck, behind us. As I piloted, Scarlet gazed sadly out the rear-view window.

The war had changed us both. It made us strong but wary, wise but cynical. It numbed and desensitized us in some ways, stirred and moved us in others. Everything was different from the eyes of a veteran. There were wounds I knew time would heal, yet others that I figured would remain open to some extent, as long as we lived. The only thing we could do now with *those* cuts was try not to let too much salt get in. Though we were technically leaving the fleet forever, I knew there really was no such thing as an ex-diver. There'd always be something about us that'd set us apart from the rest of the civilian world. We civilian-reared divers may not have been branded like our base-raised comrades, but we were still marked, in a way. I saw it in Arrhyth and Dither's eyes, when I bid them farewell. I saw it in Scarlet's emerald stare, right now. I didn't need to look in the mirror to know I had it, too. I could feel it.

When I got back to Icicle on May twenty-fifth, it was a frightening experience, to see my reflection properly for the first time in five months. I didn't recognize the hollow-faced corpse peering back at me. My health improved since then, but I still had a long way to go.

I talked a lot during the first leg of our flight to Alcove City. Scarlet listened without a word, face deadpan like Lechatelierite's always used to be. I was careful to keep my chatter light, but not cheery. She had a right and reason to be sad, after all. Eventually, I realized I was probably irritating her, so I shut up. We flew in silence for a few more hours until we landed at the Alcove City Flight School, just down the street from the hospital, where Scarlet wanted to stop before taking the plane to Conflagria. Why she wanted to visit the hospital, she didn't say.

As for me, I'd reached my final destination. My parents' home was only a few blocks away, and I'd enjoy the walk. Scarlet and I emerged from the cockpit and stood there on the asphalt beside the grey and blue jet, glinting in the June sun. I handed her the keys.

"Make good use of the plane, Red Leader," I said, jovially.

She looked up at me, eyes moist. "I will, Nurtic," she half-whispered.

"Say hello to Fair for me." I took her hand and shook it firmly. "I'll be praying for you two, and for the entire revolution."

She just swallowed and nodded.

"Who knows," I added, "maybe, we'll see each other again, someday."

"Not unless you come to Conflagria," she sighed. "I don't intend to leave the island, ever again. Tincture knows I've already done enough travel for two lifetimes."

For a moment, I lifted my eyes to the scintillating city skyline. "Actually, I do want to return to Conflagria, at some point. As a missionary."

She blinked. "You're allergic to dust."

"I can take medicine."

She finally grinned, even as a single tear escaped from the corner of her left eye. "After what happened to you, I can't believe you'd ever want to go back there."

I shrugged. "It'll probably be a while until it actually happens. First, I want to reapply to the University of Vita. UVA accepted me before I went to the Diving Academy. It'll take four ages to graduate from there. Then, after that, my Master's in Missiology will take a couple more ages. Then, I'll probably have to spend another age or so gathering financial support before I travel overseas."

"Seven ages, then." She let out a bitter chuckle. "So much can happen in seven ages." She swept a hand through her hair—an odd gesture for a mage with autonomous control over her locks. "When I was deported in eighty-seven, I had no idea what'd happen to me over the next seven ages. I wouldn't have wanted to know. Let's just say, all *this* was about the last thing I expected." She exhaled. "So, I guess this is goodbye."

My voice went small: "Guess so."

Without another word, she walked up to me and embraced me. I put my arms around her slight, breakable shoulders. But, the hug was a little bit awkward, since I was over a foot and a half taller than her.

I looked down at the top of her shiny, red head. "I stored my number in the plane's computer. If you ever need anything, don't hesitate to call."

She pulled back, bewildered. "Need anything? We'll be in different countries, fifteen-hundred miles apart."

"I have a Nurian private pilot's license that I wouldn't hesitate to use for you."

She shook her head, vigorously. "Oh, no, you've done more than enough for me already, Nurtic. I can't ask anything else of you, ever. I refuse to."

"You never know."

She smiled a smile full of pain. "We really don't know a damn thing about the future, do we?"

"Only God does, Scarlet."

I couldn't deny that I loved her, as I looked at her flushed face for the last time. But, of course, I didn't say anything, for I knew she belonged to Lechatelierite's memory and I respected that.

"Happy Summer Solstice Day," I told her.

"Happy?" she whispered. Then, she touched my hand for just a moment, blinked, turned and took off down the sidewalk, flaming hair flying behind her tiny frame. I missed her already.

SCARLET JULY

Leaving Nurtic standing there on the runway, I took off down the street, feeling the gentle Nurian sunlight filter through my hair. I ran and ran and ran, as though trying to put the last seven ages far behind me. I knew my way around Alcove City as though I were here only yesterday, working as a train conductor, sleeping by dumpsters, living off of my aura and traveling from library to library in the furious pursuit of knowledge. Little did I know just what I was preparing myself for.

I skidded to a stop in front of the Alcove City Hospital, absent-mindedly fingering Cease's Silver Triangle under the collar of my robe. I looked up at the immense building, checkered with blue-grey windows, wondering behind which I'd find Cease's mother, Qui Tsop Lechatelierite.

During the months I wasted with pushing Cease away, I believed the opposing elements of fire and ice could never successfully unify, that one would inevitably destroy the other. I thought, either the ice would melt or the fire would extinguish. But, I knew now, as I stroked my deceptively-flat stomach, that I was wrong. Our covalent son was proof enough.

Eight months remained until my due date. Eight months until February twenty-fifth of the ninety-fifth age.

The end of one Crystal was the beginning of another. The first Crystal dissolved in the intense flames, but now, it recrystallized into something new.

And, so, I'd name our child Commence. Commence July Lechatelierite. I smiled and pushed open the hospital door, even as a single tear trickled down my cheek. Cease's life ended. The System's dominion diffused. The worst of the war was over. But, for Commence and I, this was just the beginning.